*To Mich
God's bless~*

THE DAZE OF GRACE

THE DAZE OF GRACE

DONNA M. YOUNG

The Daze of Grace
Copyright © 2017 by Donna M. Young. All rights reserved.

No part of this publication may be reproduced, stored in a retrieval system or transmitted in any way by any means, electronic, mechanical, photocopy, recording or otherwise without the prior permission of the author except as provided by USA copyright law.

Published by Donna M. Young
P O Box 76, Lawton, IA 51030
dmywriting@wiatel.net

Author photo by Elizabeth Rose Kahl

Book Cover and Layout by Christina Hicks Creative
christinahickscreative@gmail.com

Published in the United States of America
ISBN: 978-1-947143-06-7
Fiction / General
Fiction / Christian General

Finally, be strong in the Lord and in the strength of His might. Put on the whole armor of God, that you may be able to stand against the schemes of the devil. For we do not wrestle against flesh and blood, but against the rulers, against the authorities, against the cosmic powers over this present darkness, against the spiritual forces of evil in the heavenly places. Therefore take up the whole armor of God, that you may be able to withstand in the evil day, and having done all, to stand firm.

Ephesians 6:10-13

CHAPTER 1

Sounds of gunfire disrupt the busy hum of nighttime, urban noise; and are rapidly followed by police sirens, whining incessantly somewhere in the distance. Grace glances nervously down at the kids tucked around her sides. Trying to judge their reaction to the noise, she concludes that exhaustion is, at last, beginning to take its toll. She crosses her fingers and hopes it will remain that way.

Not a whisper of summer breeze breaches the tenth floor window of their dilapidated, efficiency apartment, as another scorcher lays claim to the city on that mid August night. She'd tried cutting down on the amount of sun coming through their one small window during the day, patching gaps in the ancient blinds with scraps of paper, and bits of old aluminum foil; but sunlight, like laser beams, shot through every remaining tiny hole in the casement covering, and her efforts amounted to nothing.

Heat, which collected layer upon layer throughout the sweltering day found no discernible escape route, forcing it to settle hot and sticky in the cramped room, and it held on with tenterhooks throughout the excruciatingly long night. With no air conditioning, or even a simple electric fan, Grace was without a way to soften the impact of hours of stifling darkness; so, she laid awake, sweat soaked, in the dimly moonlit space; waiting out the remainder of another nighttime hell.

One small tanned leg, draped over her larger one in the tangle of bodies on the old stained couch, added to the discomfort and threw a wrench into her vain attempts at sleep. Wanting desperately to move the chubby appendage; but knowing all too well how much time it would take to get the little leg's owner back to sleep; she lay unmoving, with rivulets of perspiration tracking through every downward crack and crevice of her body.

Grace shared the old, fold out sofa with her three young siblings, and as much as she relished the warmth of those little bodies on cold winter nights, the heat they radiated in this already insufferable situation caused her to entertain thoughts of flight out that small, open tenth floor window and into the blissfully, still, nocturnal sky.

"Hottest Summer in a Hundred Years", and "Heat Wave of the Century" were recent headlines in local papers, and Grace was sure she'd never known such debilitating warmth in her whole life. Crime rates, which seemed to rise every summer with high temperatures, had this year's felony count breaking records of all kinds in the region, and would probably get worse before this cursed season was over.

As she lay in near darkness she heard volleys of gunshot grow closer; an all too familiar sound on her side of town; and she hoped that, for once, it wouldn't drift any nearer to risk waking the kids. She sighed and tried to slide over ever so slightly to remove some skin to skin contact with the biggest source of heat; but the small, sticky body, making barely perceptible sleepy noises, migrated right back to his place of safety against her side. She sighed again, knowing she wouldn't have a chance of escaping the oppressive heat tonight.

Closing her eyes, and rocking slowly to the ever present melodies in her aching head; she at last achieved a state of relative ease. Soft snoring sounds of the little ones tucked under her arms told her they were finally, thankfully, off to a deep sleep.

Just as a peaceful haze began to dim her sleep deprived mind, a blood curdling scream ruptured the quiet of the night. Her eyes flew open, and she lay for a moment; heart fluttering, and stomach churning, like a kaleidoscope of butterflies taking flight. Her breath came in small panicked gulps, as she tried unsuccessfully to pinpoint the source of the sudden outcry. Had she indeed heard a scream, or was it just another of her infamous fleeting nightmares taking hold as she'd begun to drift off? It wasn't the kids, of that she was certain, and they didn't seem to be phased by the noise. Perhaps she did imagine it after all. So she tried with all her might to relax.

Next, a series of loud thumps, which seemed to originate from the place next door, punctuated the already uneasy conditions caused by the earlier scream; and were then followed by relative quiet. Pretty sure she'd actually heard the noises against the wall, she tensed to move quickly, should the need arise.

Paper thin walls in the old apartment building, offered no genuine insulation, or sound barrier. For that matter the noise, for all she knew, may have begun almost anywhere in the maze of one room hovels making up the interior of the vermin infested structure. Grace felt the hair on the back of her neck stand on end and her skin broke out in undulating waves of gooseflesh from her scalp to her shins. The racket had stopped, but was it over? Every nerve in her body stood ready for flight, since it was impossible to predict what might happen next.

This certainly wasn't the first time she'd heard yelling, and sounds of desperation, in this dreadful place, not by a long shot. No, she'd actually, stupidly, put herself at grave risk more than once, rushing out to help others when they cried out in panic. She knew better; after getting herself into all sorts of trouble trying to be of aid; than to get involved in outside scuffles when she had the welfare of the kids to consider. But, she wasn't always a creature of logic when someone's life was at stake; so she closed her eyes again and continued, though a little more rapidly, rocking and rocking the old stained couch. All she could do was hope, against all hope, that the situation would resolve itself before she was compelled to intervene.

The loud shriek hadn't stirred the children; maybe it really had been all in her exhausted mind; so she concentrated on trying not to make any sudden moves, that might do that very thing. Rocking the sofa cushion, gently; to music that was ever present in her own head; was a habit she'd persisted in as long as she could remember. Simply her way of soothing herself; it had become her way to offer comfort to those she loved as well.

Anything to avoid the seemingly endless whining and crying which occurred earlier that evening, as she'd tried to settle the kids in for the night. That scene had come close to driving her mad; and she had no desire to repeat the whole exasperating cycle again.

This terrible heat made them all crabby, if she was to be honest, and had gone on for over two weeks now with no let up in the foreseeable future. She couldn't blame the kids for their crankiness, but if she couldn't keep them sleeping her own slim chances at getting a little shuteye would be jeopardized again. She didn't know how many more of these excruciating, sleepless nights she had in her, before her own system would begin to shut down for good.

It'd been only seconds since she'd heard the first scream, and subsequent thumping noises on the wall, before her mind began to wander to the jumble of disjointed thoughts filling her head, but it felt like hours. She weighed her options. Should she stay, or should she go? She decided to sit tight unless she heard something more.

Darkness still prevailed, and she knew all too well it wasn't safe in these hallways late at night. A fifteen year old girl was raped and killed right there on the stairs one floor below just last week. Her mother found her body, in a broken, bloody heap on the ninth floor landing, and wailed her anguish until men in white coats came to take them both away. Blood stains still covered four of the old warped steps to varying degrees; and negotiating the taped off areas carrying a baby and leading her other two little ones proved to be difficult to say the least. But she'd grown used to difficult in her lifetime. For all intents and purposes, she was practically immune to difficult.

"What can you expect in a neighborhood like this?" she'd been told over and over by her ancient neighbor, Rosie. "Stay inside where it's a little safer for you children," her elderly friend warned, "Things aren't what they used to be in the neighborhood. Not so many years ago a lady could walk down the street without fearing for her life, or her virtue, but I wouldn't dare try that today, not without a darned good body guard! God loves you Gracie and He'll take care of you. That's a promise from me!"

"Well, so far Rosie, I've gotta say He's been doing a TERRIFFIC job." Grace answered back a bit sarcastically. She wasn't trying to hurt Rosie's feelings, but she also wasn't a big fan of this God Rosie tried over and over to share with her. She was pretty sure, if He even existed, that He didn't know, or care, that she was wandering around this broken down, old building very scared and terribly lost. And she'd decided long ago, that she didn't have time for anyone who didn't have time for her.

A second scream resonated through the stairwell and this time Grace was awake and focused enough to know it definitely came from the flat to the left of her place. Her body stiffened and her rocking stopped.

Accountable for the safety of her two small sisters, Gail and Barbie, and her eighteen month old baby brother, Bobby; Gracie took her role as caregiver very seriously. Whenever her mother took off for the night; and that was often; she was all too aware, especially in the neighborhood where they lived, that their young lives were literally in her hands. A responsible girl for her age, she reasoned she couldn't leave them alone to find out the cause of the ruckus. Well, at least not yet.

"For crying out loud people", she agonized under her breath, "let someone else around here take care of it for a change." The second shout had been loud enough to rouse her siblings, and she sighed deeply as the children woke, shaken, from the sudden noise. Every muscle in her body tightened, as Bobby began, all over again, to bawl his disapproval.

Temples pounding, from a headache which threatened to undo her, she stroked her brother's back to quiet him, as she softly shook her head to sooth her own worsening pain. Then, sitting up but still content not to get unnecessarily involved, she reached out to pull the kids closer. They all huddled together wrapped in a single cotton sheet in the middle of the old, tainted sofa. "What was that Gracie?" Gail asked in a shaky, small voice. Little Gail tended toward timid, and was easily frightened, so Gracie pulled her close.

"I don't know honey. Let's just stay quiet and see what happens, okay?'

"Okay, just stay here Gracie."

"I will honey. Don't worry, you're fine. I won't let anything happen to you. I won't ever let anything happen to you. Do you hear me?"

The children latched on tighter and Grace continued rocking and soothing as best she could as she pleaded with her brother to, "Hush baby, shush now. Everything will be okay."

Not knowing the source of the noise, or the cause of the trouble, she didn't want a possible intruder in the neighbor's apartment to hear the cries of her brother and come crashing through to investigate, putting them all in danger.

A third cry, and from the sounds of it, this one originating from a place of deep anguish, ripped through the stillness of the night, and stabbed at Gracie's already churning gut. It ended in a heart wrenching moan which was nothing short of primordial.

Grace knew the young girl next door had brought her brand new baby home from the hospital only two days before and couldn't imagine what might be going on over there. Suddenly she was overwhelmed with a need to know what was happening. Perhaps, even though she knew she was probably being reckless again at her own expense, there might be something she could do to help? At any rate she couldn't just sit here now, not after that third terrifying cry for help.

Liberating her body from the prison of arms and legs, on the makeshift bed, she rose, and silently searched the cupboard for something she could leave for the children too snack on, in an effort to keep them occupied and quiet. Locating an almost empty box of Captain Crunch cereal she gave them permission to eat on the furniture, just this once, and admonished all to stay right where they were until she got back, as she left to check out the situation.

Leaving them whimpering, and sniffling, to carefully remove the chair she habitually lodged tightly under the doorknob of the front door before she went to bed each night, she quietly opened her door to the tenth floor landing.

Peeking around the scratched, and warped, wooden jamb; to see there were already two frightened, and trembling, women standing just inside their own entryways; she stepped out into the dim light of the corridor. Stumbling over her own feet trying to avoid stacks of refuse; which had been part of the building's inner landscape for as long as she could remember; Grace nodded in the direction of the two women. Trying to get a feel for what help might have already been offered, Grace asked if anyone called the police. They shook their heads in the negative.

Giving them orders to make the necessary call, Grace approached the young woman's place, and knocked tentatively. The only response she received, was more sobbing and howling from within. Turning the handle, the unlocked door opened easily enough, to the room beyond.

What she found inside didn't register at first, and when it did, Grace took one unsteady step backward. Her young neighbor sat on the floor of the small living room holding what appeared at first to be an armful of bloody rags.

Upon closer inspection the bundle turned out to be her new infant daughter, minus most of her face. The bundle was limp and in the middle of the place where her face should have been was a pink, plastic binky. It didn't take a vivid imagination to put the tragic story together in a way which seemed logical.

New mommy, who perhaps wasn't as familiar as she might have been with the rampant vermin problem in the building, put her sleeping baby to bed with milk on her face. It appeared the infant was sucking on her pacifier, for comfort, when the rats, probably attracted to the small suckling noise and the smell of milk, attacked in a feeding frenzy. The newborn didn't stand a chance. She couldn't scream, or even cry out, due to the swift assault, but rather sucked harder on her pacifier trying in vain to sooth herself until merciful death released her.

When the young mother woke in the night, and found her child still covered by the feeding rodents, she snapped. There were a dozen, or more, mangled, and dead rats laying in various places in the small room, with bright red marks on the walls all around, where sudden impact ended their noxious lives. But, it was too little too late to save the tiny baby. Mom sat, gore covered, rocking her lifeless babe;

an unnerving, blank stare on her face.

Young Grace could only stand and gape, shocked to the core, at the blood spattered room and the small dead body in her mother's arms. A flood of tears suddenly poured from her eyes and mixed with cold sweat to bathe her own flushed face. Backing slowly out to the landing, shaking her head all the way, she tripped and fell over a pile of rotting trash sending cockroaches and rats skittering in all directions; sobbing loudly now as she struggled to be free from the pile of filth, she crawled away and stood up trembling, covered in the stench, and slime, of putrid garbage.

She didn't wait there for the police. She didn't need to. The story would be revealed in all its horror, as soon as they arrived, and viewed the picture for themselves. Obviously there was no help she could offer; and she thought if she stayed any longer, the revulsion she was feeling might very well transform her own face forever into a blank staring countenance, like that of the young mom. Cops would be all too familiar with the sight; which occurred in varying degrees, ever more frequently around the city; as young girls without resources became mothers, and were forced to occupy rooms in these filthy old tenements.

Shivering violently, even in the repressive heat of the

hallway, Grace shook her head at the two women in their doorways, as she quickly opened the door to her own place and slid in. They covered their mouths in shock, and empathetic heartache, for this neighbor they barely knew; but in some tangible human way could identify with; and then they backed slowly into their own ramshackle homes.

Leaving the entrance to the young mother's apartment open for the authorities, she closed the door to her own dark, dismal space. Inside, her baby brother reached out for her, opening and closing his hands and crying to be held, but she walked past him into the bathroom, pulling her clothes off as she went. Turning the shower on she stood under the steaming flow, scrubbing her flesh till it was red and raw, until the water turned tepid, then cold, and the worst of the buggy, crawling feeling left her mind. Not knowing how many of the escaped pests might be lurking in her own room she was determined to keep her charges safe even if it meant she would never sleep another night in her life.

Grace didn't know if she ever wanted to have children of her own. At only eleven years of age, on that hot summer night, she realized she'd been caring for her siblings as long as she could remember. She loved them all very much, but sometimes; as guilty as it made her feel to admit it; she resented the fact she was always responsible for those other three lives, as well as her own. And she purely hated that she never had a single solitary moment to herself.

When she wasn't in school, or at her part time job, she was taking care of children; helping with homework; cooking whatever food stuffs she was able to procure from the small store where she worked; and trying to keep the tiny space where they lived clean amongst the filth of the building around them.

Cleaning a small area might seem an easy thing to most people, but Grace could tell you it was far more difficult than keeping a large place tidy, especially when four children were in residence, and even if their possessions were rather meager.

Grace didn't remember a lot about her maternal grandmother; from her few visits there with her mom all those years ago; but she did remember her wonderful kitchen. A kitchen of bright, yellow walls; gingham curtains; and lots of windows. Colorful sun catchers adorned every pane. That cozy, warm kitchen filled with amazing aromas, tasty treats, and a saying embroidered on muslin, which had stuck in her mind for all these years, "A place for everything and everything in its place". A sentiment rather difficult to follow in a place as tiny as this one, and she dared anyone to try.

The only other thing she remembered was a terrible argument between her mother, and grandmother, in which angry words were brandished like ice picks. Her grandmother's last words to her daughter were, "I'm tired of trying to help you, only to see you throwing away everything I worked so hard to build. If your dad were still here, he would be mortified. You make me so ashamed!"

Followed by her daughter's, "I don't want your help Mother. I don't need your help either! I never did! Gracie and I will be fine and you don't ever have to worry about seeing us again. Do you hear me? Never."

Grace missed the warmth of that homey, old kitchen, and the fragrant scent of vanilla, which engulfed her every time Grandma held her in one of her frequent, and ample, hugs. Grandmother called her 'peanut', she said because Gracie was petite for her age, with chestnut hair and huge brown eyes. "You just remind me of a tiny peanut, little one", she often heard from the most loving person she'd ever known.

And, Grandmother always fed her while they were visiting; insisting she was too skinny; delicious goodies like: homemade cookies, and cinnamon rolls; wonderful meals of roast chicken, and beef stew; smells, and tastes she would never forget, all washed down with big glasses of fresh, cold milk. She told Gracie she wanted her to grow up to be big and strong, so she should always drink all her milk. Grace wanted nothing in the world more than to please that kind woman; though they seldom had milk to drink these days; and she sometimes wondered if they would ever have the opportunity to meet again.

Given the current evidence, she hadn't grown very 'big', so far, but Grace was deceptively strong for her size, and more than a little bit crazy when backed into a corner. Once confronting four, teen aged boys who were harassing her sisters; and beating one of the boys so badly the other three ran off in fear of the diminutive girl, she proved she wasn't afraid of anything. The incident garnered her much respect, with the local hoods, and she was mostly left alone by the bullies in the neighborhood.

Known as wise beyond her years, and singularly daring against anything the neighborhood, and its ilk, could throw at her, she'd been called upon many times for advice and help by grown women in the building. But, this, this was something even she couldn't fix and her lip trembled as tears flowed for the dead baby, and her broken mother.

When police and paramedics arrived next door Grace could hear the gasps and mumblings of the officers, and ambulance workers, through the thin walls, as they went about their gruesome business. She heard practically everything as they performed their dreadful duties, which were suddenly interrupted, by the excruciating sobbing of the young mother. Screaming, and weeping, all over again, she sounded frantic as the officers took the tiny, limp bundle from her arms.

Gracie couldn't get the sight of that poor woman and her dead baby out of her mind; so, brushing aside Captain Crunch crumbs from their bed she lay down in the semi-dark room and mentally surveyed her own rather directionless and troubled life, as she once again began to rock to the music in her head. Bobby was snuggled, again, to her damp side, and his even breathing was punctuated now by small residual hiccups from his former screaming tirade.

One main room, and a tiny bathroom, with sink, toilet, and open shower, was all the space the universe had carved out for her small family. Grace never knew her own dad, and each of her siblings were fathered by different men her mother met in bars along the way. Each of those men made the appropriate promises to get what they wanted, and then when the woman was pregnant again, which she seemed to have a strong penchant for doing, they left without so much as a how-do-you-do. Grace never really got to know any of them. They weren't around long enough for that. She was glad though, because it was easier not to get attached to those who wouldn't be part of her life for long; more sage advice from her very old, very dear friend.

Grace supposed her mom wasn't the worst mother in the world, but she was convinced she wasn't the best either. She'd seen wonderful old movies that portrayed sweet maternal figures, and she longed to be loved, and cared for, like the children in the make believe families in those great films. Her day dreams included beautiful Thanksgiving tables covered in delicious food, and being surrounded by loving family members all dressed in holiday finery; Christmas trees loaded with gifts for her baby brother and sisters; and a yard where they could play and roll in the fragrant, green grass. Perhaps with a wiggly, yipping, cold nosed puppy.

Abundantly aware though, that life wasn't a movie trailer, her heart broke for the little ones who had only their eleven year old sister to depend on. She certainly didn't know much about raising kids, and worried all the time about how they would grow up with only an inadequate, adolescent protector to look up to, and care for them.

Grace's mother seemed convinced that her roll in life, or so she said, was to try and find a daddy for her children; but the hunt always seemed to entail going out to bars, drinking, partying, and doing whatever drugs were in the mix that night. Of course that sometimes meant she didn't come home for days at a time, especially in the summer. The woman got a welfare check every month and Grace became rather adept at forging her mother's signature to pay the rent, and utilities, or to pick up a few groceries. The money was necessary for survival, used in between her own meager twice monthly paychecks, from the store where she worked as many hours as she could manage to eke out of her kind employer.

She'd determined long ago there was no use feeling guilty about things she was forced to do to ensure her family's survival; so she refused to acknowledge the remorse she supposed others might assign her if they knew the depths of her depravity. Where it came to the well being of the little ones, she would do whatever she must to take care of them, and would continue to keep them safe at all cost.

When her mom was home, it was blatantly evident to Gracie, she didn't want to be there. Instead she'd rather be out having sex, and avoiding all manner of duty. Angry, and impatient with the children, whenever her circumstances cooped her up in the apartment for more than a day; it wasn't unheard of for her to go into a rage and hit the little ones.

Since Grace was very protective of the kids she always stepped in, if she was home, and took the abuse her mother was dishing out, to save her siblings the bruises they'd have suffered at their mother's hand. At times she wanted nothing more than to hit her mother back, to give her some of what she was putting out there, but something kept her from unleashing that kind of rage against the woman who'd brought her into the world. Grace learned very young to beware the difficult moods caused by her mother's bad habits, but as yet had not been able to properly tutor the children to avoid her wrath.

Grace wondered if she ought to be sad when her mom wasn't around, but if truth be told it was just easier for everyone when she wasn't there. She and her charges had their routines and by the time they fell asleep on the sofa each night they were fed and, more often than not, clean enough to get by. Grace was perfectly aware it wasn't an ideal situation, but she did the best she could with the resources available to her.

Their apartment was not large, but it contained the bare necessities. Along the front wall a sink with drain board, and a two foot long work surface; a tiny fridge; and a small two-burner stove covered the space between the corner of the room and the front door. Two undersized cupboards, above and below the sink, completed the kitchenette. Storage space was scanty, but without a lot to store, it didn't much matter.

Flowered paper, on two of the walls, curled along its edges, and peeled off in layers of crumbling shards; and aged plaster, actively disintegrating in multiple locations, on the ceiling, and walls, was further decimated by the humid weather; and the scarred hard wood floors were so uneven that walking on them felt a little like walking through an amusement park fun house. She'd learned if she dropped her pencil on one side of the room, it would roll all the way across to the other side, and slip into a crack which separated the wall, and baseboard, from the floor. Not sure where the items lost to the crevice ended up, she imagined the neighborhood rat colony might be using them for building supplies.

The only furniture in their small home was the old sofa, which served as the children's bed; an old reclining chair, where Mom slept if she was home; a small table with four mismatched dinette chairs; and an end table which held a thirteen inch black and white television. There wasn't much use for TV though, as the business of staying alive took up most of their time and attention, and truthfully, Grace enjoyed playing games with the kids if there was enough spare time to do so.

The children's few clothing items, and other personal belongings, were stored in plastic bins; and stacked in the far corner of the back wall. This kept most of the rats, and bugs out. At night they took turns showering, and dressing in the small bathroom, with Grace diapering and dressing her brother.

At eleven years old Grace was very creative, and bright, and liked to teach her siblings crafts, plays, and competitions that she'd invented for their entertainment. It really wasn't such a bad existence, as long as they had each other, she reasoned; yes, just as long as they always had each other.

The apartment next door was empty now. People came to move the unfortunate girl's few belongings on Sunday, two days after the baby died. Grace suspected the group were relatives of the young woman, because she could hear them crying as they packed up her negligible possessions. She wondered as she listened to their mourning, if their grief was due, at least in part, to feelings of guilt; as she'd also heard a few squabbles spring up while they were clearing her things out.

It sounded, from those arguments, as though the girl's family had kicked her out when she became pregnant, as so many families tend to do when they believe they are standing up for their precious moral principles. Had they come to the realization now, that if they'd offered her a place to stay the baby would likely be alive, and the young woman would still be sane? Grace didn't know the answers to those questions, but guessed she was probably right on the money. There'd been more than one young single mom, holed away in this horrid place, in Grace's years of residence; thrown away by her own parent's moral principles.

Grace didn't go next door to say anything to the girl's

loved ones, because there wasn't anything to say. Sure that the landlord would soon have a new tenant for his apartment, she just hoped it wouldn't be anyone as crazy as the guy who'd lived there last year. He'd been the main reason Grace started shoving the kitchen chair under the door handle. These places, disgusting as they were, never stayed empty long. "Someday I'll get us out of here", Gracie promised herself, "someday."

Another sizzling night had little Bobby suffering with a fever so high his eyes rolled back in his head, until only the whites were visible. The situation became more worrisome, as his body was racked with repeated convulsions. Violent and twisting, his seizures left Grace terrified to the depths of her soul. Crying, she picked him up gently, and took him to the shower where she sat with him for several hours allowing the tepid water to wash over them both.

She couldn't call for help, because her mother routinely took the only phone they owned with her every night. Rocking and rocking, shielding his face from the force of the spray, she hummed soothing tunes in his ear, from the store of melodies in her head. Eventually the fever broke, and shaking with relief, and exhaustion, she dried them both, and diapered, and dressed, her brother. Then, gently moving the sleeping forms of her two sisters, she laid Bobby in bed, covering him loosely with the lone sheet.

The hours of darkness were practically spent, and she couldn't have gone back to sleep if she tried; after the trauma of that night; so she dressed herself for the day. The girls slept through the worst of the night, and when they woke they were ready for breakfast, so Grace went about adding water to the small amount of milk left in the fridge, trying to stretch the precious liquid as far as she might.

When her mother eventually stumbled in, reeking of alcohol and cigarettes, and wearing her shirt inside out; thankfully in time for Grace to leave for her part time job; only to flop onto the recliner as if she was about to sleep, Grace couldn't tolerate the woman's uncaring, frivolous attitude for one more minute. "You certainly aren't going to lie down and sleep while the baby needs you, are you?"

"What's your problem little girl? I'm worn out and tired. I've been out all night looking for a daddy for you damn kids. The girls can take care of him if he needs anything."

"Oh is that what we're still calling it? Looking for a daddy for us kids? Well, for your information the baby was really sick last night. He had a terrible fever and I sat in the shower with him for hours to bring it down!"

"So, it's down, right? What's the big deal then? Little ones run fast fevers. He's okay now isn't he?"

"Yes he's okay Momma, but you weren't here. You're never here when these kids need you. It's always me, only me, and I'm tired of being the only one here for them. What if the shower hadn't worked? What if he'd died last night? That's what I was afraid of you know? I couldn't even call for help! What would you have done if something happened to your little boy while you were out getting drunk, and having sex with strangers?"

The slap came fast, and hard. Grace's head snapped sideways from the momentum of the blow and immediately a hand shaped, red welt grew on her left cheek. "Don't you ever talk to me like that again you ungrateful brat! I'm the only reason you eat, or have a roof over your worthless head, and walls between you, and a world full of perverts out there! You think I'm a terrible mother? I promise you there are a lot worse! I had a lot worse myself! Why do you think we don't go visit your grandmother anymore? I'm not perfect. I never claimed to be perfect, but I supply everything you've ever had, and at least I've never walked out on you! I could you know. Plenty of men have wanted me, but they just didn't want to mess with my damn brats, so be glad I didn't take one of them up on the offer!"

"Sometimes I wonder Mamma. Would we be so much worse off if you did? Listen, I've gotta get out of here or I'm going to be late for work. Just don't fall asleep in case the baby needs you. You can do that, for once, can't you?"

Mr. Rand was a pretty good sort. He'd figured out her home circumstances, without any outside help from Gracie, and allowed her to come whenever she could, to earn a bit of extra money. An excellent employee, when she could be there, she kept his shelves clean as a whistle, and the floors fairly shining. His small market boasted a meat case; which was stocked by a neighborhood butcher; and a large section for fresh local produce, dairy, and baked goods. Plus an assortment of packaged and canned convenience items. He was fair, and well respected in the community, and Grace liked him very much.

Not an old man, he was perhaps middle aged, with slightly graying temples, a swarthy complexion, and dark brown eyes in a handsome face. As far as Grace could tell he stayed unmarried, to take care of his sister who lived with him. She'd only seen the sister a few times. Usually the frail looking woman was upstairs in the tiny flat, above the shop; but even with the limited exposure she'd had to her, she thought there might be some mental, or emotional problems, of some sort. Regardless, the woman didn't help with the store, and seemed to have an aversion to people, so Gracie helped with as many hours as she was able, and that worked out pretty well for both of them.

Always looking to earn enough money to help out, Gracie attempted other part time jobs in her young life; including babysitting; but that required her to be away from her own kiddos during times when her irresponsible mother wasn't around to watch them. She'd also tried working at the bowling alley, the one on the corner at the other end of her busy city block. Filling pop machines, and cleaning; that is until the owner tackled her to the floor in the back room, one ugly day, grabbing and groping her for all he was worth. A swift knee to his groin, and a thumb in his eye, barely got her out of that one. Running for her life, she stumbled out to the street crying, and gasping for air. For that reason she was glad her new boss always seemed safe, and kind.

Getting a good amount of hours in during the summer months, would assure she had money she needed to provide for her siblings throughout the school year. And, though she hated the thought of leaving the kids with her mother, knowing she was probably sleeping and leaving them to their own devices, she didn't find she had much of a choice. With part of her summer earnings she planned to buy school clothes, and supplies, for her sisters; some much needed things for her quickly growing brother; and she even hoped to be able to save a little aside for Christmas if she could. This would all require planning, and some major deception, in order to keep the growing funds a secret from her mother.

As long as she only worked every other day, she was left with sufficient time for her siblings, and sometimes when the weather was good they'd ride the bus into a better part of the city to a glorious green park they'd found there. Things weren't always so terrible.

The kids loved the park. Swinging for hours, climbing the jungle gym, and rolling around in the grass were all things they couldn't do at home, so, they begged to go whenever Grace had a day off work. But, as much as they loved being there, they equally hated going home when the day was done, and whined until Grace had to threaten that she wouldn't bring them back again, unless they stopped. Often she would save out enough money from her check to buy them a hot dog, and an ice cream cone, from the food carts which were abundant in the park.

The children treasured those times and she felt very magnanimous when she was able to treat them in that way. She saw it was important for them to feel normal sometimes, instead of always feeling like the poorest kids on the block. She was quite literally the only person in their world, who truly cared about them, and that seemed an enormous responsibility. She was also aware they loved her like a mom. And that was an awesome, and frightening privilege.

The day of her twelfth birthday came, and went, much like any other day. She didn't say anything to the kids, because they'd only feel badly they had nothing to give her, and her mother never mentioned a thing, but, instead, got herself dolled up, and left for the night as usual. Though her feelings were bruised, Grace knew it didn't really matter. Maybe on her next day off they'd ride the bus again, and go down by the river. She'd heard of another park they could visit, and this one had a public place to swim as well.

Mr. Rand trusted her, and since she was excellent at math he let her run the register when she was done cleaning the bathrooms, and sweeping and dusting the store. He also let her take a few items home with her; some bruised fruit and vegetables, day old bread and dairy products which displayed an expiration date equal to the day's date (since it wasn't legal to sell them to the public past that date). Everyone knew milk was good for at least a week past the due date, so she didn't have a problem taking the valuable resource with her. With these riches she was able to add extra value to her family's grocery budget and the kids got some much needed milk, fruits and veggies to help them grow big and strong.

Quite honestly her job gave her a much needed break from the children too, but she wondered, and worried, about them the whole time she was gone, until she was finally home late in the afternoon.

When she arrived back at the apartment at the end of her work day she was usually greeted by grouchy, hungry children who'd been ignored all day by a sleeping, or worse, drunk and high mother. The place was always a mess, when she arrived home, and more often than not, completely trashed. A big part of her wanted to turn around, and walk back out the door; but her mom was typically sitting in her chair impatient, and ready to go out early for the evening. Normally, with ten words, or less, to say, she was off again, and Grace was left to put things back in order. Feeling a bit guilty for the thoughts of freedom, which had danced so invitingly through her head, she would take extra time to play with the kids, and show them some additional attention.

Her absence during the day was hard on the kids, but she really had no choice in the matter. Needing to get whatever hours she could manage, she was aware once school started up, she wouldn't have the option to work three full days a week as she was now. Even now when her mother didn't come home in the morning, as was expected of her, she was left without a sitter and couldn't work. Mr. Rand understood her position, but it left him in a bad situation too, and her without a day's pay. All too aware if she hired a sitter she'd be working for essentially nothing, she had to depend on her negligent mother as the only adult source available to watch the children.

†

Summer was winding down, though the heat continued

unrelentingly. School would be starting soon, and Grace planned a bus trip for the children. She'd saved her money all season, and wanted to purchase school clothes and supplies today, before going to the new park she'd heard so much about. There was a little money saved aside for lunch, and a treat, and the children were so excited they could barely contain themselves. Little Bobby, who often accidently called her Mommy, much to his mother's ire, was jumping up and down holding his arms up. "Mommy, Gracie up, up, go, go, go".

"We're going, we're going Bobby. Keep your pants on. Okay little ones first we're going shopping, and then, if you are very good we will go to the park, and wade in the water." She'd realized she couldn't take them swimming, because none of them owned bathing suits, and she couldn't swing that expense today. Besides, it would have been too hard to keep track of Bobby around deep water. But, she'd discovered, through further investigation, the park sported a shallow creek at one end which fed into the pool and eventually the dam and she knew the cool water would be a real treat for them in all this damnable heat.

"Yaaaaaaaaaaaaaaay", the kids sang out, as Grace tried to shush them, and they left their drunken mother passed out in her recliner.

Grace wasn't sure her mom would remember the conversation they'd had when she came stumbling in early that morning. The conversation where she'd told her about plans to shop for clothes for the kids, and a trip to the park. Her mother had been even more drunk than usual, which usually led to problems with her memory. She argued that there would be more important things to spend her daughter's hard earned money on, and she ordered her in heavily slurred speech to "Put that damn money away, in case I need it for something. Don't you dare spend it on those damn kids! They'll grow out of those things so quick, they'll hardly get any use out of them, I already know it, and so do you. It's not worth it Grace, you hear me?" The issue for Grace was that she considered her sisters, and brother, to be worth a whole lot more, than whatever drugs, or booze her mom wanted to spend 'her' hard earned money on.

Grace wrote her a quick note, and left with the children anyway. She knew very well what her mother considered "more important" things and she wasn't about to let her buy a night of worthless partying with her hard earned paycheck! She also knew she'd be in for a beating when they got back home, but some things were worth the pain.

With the funds she'd saved she was able to buy all the necessary school supplies she and her sisters needed, three outfits for each of them, including several for Bobby; and two large packages of disposable diapers. She even had enough remaining to help with Christmas, but was confidant she'd be able to get in a few more hours before that was a concern. Pleased as punch with their purchases they ate hot dogs and ice cream cones from brightly colored vendor's wagons, walked barefoot in the cool grass, and played for hours in the park.

Shortly before it was time to leave they walked to the creek, left their packages, and shoes and socks on the bank, and waded in the cool water. Bobby spent more time sitting than wading and his diaper soaked up creek water till he looked to be carrying a bowling ball in his pants, but he had a great time trying to catch tadpoles in his chubby fingers and they all had a good laugh as they enjoyed searching through the creek bed for smooth rocks to start a collection.

After a full day they boarded the bus tired, but smiling and happy. Riding home Grace saw the exhausted joy on their faces and wished she could give them more days like this. Her sisters looked at her with adoration and little

Bobby said, "I wuv you Gracie", as he sat on her lap in his squishy pants. Back at home her mother slapped her and dragged her across the room by her hair, all to a woeful chorus of cries from her helpless siblings. She searched Grace for the remainder of her money, folded it and stuck it in her own pocket, all the while bemoaning the waste of funds used, "To buy these brats crap they don't appreciate and are gonna outgrow faster than you can blink a damned eye."

When she'd ranted and raved sufficiently to sooth her ire, she grabbed her purse and slammed out of the apartment. The little ones, who'd been too afraid to step forward during the assault, came running to Gracie the moment their mother left. Grace comforted the children. "It's okay guys. She can't hurt me. I'm tough, remember? At least we have our school supplies and our day at the park! She can't take any of that away from us, right?" That night after showers and supper the kids laid all their new things on the couch to admire. They were proud as peacocks and anxious for the new school year to begin, only a few days away now.

Grace always loved school. It was a place where she could shine and feel good about her accomplishments. She was a natural scholar and the same creativity which entertained her siblings at home intrigued her teachers. They challenged her with new assignments and opportunities whenever they could manage to come up with something which might allow her ingenuity to flow. She was especially good at math and English and several teachers suggested she might enjoy teaching. Grace wasn't sure about that. It sounded a lot like babysitting, or being a mom and she'd already decided once her siblings were grown, she could only be happy in a role which would afford her some freedom, a commodity sorely lacking in her life now. She wanted to travel, to see the world and all the marvelous things it held and she could hardly wait to be old enough to do that on her own.

When thoughts of freedom filled her mind Gracie felt instantly ashamed. She loved her sisters and brother, truly she did, and knew they loved and appreciated her. She just couldn't imagine being happy for the rest of her life being tied down by the needs of others and never experiencing any of her own distant dreams. She dreamed of having her own apartment, her own car and most of all never having to plan her life around anyone else's schedule again. She couldn't remember a time in her life when she wasn't expected to take care of her mother's messes and responsibilities and she despised the woman for it. No, she would have her freedom and she would see the world, she was sure of it.

†

On her last full day of work, before school was scheduled to begin, Gracie and her mother argued. She left the small tenth floor room with an eye turning black from the back handed blow her mom landed as she'd turned to head for the door. The contact was enough to leave her vision blurry and her head fuzzy, but most of all she was furious and knew she'd better leave for her own good.

The children were crying and didn't want to stay with their mother, but Grace needed to head out or she'd be late for work and her temper would get the best of her. The woman was drunk as usual. Reeking of alcohol, cigarettes and sweat; her shirt on inside out, and backward, again; she resembled a raccoon for the appearance of her smeared mascara. Gracie hated her with a white hot revulsion which blocked out reason and left her sick and trembling inside. She wanted nothing more than to be done with her and her selfishness. If it hadn't been for the children, she'd have left long ago, twelve years old or not.

When she got to the landing outside their apartment

she stopped, and listened to her mother screaming at the kids. She held, white knuckled, to the railing for a moment with tears streaming down her flushed face. She felt badly leaving them, and even contemplated taking them with her for just a moment, but couldn't bring herself to go back in. Turning to go down the stairs she heard a loud slap and one of the girls screamed. She almost opened the door, but she thought she might kill her mother if she did, and ran down the ten flights as fast as her feet would carry her instead.

At work Mr. Rand looked suspiciously at Gracie's face, but didn't say anything. He'd been tempted on several occasions to call Children's Services and get that evil woman locked away where she couldn't hurt anyone anymore, but he knew the way the foster system worked, having been a product of it himself, and knew the likelihood of four siblings staying together would be worse than slim. After all, he hadn't been able to keep his sister with him until he was old enough to become her guardian, and look at the problems she lived with every day now. He couldn't imagine Grace's small sisters and brother surviving more than a minute without her, so he kept his mouth shut and hoped they'd all survive as he and his baby sister had.

My tears have been my food day and night, while they say to me all the day long, "Where is your God?"

Psalm 42:3

CHAPTER 2

The hours dragged by ever so slowly that day. And though she couldn't figure out why, she was just anxious to get home. Gracie loved working in the store, and usually calmed down quickly, from skirmishes with her mom once she was dusting and sweeping the familiar aisles. Eventually her anger at her mother lessened, but the nagging concern for her sisters and brother never left the back of her mind, and she continued throughout the day to feel guilty for leaving them with that hateful woman. She tried to shake off the uneasy feeling. It would be time to leave for home in a couple of hours, so for now Grace concentrated on doing a good day's work for a fair day's pay.

At around three o'clock a young man ran into the store yelling for someone to call the fire department. "The old apartment building behind us on the next block is burning," He yelled, "There are people still trapped inside."

Gracie froze. Though there were several old tenements on the next block she knew without a doubt he was referring to her building. She could feel the terror rising as she looked pleadingly at her boss.

Mr. Rand motioned frantically for her to go as he dialed 911. Grace couldn't say how she got from the store to her block that day, as it seemed she was teleported through time and space in the blink of an eye. But once there, choking, she held her sleeve to her face, for the air was thick with caustic smoke and lit with hot ash.

Sounds of people screaming for help emanated from windows all throughout the upper floors of the building. Fire engines and emergency rescue vehicles were arriving, and police had already cordoned off a large area. Police held her back from the flaming tinderbox; which was ablaze from about the third floor up; when she tried to push past the barricade. She yelled that her family was in the building, but officers still wouldn't let her pass. Looking up to the small tenth floor window, her gut twisted as she saw her mother hanging out the small opening, holding Bobby over the ledge by one ankle as he twisted and cried out in fear.

Hollering and motioning to her mother as loudly, and frenetically as she was able, to pull him back inside; while the din from machinery and frantic humanity screaming for their lives drowned out her attempts; she saw the unthinkable play out before her eyes.

Fire fighters yelled through a megaphone, "Ma'am hold on, don't drop the baby, we will get a ladder up to you", just as she let go of Bobby's small foot. After dropping Bobby, as if perhaps she hadn't heard the pleas of the firemen, she wrestled with, and then threw Gracie's sisters out the window one after the other. Grace watched in horror as they battled their mother for their lives, then screamed, and flailed, each in her turn, all the way to the ground. Next her mother leaned out of the small opening, and just sort of somersaulted slowly through the portal, falling limply, and so close to the building that she caught, and bounced off several window ledges on the way down. Probably still so inebriated she couldn't feel the pain of her abrupt landing at all.

Grace couldn't think, couldn't move, and could barely breathe for what seemed like an eternity. After sounds of reality began to pierce shock's dense fog, she ducked under tape placed around the scene by somber looking police. No one stopped her now. Walking slowly past trucks with newly extended ladders; hoses filling the air with powerful streams of water; black smoke billowing from windows;

and yelling emergency workers; she approached the bodies of her lifeless family on legs that felt like Jell-O. Severe heat caused mirage like images on the pavement as she walked through the mist of fire hose fallout, and absently, she noticed small rainbows in various places.

EMTs worked frantically on Barbie, who was still battling for air with tiny strangled gasps. Her innocent gaze turned to Grace, and a small smile touched her pink foam, tinged lips as she took her last painful breath. Grace watched horrified until Barbie's beautiful hazel eyes glazed over, and then she slowly ventured, on unsteady legs, toward her other sister. She was sure Gail's end had been less painful, her body hitting the ground at an angle which certainly snapped her neck on impact, but the look of fear on her face was frozen in time. Poor Gail, poor frightened girl. Her entire short life had been engulfed in dread, right down to the last terrifying second. The hardest to see was little Bobby. The back of his head was utterly crushed, though when viewed from the front he appeared to be simply sleeping. When she saw his sweet, peaceful face, haloed by a slowly growing pool of blood, she broke down sobbing, and fell to her knees on the wet, gore, and soot covered pavement.

Hearing the EMT working on her mother exclaim, "I

swear she's got so much alcohol in her system she probably didn't even know what she was doing," Gracie turned toward him. She could have told him first hand her mother spent her whole life not knowing what she was doing, but what good would that do for her little family now? As much as she thought she hated the woman, something deep down inside cried out the loudest for this broken person, who in the same circumstances might not have felt a thing for her. How could she possibly care that this worthless human being, this terrible mother, this murderer of everything she loved, was dead? Yet in the deepest part of her soul; the part which always longed for the love and approval of her distant mama; she cried, cried for the one who had destroyed everything.

Yet for your sake we are killed all the daylong; we are regarded as sheep to be slaughtered.

Psalm 44:22

CHAPTER 3

Fifty three people died in the devastating conflagration; in the fire which killed Gracie's family. Her ancient mentor, Rosie, was another of the casualties of that terrible day and Gracie's heart broke for her friend, the only voice of reason, besides her own, she'd ever met in that building of horrors. She could only imagine Rosie's fear as she watched the flames coming closer, not being able to get away from their fiery fingers. If only she'd been there. Where was her worthless God when she'd needed him? Why didn't He save her if He was so powerful?

Authorities said the number of dead would have been much higher if the blaze had occurred at night, "People in the community should be grateful that the losses weren't much greater", the Fire Chief declared in a press conference. But for Grace the loss was more than she could safely process, and she ached over the unbearable slaughter of her loved ones. Most of all she was consumed by guilt for not being there when they'd needed her, or even taking the children with her. If only she'd stayed home that day. Perhaps she could've gotten them out safely. Or, at the very least she would have listened to the firemen who were trying to help and she might have saved the kids. And, even if she couldn't keep her mother from doing the absurd, then at least she would have died with them and they could all be as one even now.

Memories of the children on their last day in the park together, the joy of playing in the grass, wading in the creek, catching tadpoles, eating ice cream and looking through their new school supplies flowed through her mind; followed by the graphic images of terror on their innocent faces as they fell to their deaths. Sounds of their helpless screaming, followed by the sudden end as they hit wet pavement, played over and over in her wounded psyche. How would she survive? How could she go on? Did she even want too? She was too exhausted to think.

Grace hid from the police. A well meaning neighbor told them there was another child who belonged to that decimated family. She knew if they found her they would likely send her off to some foster care situation and she didn't know if she could handle that on top of everything else that had transpired. For now, Mr. Rand let her clean up and sleep in the back of his store until she could figure something sensible out.

All the authorities would have their hands full for a while with so many people displaced by the tragedy, so she had a little time to outline her next move. With no possessions to worry about she wouldn't be much of a bother to anyone. Everyone, and everything that meant anything to her, was destroyed in one fell fiery swoop. She didn't even have a change of clothes, until Mr. Rand came back to the store the following afternoon, and handed her a bag with a few articles he thought might fit her.

Grateful for his kindness, she knew she couldn't stay hidden in the back of his store indefinitely, not without getting him in some kind of trouble with the law. He and his sister lived above the store in that tiny apartment, which wasn't large enough to allow for guests, not that she would have suggested such a thing anyway. He'd been so good to her already, and she didn't want to return his thoughtfulness by causing him trouble with whatever powers out there might not like his intervention on her behalf.

With no place to go Gracie was able to put in lots of hours for her kind employer, which was good for both of them. She didn't mind really. The work kept her mind busy and off the memories of that terrible day for the most part.

The details coming back to her only when she slept, causing her to wake gasping for air, and grasping for her babies.

School started, but Grace didn't. She knew going to school would require a home address, signatures from a parent and supplies she no longer owned. Mr. Rand, he'd asked her to call him Tony now, was great. He offered her all kinds of help with supplies to get back to school, but she declined. Supplies wouldn't get her the signatures she needed and if she put herself out there it would be too easy for the authorities to pick up on where she was staying and drag her off to who knows what?

When kids made their way past the store after classes, laughing and goofing around like children do, Grace's heart ached for her sisters who would never get to use their new 'Disney Princess' back packs, would never wear their new school outfits, or have an opportunity to run and play with their classmates and friends. Barbie had looked forward to starting kindergarten this year and loved her new 'Frozen' panties so much Grace had to warn her not to pull her jeans down to show them off to everyone who passed by; and Gail couldn't wait to show off her new 'Monster High' socks and sneakers to all her 'big girl' first grade friends. Now none of that would ever happen. Everything that mattered was lost.

At night when she lay on the cot in Tony's storage room, a room he'd tried so valiantly to make as comfortable as possible for her, she missed Bobby most of all. The way he'd always cuddled so tightly to her side, like a soft little extension of her own body. Now that the weather was slowly turning cooler she missed his intense heat and the sweet smell of his hair after he was freshly bathed. His chubby, baby face looking up as he reached out for her and called her Mommy on their last park trip together was etched in her memory, and haunted whatever sleeping hours she tried to attain. Those lingering thoughts troubled her so deeply she found herself relentlessly up in the middle of the night to dust shelves and arrange canned goods, all in an effort to keep from dreaming about those poor lost little faces.

Thoughts of her mother caused her conflicting bouts of rage, and anguish. At first she'd been glad the old bat was dead, hoped she'd suffered for all the evil she'd done to their weird, dysfunctional little family, and hoped she was in hell where she belonged; then she cried and grieved for the troubled woman's love, the love she'd longed for all her life. There would never be a redeeming moment in their relationship now, a coming together of mother and daughter to be grown up best friends; no movie trailer ending to this story after all.

Her mother was never the Betty Crocker type, not kind, or loving, to Grace and her siblings, but Gracie knew that without her she would not have life, or the brief time together with the kids that she did. That was worth something wasn't it? Well, it had to be, or she would go crazy. Those little one's lives hadn't been very long, but they were the most important times, and the most important people, in her life and she would never forget them, never.

All day long they injure my cause, all their thoughts are against me for evil.

Psalm 56:5

CHAPTER 4

On a chilly Friday afternoon, while Tony was at the cash register with a customer and Grace was cleaning up a broken jar of pickles in the back of the packaged foods aisle, a tall, grey haired woman sporting a tight bun and wearing a cheap, frayed navy blue business suit entered the store. When Grace eyed her she knew immediately the woman was bad news. She had to be DHS. Everyone knew those workers were underpaid and overworked, especially in this part of town, and her exhausted look spoke volumes to the frightened girl.

Gracie ducked down and worked her way around the backs of the rows of cleaning supplies, boxed goods, baked goods and produce, to her room in the rear storage area. Right before she closed the door, she spied the tall woman walking up to the counter and opening her worn briefcase. The look on Tony's face, as he flashed her a warning to make herself scarce, was positively shaken. She decided to leave the door open just a crack to hear the conversation going on in front. "Good afternoon. Can I help you?"

Looking up with a serious gaze which could not be mistaken she said, "Yes sir, are you Mr. Rand?"

"Yes I am. What can I do for you?"

"We have received information that you are friends with a girl who was recently orphaned in a house fire?"

"Are you talking about Gracie? Sure I know who she is."

"We understand that Grace has been staying with you?"

"Who told you that? I mean I know who she is, but I don't have room for her to stay here, so whoever told you that doesn't know what they're talking about. I take care of my sister and the apartment upstairs is barely big enough for the two of us."

"Oh, well certain informants have told us they see her here at all times of the day and evening, till closing time. They assumed she was staying here. She hasn't been showing up for school. Were you aware of that?"

"Well, she was stopping by to see me, since she doesn't have any other friends or family around the neighborhood anymore, and I even let her earn a few bucks working for me since I knew she was having some hard times, but I believe she's recently left the area to stay with a relative."

"Really, we weren't aware of any relatives, well, at least in the immediate area. Did she tell you where she would be going, since you seem to be her only friend in the vicinity?"

"No, no I think she said something about a grandmother or someone kind of far away it seems. Sorry I can't help you any more than that."

"Well, let me leave you my card Mr. Rand. If you hear anything from Grace, or learn where she may have gone, please give me a call; the streets are no place for a young girl."

"Sure thing," He answered out loud. Then, "Neither is foster care," Under his breath. As soon as the harried woman started her car and drove away Mr. Rand gave Gracie the 'all clear' sign. As Grace walked slowly to the front of the store he said, "I suppose you heard all of that?"

"Yes I did. I'll pack up my things and be out of here in a few minutes."

"I don't know if that's such a good idea Grace. It's getting cold out there. Winter will be here soon. Where would you go?"

"I don't know yet, but I can't stay here. Not after all the kindness you've shown me. It would just make trouble for you."

"She was right you know. The streets are no place for a young girl, Grace. You could get hurt out there and then I would never forgive myself. Have you thought about just turning yourself in to DHS? They might actually be able to help this time."

"After all the stories I've heard about the foster care system in this state, including from you, Tony, are you kidding? I think I'll take my chances out there. I'll figure something out before it gets too cold."

Tony shook his head. "I'm sorry Grace. I wish I could have done more. You've been dealt a pretty bad hand, and if there was anything I could do to change that I sure would. If there's anything I can do for you in the future, you know where I am."

"Tony, you were there when I needed a friend and a place to stay. You've been great. I couldn't ask for a better friend, or anything more, and I thank you for putting your neck on the line more than once for me. I'll be fine and I'll check back in with you from time to time, okay?"

"Sure Gracie. I wish I had more answers for you. Heck, I wish I had a house. I'd offer you a permanent home in a heartbeat, you know that don't you?"

"Hey, don't worry about it. I'm going to get my stuff together, so I can get out of here."

Once Grace had her few belongings, mostly gifts from her generous friend, together, she loaded them in a large back pack, another gift from Tony, and took one more look around. This room had offered her a place of refuge and more privacy than she'd ever had in her twelve years of life. She would miss him. He didn't judge her like most adults did, or treat her like a little child. She felt safer here than she'd ever felt in her mother's care and really had no idea where she would go, or what she would do now. But she wouldn't allow Tony to see the fear she felt, as she didn't want him to feel any guilt at her impending situation.

When she got to the front of the store Tony was waiting with a bag of food for her, and four hundred dollars in cash. "I can't take that Tony,"

"Don't be ridiculous. It's probably not even all that I owe you for the past several weeks of work since you moved in here after the fire, you work all the time and the store has never looked so good!"

"Yeah, but you've been giving me a place to sleep and feeding me and you even got me some new clothes; I really can't take it."

"I insist Gracie. I won't let you walk out of here without it. It will make me feel so much better. I want you to keep in touch too. Do you promise? I'll be wondering about you and how you're doing."

"Okay and thank you, but I'll pay you back when I can, I promise. And, I will try to keep in touch. You've been a real friend and I'm going to miss you." Grace wasn't a crier, but she could feel tears building behind her eyes and didn't want to make him feel badly when there wasn't any more he could do, so she turned to go.

"I'm going to miss you too Gracie. You've been like a little sister to me and I hate the thought of you being somewhere I can't keep an eye out for you. Take care. You know how to find me." All Tony could do now was to continue shaking his head regretfully as a single tear slid from his eye. He wished he hadn't shared with Grace so many stories from his youth in the foster care system. At least he and his sister were alive, which is more than he would be able to guarantee his little friend after a winter out on those streets alone.

Grace left the shop and started walking. After awhile the bag of groceries she carried began to feel very heavy, so she stopped at a bench and opened her backpack. Removing the grocery items from the paper sack one at a time she took inventory. A six pack of energy drinks and one of juice, two boxes of breakfast bars and two boxes of peanut butter and chocolate protein bars, several packages of dried fruit and several more of roasted nuts. Four vacuum packs of beef jerky and two twelve packs of mini Snickers bars completed her food supplies. That should be enough to keep her fed for awhile, and actually better than she usually ate at home. Those things, added to a few personal hygiene items and a couple changes of clothes and underwear she'd packed, along with the four hundred dollars Tony paid her, tucked way deep down in her pocket, summed up her current personal worth. She was twelve years old and didn't know where she would go next. Then, she wondered, did it even really matter?

Fear and trembling come upon me, and horror overwhelms me.

                                              Psalm 55:5

CHAPTER 5

Gracie walked through blocks of small, run down businesses which she recognized, and then past quite a few more blocks of buildings she didn't. Passing several bus stops along the way she finally got tired of walking and took the next bus uptown. She didn't know why she was headed uptown, there was no plan, no destination, and no map for her life.

The bus was filled with other local residents (thank goodness for free public transportation). Some, she was sure were headed for work. She knew several of them as parents of her former school mates who worked evening shifts at nice hotels and restaurants in better parts of the city. Others seemed to be riding for no apparent reason, other than they were tired of walking, just like her. She turned her face toward the window hoping not to be recognized by anyone who might give her away to the authorities.

As she watched the neighborhood landscape roll past the bus' grimy window, a picture of her grandmother's face flashed through her mind several times. She was almost certain she and her mother had taken a bus for those trips, but it was so long ago, and she'd been so young on the few visits she'd retained in her memory banks.

Her sisters and brother hadn't been born yet when she could remember journeys to that magical, warm kitchen. She didn't know her grandmother's name; all she remembered was 'Gramma'; or even what state she lived in. Heck, she didn't know if her own mother used her real last name. With absolutely no information which could lead her back to the only affectionate embrace she remembered in her lifetime, she was without resources. Not aware if her grandmother was even still alive, she couldn't begin to guess how she could ever contact her.

After all that transpired, if she turned herself in to the DHS, or the police for that matter, she would be sent off to foster care family for sure. And after the stories she'd heard from Tony and several others, it seemed care takers in the system, at least the care takers in this area, only went into the fostering business for the monthly checks they received. She didn't want to end up somebody's house slave, or baby sitter; or from some of the dark things she'd heard, worse, so she wouldn't put herself in that position.

Once uptown she dragged her pack down the steps of

the bus, pulled the straps over her shoulders, and began to walk again. The shops and businesses on this side of town were upscale, colorful and much cleaner looking. No drunks leaning against buildings, or sleeping over heating grates here. These were streets for which she was not at all familiar.

It was just about suppertime and she could smell wonderful aromas, from the menu items of several fine dining restaurants, wafting in the air. Her mouth watered and her stomach growled in response, but she couldn't afford those pricy places, she knew that without even looking at the menu, maybe someday.

As night slowly descended all the trees and shrubs lining the sidewalks in the uptown area blinked on one at a time, trunks and branches covered with tiny white lights, giving the area a soft warm glow even in the cool temperatures. "It's not even Christmas time", Gracie whispered in awe as she viewed the spectacle around her. Most of the street's decorated foliage had already succumbed to fall's chilly nights, and brightly colored, crunchy leaves lay on the ground in small piles around the bases of most of the trees, or skipped and skittered here and there, dancing in the brisk evening breeze.

But, as darkness crept in, so did a pervading sense of uneasiness. Gracie knew all too well the hell which invaded the streets, at least in her part of the city, in the midnight hours, and just like the DHS worker had said, "The streets are no place for a young girl." She didn't know how safe the streets were on this side of the city either, but she didn't relish the idea of finding out. She wasn't an idiot in any case and knew she wasn't safe outside with the temperatures getting so chilly at night, but what could she do about it?

She'd never thought she could miss the shabby little apartment she'd shared with her family, but at this moment there was no place she'd rather be. Moisture began to build up behind her eyes and she feared the dam might burst at any moment, releasing an unwanted flood of tears while she stood in this very public place. Grace had never been much for emotion. She couldn't have survived this long if she had been. But, lately she found herself crying more, and being overcome by waves of despair so strong she felt as if they would overwhelm her, to her very soul. In those moments flight off a tall building, or a quick step into oncoming traffic seemed an easy fix, and those moments were coming more frequently these days.

For twelve years she'd listened to sounds of gunshot and

sirens through the little tenth floor window of her home, but at least they'd been clear up high, away from the fear of stray bullets. She also knew how bitter the winters were in this part of the country, and though they hadn't owned much while she was growing up, her mother was right; at least they'd had a roof over their heads, and four walls to keep the worst of the cold out.

Well, for tonight she would just have to figure something out; a workable solution which would keep her in, off of those unforgiving streets, until she could come up with a long term plan of some sort. There was no time to get all weepy if she was going to figure out a strategy for the night, so she hastily wiped away a couple stray tears which slipped unbidden down her cheeks, with the back of her shaking hand, and got down to the business of figuring out how to stay alive.

With limited resources, Grace knew she had to make the money she had in her pocket last as long as possible. There were not a lot of folks out there who would hire a twelve year old girl for much of anything, and she couldn't risk endangering Tony after all he'd done for her. Just by looking around her current surroundings, she knew she couldn't afford a place in the uptown area, so she got back on the bus and rode it, this time, right back down to her old stomping grounds. Now when she tried to look out the filthy windows of the bus, in the dark, all she could see was her own miserable reflection looking back at her.

On her 'side' of town she witnessed the unpleasant, but familiar scene of dozens of drunken men with no regard to propriety propped up against, or relieving themselves on, local buildings. Instead of colorful fall leaves skittering around the sidewalks, it was discarded fast food containers and forgotten newspapers; no softly lit trees on this side of the tracks, no colorful buildings. She descended the bus' steps and noticed, maybe for the first time in her life that the smells, much different here, definitely were not as pleasant and mouthwatering as they'd been, coming from the uptown restaurants.

Standing on the sidewalk outside the bus she saw a man vomiting on the ground in front of a dingy looking bar. She had to fight the urge to retch along with him. Turning to the side to move down the street she saw, on the corner, a group of young thugs who appeared to be up to no good. They were dressed in jeans, which hung down to their knees, and dark hoodies; she just shook her head, ashamed for so much madness going on in her wayward generation.

They eyed her suspiciously, and she knew they were selling drugs to those who approached them with enough cash, so she made an about face and began walking quickly in the other direction.

Other men staggered down the street, heading for who knows where or what, even though it was still relatively early in the evening. Some of the more industrious hookers in the neighborhood were braving the chilly night in their skimpy outfits, probably hoping to lure a client who had a good heater in his car. Some people would do just about anything to get in, out of the elements.

Spying a local hotel sign, on the next block, Grace made her way as rapidly as she could without alerting those around her to the dread which was bubbling up inside. "Don't let them smell your fear", she mumbled under her breath.

Opening the establishment's front door; whose glass was held together by at least a full roll of duct tape applied in various places; she was assailed by the sights, and smells, of the place. Warily, she approached the front desk of the shabby lobby. The tiny reception area stunk of sweat, urine, and stale beer and the carpet was torn and stained with, what she estimated to be, at least a million different disgusting things. Gracie shuddered as she looked around.

The man behind the counter was middle aged and, well, greasy looking. As soon as he saw Grace his eyes got a glint in them, one which was, unfortunately, familiar to her. It was the same look her boss at the bowling alley had in his eye every day of her brief employment there, and it felt completely uncomfortable. "Hey there little girlie, what can I do you for? Are you selling Girl Scout cookies or something?"

His words, even the tone of them, struck her as dirty and made her skin crawl. "I'm looking for a room for the night mister." As he rose from his stool she backed up a step, and the look in his eyes changed to one of malice; a look she was also all too familiar with after twelve years as her mother's punching bag. She could tell that much of the foul odor she detected was coming directly from him, and her nose wrinkled in disgust.

His tone changed immediately at the look of distain he saw in her face. "Where's yer folks missy? I ain't running a baby-sitting service here."

"What makes you think I need permission to stay in your ratty old hotel? I'm a college student, in town for the night and I need a place to stay. Is my money good here, or do I need to find another place to spend it?" As she spoke she pulled the wad of twenties out of her pocket and the look in his eyes changed yet again.

"No, no, your money's good here girlie. Let me get you a key. And, that'll be forty dollars, in advance. Checkout is ten a.m., and you got room number four. Enjoy your stay." The last said with a tone as sarcastic as he could muster.

Once in her room Gracie let out a long, shaky sigh and marveled at her own brazenness. However, she didn't trust the man with the perverted look in his eyes and pulled the one chair in her room over to the door, jamming it firmly under the handle the same way she used to do at home.

She checked the window too, since her room was located on the ground floor, and made sure it was locked tight. Her view from that window consisted of a garbage strewn cement alley and an old, probably 'out of order' pop machine, so she pulled the curtains closed. Looking around the room she had a sense of déjà vu. "He must use the same decorator as the apartment buildings on my old block," she mused out loud. She walked over to the full sized bed, positioned in the middle of the far wall, and pulled down the covers. She didn't see anything crawling around, but, from the crusty look of them, the sheets were definitely not washed since the last occupant, or perhaps the last ten. There was a red, velvet picture of a naked woman, sprawled over rocks on a beach somewhere, hanging crooked above the bed; and one lamp, with a torn shade, on the bedside table. In place of a desk there was a small table with a bit of a lean, and one sloppily bandaged leg. Numerous names had been carved into the top of the little table over the years and she wondered how many of them had slept here since the last time the sheets were changed. Her one chair was currently supplying security, but appeared to have come from an old kitchen dinette set, and had a back and a seat of cracked orange vinyl.

Well, she would make do. She'd made do with this much or less most of her life. Turning the sheets and blankets around so her skin wasn't touching the strange, crunchy stains in the center of the bed would help for a start. A quick examination of the bathroom assured her that he wasn't spending his money on maid service for his paying clients. That was ok too. She could wash the tub out before she stepped in to shower and if she rinsed out her under things and hung them to dry on the shower curtain rod (avoiding the moldy spots of course) it would extend her need for a laundry facility one more day. "This could work for now." She thought out loud. She pulled a package of beef jerky out of her back pack and sat on the edge of the bed to watch television while she ate; but when she clicked the remote, to turn the small set on it only crackled. "Wouldn't you know?" She said with a scornful laugh.

In the middle of the night she awoke from her usual nightmares, to the sound of someone using a key in the lock of her door and the doorknob turning. When the door didn't open, the perpetrator jiggled the knob and fiddled with the key again. After fifteen minutes of failed attempts, the person; she was sure it was the middle aged, smelly manager, for who else would have a key to her room; left her in peace for the rest of the night. Finding sleep more difficult after being wakened she knew it was less due to the greasy manager and more because of her recurring nightmares. Smoke and the smell of charred flesh still filled her senses whenever she sought slumber, or even a moment of peace.

In the morning Gracie showered and dressed in clean clothes, retrieved her washed socks and underwear from the bathroom shower rod, and stowed them in the front pouch of her bag. She ate a breakfast bar, brushed her teeth and hair and then looking through a slit in the curtains; to be sure the coast was clear; she left her key on the nightstand and skedaddled from the filthy little room, leaving its joys for the next unsuspecting renter to discover.

She was proud of herself, however, as she'd stripped the sheets from the bed before she left. Figuring it would require the same amount of work to reapply the same old bedding as it would to supply clean, she hoped it would serve as a hint for management. Then she made her way out of sight as quick as she could, not wanting to run into the weird guy from the front desk again.

For You, O God, have tested us; You have tried us as silver is tried.

> Psalm 66:10

CHAPTER 6

With the weather growing colder and Gracie's finances dwindling she was forced to make some hard choices. She'd paid for hotel rooms at various seamy locations, on several different nights, every one as creepy and grimy as the first. But, she knew it was a luxury she couldn't continue; especially if she wanted to have a little money for laundry and food in the upcoming freezing weather. She still had some supplies in her backpack, but those were dwindling and wouldn't last forever either.

On her bus trips back and forth between uptown and downtown, as she took advantage of the heated, free transportation available in the city, she'd noticed several things. Riding the bus with the kids she'd always been too busy keeping them occupied to notice anything outside the confines of the bus windows. But, these days she was keeping a close eye on her surroundings, looking for alternatives to her situation. For one thing she noticed police rousted vagrants from sidewalks and heating grates on the uptown side, but not usually from her old side of town. It seemed they weren't as concerned for the welfare of those homeless in poorer areas, or was it something else? Perhaps the business owners uptown paid them a little extra to keep their sidewalks clean and free of human debris?

Aware that homelessness wasn't an ideal situation on either side of the tracks, she wondered if it wouldn't at least be safer for her to stay on the good side of town, but where? She couldn't find any solutions to make that happen, as there didn't appear to be any aid centers of any kind uptown. There was, from all available evidence, a concerted effort by those who 'had', to keep those who 'didn't have' out of sight; after all, "out of sight, out of mind", right?

As the weather grew colder Grace became more conscious she had to find better shelter and a warmer coat. She'd been layering her few shirts and one sweatshirt in an effort to stay warm, but that wouldn't work much longer. As it was, her hands grew numb walking the streets even in the daytime now. Hoping for a few minutes of respite one day, she entered a Salvation Army soup kitchen, a few blocks from her old neighborhood, and noticed a table full of donated coats, gloves and hats.

The sign said 'FREE', so she eagerly and gratefully rummaged through the seemingly endless piles of outerwear. Well, that would certainly solve part of her problem. She found several usable items: a good, heavy coat, with a zipper that actually worked; a stocking hat and face mask; A good pair of boots that were only a little big on her, and hey, she'd be able to wear extra socks with all that additional toe room; gloves and a few pairs of nice thick socks rounded out her haul, so she rolled the items together and stashed them, all but the coat, in her pack.

Hungry, but not wanting to appear too eager, she tentatively made her way to the other end of the room and went through the food line. The steamy soup looked hearty with big pieces of meat and vegetables in a thick rich broth, and smelled so delicious it actually made her feel a little light headed. It was served with big hunks of crusty French bread and butter and there was apple pie for dessert! She noticed concerned looks from volunteers, behind the line, as she walked through, and was immediately wary, so she tried to find a private place off to one side of the large room to eat her meal.

Noticing the serving ladies talking among themselves she wondered how long it would be before someone called DHS. Grace ate as quickly as she was able without choking. She hardly tasted her food and thought it was a shame to have to inhale it the way she did, considering it was the first hot food she'd eaten since being on the streets. But, even with its quick consumption, the meal was warm in her stomach and the luscious flavor lingered on her taste buds. Finishing her pie in four bites, she guzzled her carton of milk and wished she had another.

Cramming a few extra hunks of bread and some saltine cracker packages in her pockets she headed as quickly as she could for the door. Once there she found her way was blocked by a kindly looking gentleman, who looked to be in his sixties, wearing an apron which read 'Lean Mean Cookin' Machine'. "Hi there young lady, I just wanted to know if there was anything else we could do for you?"

"Nope, all is well. Thanks for the soup. It was great and the pie was delicious; my complements to the chef. I also got some stuff off your table over there. It said 'FREE'. That's right, isn't it?"

"Well, thank you. The chef would be me. And, oh yes, of course you can go through our 'FREE' table any time you'd like. Can I ask where your parents are Miss?"

"Sure, My Dad's at work. We've been staying with my Grandma. Things have been kind of rough since my mom died, but Dad and I are making it. I just thought I'd check things out over here and have a bowl of your great soup is all. Is that okay? I mean if this place is only for homeless people I won't come back."

"No, that's great. You feel free to come and go anytime you'd like to. Bring your Dad in too, when he gets home from work."

"Well, my Grandma has been making us some great suppers, so he probably won't want to give that up. It would just hurt her feelings anyway. But, I might come back and visit for lunch again sometime if that's okay?"

"That would be fine. You're always welcome. And what's your name young lady? Just so I know what to call you the next time you're in."

"Grace is the name. What's yours?" She hadn't a clue why she'd given her real name.

"They call me Big Mike, Mike O'Sullivan is the name. I own a restaurant on the other side of town. I volunteer to cook over here a few days a week."

"That's great. You're really good at it, and I'll bet folks really appreciate that about you. Well, I'd better get going Big Mike. I'll probably be seeing you around sometime. My Dad will be real pleased you were so nice to me. Maybe

I can even get him to stop by for a while some evening. Bye, see ya."

"Bye Grace. If there's anything we can do for you please let us know, I mean that." Mike shook his head sadly as she hurried out the door. It was clear young Grace was all on her own in the world, and he hated the thought of her out there on the streets with no place safe to stay.

There was a piece of Grace's heart that almost wanted to tell that kind man the truth, the whole truth and nothing but the truth, about her life and what had become of her family. But she didn't. What could he do but turn her over to the authorities. Gracie never had a Grandpa, but if she could pick one he'd probably be a lot like Big Mike. She'd have to be extra careful about walking into places like this from now on. She'd come very close to letting her guard down.

After her exchange with Big Mike she made her way to the local Laundromat. She would wash up her new items and some other laundry from her bag and take advantage of the nicely heated space for as long as she was able. Changing one of her twenties for quarters, she shoved most of the coins down to the bottom of her bag, where she'd taken to keeping the remainder of her money, she'd try to make the change last as long as possible. Thankfully all the clothing she owned, including her new coat, fit easily in one washing machine. From her chair in the wash area she could see all the comings and goings of the customers in the store, and she noticed one woman eyeing her suspiciously.

Picking up her pack, she rose from her seat and walked back to the restroom, ignoring the blatant stares. While she was in the back she washed her face, and brushed her teeth, then she brushed her hair and pulled it back into a pony tail with a free rubber band which had held a pair of her new socks together. Removing her sneakers she pulled another pair of socks over the ones already on her feet and pulled the new boots over them. They fit like they were custom made for her feet. Stowing her sneakers in the bottom of the bag she arranged her remaining personal items and clothing over them, leaving more than enough room for the clothes she was washing. Done with all she could think to do in the bathroom she made her way out front again. Her clothes were finished washing and she transferred them to a dryer. The woman was still watching her.

"Gracie?" She heard from behind her.

"What did you call me? You must have me confused with someone else."

"You're not little Grace from the apartment building that burned down a couple months back?"

"No, no I'm not. Sorry to hear about the fire, but I'm from out of town and I'm just here visiting for awhile."

"I'm Pam. I'm from that building, the one that burned. My kids and I got out just in the nick of time, but I heard everyone in Gracie's family, except her, was killed. I felt so bad about that. She's helped me out a few times when my kids were in some trouble and I have to say, you look just like her. In fact, you could be her twin. Visiting? Who are you visiting? Maybe I know them?"

After those revelations Grace realized she did know Pam, and felt a little guilty lying to her. She'd helped the woman watch out for her two adolescent boys on a number of occasions when they were making some rather stupid decisions. Now the situation became more uncomfortable than it was previously, and she felt a strong desire to get away before Pam figured out her deception.

"I'm visiting Big Mike. You probably don't know him. He owns a restaurant on the other side of town, but I'm staying with friends and taking the bus back and forth. Well, sorry I couldn't help you. I hope you find your friend. You said Gracie was her name? Too bad about the apartment building, that's a shame. Well, nice to meet you." Grace turned away quickly to put an end to the conversation and concentrated on her dryer. When the clothes were finally dry enough to fold, she took care of that chore quickly, returned them to their place in her backpack, turned and gave the lady a cursory smile, and left without another word.

That night, as she was scouting the area, Gracie found a dumpster outside the furniture store, a few blocks from the soup kitchen, and peeked inside. It appeared the unit was only used for cardboard disposal and didn't smell too awful, so she climbed in. The layers of cardboard would be good insulation. She wrapped up tight in her new coat and accessories and settled down for one of the worst nocturnal experiences of her life. The night was filled with sounds of gunshot and yelling. Her few moments of intermittent sleep were haunted by visions of bloody babies with binkies, flames, and the faces of her dead family.

Each time she was jarred awake by noises outside the dumpster she was forced to remember where, and how cold, she was. Finally at around six a.m., as judged by the sounds of traffic starting up around her, she opened her sanctuary's lid a bit to check for witnesses, hopped out and made her way to the nearest bus stop.

You know my reproach, and my shame and my dishonor; my foes are all known to you.

Psalm 69:19

CHAPTER 7

More bitterly cold, as winter drew near, Gracie's circumstances wouldn't work adequately much longer. Neighborhood stores all around the city were decorating for Christmas. Downtown, men dressed in shabby red suits staggered through alleys between their assigned donation buckets and local bars. Tasteless, gaudy, green and red lights, applied hastily to dirty windows, blinked on and off like dismal distress beacons.

On the other hand, uptown looked like a winter wonderland with softly lighted well thought out displays in each sparkling window encasement. Wreaths decorated doors, and garland wrapped gracefully around hand rails and window ledges. Large glowing snowflakes hung on every light post, and stunning center pieces graced intersections. A beautiful manger scene, in the middle of town square, was simply lit and humbly presented, yet elegant. Ordinarily things like that wouldn't move her, but this year the sight of the baby Jesus in his manger choked her up every time she passed by.

The biggest Christmas tree she'd ever seen stood outside the courthouse, and from what she'd heard its official lighting would occur this upcoming Friday evening. She planned to attend. Her trips to this side of town, before her current circumstances, had been infrequent and only to take the kids to the park, so she'd not been aware of the array of holiday festivities available this time of year.

She would've loved to share this Christmas splendor with the children, as they usually didn't have even a small tree for their place. Mother had thought store bought decorations, and trees, were a waste of money. Instead, each year Grace came up with craft ideas to keep the kids entertained, and their scanty decorations were all proudly homemade, and displayed in the small tenth floor window of their apartment. "Wouldn't the kids have gone nuts over this?" Grace whispered, as she took in the marvelous atmosphere. Songs of the season played from speakers in the square, and provided a perfect backdrop to the beautiful lights.

There was some snow, but not as much as there would be later in the season, and she'd been dreading the extremes which would surely hamper her comfort and safety as she slept in the furniture store dumpster. For now though, she felt wrapped in a cocoon of brilliance and didn't sense the cold a bit.

†

Halloween had come and gone this year without much fanfare, and Grace spent that whole evening, and night, hidden in her dumpster. Shaking with fear, and cold, she listened as young hooligans, with more tricks on their minds than treats, hooted, and hollered, while they plundered and wreaked destruction on the neighborhood's unsuspecting souls. She'd never understood the thrill of destroying things and scaring people, but then, she'd had a different sort of childhood; one devoid of superfluous things; so waste and destruction seemed completely unnatural, and mindless, to her.

Remembering last year's Halloween celebration brought more pain with the memories. Gail had dressed as a scary witch and Barbie sparkled as a fairy princess with her long blond tresses cascading over her shoulders. She'd made their costumes by hand, at home, and though they were far from professional, the kids were thrilled with her efforts. Since it was Bobby's first Halloween she'd dressed him in a warm hoodie with long ears sewn on and sweat pants with a poufy tail attached. A smudge of her mom's eye liner on his nose and a few appropriately placed drawn on whiskers turned him into the cutest bunny she'd ever seen. The very thought made her smile, then cry. How could they be gone? It wasn't fair. She'd spent the rest of that night sobbing into her coat sleeve inside her cold metal bin, wondering why she was still alive. If there was a God, why would He have left her here alone?

Thanksgiving, like so many things, had sort of snuck up on her and she'd made her way over to the soup kitchen. Big Mike was there, and of course he'd wondered where her dad was. She'd lied again and told him her dad had to work half a day and they'd be eating with Grandmother at four. "Well, can't you have just a taste with us?" Mike asked. "I made a special turkey with Cajun spices I'd love for you to try."

"Oh, maybe a bite or two", Gracie said. "I've never had Cajun and you are the best chef I know after all." She'd filled her tray to overflowing with that wonderful spicy turkey (even the thought of it now made her mouth water), dressing, cranberry sauce, yeast rolls and butter, peas and corn, mashed potatoes and gravy and pumpkin pie with mounds of whipped cream for dessert. She'd put two milk cartons in her pockets since there was not a speck of room left anywhere on her tray.

Mike asked if he could sit with her while she ate.

She'd responded with, "Sure, but only if you'll eat something. I'd feel funny if you just sit and watch me eat." Mike filled a tray and sat down across the table from young Grace.

Gracie immediately began shoveling the scrumptious food into her mouth. "Do you mind if I give thanks?" Mike asked.

"Oh, yeah, go ahead." Grace said a bit sheepishly, bowing her head.

"Lord, we thank you for this bounty and for good friends with which to share our table, In Jesus name. Amen."

"Amen. Sorry, I've never been much for prayers."

"Can I ask you a question Gracie?"

"Sure."

"Why are you alone? I mean it's pretty clear your dad isn't really around." Grace looked up with her mouth full and appeared ready to bolt. "Hold on honey. I'm not going to rat you out and I'm not going to grab you. I just want to help if I can."

"Listen, there's nothing you can do. Maybe I shouldn't have come here again. I'm not going into foster care and I'm making out fine, really I am."

"Oh, I'm not suggesting that you can't take care of yourself Gracie. You seem to be a very bright and capable young woman. I just don't think the streets are safe for a young lady by herself." Grace continued to shovel food into her mouth as Mike spoke. His voice was calm and reassuring, but she wouldn't be caught with her guard down, so the entire meal was consumed with her arm through the strap of her backpack, and one leg on the outside of the bench seat. She even went up for seconds holding the pack, and Mike didn't want to push things too far.

Grace hadn't eaten a meal so delicious since her grandmother's kitchen, and she barely remembered that time at all. She went through the items on the "FREE' table again and found two sweaters, which looked about the right size, a pair of jeans and several more pairs of warm socks. Loading her goodies into her bag, she told Mike she'd be back to see him for sure. He asked when. She said she didn't know and left before he could talk her into staying longer. Part of her believed Mike when he told her he wouldn't rat her out, but she wasn't going to give him her schedule just in case.

The Daze of Grace

After her meal Grace headed back to the Laundromat she'd visited on her previous trip. It'd been awhile since her last shower and she was sure her ripe body odor and greasy hair were some of the reasons Mike had been able to figure out her secret. When she entered the facility, she walked directly back to the restroom. Locking the door she stripped off her dirty shirt, jeans and underwear. She stood on her filthy clothing, to keep her bare feet from touching the even dirtier restroom floor. Pulling shampoo and body soap, wrapped in plastic baggies, from her pack she got down to business.

Washing her hair in barely tepid water, she felt like it would take forever to get all the soap out as she shivered naked in the chilly room. Pulling a handful of paper towels from the wall dispenser, she used some to dry her hair and others as faux washcloths to scrub her trembling body. Then she rinsed her face and armpits free of soap residue and dried off some more. She'd noticed lately her body odor was stronger and her chest was swollen and sore. Her lower back ached too, probably from all those nights in a dumpster. Brushing her teeth and combing her hair, she pulled it back in a damp pony tail. She was purple and covered in goose flesh by the time she was finally ready to dress.

Slipping into clean underwear and her new jeans, she donned one of her newly acquired sweaters and nodded her approval at the comfortable, if slightly large, fit. Two clean pair of socks and her boots laced up tight completed the ensemble. Gathering her dirty laundry, including her coat and the second new sweater she threw the whole mess into the nearest washer, dumped a small box of soap in the machine, applied coins and turned it on. Then she picked up a 'People' magazine and retired to a chair closest to the heat of the dryers.

✝

Christmas was still almost a whole month away, so she'd get to enjoy the lovely sights of the uptown decorations many more times on her endless daily bus rides. By now she was on a first name basis with the route's driver. "Hey Angie, how are you doing? Here we go with another great morning in the big city, huh?"

"Hi Gracie, how are ya girl, are you staying warm?"

"Warm as cinnamon toast Angie, how about you?" Angie never bothered her, never asked where her parents were, didn't tell her she couldn't ride again even if she'd already made the circuit ten times that day, and was always nice.

There were several others who rode the bus to stay warm and Angie simply figured she was paid to drive, whether the bus was empty or full, so she didn't mind helping those who looked like they needed it most, especially in the freezing cold weather.

"Well, it's getting harder to stay warm every day, but I'm grateful for my mini heater."

"We're grateful for your mini heater too Angie. Thanks for letting us share."

"Any time Grace, any time."

Save me, O God! For the waters have come up to my neck.

Psalm 69:1

CHAPTER 8

Several days after Thanksgiving another rider came and sat beside Grace after she'd claimed her usual seat. She introduced herself as Ruth. She was elderly, probably seventy or so, and had hair so white and wild that when the sun shone through it looked like an impromptu halo around her head. Grace was uncomfortable with the sudden, uninvited company, but didn't want to be rude, so she didn't say a thing right off.

"Where are you headed today, Grace?"

"Nowhere special Ruth, just thought I'd ride around a bit till I want to go home."

"And where's home, Grace?"

"Oh, here and there, why do you ask?"

"Well, I've got something to show you that I think you might be interested in."

"And, what makes you think I'd be interested, Ruth?"

"Well, the way I see it you can't keep sleeping in that dumpster behind the furniture store, especially with the weather getting so cold."

"What, how did you know I was sleeping in a dumpster?"

"A few of us have been watching you and we've seen you go down that alley. From there we just figured it out. If we can figure it out then who knows who else might have that information? I know you're by yourself Grace and I know you're probably hiding from the cops, but you need to be careful of the druggies and the hoodlums too. Do you want to see my secret or not?"

"Sure Ruth, I'd love to see your secret."

Once the bus reached the second uptown drop off the old woman nudged Grace and told her to be ready to disembark at the next stop. The girls said goodbye to Angie and climbed down the steps, Ruth a bit more slowly than Grace, and turned left on the sidewalk. Almost at the end of the street Ruth nudged her to follow, and she slipped into a slim, neat alley between two women's clothing stores. Halfway down the alleyway she came to a window, with reinforced glass, at ground level. She looked around to be sure the coast was clear and pushed lightly on the frame until it shifted just enough for her to get her arm through. She unlatched the window quickly and pushed it in. Climbing through the opening she told Grace, in hushed tones, to follow. Grace was not averse to breaking into a building or two, but looked around again just to be sure she wasn't spotted and then hopped through the gap quick as a flash.

There were wooden crates set up like steps down to the floor. She pushed the window tight and latched it shut before descending. The room was warm and it appeared Ruth had quite a good deal going here. She'd claimed the boiler room of the large building as her own, and, as long as there were no problems with the boiler system there wasn't any reason for anyone to ever come down into the deep recesses of the ancient structure. Therefore, Ruth kept the boiler area clean, and watched it for any malfunctions that might bring repairmen.

Gracie looked around and saw a nook which contained a stowed bedroll and a few personal items in a worn shoebox. A water release valve on the boiler system appeared to be where Ruth was getting her water and for all appearances would be a great source for that. There was a large basin draped with a washcloth and towel sitting slightly behind a tank and near a floor drain. Most of the basement space was taken up by the very old, very large boiler system and an array of fuse boxes and other electronic equipment. A cement floor and wood framing against cinder block walls pretty much summed it up. Grace saw a broom in the corner and an old ice chest, containing who knows what. The room was cozy and warm compared to any place Grace had seen in a long while and she nodded her approval.

"We'll have to get you something to sleep on, but it's warm and we've got all the hot water we can use. I only have three rules: you can't tell anybody about our space; you've got to roll up your bed in the morning so no one will see it, you know, if there's ever a problem that might bring them down here; and you can't be in the building from nine a.m. till six p.m., because that's when the store is open and we don't want to risk getting caught. So, if you want to stay I'd be fine with that."

"I don't know how to thank you Ruth. Yeah, that dumpster has been getting pretty cold at night, but why me? There are lots of folks looking for a place."

"I figure you're just a kid and I'd feel terrible if anything happened to you when I got this nice warm place down here, that's all."

"Thank you Ruth. I don't know how to repay you, but I'll figure something out."

"Oh, go on Gracie. Just do like I say and don't get us caught. It'll be nice to have the company. For now we've got to get out of here. We'll come back again tonight, okay?"

†

Over the next few evenings Grace and her new friend smuggled a few articles into the boiler room for Gracie's comfort: a sleeping bag, a great find from the Army surplus store; some sheets and blankets; and a couple of towels and washcloths. The concrete floor felt a whole lot better with some padding between it and her. Hot water was great! The girls woke up early each day and washed up before setting out and Grace had to admit having a roof over her head and hot water to wash with made her feel almost human again.

†

Before you knew it they'd become inseparable and Gracie was very aware that Ruth's intervention in her life had very likely saved her. The nighttime lows over the past week had gotten down below freezing and she believed she quite possibly would have died in that dumpster if not for her new friend. The deep depression which had been settling in her soul for the past few months seemed to be lifting, with a friend she could confide in, and another human being to talk to on a regular basis. Ruth was clever and funny and she'd been on the streets for a long while, so she had lots of tips and tricks to teach. Gracie was a willing and quick learner.

Friday evening came, and they attended the tree lighting ceremony together. The crowd was large, so the body heat radiated in the town square made things seem almost comfortable even in frigid temperatures. As a group they laughed and chatted until time for the ceremony. Several participants even brought their own thermos of hot chocolate and enough Styrofoam cups to share, so Ruth and Grace each held a steaming container in their gloved hands, grateful for the added warmth.

Grace couldn't remember ever feeling such a joyful sense of the holidays, and was so excited over the upcoming festivities she had butterflies in her stomach as she anticipated the grand event. It seemed almost a sin to enjoy anything this much when her family couldn't be here to share in the moment. Her guilt in surviving without them was almost more than she could bear at times. She didn't even know where they might be buried, as she hadn't stuck around for any of that. The thought of her babies lying in the cold ground, probably in the pauper's section of the local cemetery, with the temperatures so low, caused her elevated degrees of distress that she couldn't describe. If only they could be with her here, now, drinking hot cocoa, and waiting for the big tree lighting event.

"You okay, Gracie?

"Yeah, just missing someone, that's all.

"I know how you feel, but I'm glad you're here."

"I'm glad you're here too, Ruth. It's good to have a friend to share the holidays with."

The time came for the celebratory lighting of the tree and the whole assembly counted down, three….two….one; and with a flourish the mayor flipped the switch. Hundreds stood in awe, many ooohing and aaahing at the tens of thousands of multicolored twinkling lights. Loads of people had tears in their eyes, including Grace. Someone in the back of the crowd began in a soft voice to sing, "Silent night, holy night," and pretty soon the whole congregation joined in. The song was beautiful, the tree was lovely, the moment was ethereal and the entire evening was something Grace would always remember.

✝

Ruth was protective of her new charge, but Grace was

every bit as protecting of her. Ruth knew the ropes, as she'd been on the streets much longer, and knew where to forage for the best stuff, but she wasn't very quick anymore and that's where young Gracie came in. Grace still had some cash too. She'd been very frugal with her limited funds, and that came in handy as they were able to do their laundry on a regular basis. They'd also salvaged and saved an empty large plastic bag on one of their scavenging expeditions, and picked up redeemable cans along their route each day, turning them in for cash. Ruth was full of good ideas like that.

After a while they began eating their main meal together, every day, at the soup kitchen, and when Mike came in for his next scheduled volunteer day he seemed genuinely excited to see Grace again. The girls told him Grace was staying with Ruth now, of course leaving out the fact that their domicile was in the boiler room of a women's clothing store, and he was pleased and obviously relieved about the news.

"I'm so glad you've got someone looking after you Grace. I've been pretty concerned, especially with the weather so much colder outside."

"I told you that you didn't have to worry about me

Mike. We've got it covered and we're in a nice warm place."

"I'm very pleased to meet you Ruth! It's good to know there's someone interested in the well being of our young friend here. If you two need anything please let me know."

"Nice to meet you too Mike, Gracie has talked about you non-stop. I'd have to say Gracie looks after me as much as the other way around. Anyway, it's nice to have the company. It hasn't taken long for Grace to feel like family to me and I'm glad to have her around."

"Well, you ladies eat up. I'm going to fill up a bag for you to take home."

"Thanks Mike, Ruth and I really appreciate you."

Gracie dug through the 'FREE' table again, and came up with a new heavy coat plus additional warm items for her friend, and a new pair of jeans for herself. She promised Mike they would continue to come see him every day for lunch, but he still loaded up a bag with leftovers for their supper, and some donuts for breakfast, anyway. Grace hugged him before they left and promised for the tenth time not to be a stranger. "Don't worry Mike, I'll see you tomorrow."

Back in the boiler room that night the girls ate their leftovers and talked. "Ruth?"

"Yeah honey?"

"Why are you alone?"

"Well, I'm not alone anymore Gracie."

"You know what I mean. Why do you live on the streets? Did you ever have a house of your own?"

"Yes I did. I had a home, a nice one, plus a husband and two kids, once."

"What happened? Where is your husband? And, what happened to your kids?"

"My family died in a fire Grace. They died and I survived, and for a long time I couldn't live with the guilt of going on without them."

"Oh, I'm so sorry Ruth, but I know exactly how you feel, my family died in a fire too." And then Grace relived the entire horrible day in the retelling.

"My word Gracie, you poor child; I didn't know, and I'm so sorry for your loss."

"Thank you. So your house was lost? Where did you stay?"

"I told you I couldn't handle the guilt of surviving. I lost my babies and then I lost my mind, Gracie. I just lost my mind. They locked me up for a long time, and I wandered the green halls of the sanitarium, reliving that day over and over. Then, one day the doctors came in and told me that their budget had been cut, and they could no longer keep me. Since I wasn't a danger to anyone they put me out and I've lived on the streets ever since."

"That's terrible! Where did they expect you to go? Do you have other family?"

"My parents passed away years before and I didn't have any brothers or sisters, so no, I had no one, but now I have you and I feel like we are family."

"I do too Ruth. I feel closer to you than to anyone. As far as I know you're the only family I've got. So, how long were you in the sanatorium?"

"Twenty five years. I've been out for sixteen years now. I stayed in a half way house for awhile, oh, about six months or so, but they had younger girls with children who needed the space. I'm seventy four now Gracie and there aren't very many places that care if an old lady has a roof over her head or not. Especially an old lady without money."

"Have you ever thought about a nursing home?"

"Not much. Those places are income based like most things these days and the type of place I'd have to go, with no funds, well, I'd rather be dead. Have you ever walked through one of those places? The way they smell. A bunch of old people in diapers, staring at walls; like I said, I'd rather be dead, that's all."

"That's how I feel about foster care. I'd rather be dead than end up as someone's slave, or worse. Mr. Rand, well, Tony, I'll have to take you to meet him soon, and his sister grew up in foster care, and she's kind of crazy now. He owns a store where I used to work and he takes care of her."

"That's too bad. There are some horrible things in this world. I figure all we can do is our best. I've been in this basement for close to six years now and it's worked out for me. Before that I stayed in shelters when they had room, and then usually under the big bridge in nice weather if there wasn't room at the shelter."

"Under the bridge, you mean the old one; that must have been scary. I can't stay in a shelter because they ask too many questions. Everyone wants to know where my parents are."

"I can see how that would be difficult. I didn't have much trouble under the bridge. I didn't have anything to steal and I'm not young, or pretty, anymore, so the men didn't bother me much, except to make rude remarks. There was a girl I knew for awhile who was raped and murdered under that bridge though, and lots of people have been robbed of what little they had, so I wouldn't recommend it to everyone. But we do what we have to and I had to have a place to sleep. As you might have noticed, the police won't let anyone sleep on the streets on this side of town and the gunfire on the other side of town is way too dangerous. I'm lucky that I happened upon this place."

"We're both lucky, as far as that goes Ruth. I don't know what I would have done without you. You've been like an angel to me."

"Well, angel is going a bit far, but I feel the same way about you Gracie, and that's just what family does for family. Now let's get some sleep or we won't be able to get up in the morning."

Grace woke in the night to terrible cramps in her abdomen. She rocked and cried, but nothing helped. She thought of waking her friend, but what possible good could come from them both losing sleep? After very little rest, she rose in the morning to wash up, and noticed a good amount of blood in her underwear. She remembered her fifth grade hygiene class and found herself at a loss for what to do next. For now she folded several paper towels, taken secretly from the Laundromat bathroom, and placed them in the clean pair of underwear she'd put on; then she rinsed the blood stained pair and hung them to dry, pouring the dirty water down the drain and rinsing the basin for its next use.

Ruth rose to wash up. "Are you ok Grace? I heard you crying last night. I didn't want to bother you if you were missing family."

"I didn't want to bother you either. To be honest I thought I was dying because I was cramping up so bad, but I woke this morning to find I've started my period. How great is that? I really don't know what I'm supposed to do, or what supplies I need. This couldn't have happened at a worse time in my life."

"Hey Gracie, it's just life that's all. If I was your mother I'd probably give you a nice speech about how you're a woman now, and you should be proud that your body is doing exactly what it's supposed to do."

"Well, just from that comment alone, I can tell you never met my mother. My mother would have slapped me and told me I was just causing more bother for her to deal with."

"I'm sorry to hear that Grace. You really didn't have an easy time of it, did you? I think I know where to take you to get some help though; we'll head there after I get cleaned

The Daze of Grace

up. Why don't you pull out some of those delicious looking donuts and we'll eat before we go."

They hauled their laundry along, since they'd be right in the vicinity anyway. Ruth did indeed know where to get help; she took Grace to the free clinic downtown. Grace had never been in the health center before, because it was one more of those places where they asked too many questions, but Ruth handled it quite nicely. She told the receptionist that Grace was her granddaughter and pretty soon they were in to see a nurse. When they explained the situation the nurse smiled kindly and left the room. Pretty soon she came back with a sack of supplies, and told Grace she could come back for more whenever she needed to. She used the ladies room and removed the scratchy, paper towels to replace them with a soft pad.

They thanked the nurse and left. "Do you feel better now?"

"Yes, thanks for taking me. I don't think I've ever been to a doctor's office before, at least not one I remember. I don't know what I'd do without you Ruth. You're the best."

"Oh go on now, that's just what family does. You know I didn't get to see my own son and daughter grow up, and I never had any grandkids, so it's a real treat to me that you let me be part of your life like this."

"Part of my life, Ruth, these days you are my life; and I can't imagine my life without you in it, sweet lady!"

After the clinic, they walked the few blocks to the soup kitchen for lunch. By the time they arrived they felt half frozen, so the warmth which hit them square in the face as they opened the kitchen's door, and the smells emanating from the building, seemed more than heavenly. Mike was there and without understanding why, as soon as she saw him, Gracie's face turned beet red. She hoped he couldn't sense a change in her; she was embarrassed about her body's recent changes. Mike asked what was going on and she told him nothing, nothing at all, all the time wondering if he could tell there was something different about her.

Lunch was meatloaf with mashed potatoes and gravy, green beans, peaches and chocolate cake for dessert. She and Ruth both went up for seconds, and again Mike sent them home with leftovers, and homemade cinnamon rolls for breakfast. The girls promised they'd be back and Mike quipped "You'd better be if you know what's good for you." Grace hugged him tight, thinking this must be what it felt like to hug a dad or a grandpa, a feeling she'd never experienced before Mike, and they left.

Ruth was as familiar with the Laundromat now as Gracie was, so she went to purchase a box of soap from the machine while Grace headed for the bathroom to freshen up. This whole 'being a woman' thing was going to be a huge inconvenience to deal with every month. Once their laundry was done; they could still fit all their clothes in one large machine; they walked back to the bus stop with their day's acquisitions and headed for home.

While they rode, Ruth nodded off, and Grace watched her lovingly as she snoozed; tiny wheezing noises escaping the small opening in her pale, relaxed lips. The way the last rays of sunlight danced in her mane of untamed, fine, white hair made Grace smile, but the prominent veins in her neck and hands made her look vulnerable, and, well, old. She reached over and placed her hand over the hand of her friend. She loved Ruth and she knew Ruth loved her. They were family and she thought she might just make it now, as long as she had this great lady beside her.

†

With Christmas only three days away, the girls made a deal. They would each take two dollars from their accumulated can redemption money, and buy a gift for the other. Deciding on the 'Dollar Store' for their purchases they were as excited as if it was 'Tiffany's'. Each had ideas in mind for the other and intended to keep their gifts a secret until Christmas morning. Wandering the store separately, laughing every time they encountered one another at the end of an aisle, they were thoroughly enjoying their shopping experience. Ruth finally settled on a set of hair combs and a lip gloss for Gracie and Grace chose a lovely, colorful scarf for her friend. Picking up a scented, red candle for decoration and ambiance, a few assorted Christmas candies, a small bag of red tissue paper for wrapping, and two bows, they were all set. All the way home they snuck peeks at each other and giggled like little girls. Ruth couldn't remember the last time she'd been so happy, she was as giddy as a schoolgirl, and Grace was just grateful to have a friend, and someone to spend Christmas with.

Sneaking a peek sideways Ruth teased, "What did you get me?"

"I'm not telling you. It's a surprise! What did you get me?"

"No Gracie, you'll just have to wait for Christmas morning young lady,"

The Daze of Grace

✝

Two days before Christmas Gracie decided it was time to visit Tony. She wanted him to meet her new friend, and to know she was safe. It had been far too long, she realized, and actually felt a little ashamed she hadn't contacted him before this. She wondered if he'd been worried about her at all.

When the ladies walked in off the street, Tony looked at Grace as if he was seeing a ghost. He banged his hip into the counter, in his haste to be free from the register, and then practically ran to her. Wrapping her in his arms, he lifted her in the air, and gave her the biggest hug ever. "Gracie, how have you been? Where have you been? I've been worried sick about you. It's been so cold out and you didn't let me know. You promised you'd let me know."

"I'm sorry Tony. I, I didn't mean to worry you. I was trying to get situated before I let you know what was going on. We came to visit, because I wanted you to meet my friend Ruth. She took me in, and I've been staying with her."

"You look great Grace, better even than when you left here. I've thought about you every day, and wondered how you were getting on. I've missed ya kid, I mean really missed ya. I haven't found anyone who keeps the place up like you did."

"It's good to be missed Tony, and I'm sorry you haven't been able to replace me, but maybe I could come in and get a few hours now and then? Have you heard anything else from DHS?"

"Not since the beginning of December, where were you staying before that?"

"Well, we won't talk about that, but I will tell you that Ruth stepped in right in the nick of time. I'd have to say she saved my life. Oh, Tony, I want you to meet Ruth here. She's the friend I've been staying with."

"Well then, Ruth, I'm very glad to meet you; any friend of Gracie's is a friend of mine, and thank you for being there for her. Thank you with all my heart."

"You are welcome Mr. Rand. It has been my great pleasure, and Gracie makes more of it than there is. Actually I think she has saved my life much more than I have saved hers. I've come to count on her a great deal."

"Please call me Tony, Ruth. And yes, I know what you mean. Grace has that effect on everyone she comes into contact with. We think we are helping her, and she swoops in and saves us. I'm just glad she has someone looking out for her now. And yes, Grace, I'd love to have you come back if you think it's safe for you."

"Well, maybe it would be best if I waited a bit longer, just to be absolutely sure. I don't want to walk right into their arms. But, when I'm ready I'd be grateful for any hours you could give me. How's your sister Tony?"

As soon as the words came out of her mouth, and she saw the look on Tony's face, she was sorry she'd asked. "She passed away two days before Thanksgiving, Gracie. I didn't cook. There wasn't any point in it. And we had a quiet memorial service the Monday after. We didn't have any family except each other you know. It was just me and a couple of people from the neighborhood at her service. You know she had a hard time with people, because of a lot of things we went through as kids, but she was my little sister and I've always tried to be there to take care of her, at least since I turned eighteen, so it's been hard knowing she won't be here for Christmas."

"I'm so sorry, Tony. I didn't have any idea. I wish I'd known. Now I feel worse about not contacting you sooner. We've been eating lunch at the soup kitchen just a few blocks over from here, and doing our laundry at the little place about a block up from there. I would have come sooner if I'd known. I should have come sooner, and you wouldn't have had to be alone on Thanksgiving. I feel terrible."

"That's okay, Grace. I didn't feel much like celebrating anyway, and now you're here and I feel much better knowing you're okay! You have to promise me that you'll come back to see me more often."

"We will Tony. We were headed over to eat at the soup kitchen. Do you want to come along? We can wait till you lock up."

"No, I'd better not. You know I get a lot of traffic over the lunch hour. I'll be fine here. You girls go along and have fun. Just promise me you won't stay away so long."

"I promise. We will check back in with you soon. Mike is making a special meal for Christmas Eve at the soup kitchen. We're planning on going. Can we come by and pick you up? We could all go together."

"That would be nice. I think I'd like that. Maybe we could come back here after, unless you ladies have something special going on somewhere else that day?"

"What do you think Ruth?"

"I think it sounds great to me, if you two don't mind an

old woman tagging along."

"I think it sounds great too Tony. We'll be by to pick you up a little before noon on the day after tomorrow and we'll plan on spending the day together. You'll get to meet Mike too. You'll like him. Well, we'll get going for now. Can't wait to see you again Tony, it's been great."

"For me too, Gracie, nice to meet you, Ruth, I'll be looking forward to Christmas Eve."

"Nice to meet you too, Tony, I think it'll be a very nice time."

"Great, we'll see you then, Tony. Come on, Ruth, Mike will be wondering where we are, and I'll never hear the end of it."

On the way over to the soup kitchen the girls talked about Tony, about the loss of his sister and the upcoming plans for Christmas Eve. They decided to dig a little further into their budget, and come up with a little something each, for Mike and Tony. They would take care of that right after lunch and laundry.

"Hi Mike, we're going to bring another for Christmas Eve, will you have enough food? He's a friend I haven't seen in months and he's anxious to meet you," Grace chirped as she entered the warm kitchen and proceeded to remove her coat and gloves.

"Who's that Gracie, is that your boyfriend?"

"What are you talking about, Tony? Yuck, he's an old guy; well, not as old as you, but old! He's the man who helped me right after my family died. He's just a friend, that's all."

"Oh, Gracie, I didn't even know about your family, I'm so sorry."

"I, I guess since I told Ruth I thought I'd told you too, Mike. I was pretty messed up for a long time. I'm sorry. I didn't mean to spring it on you like that."

"No, no, it's okay, Grace; it explains a lot I guess. And, I'd love to meet your friend, even if he's an old guy like me."

"No, I said he wasn't as old as you. You're still the oldest guy I know. What's for lunch?"

Ruth just shook her head and smiled, following the two in front of her as they kidded and jabbed at one another. "I'm going to look on the clothing table before I go through the lunch line if that's okay with you two goofballs." The change she'd seen in Grace in the month she'd gotten to know her was amazing. The girl had been through some of the most devastating tragedies she'd ever heard of, and she was bouncing back. Her own troubles had kept her down for decades, but it seemed nothing could keep Gracie low for long. She was so grateful to have this spunky young lady in her life; almost forgetting until now what it felt like to have a real family. How could she have ever guessed her offer of sanctuary, which she meant to save the life of the child, would ultimately be her own salvation?

"Okay, look away, Ruth. If you see anything that will work for me grab it would you? I'll get you a tray too, that way you don't have to go through the line."

"Great Gracie, I'll see you over there then."

Lunch today was beef stroganoff, in a thick, mushroom gravy; with big, fat, buttery homemade noodles; garlic bread; salad with tiny tomatoes, and cucumber slices; and banana cream pie for dessert. "If I keep eating like this, nothing on that table will fit me, Mike!"

"I wouldn't worry about that Grace; you're one of those girls that'll never have to worry about your weight! You're just a little bit of nothing packed into a pair of jeans and a sweater."

"Hey, watch it buddy, you don't want to hurt a girl's feelings do ya?"

"Well, you'd be the first girl in the world who ever got

her feelings hurt because someone told her she wasn't fat!"

Ruth met them at the table and laid her finds out for her friend to see: a pair of nice pants and sweater for herself, and a Christmas themed sweatshirt for Grace plus some new heavy socks for them both. "I found something to wear for Christmas Eve!"

"That's great, Ruth! And, I love the sweatshirt. It'll be perfect!"

"I'd like to offer a blessing," Mike said. Grace was used to Mike, and his prayers, and Ruth was beginning to get used to them too. "Lord, thank you for friends and family, for holidays and hope, for the wonderful meal we are about to receive, and for bringing us all together to share. Amen."

Gracie always felt a little guilty that she didn't share Mike's love for this God he prayed to. She knew how important it was to him, but after all the things that happened in her life, she didn't think his God was spending too much time looking out for her. Ruth on the other hand, believed in Mike's God once, until He took her family from her. She had stood up in front of her church as a small child, and asked Jesus to be her savior, and then was baptized. Gracie had heard all the stories.

Mike's prayers tugged at Ruth's heart and she thought

she might ask him some questions the next time they were in after Christmas. She wasn't getting any younger, and wanted to make sure she was set for eternity, when she left this place. It certainly couldn't hurt.

How they are destroyed in a moment, swept away utterly by terrors.

Psalm 73:19

CHAPTER 9

Christmas Eve dawned bright and cold. Ruth and Grace decided they would stay put until it was time to head over to the soup kitchen. The store above them would be closing at noon today, and they were very busy with last minute shoppers, so there was little chance they'd be discovered.

They took turns at the hot water spigot and washed up meticulously. Ruth dressed in her 'FREE' table finds from a couple days ago; combing her wild mane down with plenty of water, only to have it spring up, and float about her head again as it dried; and Grace wore clean jeans and the Christmas themed sweatshirt her friend had discovered, pulling her chestnut hair back in a neat ponytail to keep it out of her face.

Her new shirt was red with the words 'Santa's Favorite Elf' printed on the front in green. They'd picked up an apron for Mike which read, 'World's Best Chef', and a nice pair of gloves for Tony, and they wrapped the gifts in some of the red tissue paper left after packaging their own presents. They'd decided to use the bows they'd purchased on the gifts for the men. Loading their treasures in Gracie's backpack they were as excited as a couple of kids to get the holiday festivities started, when, just as they were about to climb out the window, Ruth doubled over in unbearable pain.

Grace helped her back down and unrolled her bed, aiding her as she lay down. Ruth told Gracie to go on ahead without her and enjoy herself.

"I'm not going anywhere without you, Ruth. If you aren't feeling up to it we'll just hang out here."

"Grace, your friends won't know what happened to us, and they will be worried, just go on without me." Ruth curled up into a fetal position on her bed and moaned lightly under her breath.

Grace had never seen her friend sick before, and knew she couldn't leave her, but was she being smart? Should she go for help? "Do you want me to go for help Ruth?"

"Don't be ridiculous Grace; I've probably just got bad gas or something."

"Gas, you want me to believe you're doubled up like that over gas? I'm going for help and that's all there is to it."

"No, Gracie, please don't leave me. Just stay. I'm sorry

I'm ruining our celebration."

"It wouldn't be a celebration without you, Ruth. I'm not going anywhere. I'll just stay right here with you."

"Do you promise? I don't want to be alone."

"I promise, Ruth. I'll never leave you."

"Family, Gracie?"

"Yes, Ruth, family forever."

"I love you, Gracie."

"I love you too, Ruth."

Throughout the night Ruth became hot to the touch and moaned incessantly as she thrashed about on her pallet. Grace cried and thought more than once about going for help, even though she'd promised she wouldn't. She'd told her friend she would stay, so she stayed. Where would she get help on Christmas Eve anyway? All the stores on the block had closed at noon. There were no outdoor pay phones on this side of town, as everyone had their own expensive cell phones in their pockets these days. The world was different on this side of the tracks, and that could be good, but tonight it was only lonely.

Ruth reached for Gracie several times in the night, telling her she loved her, and Grace held her hand, wiped her brow, and even lay down beside her to rub her back. She rocked her friend's pallet softly, the only comforting thing she knew to do, and sometime in the night, completely exhausted, they both dropped off to sleep.

When Grace woke and saw light filling their little window she got up to wash herself. At least Ruth appeared to be sleeping quietly now. So what if they had missed their Christmas celebration with Mike and Tony; as long as her friend felt better they could figure it all out later. After she was cleaned up she rinsed a washcloth and made her way to Ruth, who still hadn't moved from the spot where she'd fallen asleep facing the wall. Grace sat on the bed beside her friend and knew immediately something was terribly wrong.

"Ruth, hey, Ruth, sweetie, are you okay?" Grace put her hand on Ruth's left arm and felt the cold. She shook her lightly, and then a little harder. Ruth rolled limply onto her back, eyes wide open. Grace saw her friend was no longer there. She collapsed onto Ruth's chest, clutching her and sobbing. She tried CPR and shook her again, harder. If only she'd gone to get help. It was all her fault. It was always her fault. Ruth had been more than a friend to her, she was family, the only family she had left, and now she was gone and Gracie was all alone, again.

Curling up next to her companion she cried for hours and when she thought she'd cried all the tears she could cry, she cried some more. Finally, when she didn't have a drop of moisture left in her body to cry with she sat up, dried her face and tried to make up her mind what to do next.

She'd have to get help. She couldn't leave Ruth here in this place alone hoping someone would find her, but she knew she couldn't get her up the steps by herself either, so she spent Christmas day in the basement with the only family she knew. She'd never seen a rat in this place, but wouldn't leave Ruth by herself to take that chance. She opened the scarf she'd wrapped as a gift and laid it lovingly around her friend's head, gently closed her eyes, smoothed her holiday outfit over her motionless body, crossed her hands over her chest and waited for this dreadful Christmas to come to an end.

In the morning, early, before the store was open, she would pack up her belongings and write a note to leave with the shop's owner. They would find Ruth and someone would be able to take care of the things she couldn't, but she'd never be able to come back here. They would know about her sanctuary now, and she could never risk going back there ever again.

Next morning she looked around the little room which had been her residence for only a little over a month, but felt more like home than anywhere she'd ever laid her head; she gathered the last of her things, took the can money they'd collected from the small box in Ruth's cooler, kissed her friend on the forehead, pulled the window open and crawled out. It was cold, but she'd been cold before. She'd dressed in layers and wore three pairs of socks plus her face mask. She left the note she'd written, which explained the situation they would find in the basement, on the door of the shop upstairs and made her way to the bus.

"Hi Gracie, where's Ruth? Did you two have a nice Christmas?"

"Ruth's dead Angie and I don't want to talk about it, okay?"

"What? Ruth's dead? How, what happened?"

"I told you I don't want to talk about it Angie. You wanna let me off at the next stop?"

"Sure Grace, hey, if you need anything you know where I am right?"

"Yeah Angie, I know where you are."

The bus stop where she disembarked, to avoid more painful conversation, was miles and miles from any of her usual destinations, but she really didn't know where she was going anyway. She seemed to bring death to anyone who got close to her, so she'd already come to the conclusion she wasn't going to get any closer to Mike and Tony, or Angie for that matter. It was a day after Christmas and she was on her own again, she would just have to figure things out. She'd been pretty self sufficient when she lived with her mom, and she'd just have to manage without a friend; she didn't want to risk anyone else being hurt, not because of her.

Without a clue as to where she might be spending the night, she thought she'd make her way out to the old bridge, where Ruth had spent so many nights, years ago, and check it out. She would miss her dear friend, but that would be the last time she opened herself up to the pain of relationship, and she knew Ruth would want her to go on.

O God, why do You cast us off forever? Why does Your anger smoke against the sheep of Your pasture?

Psalm 74:1

CHAPTER 10

With homeless shelters around the city packed to the rafters, the overflow of destitute had created a cardboard and tin village, under the old bridge, years ago. A large overhang, from the aged viaduct, kept out most of the rain and snow; especially if yours wasn't one of the unfortunate outside structures in the scramble of that rickety village. The word structure could only be used in the loosest of terms, in regard to the small hovels pressed together in the concrete depression under the bridge. Only the hardiest survived in this desolate place, those who were willing to do just about anything to stay alive.

As in all societies, democratic, socialist, or communist the strong tend to prey on the weak. We'd all like to think as civilization evolves it no longer has that inclination, but if we are to face reality we soon realize that in an evolved culture, the strong just become cleverer about their deceptions, and their tactics a bit more subtle. The village under the bridge was sadly, no exception.

It took Grace Hours to make her way to the small improvised community under the ancient railway bridge, and when she arrived she saw several faces peering at her from cracks in their crude homes. The snow outside the overhang was grey and trampled, obviously from the comings and goings of the makeshift town's inhabitants, and the snow free space directly under the protective covering was frozen solid. From the looks of it the whole area became muddy mire when the snow began to melt. "Hello?" Grace shouted to anyone who might be able to hear her and come to her aid. "I can see you watching me. Is anyone going to answer?"

"Who are you?" A voice answered from the depths of cardboard.

"My name is Grace and I'm looking for a place to stay."

"Go away. We ain't got any room for ya here. Just go away."

"Whoa Frank, you don't speak for everyone here, so just shut up. What did ya say your name was, Grace?" A middle aged, grey haired man in a patched, brown leather jacket said, as he walked out from the back of the largest hovel in the neighborhood. What are ya looking for little girl. As you can see we're pretty full up. We only take new occupants who can offer something to the group. What have you got that's worth a damn to us, pretty girl?"

The tone in his voice, and the look in his eyes, gave her the same creepy feeling which had accompanied her conversation with the greasy hotel manager all those months ago, but what choice did she have? "I've got a little cash from collecting cans and I've got some donuts left. They're a little stale, but I'm sure they're still okay."

"Hey, cash and donuts, that's better than you brought with you Frank. Maybe we ought to give her your place. I think we just might be able to help you little girl."

"My name is Grace. What's yours?" Grace stated with a defiant glare in her eye.

"Oh, she's got some spunk too. Tom's my name. Let's see the cash Grace. I'm not calling you a liar, but I've gotta know you're on the up and up."

"Here you go Tom." Gracie said as she pulled a wad of ones from her pocket. "It's all I've got," she claimed, pulling her jean pockets inside out and then tucking them back in. She'd hidden her larger bills deep inside a double pair of socks at the bottom of her backpack; she kept only change in the small coin purse in the front pouch of her bag, currently five dollars and seventy five cents left of her laundry quarters; remembering the words of warning, from Ruth, about the rampant robberies in this place.

Tom took the cash from her and counted it out. "Twenty one dollars, not too bad Grace, how'd you come by the money? We don't want to be harboring any fugitives."

"Like I said, from collecting cans, I've been doing it for awhile. A friend was helping me and letting me stay with her, but she died and I don't have a place to sleep anymore. I wouldn't even ask, but it's pretty cold out."

"You're right Grace, it is cold out, so I'm gonna keep the whole twenty one dollars. Have you got a problem with that?"

"Nope, it's all yours just so long as you give me a warm place to sleep."

By this time most of the residents of the slum had exited their dwellings and were standing around stomping their feet, and slapping their arms, to keep warm; some smoking; all watching the exchange. Many of them were wrapped in dirty blankets, which hung over their clothing, and they still appeared to be colder than she felt. She heard lots of coughing, some of it deep, and wet sounding. She hoped she hadn't made a foolish decision coming here, but she couldn't stay out in the elements with no shelter of any kind. "I can't promise how warm you'll be, but at least it's better than nothing," Tom stated flatly. "I'm gonna let you bunk in with Wendy."

"Aw Tom," Wendy whined. "You know I gotta have my privacy."

"What privacy Wendy, you know damn well you ain't got no johns coming down here in this cold. When the weather warms up we'll figure something else out; that is if our little princess lasts that long."

"Oh, all right, come on then little girl."

"My name is Grace."

"So you are a spunky one, okay Grace, come on in and make yourself comfortable. Did you say something about donuts?"

Grace took one look back at Tom and the others who were still standing around outside as they began to file slowly back into their separate units.

Wendy's small, semi dark residence was almost directly at the center of the improvised village, meaning that very little cold wind made its way that far and her dwelling was a bit warmer than the units closer to the outside walls. Grace could see as she walked through, ducking now and then to avoid hitting her head on low hanging boards, that the bee hive of living chambers was actually quite ingeniously constructed. Once she began examining her surroundings more closely, she could see that four or more layers of cardboard, in some cases, or two layers of plywood in others, made up each wall; additionally the walls were linked together with boards to strengthen each one. Floors were created with cardboard, or plywood, covered with scraps of discarded carpet and old blankets for insulation. The roofs on some units were plywood, on others corrugated tin and the dwellings were all attached through a series of covered, plywood breezeways, for additional strength and covering against the worst of the cold. The situation wasn't ideal, but a far cry better than living in a dumpster.

Looking around the rather meager space, Grace saw there was no electricity available in the room, so she understood then when Wendy was thrilled to find out she had a large, scented candle in her pack. Wendy was also tickled to find out there was Christmas candy to go along with the donuts, even if those donuts were a bit stale. Grace's sleeping bag, along with her sheets and blankets would keep her warm enough in even the worst of winter as long as she was securely tucked away, here in the center of the complex.

As Wendy lit the new candle and munched on a stale

donut Grace tried, as inconspicuously as possible, to size her up. Thirty or so, with bad skin and bleached blonde hair; she had three or four inches of roots that needed attention, and wore way too much eye makeup. Her body odor was tolerable, but certainly not spring time fresh. She went on and on about having a candle and she was almost giddy with delight over a stale donut and some candy. A bit on the hefty side, but not altogether fat, she definitely looked haggard for her age. Tom had mentioned johns, so her profession was clear, but as long as Grace didn't have to be present while business was conducted, she wasn't anyone's judge.

After she got situated Frank let her know that Tom wanted to speak with her. He led her to Tom's dwelling, which seemed to be of a little better construction than all the rest. He had a small generator outside his unit, and even in the waning light of evening she could see evidence of his conveniences. He had an old lamp, with a battered shade, that he'd rescued from the dump; a newer looking space heater; a small black and white television with bent rabbit ears, which reminded her of the little set in her old apartment; and a dorm room sized refrigerator; all the comforts of home. So, his need of money wasn't just for food. He would also require gasoline for his generator, to maintain the life style he was accustomed to living. That would be her bargaining chip. She could collect cans and give a portion of the money to Tom for his fuel, in exchange for his protection.

Tom invited her in and motioned for her to sit in a stained, lopsided bean bag chair. "So, Grace, did you get settled in?"

"Yes, thank you, I think I'll be quite comfortable.

"I wanted to visit with you so I could go over the rules."

"Great, I like to know the rules right away, so I don't get on the bad side of anyone."

"Good, we're on the same page then. So, I'm sure you figured out that I'm in charge around here?"

"Yes sir, that was pretty obvious."

"And, you probably know that I can make things happen, or keep them from happening?"

"Yes sir, I would guess that."

"Most people who live in my little community donate something to keep things running smooth; you know, money, or a service, you get my drift?"

"Yes sir and I've already been thinking about how I can contribute."

"Good girl Grace. I knew you looked like a smart girl. Tell me how you think you can contribute and then I'll tell you my ideas."

"Well, I told you how I collect cans, right? I can split the money with you. That way I have a roof over my head and I can still buy food and personal things, but you will have money for gas to keep your generator going, even in the cold. You can count on me to keep your gas can full; though in return I would also expect your protection."

"Well, I had some other things in mind that sounded more fun, but come to think of it that actually sounds like a pretty good exchange; a roof over your head and protection, for gas to keep my generator going. Okay Grace, you've got a deal, for now. Understand though that our little contract is subject to change if I don't feel like I'm getting the best arrangement for my money, got it?"

"Yes sir. I do. Good then, I'll head out tomorrow to hunt for cans. Thanks Tom, I appreciate your help and I will depend on you to watch over things." Gracie had the feeling, as she left his warm space that she'd dodged a bullet somehow and she felt his eyes on her until she was safely out his door. When she stepped into the breezeway a shudder ripped through her from her head to her toes and she knew it wasn't just from the temperature change. "I'll have to keep an eye on that one," Grace muttered to no one in particular. Her new situation could never feel as comfortable as her time with Ruth, but she was a survivor and she would make do the best she could with what she had.

When she got back to Wendy's space she noticed her backpack had been moved. She opened her front pouch and pulled out the coin purse which was stowed there. Her purse was empty and she looked up at Wendy who was trying, without success, to look innocent. She couldn't say much, because she'd told Tom that twenty one dollars was all she had, and to yell thief now would put her own word at question. She'd have to eat the loss and be more careful in the future. Obviously her roommate couldn't be trusted. She'd wait to check the cash in her sock bank until later, but was pretty confidant Wendy hadn't had time to dig that deeply into her personal items in the time she was gone. Well, her pack would make a good pillow and from now on it would go everywhere she went.

Wendy snored, farted, and talked in her sleep. Grace was a nervous sleeper, especially these days, and every noise woke her. She was surprisingly warm in her sleeping bag and her backpack actually made a fairly comfortable pillow, but she still lay mostly awake all night. She'd waited for Wendy to fall asleep, before checking her bank, and was pleased to see that her bunkmate hadn't found the stash of cash in her socks. Eighty five dollars was still folded and stuffed in the toe of the inside pair of socks. She wrapped the second pair of socks tightly around the first and shoved the bundle back down to the bottom of the bag. She wouldn't make that mistake again. No one could be trusted.

Gracie was up and out before Wendy woke. She didn't want to talk to her and if she was going to earn her keep, she'd need to collect lots of cans. Grace wouldn't be able to avoid the bus, but she might be able to evade Angie. Walking to an alternate route she boarded a bus with an angry looking older gentleman driver. Disembarking at a stop not too awfully far from her regular Laundromat she made her way into the building and back to the restroom straight away.

She was still wearing her 'Santa's Best Elf' sweatshirt and wasn't sure what to do with it once she had it off. She didn't want to throw it away since Ruth had found it for her, so she figured she'd wash it and store it in the bottom of her pack.

Once she was stripped down and standing on paper

towels, she washed her hair with lukewarm water in the small, dirty sink. Scrubbing herself all over with a soapy washcloth, she proceeded to rinse. All too aware how much she missed the hot water spigot in the basement space she'd shared with her friend, but, most of all she missed Ruth; good old Ruth with her crazy, wild hair and sparkling blue eyes. Thinking about her friend, brought a smile to her lips, and moisture to her eyes.

Soon hot salty tears tracked down her face, mixing with soap suds yet to be rinsed away. Ruth had loved her, more than her own mother ever had, and she'd loved Ruth right back. Where was this damned god everyone talked about? Why did He keep taking everything she cared about from her? Drying herself briskly with her only towel, she wiped her tears away, and shivering almost uncontrollably now, dressed in clean jeans and a sweater.

Pulling her hair back in her usual damp ponytail she stood and looked in the mirror for a minute, something she rarely did. Years of her mother's verbal abuse had made her very self conscious, and she'd never felt like she was much to look at. Turning from side to side, she examined her face and decided she probably wasn't the ugliest girl in the world, though her mother had spent a great deal of time trying to convince her she was. She had thick chestnut hair, which fell well past her shoulders now and large brown eyes with thick, long lashes. Her nose was straight, without the cute turned up end like her mother's, but it seemed to be about the right size for her face. Her smile was a little crooked, in part because of the dimple on the left side of her mouth, but her teeth were straight and white. She'd brushed them regularly, since kindergarten when the dentist's assistant came to her school to demonstrate proper oral hygiene; so she had no cavities; and she had a good, strong chin. Her skin was clear; though she'd seen many of her school mates begin to break out with pimples at about the time they began bragging they'd started their periods; but it was dry from the harsh weather and she wished she had a little lotion to sooth it.

Twelve years old and only about four foot ten, at least at last measure, she was much shorter than most of the girls in her grade; but she wasn't fat like Lois, the only other diminutive girl in sixth grade. She should have been in junior high this year and had looked so forward to the new challenges of that grade, but was sure she'd be so far behind by now, that even if things in her life got figured out she'd never be able to catch up.

Putting on three clean pair of socks, she pulled on her footwear and gathered all her dirty things for a load of wash. Propping her foot on the edge of the sink she cinched her laces tight and tied first one boot and then the other. She was toughening up for sure, and she knew it, but she would have to be very careful in her new digs. It was obvious that each one there was only out for his, or her, own welfare and she didn't know how much she could count on Tom's so called protection.

After her laundry was finished she made her way to a small local market, and picked up a package of crackers and a small jar of peanut butter for brunch. A hot cup of coffee with lots of cream and sugar completed her meal. She'd been forced to break another twenty, due to her roommate's sticky fingers, so she folded the bills and dug back down to deposit them in her bank and slid the change into her pocket. When she was done she pulled out her plastic sack and headed outside to rummage through the local trash for redeemable cans. After a six hour day in the elements Grace could claim only twelve dollars in earnings. Not a huge haul, but Tom's half would be more than enough for a couple gallons of gas for his generator, so he should be happy. Her half went for some additional groceries: a small loaf of bread, to go with what remained of the peanut butter; a couple apples, a box of donuts and two cans of soda, which she was sure she'd be sharing with her thief of a housemate. She wouldn't complain though, she was glad to have a roof over her head.

Walking back to the bus stop she passed a pawn shop and something caught her eye. Stepping in to take a better look she decided that eleven dollars was fair for some additional protection. She dug down to her bank once again and came up with the price of a nice hunting knife and sheath with leather straps. She wasn't altogether sure she knew how to use a knife for protection, but just having it around would make her feel better protected. She tucked the purchase far down into her bag and headed for shanty town.

†

"Hey Grace," Frank shouted at her as she walked up to the village.

"Yeah Frank, what do you need, I'm tired."

"Tom told me to tell you he wants to see ya when you get back."

"Fine Frank, I'll take care of it." Grace headed to Tom's

shelter to hand over the six dollars she had for him."

"Hey Tom, you in?"

"Come in Grace. Glad to see you're finally back. I was getting worried about you."

"Worried about me, Tom? You mean worried if I was going to come back with any money for you?"

"Well, one goes with the other I guess you'd say Grace. How'd you do today?"

Grace pulled the six dollars out of her pocket. "Here's your half just like I promised."

"Six bucks Grace? That ain't gonna hack it. You're gonna have to do better than that little lady, or I'm gonna need something else besides."

"What are you talking about Tom? We agreed on half of a day's take. Half of twelve dollars is six dollars and that's fair."

"You gave me twenty one dollars the first time Grace. I was expecting results when I agreed to your proposal."

"Twenty one dollars was from days and days of collecting for me and my friend, Tom. You knew that and you agreed to that. I told you I'd keep your generator in gas and six dollars will put two gallons in that thing. I'll be back out tomorrow, and all the days after too, so don't worry, you'll have your fuel."

"I'd better Grace, or we're gonna have to have a little talk, you get me?"

"Yes Tom, I get you."

Back in the room Grace noticed Wendy was still in the same clothes she'd had on when she left. She smelled a bit riper than she had that morning, and her makeup was smeared. Perhaps the woman didn't bathe very often. She hoped that wasn't the case.

"What's going on Wendy?"

"I'm just chilling Grace."

"Have you been out today?"

"Just over at Tom's paying my rent."

"Did the five seventy five help?"

"I don't know what you're talking about, but that ain't how I pay my rent. I take care of mine in services if you know what I mean."

"Yeah Wendy I know what you mean, sorry to say. I brought some groceries if you're hungry."

"I'm starved! What did you bring?"

✝

Grace continued rising each morning before dawn and

making her way to the bus stop to begin her long day of collecting cans for redemption. When she woke in the morning, before heading off, she strapped on the knife. Wearing it on her hip gave her a feeling of comfort and safety. She would carry the knife every day going forward.

She wanted to spend as little time as possible in the shanty town, and as little time as possible around its inhabitants. Regretfully she could no longer work in Tony's store; as the money there had been much better, and the work less dirty; because she'd promised herself she would never again put her friends in danger, by their mere association with her. She knew with every fiber of her being the only reason her family, and Ruth for that matter, were dead was because they'd known her, and been a part of her life. The hours were long, and the profit minimal, redeeming cans; but there weren't many jobs for twelve year old girls, so she would do what she had to do to pay for her keep.

Tom continued to make threats about additional forms of payments, if Grace didn't bring in more money, so a few times she'd added cash from her sock bank to the days take, to keep him at bay, but that would only last so long. It'd likely be another six to eight weeks before winter relaxed its icy grip on her part of the world, so she had to stay on his good side until then. Grace thought often about finding another place to stay, once the weather broke, maybe even heading out west after spring arrived.

She was lonely in this place. Hard as she tried to be nice, she just couldn't be friends with Wendy. The woman was selfish and sneaky and reminded her to much of her mother. As winter wore on, the small shared space became harder to bear. Wendy's body odor got so bad, Grace didn't know how she could even stand herself. Every day when Grace got back from hours out in the cold, her roommate wanted to know what she'd brought her, and Tom demanded to see her in his room for his cut of the profits. He was becoming more aggressive and demanding every day, and Grace's nerves were very much on edge.

☦

It was right around the end of January, when Grace's redeemable can hunting business took a turn for the worse. The average day's haul lately was running five dollars or less, way down from her fall numbers in the double digits. Tom was not pleased with his share, and she could, if grudgingly, understand why. Their agreement had assured him enough to keep his lights on. Two dollars and fifty cents didn't cover even one gallon of gas for his precious generator, so he was wanting something more from her to pay for her keep. She'd used up the money in her sock bank trying to keep him happy, and paying for groceries and laundry, so her alternatives were slim.

Today when she came in from eight hours in freezing temperatures, hands, back and feet aching, he would be waiting for her with an angry and impatient look on his face. She couldn't lie to him, she had only four dollars and twenty cents to show for her efforts out in the cold, and he'd likely pitch a fit when she told him. Her psyche, already beat up from her lack of success on the streets, deflated more as she approached the edges of the slum village, and his predictable wrath. When she relayed her unwelcome news, he back handed her, knocking her to the floor.

Something rose up in her as her body hit the ground. She'd been knocked around all her life by her mother, and she sure wasn't going to take the abuse from him! As she stood up, a glimmer of black thunder filled her eyes; a look bordering on crazy. Her hand disappeared under her coat, and when it reappeared it held a very long, very sharp knife. Tom backed up a step, and his look changed from anger to fear. This young woman was not the same compliant little girl he'd been dealing with up to this point. "Hey Gracie, let's not get carried away here now. You hear me? You're acting a little crazy girl."

"You will never lay another hand on me Tom. Do you understand?"

"Sure Grace. You know you ain't been filling your end of the bargain. We had an agreement. I just got a little carried away. It ain't gonna happen again. I swear. We okay?"

"Yeah, Tom. We're okay. I'll get it figured out. Just know if you ever lay another hand on me, you will live to regret it."

"Okay. Understood. We'll talk about this later, when we've both cooled off. Deal?"

"Yeah, right, deal."

You have put me in the depths of the pit, in the regions dark and deep.

Psalm 88:6

CHAPTER 11

Crammed in her mouth, and half way down her throat, before she could scream; the filthy rag was gagging her as she woke disoriented and hopelessly tangled in her sleeping bag. She tried to sit up, but only made it halfway, and on to one elbow, before she was slammed back down by unknown assailants. The room she shared with Wendy was pitch black and as she reached for her knife, which was still hidden beneath her coat, her hands were seized and jerked behind her back. Her attackers fastened them with a zip tie that immediately cut off her circulation. It was almost as if they'd known about her hidden weapon.

She never saw their faces. Struggling to free her legs from the night's covers, she tried kicking her ghostly assailants, but they caught her feet, and wrapped them in what felt like yards and yards of cord. A bag over her head would assure their anonymity as they emerged from her shelter, carrying her between them by her arms and legs, into a moonlit night.

Tossed onto the floor of a running vehicle, like a sack of laundry, she tried again to sit up; only to be knocked over, slamming her head into the van's wheel well as the engine revved and took off at break neck speed. She laid still. Who were the men who'd attacked her and where were they taking her, were a couple of the questions speeding through her confused mind. She heard them speak. "Hey, she still alive back there? She hit the wheel well pretty hard." A hand grabbed her neck to feel for a pulse.

"Yeah, she's just out cold. She'll be okay."

"Well be sure she stays that way. Tom would be pretty pissed if anything happens to her before he gets paid."

"Ain't she gonna be surprised when she wakes up? I'd love to be there to see the look on her face when she realizes he sold her to the Russian mob! What a hoot. Guess that'll teach the little whore not to pull a knife on the man in charge, huh?"

"Yeah, that'll teach her for sure."

Sold to the Russian mob? What did they mean sold to the Russian mob? So this was all Tom's doing? That would explain how they knew about her hidden weapon. She wondered if Wendy had been in on the whole thing, or just watched it happen without attempting to help? It didn't surprise her. She'd known from the beginning her roommate was one of the most self serving people she'd ever met and now she'd have Gracie's sleeping bag and pack along with all her other supplies for her trouble. It was certainly worth it to the slut, to turn a blind eye to the young girl's plight if she could benefit that much by keeping her pie hole shut.

Grace tried to hold very still, listening for any clues as to where they might be taking her. The men laughed and joked at her expense, but didn't give her any more information through their animated discussion. No, but wait, those were railroad tracks they just drove over and wasn't that a barge horn? Like the ones she heard when she was down by the river? When the van stopped, Grace found herself being handed off to two men who had, what sounded like, heavy Russian accents. She could hear the sounds of river vessels and loading docks mingled in with other background noise. She was carried into a building, down what seemed like a very long hallway, through a set of doors, down another long hallway and then unceremoniously dumped in a room on what felt like a padded surface of some kind. The two men left the room and closed the door behind them. She heard a bolt slide home. Grace struggled in her restraints, with no success, until she heard soft footsteps coming back to the door.

She lay quietly until the door opened, light footsteps approached her and a hand pulled the hood from her head. A girl of perhaps thirteen, or fourteen, with hair blue black as raven's wings, and large brown almond shaped eyes, looked pityingly down on her. She took hold of the rag still firmly lodged in Grace's mouth and began to remove it, causing her to gag all over again. Grace choked and tried to ask for water, but no sound came forth. The beautiful girl seemed to know her request though before she asked it, because she'd brought a bottle of water and a knife with which to cut the binding from her hands and feet.

Gracie guzzled the whole bottle of water and then rubbed her bruised and bloodied wrists. "Where am I and who are you? What is this place? I demand to talk to the person in charge! You can't keep me here like this. This is against the law!"

The Raven haired girl spoke with a slight Asian accent of some sort, though Grace didn't know enough Asian people to pin it down, and a soft voice. "Try to calm down. If they see you like this they will only beat you and I don't want to see that happen. I am a prisoner, just like you, though I have been here since I was six years old, and I am afforded a bit more freedom when it will suit their purposes. You are in a compound run by the Russian mob. The people who now own you."

"Own me? They can't own me. It's against the law to own another person. I want to talk to the person in charge, who is that?"

"Believe me my dear, you do not want to talk to the person in charge. If he ever has to come talk to you, you will be very sorry indeed. And yes, they are very aware that what they are doing is against the law, but I am guessing that is why they make so much money doing it. Now you must calm down if you don't want to be in further bad circumstances."

"Are you going to stab me with that knife? If not, I'm going to leave now. Will you try to stop me?"

"You won't make it ten feet my dear. They only trust me to cut your bonds, because they are armed with AK-47s, which this knife would do little to stop. This building holds the receiving cells for a brothel which is owned and operated by the gentleman who now owns you, just as they own me. There is no way to escape. Believe me. I have the scars to prove that it cannot be done. I am here to reveal to you your circumstances and to prepare you for the house."

"A brothel. You mean a whore house? I'm twelve years old. You can't be serious. I don't want to be prepared for the house. You know your way around the place, don't you? You could help me get away couldn't you? Please, you have to help me."

"This place is very well guarded my dear. Even if I could, I wouldn't. I would be responsible for your escape and I would be severely punished for that. You may as well accept your fate as we have all done. There is no escaping, except through death. There are over two hundred girls here, some as young as eight and some who have been here as long as ten years. I too have many times wished for death in this past two years, but now I am trusted to prepare the new girls and it keeps me out of the bed, so I will not jeopardize that role. I am to take you to the restroom to clean you up and from there I will take you to your assigned room."

"Grace, my name is Grace. You keep calling me 'my dear' and I want you to know my name is Grace. The girl you refused to help today, goes by the name of Grace."

In the bathroom Grace was stripped of her clothes and ordered to shower. Supplied with only a sheer night gown and flip-flops she was shamed and embarrassed. She knew everyone could see right through her clothing and guessed that helped to keep the girls in their rooms. Grace had always been shy. Her mother's constant putdowns had left her with almost no self esteem at all, and she'd never dressed provocatively as some of her developing school chums had. She couldn't understand how any girl could do this to another; sure that if placed in the same position she'd have rather faced death than take the responsibility of destroying another's life.

As she walked with her guide, past leering men, to her assigned room, tears shone in her swollen eyes and slid down her reddened cheeks. When she managed to escape this place, she planned to find Tom and kill him, but not before making him pay in ways she would invent, with great pleasure, for his suffering.

†

No one came to her the first day and she was given two adequate meals; the first was some sort of tasteless porridge, but it was warm and filled her empty stomach, and later a vegetable and meat stew with bread. She checked the door finding it securely locked, and found no other way to escape. There was no window and she still had no idea where she was. Supplied with a mattress, sheets, a blanket, chamber pot and some personal hygiene items, she was again led to the bathroom to shower and empty her pot. Well, at least they were going to allow her to bathe each day. That was a relief, though each trip meant walking past the same leering guards. The second day, however, a man who appeared to be in his late fifties or sixties, was ushered into her room by one of the guards. The door was shut and locked behind him.

The look in his eyes was unmistakable; and once again she hated that she knew that at only twelve years old. As he came closer Grace jumped up and her blanket fell to her feet. There was no denying his intent, and once he had her cornered and began groping and pawing, self preservation mode kicked in; which caused her knee to rise and connect with his unprotected groin hard enough to crumple him to the floor. There was nowhere to run and Grace began to cry. The man yelled for help, and two guards entered. They ushered him out, as he cursed and swore at, "that little whore" all the way down the hall. She knew she'd most likely get it now.

Within what seemed like less than an hour she heard footsteps approaching her room again. Stomach tied in knots, she guessed this was probably the mob leader come to kill her. Instead, when the door opened it was her Raven haired guide once again, followed by two armed guards. She directed Grace to follow her and as they walked the girl revealed, "I'm taking you to meet the man who owns you. He is very upset, because he paid a high price for you and he expects to get his money back from the services you will provide for his clients. The customer you injured paid a very great deal to spend the night with a young virgin and he has now received his money back. I would not want to be in your shoes, but I wish you luck."

Grace was led into the presence of a tall man; with dark hair, graying at the temples; piercing blue eyes, that radiated malevolence; and a square jaw set like iron. He emanated an evil power which frightened her to the very core of her being. She suspected if there was indeed a devil, this man might be he. Though to infer there was a devil, she might have to conclude there is a God and she wasn't willing to go that far, especially in her current circumstances. The man opened his mouth and spoke in a thick Russian accent, "Hello Grace. I am the man who has purchased you. You belong to me now and you will do as I say. Do we understand each other?"

"I don't know who you think you..."

"Shut up Grace. You are a young lady with many opinions and a very big mouth. Since you do not seem agreeable to doing my bidding upon request. I do have other means with which to persuade you." At that he removed his belt, doubled the leather strap in his fist and began to beat her, until she eventually passed out from the pain. Toward the end of her punishment he was grunting, with the effort he used to whip her into submission, and covered with a thick sheen of perspiration. When she woke she was back in her room. Her body, covered in bruises, ached so badly she could barely move for a full day after the beating. No one came to bring her food, or to lead her to the showers for three days afterward, as she was left alone to deal with her injuries.

On the fourth day breakfast came. She was ravenous, eating the entire bowl of porridge without once looking up at her guide. She was led, with her very full chamber pot, to the bathroom, for a chance to shower. With her sheath removed, the bruises, already turning green and yellow around the edges were shocking in their size and number. He'd been very careful not to touch her face, but it would take many days before her body was free from the effect of his brutal whipping.

The following evening, as she napped, her door was unbolted and she woke with a strange little man standing over her bed, the intent of his visit and gleam in his eyes more than apparent. Again the self defense mechanism switched on in her head, and she kicked him squarely in the gut as he approached. Punching him in the nose, and kicking him over, and over as he tried to ward off her attack, he screamed for help. Guards came swiftly to his rescue. More frightened than she'd ever been in her life she tried to pray. Rosie had told her God loved her and would take care of her. She'd promised her young friend that this God of hers would protect her. "God, I don't know if you're even there. My friend Rosie knew you and she told me you would protect me. I really need you now. I'm so scared."

Before she knew it the guards were back, with her young raven haired guide, and they were leading Grace off to the rooms of her owner. As the girl stood in the hallway watching Grace being dragged into the room she shook her head solemnly, turned and walked away. This time the guards held her down, as she tried with all her might to kick and fight against the inevitable. With a room full of men watching her humiliation, he raped her. Once he was finished he beat her mercilessly. This time though, he didn't spare her face. As she lay bleeding, losing consciousness, he grabbed her face roughly in his hand and said, "Now it's done. You can quit fighting it Grace. You are no longer a virgin. You can no longer think yourself better than the rest of the girls in this place. Do you hear me? Accept your fate, or you will surely die by my hand."

She woke shaking from the pain. Back in her room once again, she didn't try to rise. Badly hurt, she ached all over, but worse, she felt dirty and used, and as the memory of what had transpired washed over her she retched. Shame overwhelmed her, but now she didn't want to cry, she only wanted to kill. She'd asked Rosie's God to save her, but He'd left her on her own, just like every other day of her life. There was no God. For if there was and He didn't care enough about her to save her from this evil place, then He was much worse than absent.

Days turned into weeks, and weeks into months. She stopped fighting her fate, and men came to her room to use her, terrible perverted old men; she ate, showered, slept and hated. No, there was no God, not in this place. It seemed like years since Ruth had died, since she'd last seen her family. The nightmares had stopped. She didn't dream at all anymore. What was the use?

†

Girls were generally taken off the floor during their cycle; and as much as Gracie dreaded her period before, now she looked forward to it as a mini vacation from the terrible reality of her existence. When it was time for that event in her third month of imprisonment and nothing happened, she was puzzled. When another month passed she knew she must be pregnant. Afraid to tell, for fear her news would earn her another beating, she kept the information to herself for three more long torturous months.

Her little secret kept her going. The thought of having a baby, after the loss of her siblings, became the one positive thing in her mind. She wondered whether the child would be a girl or a boy. This expectation became her reason for living, for going on. She knew she was young, but being this child's mother would give her life purpose. As near as she could figure it was the end of May, or beginning of June. She hadn't seen sunlight for months, so she couldn't be sure, but she thought if she could just figure out a way to escape, she could make it on her own if the weather was warm. She'd been taking care of herself before she was kidnapped, and she could take care of a baby too, she was sure of it. Her thirteenth birthday passed without a nod.

Beginning to show, she'd already felt the baby kick and at the thought of having a small warm bundle to love, and hold, she cried. Not being noticed was becoming harder to do. Her guide began to look at her suspiciously over the next few weeks as she showered, and Grace knew it would only be a matter of time before someone called her out on her deception. Finally a client who had been a regular visitor mentioned something to the man in charge and she was called to his quarters. "Hello Grace. Why did you not tell us you were with child?"

"I'm not, well, I mean I just started to figure that out myself. It's okay though, I'll be fine and the baby won't be a bother. I can take care of him when I'm not with customers."

"You don't understand Grace. You belong to me and I do not allow my girls to have babies. Motherhood detracts from their duties. We will arrange a visit from the doctor."

"No, please, I promise I won't be distracted. You can't...." His slap snapped her head sideways and the guards escorted the crying girl back to her quarters.

The following day she was led, crying and begging, to a room in the back of the building. Once there she pleaded with a small dirty man who wore a blood stained smock and seemed to be in charge of this room of horrors. As she pled for the life of her child, while surrounded by containers of tiny, bloody body parts, she knew her fate was sealed. He was unaffected by her situation, or her pleas, and gave her an injection which knocked her out almost immediately. When she woke in her room later and moved her hand to the place where she'd felt her baby kick only the day before, her abdomen was almost flat and she knew he had ripped her unborn child from her body. She was horrified.

Inconsolable, Grace decided she no longer cared to live, and did everything in her power to ruffle the feathers of those who might be in a position to help her to that end. Refusing to service customers and throwing her food at guards was only the beginning. When she was taken to the rooms of her owner he told her he was giving her one more chance. "I don't want one more chance. You can beat me, starve me and do whatever you want to me, but I will not take care of your clients, and I swear I will make your life the same living hell you've made mine. You killed my baby. You're done. Don't you understand? You can't hurt me anymore than that."

The Russian smirked, pulled a gun and pointed it at

her head. Gracie knew she ought to be frightened, but she wasn't. She didn't know if there was a God, or a heaven, but if there was then maybe she would see her family again. Perhaps she'd have the chance to hold her baby there since she'd been denied that opportunity in this world. She looked him square in the eye and spit in his face. He knocked her to the floor, stood over her prone body and blasted her in the back of the head. "Get her out of here and get rid of the body. You know the drill. And somebody get her room cleaned out. We've got some new girls coming in."

He who dwells in the shelter of the Most High will abide in the shadow of the Almighty.

Psalm 91:1

CHAPTER 12

When Grace opened her eyes in the gloomy darkness, she figured she must be dead. She'd not been at all frightened to die when the tall Russian pointed the gun at her head, but she was terrified about where she was now, and what might be coming next. Though the place had no discernable light source she was swallowed up in layer upon layer of shifting shadows. The weight of absolute, abject despair was palpable here and her ears were filled with the sounds of sadness and great suffering coming from every quarter. She wondered if this was hell. It couldn't be heaven, but she didn't know.

She saw no pearly gates, no golden streets and no throne. Mostly she didn't see Jesus, well, assuming He could be seen, and assuming she would know Him if she saw Him. As a matter of fact, she didn't see anyone. That had to be the most disturbing aspect of her present situation. The complete and utter emptiness of the place. She called out and her voice echoed back to her without response.

Her fear deepened as she rose and walked. No, this

couldn't be heaven. Rosie told her in heaven she would be filled with peace and joy; that she would feel the love of God like a big hug. All she felt here was loss. Well, Rosie's Jesus had never been there for her while she was alive, what could she expect from Him in death, or whatever this was? The sorrow of knowing she'd thrown away numerous opportunities to share her life with Him, the way Rosie did, was intensified in this miserable place. Something deep inside her mourned for the chances she'd missed. But, it was too late now to come to know her friend's Jesus, wasn't it?

She didn't see another soul, but knew that every other presence here, cut off from all loving contact, was tormented and alone just as she was. Maybe the very definition of hell was the loneliness and separation she felt? The longer she walked, the more oppressive the hopelessness and desolation became, until her very heart felt like an enormous weight in her chest. How could she spend eternity here? How could she spend eternity alone? She'd never thought of herself as much of a people person, but the idea of spending millennia without the presence of another human being, or even the face of the God she'd rejected, was overwhelming.

The Daze of Grace

✟

"No officer, we were just messing around down here by the water and we saw her laying on the rocks. She looked dead. Well, we didn't know if she was dead, since we never saw a dead person before, but we called 911 right away. Is she dead? We told you everything we know, really. We didn't see anything, 'cause she was just there like we told you, and we didn't touch her, I promise. I never saw anyone dead before."

"Sorry Jimmy. I don't know any more than you do at this point. It was the ambulance that took her away though, not the coroner's van, so that's a good sign. They're taking her to the city. I've got your number on the report. Since you're thirteen I have to talk to an adult with any new information I receive. I hope you understand. I'll call your folks as soon as I hear anything, okay? You just might have saved that girl's life young man."

"I hope so. She's sure not very old. It would be sad if she was dead. We just came out to fish. Never knew we'd find a girl on the rocks. Boy that's something huh? I'll bet nobody at school will have a story like that when we get back!"

"No they won't Jimmy. I can pretty much guarantee that!"

✝

"She appears to be stabilizing Doctor."

"What's her BP?

"Ninety over forty five."

"That's still pretty low. Give her another unit of blood. From the looks of it she'd just about bled out. What is it now, four? She's lucky those boys found her when they did, or we'd be having a very different conversation."

"Yes Doctor. I'll get that going. Has anyone been able to find out who she is?"

"For now she's still a Jane Doe. We may never know. She's fortunate to be alive, but who knows how much will be left after that surgery? I had to dig around in her head quite a bit to retrieve the bullet fragments and stop all the bleeders. For crying out loud, who shoots a kid in a nightgown in the back of the head?"

"Well, there are some real creeps out there for sure. My friend Becky tells me about some of the cases that come in through the E.R. doors. She's covered with bruises and they aren't all from her trip down the river. They appear to be from a series of beatings over a long period of time. She's blessed for sure, whether or not she knows it. How anyone survives a bullet to the head I couldn't tell you, but she wouldn't have lasted much longer on the rocks, so if you ask me that looks like the hand of God."

"You could be right. I just don't know Nancy. I think this girl is a survivor if I've ever seen one and she's probably got an unbelievable story if she lives to tell it, or can remember any of it. I think whoever threw her into that river figured the water would finish what they started. What they didn't count on is that the temperature of the water might have slowed her system down enough to staunch the bleeding and preserve just enough heart rate to keep her alive. It will be interesting to see how this plays out."

"Well she's lucky you were her surgeon. If anyone could get that bullet out with as little damage as possible, it would be you, Doctor Phillips. We'll watch her and I'll let you know the minute there's a change, or if she starts to wake up. You go home now. You must be exhausted and I'm sure Rachel is wondering where you are."

"Yes, I think I will Nancy. The life of a surgeon, huh? What most people don't realize is it's not nearly as difficult as the life of the head surgical nurse! Say hi to Mike for me. He's a lucky man."

"I will Doc, and actually, I'm a lucky woman. I'm married to the greatest guy in the world."

She presented a pitiful sight, this young girl of about twelve, or thirteen. She was pretty, if you took away the bruises and swelling, but small for her age. If she survived it would take awhile for her hair to grow back in. They'd shaved her head for the surgery and the swelling and bruising was extensive, even to the swelling shut of her eyes. There was a sadness about her, even in sleep. Nancy sat next to her, in I.C.U., for several hours that night and prayed. A news report at ten mentioned the young girl who had been retrieved from the river alive; a girl who'd been shot in the head.

In a cement block building near the river, a certain Russian mob boss heard the news report with a high level of anxiety and began immediately to make plans to cover this oversight.

A young raven haired girl, in the same room, looked up with hope in her eyes and then quickly back down again. Was it possible Grace had survived? Her owner dressed quickly and left the room. Two of his men received instructions to make their way to the hospital. They were ordered to be sure the girl didn't awaken. Though he was sure Grace didn't know the location of the brothel, she could positively ID him and he wouldn't let that happen. He'd only been in the states for twelve years, but this country had definitely proved to be a land of plenty for him. He wasn't about to have that little whore ruin it.

†

Nancy came to visit the girl every day. She didn't want her to wake alone. Not that she was ever really alone, not in the I.C.U. The nurse's station was only ten feet away. Close enough for the ladies to keep a constant watch over her, and also close enough that the men who'd been sent to kill her, who were lurking in the halls, would definitely risk being spotted if they tried anything now. They reported back to their boss that the girl was in a coma, and they didn't think there was anything to worry about. He informed them in his anger that it wasn't their job to think. He knew he would have to come up with something soon. If she wasn't dead there was always a chance she could wake up and finger his organization. They'd been getting enough heat from the authorities lately as it was.

†

Eternity would be a long, long time in this place. She

wondered where the fire was, all the hell fire she'd heard about. If there was no fire, was this hell? And, if this wasn't hell, where was she? She couldn't tell which was worse, loneliness, or fire. If she had a choice, it would be a quick end in fire, versus the emptiness she felt now. Grace wondered if her sisters and brother were here in this place. She hoped not. They were so young. She knew she'd done plenty to deserve hell, but the kids? They were innocent. If there was a heaven she hoped they were running and playing all over the golden streets there.

She figured her mother was roaming around the same place where she was now, and probably felt as lonely as she did. Except she was sure her mom was dead, and she didn't really have a clue as to her own condition. The more she thought about it, the more she hoped the woman, as much as she'd done to make her life miserable, had been spared this fate. Her life of men, booze and pills had certainly been filled with enough sadness and despair already. Grace decided she wouldn't wish this feeling of abandonment on anyone, even her mother. Nothing she could think of caused her more fear than the idea of imprisonment in this place forever, alone.

The Daze of Grace

✝

"Something bothering you Nance?"

"Oh, nothing Mike. Just thinking about the little girl in I.C.U. again. No one has come looking for her. No missing persons report. She just looks so small and alone in that bed. I've been sitting with her for awhile every day, but so far, nothing. I pray for her hours on end, and I've even tried reading to her; you know the experts say that even in a coma patients can hear."

"Well, if anyone can make a difference Nance, it's you. We both know the power of prayer. If she wakes up it will be nice for her to see a friendly face."

"When Mike."

"What?"

"You mean when she wakes up, not if."

"Sorry. When she wakes up. And hey, I know how attached a person can get to those kids who don't seem to have anyone to take care of them. You remember me telling you about that girl Gracie who used to come into the soup kitchen? How she didn't show up for a while and then when she did she had the elderly lady, Ruth was her name I think, with her? When you came with me on Christmas

Eve I was planning to introduce you to them, remember? They were supposed to pick up Gracie's friend Tony, the one whose sister passed away before Thanksgiving, and they were all going to spend the day with us. I never figured out why they didn't show up, but at least I knew Grace had someone who cared, so she wasn't alone. Strangest thing. I don't know if I ever told you that Gracie's friend Tony came in asking if I'd seen her. She never stopped by to see him either, and he seemed pretty worried. What do ya do though, you know? We can't save them all I guess."

"That's not like you Mike. I think your feelings were hurt that she didn't show up for Christmas Eve, and you're trying to act like you don't care, but you're still worried about her."

"You know me too well Nance. Yeah, I guess I did get my feelings hurt a little. I just hope they're both okay. I still pray for the kid all the time."

"I know you do. While you're at it please pray for the little girl in I.C.U., would you?"

"Of course Nance. Anything for you."

✝

At first, no one noticed the tall Russian with piercing

blue eyes standing in the hallway just outside the hospital's I.C.U. unit. Each time the doors swung open he took in the layout of the space. He was memorizing the exact location of her bed. So far she hadn't come out of her coma, but he wasn't taking any chances. She was hooked up to oxygen, so it wouldn't be too difficult to have someone create a distraction, which would allow one of his men to disrupt the oxygen flow. He would have to work on that one. He still couldn't figure out how the little whore lived through a blast to the back of her head, and a trip down the river, but he wasn't about to let her ruin his life. He intended to keep a very close eye on her progress and stop it dead in its tracks any way he had to.

†

Nancy's surgical shift was done and she headed to I.C.U., her usual haunt since the young girl was brought in over a month ago. Wow, had it been a whole month already? The tall man with the evil aura, and piercing blue eyes, didn't seem to be around anymore. She'd reported his presence several times, so maybe the security guards had finally managed to ask him to leave. He didn't have a relative in the unit, so there was no good reason for him to be hanging around; and if she was honest, he just plain creeped her out.

As she went in to sit with the girl she saw a male nurse checking vitals, so she hung back to stay out of the way. Nancy didn't recognize him, and she was sure by now she knew all of the unit's nurses. He must be new. She checked him over and saw he wasn't wearing a name tag, which seemed a bit odd. Just then he reached for the oxygen line and looked to be switching it out with a tank of some sort, something she hadn't seen done before, since the room's oxygen and other gasses were supplied through wall outlets. She walked up behind him. "Hey, is this something new? What are you doing. Do you have an order for that?"

When he swung around she saw in his eyes something that made her grab the hose from his hand. "Hey, somebody get in here. Right now, somebody get in here," she yelled. The man looked menacingly at her, and turned to flee. "Grab that man. Somebody grab him." She yelled as he pushed his way through a bevy of nurses, and a security guard, who'd come running in response to her cries. He got clean away. "What is this hose? I need to know what's in this tank! Somebody tell me what that guy was doing in here, and how he got past security?"

"I don't know Nancy. Let me check what's in the tank. I'm not sure how he got past security, but it won't happen again."

"Why would anyone be trying to hurt a homeless girl? Somebody get her oxygen hooked back up! We need to find some answers, but we've got to keep her safe while we do. Do you all understand? We're all she's got."

"Don't worry Nancy. Carla is calling the police, and one of the techs is checking on the contents of the tank. I'll let you know as soon as we have answers."

"I'll be sitting right here until you do. And, has anyone noticed if the tall fellow, the one I reported the other day, has been back in the halls? I want to know if anyone sees him. I have a feeling he has something to do with all this. I want him kept off this floor, understand?"

"Yes ma'am. I'll send the police in as soon as they get here." Nancy stepped into the hall and pulled out her cell phone. She was shaking as she called. "Hey Mike. I'm going to be late. Probably very late."

"Why, what's going on? Is everything all right?"

"We're checking on a few things, but I'm pretty sure somebody just tried to kill my little coma victim, and I don't want to leave her."

"No, of course not. Wow! I'll tell you what. I'm just leaving the restaurant. Let me grab a couple of to go boxes and I'll bring you supper. You could probably use a friendly face right about now anyway."

"That would be great Mike. Some of your pasta with that great meat sauce and a salad would be super! I'll see you soon honey."

"Yep, see you in a bit doll face."

✝

"Yes officer, the man was wearing a nurse's uniform, but he wasn't wearing a name tag, which seemed suspicious to me. He was about five foot ten, kind off stocky, with dark hair and very hairy arms. He had a long scar on his left cheek and wasn't very friendly, to say the least. Our tech just got back to me and the tank he was trying to tie in to her oxygen line was carbon dioxide, which would have been fatal. There has been another man haunting the halls lately, well, at least since the girl was brought in a month ago. He's tall, about six foot three, or four; dark hair, with graying temples and piercing blue eyes. there's something about him that just strikes me wrong. I had security show him the door, but he may have others working for him."

"We'll keep our eyes open for him. My guess is that the girl saw something she shouldn't have seen. Maybe she has information that could identify someone. It would be fair to say that whoever shot her, and dumped her in the river, probably had something to do with today's attempt on her life. We'll post a guard outside the I.C. U. and check badges for anyone trying to enter. Is everyone here okay?"

"Yes officer. We're all fine here. Just concerned about our patient. Thanks for coming so quickly. I'll trust that you can keep our girl safe."

†

Reporting back to the brothel, with news of his disappointing failure, the young man pleaded for mercy; but the tall Russian disciplined his man in the only way he knew, without compassion. Tomorrow another body, with a hole through its skull, would be fished out of the East river. This one wouldn't be so lucky though. The bullet did its job.

†

"Hey babe. How's it going? You look pretty shook up."

"Yeah a little. Mostly just tired I think. The police were

here and they left an officer to guard the girl. I'll go back up in a minute. I just thought I'd come down and get a little fresh air while I was waiting for you."

"Well, I brought some of my famous mushroom stuffed ravioli with meat sauce and a big salad with garlic bread. Just what the doctor ordered! Why don't we eat first and then you can go back up. It sure wouldn't hurt you to take a break."

"Sounds great. I Love you ya know."

"Yep, I do know Nance. I hope you know how much I love you too. I'm just grateful that a beautiful girl like you could love a broken down old man like me. I will always be here for you babe. You can count on that."

"I know Mike. And you have no idea how much that means to me. You're my hero. And by the way; I'm no spring chicken either."

"Aw shucks, just doing what any average super hero would do. Anything for you Nance. And you'll always be a young chick to me, you pretty little thing."

"Oh, go on with you. Maybe after we eat you could come up with me. We could pray for the girl together. Does that sound all right?"

"Sure, whatever you want Nance."

The Daze of Grace

✟

"Hello? Hello? Is anybody here? Can you hear me? Please. Can't you hear me? I'm all alone. Are you here Jesus? I know I don't deserve you after all the things I've done and the chances I was given to know you, when all I did was turn away. It's probably too late for me, but I don't want to be alone. Please. I just don't want to be alone anymore. If you're real please show me, please save me."

✟

"That was delicious! You are the best cook I know and you're all mine!"

"Thank you my dear. I am at your service. I saved the best for last, Boston cream pie."

"Oh Mike, I don't know if I can eat another bite! Why don't we go up stairs first and then we can come down and have dessert later. How does that sound?"

"Sure Nance. Whatever you want. Lead the way."

"Here, let me check to be sure the nurses aren't in the middle of a procedure before we go in. Wait for just a minute, Mike."

"Sure, Nance, I'll wait right here. Take your time."

"Hi Carla, how's our girl?"

"She's doing fine. I just took her vitals. She's pretty lucky to have you looking out for her, Nancy. I hate to think about what might have happened if you hadn't caught that hoodlum!"

"I know. I think God is watching out for that girl. My husband is here, Carla. Do you mind if I bring him in so we can pray together?"

"No, not at all. I think that's a great idea. Take all the time you want."

Opening the I.C.U. doors Nancy waved Mike in and they walked hand in hand to the girl's bed. Once there Nancy was puzzled at the look on Mike's face. "You okay honey?"

"Nance, oh sweet Jesus, that's Gracie. The little girl I told you about. She's scrawnier than the last time I saw her, and pretty bruised up, but that's her for sure. I can't believe it!"

"Are you really sure Mike? I told you no one has come for her. You told me she had a friend. Don't you think someone would have reported her missing?"

"I don't have all the answers Nance, but that's Gracie. I'd bet my life on it. What could have happened to her? I don't know what has become of her friend Ruth, but it looks like she's been through hell and back. "Gracie. Hey, Gracie. It's Big Mike, from the soup kitchen. Wake up Gracie. We're here for you, and we won't leave you alone. Please wake up Gracie."

†

Trapped in the murky darkness and growing more desperate Grace stopped and closed her eyes. A voice. A voice calling her name. The voice was familiar and she longed to follow it to its source. Suddenly she was caught up in a tidal wave of emotion like hurricane winds, and she began to cry, begging to be released from this dark place.

†

"Oh, my gracious Mike. Look, tears. She's crying. I think she heard you, Mike. Keep talking to her, I think she really heard you."

"Gracie, honey, it's me, Big Mike from the soup kitchen. I've been so worried about you. When you didn't show up for Christmas Eve I tried to find you. Tony too. You had us both worried little one. I wish I knew where Ruth is. I can't figure out why she hasn't come for you. Please Gracie, come on honey, won't you open your eyes?"

"Oh, Mike, look! I think you're getting through. All she needed was to know there would be someone here who cares. Someone waiting for her when she wakes up!"

"We're both here Gracie. My wife Nancy and I. She's the one who's been praying for you every day. Now we're both here to pray. Jesus loves you little one. We're not going anywhere Gracie. When you're ready to wake up, we're right here."

Hear my prayer, O Lord; let my cry come to You!"

Psalm 102:1

CHAPTER 13

I.C.U. became Mike and Nancy's daily meeting place as they prayed for young Grace day after day. "Do you think we're reaching her Nance?"

"I know we are honey. You already know how powerful prayer is, and I know God loves this girl. I feel it with everything in me. We just have to remain faithful, Mike. God will save her, I know He will."

†

Grace was sure the voice was real, it had to be, she'd heard it over, and over, now. Again, and again, it reached out for her, but she wasn't strong enough yet to get there on her own. Still caught in the darkness, she cried out in desperation. "Jesus, I can't take this loneliness anymore. I know I don't deserve it, but please save me, please come live in me!" The moment the words were spoken Grace felt swept up in a wave of love so deep and strong she was overwhelmed beyond imagining, and began again to cry, but this time the tears were not tears of fear, she was crying for a sense of acceptance she'd never known in her thirteen years of life. Nancy noticed the tears again on Gracie's face, and she nodded to Mike. He looked at the girl on the bed, and then he too had tears in his eyes. Her fingers moved and Mike, excited to see the movement, took her small hand in his. She squeezed his thumb ever so lightly and then her eyelids fluttered, and opened.

Mike didn't know if Grace would recognize him, and he didn't want to frighten her. The doctors had been so specific about the possibilities of brain damage, and the things they might expect from her as she was recovering, if she ever woke at all. He wondered how much of the Gracie he knew was left. She tried to speak, but the intubation equipment made that impossible.

Nancy rang for the on call nurse, and before they knew it the small space was filled with medical staff taking vitals, removing tubes, and making a fuss over the girl they'd thought was finished a mere five weeks before. Once the tubes were removed Grace tried again to speak, but her throat was sore. Nancy brought her a glass of cool water with a long bendy straw. After some sips of the cold liquid she managed a few words. "Mike, you're here. I can't believe you're here." After a few minutes Gracie's eyes began to close again, so Mike and Nancy left her to rest.

The Daze of Grace

†

The next day Mike and Nancy were again sitting by her bed when she woke. She began in a hoarse voice to explain to Mike why she'd stayed away. "After Ruth died I figured it must be me. I must be some kind of bad luck charm, or something, with everyone I loved being taken away. What else could explain so many people I know dying? And I just knew if I carried some kind of evil luck I didn't want to jinx anything or anyone I cared about. That's why I couldn't come see you, or Tony. I hope you understand"

"Oh Grace, Ruth died? I didn't even know she passed away. I'm so sorry. But where have you been staying? You really should have told me. We could've figured something out. I've been so worried about you. Of course you aren't some kind of bad luck charm, honey."

"I know you were worried, Mike. And, I felt terrible putting you through that. It just seemed like everyone I cared about was dropping like flies and I didn't want to risk hurting any of you, so I left." They hugged, and Mike introduced Grace to Nancy. After a brief visit Grace began to yawn and her nurse suggested her friends leave again so she could sleep.

"You're welcome to come back later, Nancy. I'm sure the rest of your questions can wait till then, can't they?"

"Sure, Carla. We'll be right downstairs if you need anything. Just take care of our girl would you?"

"I definitely will, Nancy. Now you two go on. I'll never get her to sleep if you folks are hanging around."

"You're right, Carla. We'll let Gracie sleep, Mike. There will be plenty of time for catching up later. You get some rest, Grace. We'll be back."

"Okay, but don't stay away too long. I don't want to be alone. It's sure nice to meet you Nancy. I can see why Mike loves you so much."

"And it's a pleasure to meet you, Gracie. Mike has talked about you non-stop, so I feel like I already know you. Now, get some shut eye."

"Hey, little one. We'll be back. Rest well."

"I will, Mike. For the first time in a long time, I will."

✝

Later, while Mike was at the restaurant, Nancy sat in the small room with Grace, acting as her advocate, as police investigators gathered information, which they hoped would lead to an arrest. She halted questioning when she noticed Grace becoming exhausted again, and made her get some rest before continuing. Mike had the restaurant and soup kitchen to look out for, but made his way to the hospital every night. He and Nancy prayed with Grace, and she told them about the dark place where she'd cried out to Jesus and heard a voice that led her back to the hospital. Mike and Nancy looked at each other meaningfully over the top of Gracie's head.

While Grace slept Nancy filled Mike in on all she'd heard the girl tell police. The horrible death of her family; the dumpster; the basement room; Ruth's death on Christmas eve; her attempt to keep her friends safe by staying away from them; the shanty town; her can collecting business; being sold to the Russians by Tom; the brothel; the child who was ripped from her body; the tall man, with piercing blue eyes; and the last thing she remembered, being shot, before she eventually woke in the hospital.

Nancy knew now that the creepy man who'd haunted the I.C.U. halls was the same man who'd shot her young friend, and she could describe him as well as Grace could. Before the afternoon was out the police had brought in a department artist and they had sketches of both Tom and the tall Russian.

The emotion on the girl's face, as she related her story to the investigators, was heart breaking. Nancy cried as she filled Mike in, and he cried when he heard the horrific tale. They decided that when Gracie was ready to leave the hospital she would be moving in with them, if she wanted to.

†

Grace couldn't imagine anything more wonderful than moving in with Mike and Nancy. To have a real home, to feel safe, really safe, for the first time in her life was more than she could comprehend. She moved from I.C.U. into a room on the sixth floor of the hospital. Hospital administration and police thought she would be safer in the psychiatric ward, which was already secure and where it would be easier to post guards outside her room without drawing unwarranted attention.

It was while she was on the sixth floor, that the headaches began. Her doctor told her it was common after a brain trauma, such as hers, to experience headaches; but that they should soon go away; after two weeks they hadn't. When she was released, she was sent home with a month's supply of pain pills; which didn't do much but make her nauseous; and directions about how to deal with migraines, which didn't seem to work either.

Even though she was actively dealing with sick headaches Grace was wildly happy. Mike and Nancy lived in a hundred year old Victorian home, which they had lovingly and laboriously brought back to life. The house looked like a mansion to Gracie, who'd never lived in anything larger than the apartment she'd shared with her mom and siblings. Their home was decorated to period and had an elegant feel, which made Grace feel like a princess, as she walked through the enormous, beautifully appointed rooms.

On her first day home Grace was shown to her room, by Mike and Nancy, they were very excited and the excitement was contagious. Her new guardians never had children, but had hoped and dreamed for years, before realizing that must not be God's plan for their lives. In their years of dreaming, however, they had decorated one of the eight bedrooms upstairs appropriately for a boy and one for a girl. Gracie looked wide eyed and open mouthed at her surroundings; which included polished wood floors, topped with pink and burgundy oriental rugs; a large canopy bed with pink and burgundy bedspread and pillows; a cherry wood vanity table with antique mirror; large matching desk; and highboy dresser; and a huge cherry wood armoire.

The room also boasted a fireplace; a large window seat loaded with pillows, and throws; and lacey, pink ruffled curtains with ties. The bathroom she would use was beautiful as well, with a giant claw foot tub, and hand painted tiles on the walls and floor. She was pretty sure the bathroom here was bigger than her whole apartment had been. She'd never seen such magnificence in her life, and she turned to her hosts with a look of humble surprise. "Is this for me? I, I can't, I've never seen anything like this before. I can't take all this."

"Of course you can, Gracie. It's like I was decorating this room for you. God knew that someday you would come to live with us, and he helped me prepare a place just for you."

"Thank you, Nancy. I can't tell you how beautiful all this is, how grateful I am. And, you too Mike."

"Whoa, you can't thank me for this one. This was all Nancy. In case you couldn't guess, I'm not much of an interior decorator. Nancy always knew we'd have a little girl to put in this room and here you are."

Grace nearly threw herself into Nancy's waiting arms; and gave herself over to the years, of bottled up tears. All the fear and anxiety of the past months seemed to melt away. To be part of a family, a real family was more than she could process all at once.

Be exalted, O God, above the heavens! Let Your glory be over all the earth!

Psalm 108:5

CHAPTER 14

Within a month Gracie's headaches, which had plagued her since her hospital stay, were so severe that Nancy was forced to take her back to the Neurologist for further tests. Not able to detect any physiological reason for the pain she was suffering he offered several potential solutions, but each failed, and Grace was left looking at a future of constant pain. Mike and Nancy refused to give up and prayed over the young girl every evening, anointing her with oil. Grace eventually fell asleep each night from pure exhaustion, though nothing seemed to give her the much needed relief she sought, and her nights were fraught with pain, and nightmares.

She'd begun attending church with her new foster parents every Sunday morning and Wednesday evening, or whenever the doors were open, and was also getting a great deal out of a youth Bible study, which helped her learn to better decipher scripture. Consequently, through much study and prayer, she felt closer to God than she'd ever thought possible; all this worked to wipe away years of guilt, and condemnation, which had once overwhelmed her, as she learned of God's abundant grace and love for her; so she was confused over the little matter of unanswered prayer concerning her migraines; until, laying in bed praying one night she felt a strange heat surging through her body. She was elated, believing this to be her long sought after healing. She sat up smiling, and a sudden flash of white hot light filled her head, blinding her completely.

She cried out, and Mike came running. "Mike, I can't see. What's happening? Please help me I can't see." He yelled for Nancy's help and together they drove Grace quickly to the hospital emergency room.

Once she was loaded on a gurney in the E.R. and being wheeled to an exam room the convulsions began. Nancy cried out when she saw her new daughter's body rigid in seizure after seizure. "Oh, Mike, this can't be happening. We can't lose her. We've only just found her."

"Don't you dare lose hope, Nance! We have to trust God. He brought Gracie to us, and it's up to Him. It's all up to Him. Now come pray with me. There's nothing we can do standing out here in the hallway."

For what seemed like hours they waited, until an exhausted looking emergency room doctor came to the waiting room to talk. "I'm sorry you've been waiting so long. We've only just calmed her down, and I really wanted to have better news than this when I talked to you."

"What's going on Doctor? She's been suffering with these terrible migraines and now this. What could be causing her seizures?"

"We haven't been able to determine that yet, but our testing shows some swelling in the soft tissue of the brain. I understand she's recently been through some serious head trauma?"

"Yes, she was found washed up on the bank of the river. She'd been shot in the back of the head. She's been suffering from headaches since before leaving the hospital, but no one has been able to give us any definitive answers about causes, or solutions."

"Well, for now at least, until we can reduce pressure on the brain, we've placed Grace in an induced coma. I promise we will get to the bottom of this. Why don't you two go home and get some rest. We'll call you if there are any changes."

"Oh, Mike, what are we going to do? I hate to leave her here alone."

"Well, we're going to go home, just like the Doc suggested, and we're going to keep praying, Nance. God's got this. I feel it in my bones. Gracie's going to be fine." Mike was speaking with a lot more confidence than he was feeling, but they went home and began to pray in earnest."

✝

Grace found herself in a place filled with soothing, soft light. She knew somehow that this place wasn't heaven, but, even so, she felt the presence of God all around her. This was a place of rest, and she was fine being here as long as He wanted her to be. She hoped Mike and Nancy weren't worried about her. Having relief from the paralyzing headaches she'd been experiencing was a miracle. And she wanted to stay in that miracle as long as possible.

"Grace."

"What? Is that you Jesus?"

"Yes, Grace. I want you to know that you were blind, but now you will see."

"Lord, I'm not sure I know what you're saying. Before I came here I was made blind."

"Ah, Grace, but I can use all things for your good, and my Glory. Do you believe?"

"Yes, Lord, I believe. I will go anywhere you want me

to, do anything you ask me."

"For now, Grace, it is enough that you rest in me. You are safe in my arms. The time will come soon when I will ask you to put your faith to the test and follow me. You will be able to see things not visible to the world, and reveal truth to a deceived and confused generation. A time will come when you will be mocked and persecuted for my sake. Are you ready?"

"Yes, Lord, I'm ready. Send me."

†

That night Dr. Phillips was called in. With permission he removed part of Grace's skull to allow for the swelling which proved to be slow, but constant. Doc explained to Mike, and Nancy, that Grace's brain had most likely been distending; due to the trauma of her gunshot wound; since the initial shock took place; but had simply not been detected before this, solely because ongoing progression of the inflammation had been very slow until now. This had also most certainly been the cause of her unrelenting headaches and subsequent blindness.

Now that they knew what they were dealing with, they had only to allow time for the tissue irritation to pass and the brain to return to normal size. They were assured that removal of a large piece of her cranium would allow tissue to expand without putting further pressure on the brain and shouldn't result in further brain damage; though, the doctor concluded, nothing could be promised. And, he added, that until she woke, they wouldn't know what damage might have been done before the preventative surgery was performed.

Weeks passed, and Grace's bedside was where Mike and Nancy spent as many hours as possible. Here they talked about their days, prayed, ate their meals, played board games and prayed some more. Tony began to stop by for visits, after Mike called him to report on Grace's condition, and he also spent endless hours with his new friends there at the hospital. Their pastor and church family, along with Gracie's new Sunday school friends, made regular stops and filled the halls with the sounds of prayer, praise, and worship.

✝

In the Lord's resting place, Grace filled herself with His presence, and drank in His Word. She loved it here and loved the peace this place afforded her, but knew she must soon go back, and tend to His will for her life. She couldn't wait to experience what her future held. She only waited for His voice.

The swelling began to recede.

†

"Mike! Dr. Phillips told me the swelling is going down! He's very optimistic about Grace's prognosis now. Isn't that wonderful?"

"That's great Nance! Let's go in and see our girl, then we can eat okay?"

"Great! I'm so excited! God is so good."

"You said it girl! He sure is, all the time."

Help me, O Lord my God! Save me according to Your steadfast love.

Psalm 109:26

CHAPTER 15

On a beautiful, peaceful Sunday afternoon more than two months after Grace had been put into a medically induced coma; with a large part of her skull removed to reduce the risk of brain damage due to swelling; dozens of members of their church family, and most of Grace's Sunday school class were packed into her hospital room, and out into the hall, surrounding her door. Through much prayer, and by the Grace of God, the swelling in her brain diminished greatly, and they were all present to praise God and thank Him, for the miracles they were seeing daily. They began to sing, a few voices at first, softly, then all joined in and the beautiful chorus rose to fill the room, the halls, the building. Somewhere far away, and yet ever so close, God heard the beautiful music of a grateful choir, and He opened Gracie's ears to the sound of the melody. Grace smiled. Those close to her saw, and began to nudge others until all were aware of the faint, slightly lopsided grin. Hope filled the space, and the very air exploded with anticipation of a miracle. Her doctor had already, and repeatedly, tried to tamp down their expectations, knowing there might be extensive brain damage in his young patient due to the brain trauma she'd experienced; but their collective spirit wouldn't hear of it. They knew the power of Jesus, and they weren't letting go of the healing authority of His Name!

Over the next two weeks her room was never empty. Either Mike, Nancy, or both; and any number of church family, and friends, were in her room praying, singing, and praising God; and somehow, as if a walkie-talkie was feeding into her peaceful place, she heard every faith filled word. Their worship and praise of God fed her and her heart swelled with gratitude for the Lord and the things He was about to do through her.

On another Sunday evening, after a day of visitors and fervent prayer, Nancy sensed an electricity in the air which had not been present before. "Do you feel it Mike? There's something in the air tonight. An energy that wasn't here before. I feel the presence of the Holy Spirit so strongly, don't you?"

"Yeah I do, Nancy. There's something going on. I think God is about to do something really, really great, and I can't wait!"

They both felt a spark and turned to look toward Gracie at the exact same instant.

Her eyes opened, and praise God, she could see!

At first the sight of a full room didn't confuse her because she'd heard so many praying and singing earlier that day, but then she realized many of those currently present were very tall, perhaps ten to twelve feet tall, and had huge, beautiful wings on their backs. These beings seemed to glow with an ethereal light and stood all around and behind her parents as if to protect and encourage them all. Mike and Nancy saw her eyes were opened, and they were immediately in tears. Gracie tried quickly to assess whether or not her parents could see the tall individuals too, but saw no evidence of that. "Call the nurse, somebody call the nurse." Nancy stammered between sobs.

Gracie took in as much of the scene as she was able. Her parents, and a couple of their friends from church, who all seemed oblivious to their heavenly company; and the giant beings who filled every remaining inch of the space in her room. She wasn't afraid. She gained a sense of peace from these enormous beings. With wings on their backs Grace assumed they must be angels, but her imagination had always told her angels were soft, and sweet, little creatures sitting on fluffy clouds playing harps. These were neither soft, nor sweet looking at all. Their appearance was strong, and warrior like, with rippling muscles, armor and swords; she felt completely safe in their presence. They didn't speak, but she knew they were here to look after her. She was positive now, from the lack of reaction of those in the room, that she was the only one able to see the angels. Was she hallucinating, or crazy? She didn't think so. Perhaps this was what the Lord had meant when He'd told her she was blind, but now she would see.

As nurses and doctors ran in to fill the space her angelic protectors stepped back, but they were never out of her sight. Again, she could tell the newly arrived humans in the room were unaware of the heavenly host only feet from them. Amazingly, she knew she was witnessing inhabitants of a realm not visible to very many, and she was sure this had something to do with God's plans for her future. "Mike, Nancy, you're here."

"Where else would we be baby girl? You had us pretty worried, didn't she Nance?"

"You sure did honey, but God had you in the palm of His hand."

"I know. He still does." Mike and Nancy glanced at each

other. There was something different in Grace's voice. An assurance which hadn't been there before, and they wondered.

✝

Grace's recovery progressed rapidly. She defied the predictions of all the doctors and surgeons. She was a young lady, with a purpose, and a plan. She amazed her parents, and where, not long ago, their hearts were heavy with grief, now they overflowed with joy.

Involved in every Bible study and outreach program she could find, Grace's hours were filled to capacity and her parents hoped she wasn't pushing herself too hard.

Grace's eyes were opened more and more to a spiritual realm not visible to many and now as she walked down the sidewalks of her town she saw more than angels. Some people she encountered were surrounded by dark clouds and beings so hideous she knew they must be demons. Those demons held on with long, yellowed talons and shrank back when they realized Grace could see them. There were others though, such as herself, who were flanked by guardian angels, warrior angels decked out in full regalia.

What she found even more curious was that the people encompassed in darkness and attached to demons were so much more common, maybe by four or five times, than those encircled by heavenly host. Even more concerning was that the ratio didn't change when she walked into the church building; perhaps even growing in favor of the dark side. However when she went to places; such as the soup kitchen, to help serve food, most of the people there helping were protected by angels. She guessed that those who truly trusted Jesus, and turned their lives over for His purpose were more likely to have angels; and those who hadn't given their lives to the Lord, but were more focused on self were afflicted by darkness. She decided that wasn't hers to know or judge. She was here to minister to hurting people.

More and more Grace went with Mike to the soup kitchen to serve and to touch lives. She really had come full circle. Many remembered the lost girl who'd come to them for help and marveled at the changes they saw in her; but even more than that, they drank in the feeling of joy she radiated everywhere she went.

Grace found that as people walked through to get their meals she was able to determine quickly who needed the Lord. She would wait till they were seated and make her way to them for a friendly chat. Not everyone listened as she spoke of freedom in Christ; and at every table which was surrounded in darkness the attending demons hissed and screeched at her, cowering from the power of the Name of Jesus. As she shared, many came to trust the Lord. And, as they trusted the Lord their demons were forced to flee, to be replaced by protecting angels. It was a beautiful and miraculous process.

Walking outside Grace adopted a habit of looking into the sky to see the clouds of demons waiting to pounce on those unsuspecting souls who hadn't trusted the Living God for their salvation and hope; and each time she sent any of those revolting beings back where they came from, as more lost souls came to know Christ, she rejoiced right along with the angels of heaven.

Grace was asked to speak in church and spoke with such knowledge, and authority, about the power of God's love and Grace; though she'd not grown up knowing Him at all; that she was invited to speak in more services, and at more churches in the city. Mike and Nancy were amazed, and proud, as they heard their daughter talk about her past, her transformed life, and the power of God to use all things for good, for those who love Him and are called according to His purpose. They saw lives change, and people come forward who they'd known in church for years, and had assumed already knew the Lord.

Soon Grace's name spread throughout the city and in every church where she was scheduled to speak there was standing room only on the day of her appearance. But, Grace remembered where she came from, and the recognition didn't go to her head. God and His love, His Son, the Salvation and Grace of Christ, the hope of glory through Him was her only goal. She knew she was blessed and she used every opportunity given to her to spread the Gospel.

One day as she was about to begin speaking, she looked out over the congregation and at all the attending angels and demons, suddenly her gaze fell upon a pair of piercing blue eyes encased in a face of hate that she remembered all too well. The tall Russian glared at her with a loathing most palpable. His demons hissed and screeched, but her gaze remained steady and her look turned to pity. He turned and stormed out of the church in anger, and Grace knew without doubt that God was going to direct her to do things that only months ago would have made her writhe in agony. Nancy saw the tall Russian at almost the same instant and sent ushers to follow him. They managed to take down his license before he sped from the parking lot.

The Lord says to my Lord; "Sit at My right hand, until I make your enemies your footstool.

                                                      Psalm 110:1

CHAPTER 16

The knock on her front door was rather insistent and Grace was the only one home, so she jumped up from the table where she was studying scripture for tonight's lesson. Looking through the peep hole to see two uniformed policemen and the detective who'd interviewed her in the hospital several months ago, she opened the door. "Hello detective. Can I help you?"

"Hi Grace, are your folks home?"

"No, they're both at work, but I can call them if you need me to."

"Yeah, why don't you do that. I've got some news you're going to be happy to hear and a lineup or two that you're most welcome to attend, but I'll have to have your parents there with you since you're a minor."

"You got them?"

"Yep, and I believe we've got enough evidence to put them both away for good. They've been busy little bees and you aren't the only young lady who will be viewing their lineups."

"I'm sorry to hear that there have been more. I know there were dozens of girls, maybe hundreds, at the brothel, but I didn't think you'd ever find that place. I'm grateful you kept searching."

"Well, we followed the lead your Mom sent us and the license plate led us right to his front door. He just might end up regretting, going to your meeting the other night, for a very long time."

Grace called Mike and Nancy, who rushed home to hear the good news. They prayed together before heading off to the precinct and Grace nodded to their guardian angels. She, more than most, knew about the battles being waged in heavenly realms and she felt a big one coming on; however, she also knew, more than most, that God is good and that He is still on the throne!

✝

The viewing room at the precinct was dark and the whole place smelled like sweat and vomit. As the detective led Grace and her parents into the screening space they were directed to remain silent until the prisoners were brought in. Five men were led into a lit room on the other side of one way glass and Grace recognized Tom right away.

His eyes were filled with disdain for the proceedings, and for all those involved; and his demons held on with sharp, twisted talons. She didn't think Tom could see her, but she was sure his evil spirits could, as they jeered and murmured in her direction. "Shut up, in the Name of Jesus", Grace whispered under her breath.

The demons were silent.

"What did you say Grace? You'll have to speak up."

"I said it's him. Tom, from the town under the bridge. He's the third one in, right in the middle. He was in charge and he's the one who sold me to the Russians."

"Are you sure Grace?"

"Yes, I'm sure. I would recognize him anywhere. I had to pay him protection money every single day for a safe place to stay and we all know how that turned out."

"Good Grace, we'll have you wait out in the hallway with your folks for a few minutes. We have one more witness for this line-up; then we'll call you back in for the second viewing, okay?"

"Sure, just holler when you need me." With that, Grace, Mike, and Nancy filed into the hallway, and another young lady that Grace thought she recognized from across the hall was ushered into the dark room.

"Are you okay, Gracie?"

"Sure, why wouldn't I be?"

"Well, it must be hard seeing these faces again."

"Like I said, I'm fine."

"Mike is just trying to watch out for you Grace."

"I know, Nancy. Sorry Mike. I didn't mean to snap at you. Actually I'm fine. I'm a little aggravated that I feel a tugging in my heart, which I know is God telling me I'm going to have to forgive these men. He's telling me I'm only hurting myself by holding hatred in my heart, so I know that I'm going to have to forgive them sooner or later. It's just a hard concept, and it may take me a little while to really mean it."

"Just remember baby girl, forgiveness doesn't mean that you can't also do the right thing to be sure they never do these things to any other innocent girls."

"You're right, Nancy, but I have to be sure that's the reason I'm doing it, and not just for revenge, do you know what I mean?"

"Yeah, we get it Gracie. We're right behind you and we'll have your back no matter what."

"I know that, and I love you guys."

"We love you too little one."

After a few minutes the other witness was led out crying, and Grace was guided back into the viewing space. She was a bit shocked to see that the new group of prisoners were already in place and those piercing blue eyes were fixed on the one way glass at the exact spot where she was standing. Again his demons were mocking and taunting her as she waited in the darkness. "He's the second from the left. I could never forget those eyes, and the set of his jaw, as he looked down at me. That's him, I'm sure of it."

"Okay Grace. My assistant will lead you to a conference room. I'll see you out there in just a few minutes. Thank you for your strength and conviction. I know this had to be difficult for you."

"I'm just glad you caught them both. When will we be going to trial?"

"That isn't for me to say young lady. The district attorney's office will let us know all the charges and particulars, but I have to believe this one will be a slam dunk if I do say so. Lots of evidence, witnesses and prior convictions in both camps. We'll make sure you get justice Grace."

"Thank you, and thanks for all you've done to make this process go so quickly."

I can do all things through Christ, who strengthens me.

Philippians 4:13

CHAPTER 17

She would be testifying in two trials. One for Tom and one for Vladimir, yes she finally had a name to go with the piercing blue eyes, Vladimir Slochik. He was a kingpin in the Russian mafia and the city had been trying to get him off the streets for over a decade. Until this last bust they'd never been able to come up with a case strong enough to get a conviction. This time, however, they were more than hopeful that the testimony of several young victims would seal the fate of this man.

Police escorted Grace and her family back and forth to the attorney's office, court house, home, hospital, and restaurant. Mike felt it necessary to be sure his little family was safe, but Grace knew she was secure with her heavenly guardians. She'd been trying to find a way to tell her parents about her newly extended sight and those angelic protectors, but hadn't found the right time yet. She was certain they would think she'd slipped off her gourd and was letting the stress of her situation get to her. Perhaps this wasn't a thing to share? She didn't know. Possibly at another time when the stress level for the whole family wasn't at peak levels.

†

On a day trip to a local clothing store to outfit the family for their first day in court; surrounded by plain clothed officers, and their guardian angels; Gracie's family were suddenly encircled by more than a dozen men with assault rifles. These were most assuredly sent by the mob to dispatch the prosecution's key witness. One of the officers went for his side arm and was shot. Watching him fall to the ground to be encircled by an ever widening pool of blood felt surreal. The leader of the assailants ordered Gracie's guards to put down their weapons. They looked sideways at each other, as if questioning what to do with those ludicrous orders, until the gunmen grew impatient. Another officer was blasted in an effort to move things along. Finally relinquishing their arms to the gangsters they were rounded up like a herd of sheep as a large van appeared on the scene.

Out of the blue, as if right on cue Gracie's angels made themselves visible to the armed mobsters, in all their light, and warrior's glory, and the men's eyes grew big as saucers. Much to the surprise of everyone present, they dropped their rifles and ran. The remaining officers, and Grace's family looked around in wonderment. Everyone present was puzzled, except for Gracie. "Did you see that baby girl? What could have frightened them away like that?"

"I'm sure God has His hand on the situation, Mike. You know He watches out for us." An officer called for an ambulance to aide his downed comrades and the family was ushered quickly into the nearest store.

"Do you want to stay, Grace? After all that excitement, would you rather just go home?"

"No, Nancy. I won't let them control me like this. I know they were trying to scare me so I wouldn't want to testify, but I won't fall for their fear tactics."

"Good for you baby girl! That's my Gracie! We will not let them intimidate us and they will finally get what they deserve!"

"You're right, Mike. I won't ever be intimidated by these people again. Not when I know God watches over me. And, whether I can see Him or not, I know He watches over me!"

†

Bright and early Monday morning Grace and her family were escorted to the court house to begin Tom's trial. Crowds outside held picket signs cheering Grace on, or condemning her, and some even became rowdy, but her escorts got her safely to the doors. The jury was already selected, and seated. The prosecuting attorney's assistant met Grace and her parents in the hall and led them to a conference room where Grace was directed to wait until called to testify.

"Do you want us to wait with you honey? We don't have to go in yet if you want us to stay."

"No, Nancy, you two go in. I'll see you in awhile. I'm fine, really, God's got my back and I'm not nervous, really I'm not."

"You're a brave girl honey. Much braver than I could ever be, and we are very proud of you."

"Thank you. I love you guys. Thanks for standing by me through all this."

"There's no place we'd rather be Gracie, no place at all."

Mike and Nancy moved to the courtroom to find seats in the already crowded space. News of the trial had spread far and wide, and local interest was high, due to the proximity of the shanty town to the city in general. There had been much controversy in the past over the shady goings on there, and now there was non-stop talk about tearing it down to get rid of the bad elements. Though, in all the talk no one had thought much about what would happen to those poor individuals who considered that place their only home.

Gracie wouldn't be the only witness against Tom. It seemed she hadn't been his only sale to the Russian mob. The stand was occupied that day by one after another of his young victims who sobbed, and hiccupped, their way through testimony of heinous treatment, and then it was finally Grace's turn. The courtroom grew quiet as she took the stand and was sworn in. She was asked her name, and then proceeded to give very graphic details of the evils done to her by the man in question. "Do you see the man who committed these acts in the courtroom today?" The prosecuting attorney questioned.

"Yes I do. He's sitting right there."

"Let the court records indicate that the witness has identified the defendant."

The jury deliberated for only an hour before coming back with a guilty verdict. The next day, in the sentencing portion of the trial, Tom was given an opportunity to apologize to his victims, and declined in somber defeat. His victims, and their families, were given an opportunity to speak to the court, and several took advantage of the occasion to express their hatred for the man who'd put them through hell. When Gracie's turn arose she walked to the podium provided for her, and looked over at her persecutor. "I've thought long and hard about what I might say to you today if I had the opportunity. Tom, the things you've done to these girls, to me, are without excuse. No one has the right to sell another human being; and in each of these cases it seems you did it as much for revenge, over supposed wrongs, as for any other reason. It's clear you don't know anything about Jesus and His saving Grace. Well, let me introduce you to my Lord and Savior, my friend. I forgive you for all you did to me. I will abide by whatever punishment the court deems right, but I forgive you. I pray that you find peace in the truth of the Son of God, and that you will have lots of time to read, and discover, His infinite love for you. I will be sure you have a Bible in your cell wherever you are incarcerated."

Audible gasps filled the courtroom and then an air so silent you could hear a pin drop. And, yes, if you had looked closely you would have seen a lone tear tracking down Tom's weathered, and worn, face. He was after all just a broken, flawed human being, and seeing him now, in these circumstances, Gracie could see how vulnerable he was. His demons looked frightened, and held on to their victim tighter, but Grace could see that their hold was tenuous at best, and intended to follow up with a visit to this hurting man once he was safely back in a cell.

Tom was sentenced to forty years for seven counts of kidnapping and unlawful imprisonment. He was devastated, but trying to look tough through it all.

"Gracie, you are one good kid!"

"No Mike, I'm just trying to listen to what the Lord is telling me to do. He's the only good one. If I'd done what my anger told me to do, I'd have told him off like the rest of the girls did, but then he would never understand Grace."

"Okay, I get it. But, I've gotta say baby girl, that took guts and we are very proud of you."

"Thanks you guys. I think I'm starting to get it. The only way we can really break Satan's hold is to find ways to hand the situation over to a forgiving God, and move on. That's all I really want to do. I just want to share Jesus."

"Whatever you want and however we can help Gracie, we'll be here for you all the way."

That night Gracie spoke in another local church, and

again the house was packed. Word had gotten out about her magnanimous gesture toward the man who'd sold her into slavery, and many wanted to see the girl who'd done something most of them would never have considered. She was becoming a bit of a cultural hero, though she insisted to any who asked, that God deserved all the glory, and she wanted none of it.

†

Vladimir Slochik's trial was scheduled for the following week and the media were going crazy following Grace, and harassing her for interviews. She made a trip to the county jail, where Tom was being held before transport to a federal facility.

Standing outside the county lockup she watched as swarms of demons circled the air above the facility. Darkness was doing its best to overwhelm everything within its reach. She wasn't sure Tom would see her, but then, when she felt she'd been there so long she was sure she'd been turned away, she was ushered through a huge metal door and led to a visitation room. She sat in a peeling, blue, metal chair, facing a large pane of glass, waiting for Tom. Soon guards led a shackled prisoner to the other side of the glass. He sat with his head hanging low. She picked up the intercom receiver and when she tapped on the glass, Tom did the same. "Hi Tom." At the sound of her voice Tom's eyes grew misty, and his demons cringed and hissed.

"Hi Grace. Thanks for coming to see me, especially after everything that's happened." He looked so different, no longer the cocky man in charge. Now he looked smaller somehow, beaten and defeated. Grace knew from personal experience that this was the best time of all to introduce Jesus into the equation.

"Sure, Tom. I was serious when I told you I forgive you. I brought you a Bible. The guards told me they'd make sure you got it when you went back to your cell. I've marked some of my favorite passages, you know, some of the scriptures that have gotten me through a lot in my life."

"Thanks, Grace. I really wasn't expecting anyone to do anything nice for me, especially you, and especially not after all the stuff I've done in my life."

"We've all messed up Tom. I've come to understand that God knows we're a mess and He loves us anyway."

"Yeah, well the kind of things I've done don't deserve forgiveness Gracie. I've done some really bad things."

"I know, Tom. I think we've been conditioned to think

that there are some sins which are worse than others, some things that are too big for God to forgive. God just sees it all as sin you know, and since none of us is perfect, He sent His perfect Son to pay the price we couldn't pay, so that we could receive the Grace we didn't deserve. I don't deserve His forgiveness any more than you do Tom, but I accept it, and I know He loves me. All you have to do is believe, and trust Him."

"So all I have to do is believe? How can that be? I don't understand how He could love me, or why He would even want to. I'm just afraid, Grace. What if I ask Him to forgive me, and He won't?"

"Tom, He doesn't turn away any who would truly believe. All you have to do is confess that you are a sinner, and you know He died for you, trust Him, and believe, and He will fill you with His Spirit."

"Will you help me Grace?" At that question the demons surrounding Tom began to shake, and hold on tighter, screaming and twisting in agony.

"Sure, Tom." With that Grace led her new friend in a sinner's prayer to invite Jesus into his life. Tom prayed with tears streaming down his face, as his evil spirits were wrenched from his sides to be replaced by guardian angels.

Grace watched and knew she could never tire of the whole beautiful process.

Tom asked if she would write to him, and she agreed. The terrible toll that sin waged on the souls of this planet weighed heavily on the young evangelist's heart, and she simply knew she had to reach as many as possible with the Word of the Gospel. Gracie knew that when it came right down to it; the battle of the ages, between light and darkness; was being waged before her eyes. A conflict between good and evil, one which had been fought since mankind first walked the earth, consumed everything in its path. She knew too that she'd been called as a warrior into the fray and she decided that no matter what, she would fight until she could fight no more. The more people she won to Christ the less her own heart ached from the wounds of her terrible past. God was using her, and that was all that really mattered.

For we do not wrestle against flesh and blood, but against principalities, against powers, against the rulers of the darkness of this age, against spiritual hosts of wickedness in the heavenly places.

Ephesians 6:12.

CHAPTER 18

Undulating waves of evil filled the morning skies above the city, adding more gloom to its current veil of darkness with each passing moment. A faint smell of hot ash and sulfur filled the air, reminding her of tragedies long ago, and undermining her peace for a split second. Then she remembered quickly enough who still occupied the throne. Grace sat and watched the unfolding scene in confidence, and without fear; because for the past week she'd been asking for prayers for the city, for the trial proceedings, and for herself from each church group and interview event she'd attended. She could see the clouds of malevolence gathering overhead, but she could also see the armies of the Lord increasing with each added prayer. Brigades of mighty glowing warriors in full battle gear multiplied by the minute, creating an impenetrable wall of protection around the courthouse and her family. She felt the electric energy building, and knew God was planning a great show. Knowing now how much her Lord loved her made it hard to remember the years of her life when she'd thought He didn't care, and she was grateful He'd intervened so persistently in her life, pursuing her until she'd finally given in to His love.

She could see her purpose vividly now. To share Jesus, and His Grace, with a frightened and dark world. She knew God was making a way where there had previously been no way, and she praised Him for His goodness. She bowed her head in prayer again, and when she was finished she came up smiling. Let them come. She was ready for anything.

The city had been actively preparing for the circus, which would be Vladimir's trial, all week. Extra security forces were put in place to keep another episode like the one outside the clothing store, last week, from being possible again. No one believed the mob had simply given up any attempt to turn the prosecution's most important witness. Many in the community had come to love and support the plucky, brave young girl who'd miraculously escaped death, but there were also plenty who disagreed with her Christian views, and she faced strong opposition of her public evangelism tactics at every juncture.

Picketers lined the streets outside the courthouse. On one side of the street, signs with sentiments like: "God hates the mob" and "Kick butt Gracie!" waved. On the other side of the street, "God doesn't belong in our courthouses", and "Separation of church and state, NOW!" were a common theme. There was even talk that many of the protestors were being paid by a liberal group who seemed to hate anything remotely related to Christianity. Grace shook her head as she was ushered into a safe room where she would be kept until it was her turn to testify. A security guard stood outside her door, though she knew her safety wasn't in manmade efforts, but in the God of the universe who watched over her even now. She also noticed guards standing outside of two more doors, and wondered if there were, indeed, more witnesses for the prosecution.

She felt the explosion, as much as heard it, and suddenly the room where she was being held was filled with smoke. Gracie stood, and looked in the direction of the door just as it burst open. She was grabbed, and flung over a man's shoulder. Sounds of automatic gun fire filled the halls. She knew her guardian angels were close, but they didn't make themselves known to her kidnappers, or make any effort to rescue her. Before the smoke cleared she was carried out a side hall, through a brand new hole in the brick wall of the courthouse, and thrown into a running van. She struggled to be free, but was slammed to the vehicle's floor, bound and blindfolded, before a hood was pulled over her head. Two other bodies were dumped on the van's floor beside her and she heard faint whimpering from one. "Oh God, not again." She moaned under her breath. "Lord, I am in your hands. Only you can save me now. I trust you, and I trust whatever you are going to do for your glory in this." As she softly spoke these words a sense of peace settled over her.

Back in the court room panicked people ran for cover, and police tried to gain control of the situation. Mike and Nancy knew immediately that Grace was in danger, and tried to leave the scene to check on their daughter, only to be stopped in their tracks by court house guards.

As order was restored, and damage was assessed, it was discovered that all three of the prosecution's witnesses were gone, as well as the defendant. It had to be an inside job. That was the only way the perpetrators could have known which rooms held the witnesses in order to be able to pull the whole thing off.

Mike and Nancy were beside themselves with grief, and demanded that a team be assembled to search for the girls, but even as the panic was subsiding at the courthouse, the girls were being driven across town to an empty warehouse.

Once on the warehouse property they were carried to a room in the back of the building, and unceremoniously dumped on a cold cement floor. The door to the room slammed shut, and a bolt slid loudly into place.

Grace lay still for a few moments in an effort to judge if they were finally alone. One of the other two girls whimpered, and cried, until Grace couldn't stand it anymore. "Stop it! Right now, stop it. Crying isn't going to save us. Only the Lord can do that!"

"But I'm scared!"

"Be brave. God will see us through."

"Well, where was your God when we were kidnapped? How did we end up here? Did He suddenly stop watching over us?"

"Listen, I'm not sure how God is going to use this, but I know He can use all things for our good, and His Glory, so I'm going to trust Him!" Suddenly, Grace could feel the bonds loosen from her hands and she was free. She reached up, and removed the hood, and then the blindfold from her eyes, looked around the room, and saw divine soldiers all around. She set about to free the other two girls, and pulled off their hoods, to find that one of the girls was her raven haired friend from the brothel. As she set them free, she tried to comfort them; all the while noting they were surrounded by demons. Demons who clung tightly to their human hosts; while they cringed, and hissed, at a room filled with heavenly host. "God is watching over us girls and He is working on a plan for our freedom. All you have to do is believe."

The girl Gracie didn't know spoke first. "Believe? Believe in what? You have no idea what I've been through in my life! If your God was real, or He cared about me, why would He let me go through all this?"

"Listen, I used to think the same way you do. And, yes I do know the things you've been through. You haven't cornered the market on human suffering. None of us has. But, you can choose to be a victim of your circumstances, or have victory over them! All you have to do is believe in Jesus, and trust Him, and you will be saved."

Then the raven haired girl spoke. "Why would you even want to help me, Grace? I am the one who could have helped you to freedom, and instead I watched while Vladimir put a bullet in your head."

"I know the situation you were in. I hated you for a long time, and in fact, I thought I would hurt you, if I ever saw you again. But, then Jesus came into my life, and taught me how to love. I forgive you. I forgave you long ago. However, I don't even know your names, and since we are in this together, it would be good to start there."

"My name is Lilly, Grace. I am truly sorry for what you have suffered at my hand."

"Like I said, Lilly, I forgive you. You were in the same frightening position I was in. No one knows how they will react in a situation like that. No one should ever have to know. And, you. I need a name, so I'm not calling you, you."

"I'm Bella. And I'm still wondering how to trust your God, Grace. I don't know how to do that. How can I trust anyone?"

"Well, I can promise you, Bella, God loves you. Do you want to believe that?"

"Sure, who wouldn't want to believe that? But how do I believe?" Demons began to squirm and hold on tighter with their long, discolored talons.

"Just have faith in a God who came to earth and died in your place. A God who was willing to take on the sin and suffering of the world to give us an eternity of peace. He loves you, and sacrificed Himself for you, covering you with His Grace when all you deserved, all any of us deserved is death."

"But I don't know how to do that. What do I pray and how do I know He will even listen to me if I do?"

"Would you really like to know my Savior? I can introduce you."

"Yes. Can you help me?" There on a cement floor in a broken down old warehouse, where only moments before they had all been bound; Grace led both of those tired, frightened girls to the Lord. As they gave their hearts to Jesus their demons were violently wrenched from them, screaming and screeching, to join the dark cloud of evil swarming high over the metropolis. Just as quickly, each girl was surrounded by guardian angels they couldn't see, and as they looked up at Grace she watched their faces completely change from fear to hope.

Lilly was beautiful, with golden skin; huge, brown, almond shaped eyes; and hair so black it shone in the light with a bluish hue. Bella was blond; with large green eyes; porcelain skin; and a long graceful neck. Gracie knew these girls had been valuable to the mob for their great beauty, and understood why it was so easy for Vladimir to toss her aside when she didn't submit to his authority. She was nothing special, with chestnut brown hair, and large brown eyes in a rather average looking face.

The room was cold, and the girls huddled together, in their cement prison to stay warm. As they shared their warmth they also shared their stories and got to know each other better. When Grace began to relate her history to her new friends they were astonished at the strength they saw in this amazing young woman who had just led them to Christ.

✝

Grace thoroughly checked out their prison, even climbing a wall to test a barred window, which turned out to be an impossible source of escape. Just as she was shimmying back down the wall she heard noises in the warehouse. The three girls huddled together in a far corner waiting for their captors to present themselves. Pretty soon they heard the bolt on their prison slide free, and the metal door swung open to reveal none other than, Vladimir Slochik. He wore an expensive, black, silk suit, and a look of arrogant victory. His eyes glowed with a malevolence Grace could clearly see. He was surrounded by a particularly large group of hideously deformed demons, and they didn't seem to be very bothered by the presence of either heavenly host, or Gracie; which confused her greatly; until they were joined by a larger, and more evil force than any she had encountered previously. Obviously this demon thought he could withstand anything this slight girl threw at him. But, this demon hadn't met Gracie, and was clearly not aware of the power of an almighty God, when invoked by a trusting young lady.

As Vladimir walked menacingly toward the girls, with a smile on his face that could only have come from the deepest pits of hell, Gracie stood, and spoke. "Demons, I command you to leave, in the name of Jesus!" At that, those evil entities surrounding her enemy loosened their grip, and the smile on his face turned to a look of confusion.

"Again, I say, demons, I command you, in the Name of Jesus Christ, Lord of Heaven and earth, to leave. Be gone in Jesus' Name!" Suddenly, the air whirled and spun, as if the interior of the room was caught in the grips of a tornado; and, the faces of the demons surrounding Vladimir twisted in fear, and agony. Even the larger force looked as if he was trying, with the very last of his strength, to hold tightly to his host; but in the end, even he could not overcome that Name. Grace watched as the evil flew backward, screeching, grasping, and moaning, through the ceiling; and gathered, she was sure, to the mass of demonic forces swirling in the sky.

At the very second that Vladimir was released from the grips of his evil oppressors, he stumbled and fell to his knees. Dumbfounded by the sudden, and inexplicable, change in his emotional surroundings, he reached for, and drew his pistol from the inside of his coat; but just when he thought he was again in charge, one of the heavenly host held his arm; and Grace deftly kicked the gun from his hand. Meanwhile, Lilly dove, and scrambled to retrieve the weapon.

Gracie's warriors from glory never revealed themselves in the room, so Vladimir never knew that an angel stayed his arm, and he was shocked that the slip of a girl had gotten the jump on him. Lilly, for once, in a position to pay back the man who'd held her prisoner for years, was suddenly overcome with emotion, and the desire to seek revenge for all the wrongs he'd perpetrated on her and others. Grace, seeing the change on the girl's face spoke softly to her friend.

"Lilly, honey, give me the gun."

"No Grace. He has to pay. He can't keep getting away with this. I can't let him ruin anymore lives, like I let him ruin yours."

"No, no, Lilly. That wasn't your fault, and we can't let ourselves become like him. Do you hear me? We have to let the authorities take care of it. We don't have the right."

"What do you mean we don't have the right? If we don't have the right, who does?"

"Lilly, clearly I know where you're coming from. Bella, and I, were right there with you, but this isn't the way."

"No, Grace, you don't know all the things he made me do for him. The ways he made me hurt the other girls. I can't let him get away with that!"

"Then we will make sure he gets put away for a very long time, Lilly. Please, honey. Let's do this the right way. We don't want to have to spend the rest of our lives regretting what we do today. There are enough regrets already. Please, give me the gun."

Throughout the exchange Vladimir remained on his knees, with his arm firmly secured in the hand of an angel. He didn't know why he couldn't move his arm, but his expression was becoming more frightened by the moment. He was sure Lilly would shoot him, as he would have done in the same position; but finally she broke down in tears, and handed the gun to Grace. As Grace took possession of the firearm, she wrapped her arms around the sobbing young woman, and then Bella joined in.

In the distance, the whining of sirens, growing louder, as they approached the Russian's den of evil. It seemed that a bystander, who'd witnessed the explosion from outside, followed the kidnappers, while giving the authorities step, by step instructions to the warehouse. Quite a God moment for sure. A gunfight ensued, outside, in which Vladimir's guards, and the kidnappers, were killed. Mr. Slochik was apprehended, on his knees, in the room where he had imprisoned the girls, and he was taken back to the courthouse under heavy guard.

When the girls arrived, also under heavy guard, Mike, and Nancy, ran to embrace Grace. And the other girls, excited by what they'd witnessed, proceeded to tell anyone who'd listen, how Grace had overcome the bad guys. "No, you're wrong, girls. It was the Lord. Just like I told you. He was watching over us. And, now you've seen, in person, how much He loves you too. Mike, and Nancy, these girls were locked up in the brothel with me. This is Lilly, and this is Bella. Neither of them has a place to go. Their families are dead. Lilly is fourteen, like me, and Bella is thirteen. I don't know if there is a way we can help, and you've already done so much for me, that I hate to even ask, but they will have to go into the foster system, if someone doesn't take them after the trial is over."

Without skipping a beat, Mike, and Nancy, looked at each other and smiled. "Well, Gracie, as soon as we can arrange it, you will have two sisters, if they are agreeable." Grace smiled, and the girls fell all over themselves accepting the invitation.

Nancy would get onto redecorating a third, and fourth bedroom, as soon as she got home, until then the girls could bunk in with Grace. She was sure they could dig up a couple of cots to use temporarily. What a blessing! Childless for all these years, and now, three daughters. She would check into getting them all into classes to get caught up to the other students their age, but these were three girls with more spunk than most, to have lived through the horrors that afflicted them, so she was sure they would do well. First though, they would get through this trial.

By the time everyone got back to the courthouse, the day was almost done. The judge gave the girls two options. They could resume the trial, the following Monday, or they could reschedule. After careful consideration, Mike and Nancy asked the judge to reschedule. This would give the girls a chance to breathe. But, since it might also give

Vladimir a chance to shore up his defense, and give him another opportunity to get to the prosecution's witnesses, they would take all the help they could get from the court. Gracie wanted to get the whole thing over with, but she could also see the toll it was taking on her sisters, and agreed to allow the court to reschedule. The court assigned deputies to guard the girls. They would be under constant surveillance until the upcoming trial date.

In You, O Lord, do I take refuge; let me never be put to shame! In Your righteousness deliver me and rescue me; incline your ear to me, and save me! Be to me a rock of refuge, to which I may continually come; You have given the command to save me, for You are my rock and my fortress.

Psalm 71:1-3

CHAPTER 19

Mike and Nancy took their three, beautiful girls home for the weekend. Nancy was walking on clouds, with so many to care for. She was a natural nurturer, and tended to spoil Mike half to death, which he, usually, patiently tolerated. She'd been thrilled to add Grace to their little family, but now she'd have three girls to take care of and raise. Oh, she was sure they would have their little differences, but so far Grace had been an angel. The girl was so grateful for the love, and attention she received now, that she never wanted to create a problem for her new parents. So far their little family was a perfect picture of peace.

Lilly and Bella were timid at first, just as Gracie had been. They didn't want to be a bother, and weren't used to being fussed over. Both so in awe of the beautiful Victorian house they would now call home, they had a hard time accepting that this was truly to be their new life. Perhaps Jesus did love them after all, just like Grace said. And, perhaps it was okay for them to stop being afraid, and learn to be part of a family again.

On the way home that first day, Mike and Nancy, stopped to buy some clothing for the two newest additions to their family. Following their short shopping expedition they picked up pizza, and a movie, and headed home to relax.

The girls all took baths, and changed into brand new pajamas. Then, with a big bowl of popcorn, and large pepperoni pizza in tow, they piled in to watch 'Forest Gump'.

While the movie played, Grace watched Lilly's, and Bella's faces, both so beautiful in completely different ways, as the varying light from the television danced across their features. They seemed genuinely happy, and she was happy for them. Lilly fairly glowed in her new circumstances, and at least once, when there wasn't even a sad scene playing in the film, she saw tears in Bella's eyes. By the end of the film, they all came to the general consensus that they really made a pretty darned good family.

In bed that night Mike and Nancy talked. "Are you sorry we took the girls in?"

"Not at all, Nance. They really seem like good girls, and it's high time somebody gave them a fighting chance. How about you?"

"I'm sure you can tell how I feel, Mike. I'm in seventh heaven with babies to take care of."

"Well, I want you to be careful you don't overdo it. These girls are big enough to help, and from the looks of it, they wouldn't mind learning a couple things from you."

"Oh, do you think so? That would be wonderful. I would love to help them get ready to meet the world on their own terms. The poor dears have had a whole lifetime of misery, packed into their short lives, and whatever I can do to help them would feel like a blessing. I especially worry about Bella. She seems so fragile."

"I'm sure they would all consider it a blessing to have your help too, Babe. I guess we're going to have quite the carload for church on Sunday. Won't that be nice?"

"It sure will. I do love you, Mike, so much."

"And, I love you, Nance. You make a fine mom. I want you to know that, and I hope the girls will appreciate all you do for them."

Lilly and Bella had been under the protection of the state, since their rescue from the Russian brothel. Though, as far as they were concerned, that new veil of security had amounted to going from one terrible prison, to an only slightly better one. Being in this home, now, with parents who seemed to want them; and having access to all the material things they'd never had before; was like a dream. They were both grateful for the loving attention from Mike and Nancy, but it would take awhile to get used to it, or for any of it to seem real. Both girls lost their families very young, and both had been on their own for a while, before men like Tom stepped in and sold them into sex slavery for the Russian mob. Neither of them could really remember having a normal life, and they longed to fit in. They were willing to do whatever was necessary to make that happen. Now though, they would have to be careful until the trial was over. It was highly possible that there were still individuals out there that would do them harm, to keep them from testifying. Their court appointed deputies became a part of their day to day lives.

Sometimes fitting in can be harder than it looks. Both girls had nightmares for a time, and the family got used to waking up to screams in the middle of the night. Loud enough to draw the attention of deputies outside. But, the bad dreams eventually subsided, and they seemed to enjoy church with the family, Sunday school, and the friends they were making in high school. Grace was careful to not get in the way. She didn't want to hover, and instead allowed the girls room to make friends on their own. She didn't want to be the reason they didn't succeed with their peers, but she did remind them that they had to lay low until they'd had the opportunity to give their testimony in court.

Each of the girls had her own distinct style, and Nancy loved to take them shopping. Grace wasn't a clothes horse; it just wasn't something that was important to her; and she tended to dress very conservatively. But, she always thanked Nancy profusely whenever she bought her some new item for her wardrobe. Lilly's taste, however, was elegant. She enjoyed classic styles, wanted to choose them for herself, and knew how to wear them, by some innate fashion gene. Bella tended toward flashy, and even downright tacky sometimes, wearing whatever un-matching items were in vogue that week. Nancy was careful about what she bought and paid for, but it didn't take much to roll a skirt up, to make it shorter, roll a waist band down to show more midriff; or pull a shirt down to show more cleavage than was seemly. She took to wearing more makeup than was widely acceptable, painting butterflies on her cheeks, and flirting with all the wrong boys at school. Pretty soon she was creating quite a reputation for herself, and hanging out with known drug users.

Grace was becoming concerned for her friend. She noticed the girl's angelic guard holding on tight, and snarling demons waiting around every corner. Mike, and Nancy were at wits end, blaming themselves, and wondering what they might be doing wrong. DHS suggested family counseling, and the couple agreed. Once there, they discovered Bella was having more problems than they realized, due to her life of living in the sex trade, and that she might need years of treatment going forward. They were more than happy to supply all the help she needed, but were confused, as these were issues that didn't seem to be ongoing with Grace, or Lilly. Simply put, the counselors confided, some people are emotionally stronger than others, and come to terms with the repercussions of their previous life better than others do. Mike and Nancy did want to be good parents to Bella, so they signed up for all the help they could get.

Counseling can only help, though, if the patient is diligent to work in that direction, and that didn't seem to be the case with Bella. Counseling sessions constituted a burden in her mind, and she basically quit showing up, first emotionally, and then physically. The family continued to remind her that there might be forces in the world, which would love to see her dead, before she could testify, and they only wanted to keep her safe. But, their safe, was her prison. She seemed happiest when unfettered. She was a free spirit, caged for far too long, and she would not be tied down anymore. Within months of coming to live with her new family; she was sneaking around to hang out with some of her less than desirable new friends. She became an expert at outwitting the deputies assigned to protect her life.

Mike, Nancy, Grace, and Lilly were all heartbroken when Bella was hauled home, more than once, by concerned police officers who'd caught her in compromising situations. Bella began skipping classes, and then stopped going to school altogether. Pretty soon she was arrested again, but this time she'd been caught turning tricks for extra money. Her folks wondered why?

Nancy began to wonder where she went wrong, and cried herself to sleep more nights than she cared to count. Mike started to wonder if they'd done the right thing, taking on so many responsibilities. And, Gracie began to wonder what tragedy might befall her friend, if she didn't straighten up. Whenever Grace was near her foster sister now, she felt the turmoil in her soul. It was strange to put it that way, to say she felt the chaos, but that was the best way to describe how it was. It broke her own heart to see her friend so wrecked, but she didn't know how to fix this.

One night, very late, the doorbell rang, and everyone in the house woke, knowing the news must be bad.

"Hello Sir. Do you have a teenage daughter?"

"Well, yes officer, we actually have three teenage daughters."

"Oh, I'm sorry Sir. Do you know if all three of your girls are at home?"

"I'm sure they are. It's after three in the morning, and as you can see we have a deputy's car stationed outside of our house."

"May I ask you to check, Sir?"

"Certainly. Nance, will you check that all the girls are accounted for?"

After checking, Nancy called downstairs. "Mike, I can't find Bella. Her window is open. It looks like she might have crawled down from the back side of the roof, on the trellis."

"I'm sorry officer. Evidently I don't know where my daughter is. I'm going to need to go find her. Where in the world could she be at three a.m., and how did she get past the deputies again?"

"Sir, that's why I'm here. We found a girl tonight, who

meets your daughter Bella's description. I'm very sorry to tell you, but your daughter was discovered unresponsive in the park. I will need you to come with me to make an identification."

From somewhere behind him, Mike heard a strangled gasp, and then Nancy began crying. He thought of stepping back and trying to comfort her, but decided he might need to leave that up to the girls for now, because he was barely holding on to his own composure at this point, and didn't feel prepared to comfort anyone else. Grace wrapped her arms around Nancy, as Mike grabbed his coat from the rack near the door, and followed the officer to his waiting car.

☦

The officer was kind and wanted to comfort the grieving man beside him; after all, everyone in town knew about Big Mike, and the generosity of his heart; but the ride to the hospital morgue felt surreal, and the conversation became stilted. Mike was trying to keep it together, but his mind drifted to a time, not so long ago, when the family shared popcorn, pizza, and a movie; and many other wonderful family nights. He remembered the smiles and laughter of all his girls, and a small grin curved his own trembling lips. All he could do was hold on to hope that this girl, found in the park, wasn't their sweet Bella. Gentle rain began to fall, and the sound of the wipers coming on startled him back to reality. "Which hospital are we headed to, Officer?"

"Westwood General, Sir. We should be there in a few minutes."

"Do you have any children, Officer?"

"Yes Sir. My wife and I have three little girls. I can't even imagine what you're going through, or how you're feeling right now, Sir."

"I only wish we'd had these girls from the time they were little. Maybe that would have made a difference, but who knows. You hear so much about the things kids are doing these days. You know, all three of the girls we've taken in had terrible hardships growing up, and saw things they shouldn't have, but we have three totally different results, three completely different individuals. How do you explain something like that?"

"I wish I knew, Sir. Who knows what causes one to go down a good path, and another to take the wrong path? If I had the answers to questions like that, I'd probably be rich."

"I suppose you're right."

"Here we are, Sir. I'm going to pull up in front, and we can go in together. I'll be here to drive you home afterward as well."

"Thank you officer. I appreciate all you've done."

The pair entered by the front door, and the officer walked to the front desk to announce their arrival. Well worn rugs covered the floors near the doors, presumably to catch the wet from people's feet before it got to the newer carpet, but the reception area was decorated nicely in various shades of blues and tans. Two vases of flowers; one with a large Mylar balloon attached, reading 'Get Well Soon'; and one with a small stuffed bear, holding a bag of chocolate kisses, tied to the name tag; probably waiting to be delivered to hospital patients; sat on the counter top. Soon, an attendant from the hospital's morgue stepped off the elevator, and walked up to the two men. "Mr. O'Sullivan?"

"Yes, that's me. I've never done anything like this before. You'll have to tell me what to do."

"Yes Sir, please just follow me."

The attendant led them back to the rear, employees elevator, and pushed the button which would take them to the basement level. He supposed it made sense. The basement would be the coolest floor in the hospital, and a morgue should probably be cold. A poster inside the elevator promoted a local theater group's upcoming performance of 'No No Nanette'; however, the performance had ended over two months ago, and someone had drawn obscene doodles all over the advertisement. There were several long scrapes in the metal on the far wall, which looked for all the world like someone's attempt to escape the moving cubical through the small hatch on top. He absently hoped the contraption wouldn't fail now, as it would be impossible for him to fit through that tiny hole in the ceiling. When the conveyance stopped, and the door dinged open, the attendant walked out and urged him to follow. He wasn't sure he wanted to, but knew that was ultimately why he'd come.

The hallway was long, and lacked the coordinating amenities of the halls upstairs. No new carpet, wallpaper, or paintings by local artists to adorn the walls. The floors, and walls, were simple concrete with painted arrows, stating 'Morgue', pointing in the same direction they were currently traveling. The lights flickered, and Mike hoped they wouldn't go out, as it didn't appear there were any windows down there. The rhythmic sound of shoes slapping softly, on a cement floor, echoed through the space; and as they came closer to the door at the end of their long walk, a smell of bleach, and other less familiar chemicals, grew stronger.

The morgue attendant turned to look him in the eye, and asked, "Are you ready?"

"I guess so. Is anyone ever ready for something like this?"

"No, I'm sure they aren't." Turning the handle she pushed against stainless steel and glass, and walked in the morgue's outer room; then she held the door for Mike to enter. The lights were bright, after so long in the semi dark of the basement hallways, and he blinked several times to adjust his vision. The room was white, with lots of stainless steel, and glass, and the same smooth cement floors they'd walked to get there. Mike saw another door, and just inside that doorway, a table against the wall, which held, what looked like, a body covered with a bright white sheet. He began to sweat, and his stomach turned so that he thought he might be sick. Shaking, he followed the attendant to the table, and steeled himself for the worst.

When the cover was pulled back, he gasped. It was Bella. Her face had relaxed in death, and she looked much younger than her barely fourteen years, but it was her. If there had been any doubt, the brightly painted butterflies on her cheeks would have given it away, but no, this was his Bella. Poor, sweet, confused Bella. He swallowed back tears, and nodded his acknowledgement to the attendant. She touched his arm, and gave him a look of sympathy. There would be an autopsy. Authorities were fairly certain the cause of death would prove to be a drug overdose, as there weren't any external injuries. He signed several papers the attendant held steady for him, and then turned to go.

So sad. After so many years in the meanest of circumstances, she'd been unable to handle a life of love, and acceptance. He had much to learn about these girls, but none of it would help poor Bella now.

Following the morgue attendant back out to the dark hallway, up the elevator, and out into the reception area, he thanked her and turned to the officer, who was still waiting. The look on the young officer's face, was one of sympathy, and he returned a half smile. I'm so sorry for your loss, Mr. O'Sullivan. There will be some papers for you to sign at the precinct, but then I can return you to your home. "Fine. I understand that there is red tape, but is there any chance all of that can wait until tomorrow? I'd like to get home to my wife and girls. I'm sure they're all worried sick by now. I can come by the district tomorrow, to sign anything you have for me."

"Certainly Sir. I'm sure that can be arranged. The hospital will also need to know which mortuary you would like them to contact."

"I, I hadn't thought about any of that, I guess. I'd like to talk to my wife first, if that's okay."

"Sure, Mr. O'Sullivan. I'm certain all of that can be worked out. Let's just get you home for now. I'll have someone get in touch with you in the morning."

The ride home was pure torture. How would he tell Nancy and the girls? He was sure they were all hoping there'd been some kind of error, just as he had, and now he would have to tell them there was no mistake, their Bella was gone. He was frustrated with everything to the point that he was feeling angry with God. Hadn't they all been happy? Why would God allow this young lady into their lives, just to take her away again so quickly? What had happened to this confused child, and how would he live with himself now? Obviously, he hadn't done his job very well. He was her foster dad, it was up to him to keep her safe, and he hadn't protected her. He closed his eyes for the rest of the trip, concentrating on the pulsing light behind his eyelids.

✝

The morning of Bella's funeral dawned bright, cloudless, and chilly. Everyone in the family was numb with grief. Gracie looked around and noticed there were precious few at the service; and most of those were close friends of Mike and Nancy, or those who had been touched by Gracie's ministry, and who'd come to offer their condolences. No young people at all. Such a sad thing. Had lovely Bella touched so few lives? Her cherry wood coffin gleamed in the sun, as it sat perched above the recently dug grave, which was loosely covered by a sheet of green indoor, outdoor carpet. A large spray of flowers, from her family, decorated the top of the coffin; and was arranged using daisies, carnations, and several other brightly colored spring flowers. Bella would have been pleased with its variety, and colors, of blooms. Only three other flower arrangements had come, and those were from the hospital, the soup kitchen, and Mike's employees at the restaurant

The green canvass tent, where the family sat, cut back on some of the glare from the sun, but a cool wind swept through the temporary structure and caused Grace to shiver uncontrollably. They'd all been provided with metal chairs, covered in green velour; which were placed in a line and pointed toward the camouflaged opening in the ground; but the chairs were hard, and cold seeped through the covers adding to the chill. Pastor from their church would be presiding over the burial, but he seemed to be running late.

As Grace sat, cold; and rocking herself slowly, as was her habit; she looked around at her family. Mike and Nancy were pale, and looked as though they'd probably been crying all night. Lilly stared at the ground, but when she lifted her miserable gaze it met with a similar saddened look from Grace. They gave each other a small reassuring smile and Grace patted her hand; then Lilly went back to staring at the ground. Grace wished she could tell her family that their guardian angels were all around, so there was nothing to fear; but that seemed like an empty assurance with Bella gone. Where had her guardian angels been when she was injecting poison into her arms? Gracie had been crying out to the Lord for days, asking for an answer to her pain, but so far He had been silent. In the back of her mind she was reminded to, "Trust Me", but she was feeling very angry.

Out of the corner of her eye she spotted movement behind a nearby tree and turned her head. A young man stood not far off, and was looking in their direction. She got up from her cold, metal chair and walked, arms crossed over her chest, to his location. He didn't run, and as she drew closer she could see he'd been crying. "Hi, I'm Grace. Were you a friend of Bella's?"

"Yes. I didn't know if I'd be welcome, so I tried to hide."

"Of course you are welcome. Why wouldn't you be welcome? Why don't you come down to the tent, before services start? Can I ask what your name is?" Gracie noticed his angels right away, and was comforted in knowing that Bella had a Christian friend.

"Sure, my name is David. Bella was everything to me. She was my only friend. If I hadn't met her, I wouldn't have met Jesus. I don't know what I'm going to do without her."

"So, Bella introduced you to Jesus? That's wonderful. I had no idea that our little Bella was an evangelist. David, how long have you known my sister?"

"I met her the first day she started school. I'm afraid I'm the one who tried very hard to get Bella to do drugs with me. She told me she'd done that sort of thing before, but she loved her new life now, and would never go down that road again. I know they're saying she died of a drug overdose, but I can't believe that. She's the one who helped me stop using. She saved my life in more ways than one."

"I see. But, now you say you know the Lord, is that right?"

"Yes. I was such a mess, so many problems. I'd even tried to commit suicide, twice. Bella told me about you, Grace, and all about her years in the brothel, all the terrible things that happened there. She was so happy with Mike and Nancy, but she felt guilty about her life, the things she'd done, and things that were done to her, and she was having a hard time trying to fit in. You know, she asked me to go to the park with her that night, she wanted to run barefoot in the grass of all things, but I told her it was too cold outside and I wanted to stay in and watch Netflix. If I'd gone with her, she'd probably still be alive. I know she was searching for her purpose, always afraid that her time here on earth wouldn't mean anything, so I can't believe she would take her own life this way. She cared about making a difference, and now she's gone."

"Oh, David, you can't take responsibility for Bella's life, or her death. We would all strangle ourselves in guilt if we did that. And, I can tell you that Bella's life did mean something. If she hadn't lived, you wouldn't know Jesus. She had a choice to make. 'Do I share the best thing in my life with this young man, or do I keep this wonderful Savior to myself?' She chose to share, and I think that makes her pretty special. All I can say to you is welcome. Come on. Let me introduce you to Mike and Nancy. They will be so pleased to hear about your special relationship with Bella, and I think you should tell them everything you just told me, they could really use some good news right about now." As they spoke they walked back to the larger group.

"Mike, Nancy, this is David. He was a friend of Bella's. He's told me that Bella introduced him to Jesus."

Nancy approached David with her arms out, expecting a hug, and David practically fell into them."Oh, David, thank you so much for coming. Praise God. So our Bella was an evangelist? How wonderful. That makes me so happy, so very happy."

Mike held his hand out. "Welcome, young man. We're so glad you came. Come. Sit here with the family."

Pastor had arrived, and the service proceeded. Mike sat, with Nancy to his left, then Lilly and Grace, and David. As Pastor spoke, Nancy cried, and Mike put his arm around her shoulders in an effort to comfort. Grace looked at Lilly, and saw that the usually stoic girl had tears running down her face, so she reached out and placed her hand over her sister's. The gesture was met with a soft smile. She then turned toward David, and saw that he, too, was quietly crying, so she placed her other hand over his. At precisely that moment, a beautiful butterfly danced through the air and landed on her hand. She smiled, as the butterfly appeared to soak in the outpouring of love, then it fluttered to the spray of flowers on the gleaming casket. Several people gasped, and the small crowd broke out in soft murmurs concerning the appearance of the lovely creature so closely associated to their beloved Bella. Suddenly, the butterfly flitted into the sky, soaring higher and higher, right along with Grace's heart.

Let brotherly love continue. Do not neglect to show hospitality to strangers, for thereby some have entertained angels unawares.

Hebrews 13:1-2

CHAPTER 20

Since Bella's death Grace had questioned her own relationship with the Lord. Why was she still alive, and poor Bella dead? Why was her family dead; and what about Ruth? Certainly her own life was not more valuable than the lives of all these. What sense did it make for her to see angels, and demons, if she couldn't thwart an evil plan? The day that an angel had stayed the hand of Vladimir, to save her life, surfaced in her mind and confused her. What was the use of her abilities if she couldn't save her own sister?

Several days later the family received news that Bella's autopsy had been completed. Mike went, alone, to the hospital to receive the news. The conclusion was that Bella had indeed died of a drug overdose, but the coroner didn't think she had administered the lethal dose herself. He'd noticed heavy bruising on her wrists, and ankles, with no evidence of recent sexual contact, which would be consistent with someone holding her down, most probably for the purpose of injecting her. This indicated to him that an outside source had been involved in the overdose. The amount of drugs in her system would have killed ten people of her size, immediately, which was at least some small comfort, since they knew she didn't have to suffer for long. The coroner also wondered if Mike was aware that his daughter was pregnant. He wasn't, and his heart broke for what poor Bella must have been going through, with this new revelation. When he got home he took Nancy aside and shared the new information. From the other room Grace could see Nancy's hand go to her mouth, and her head shake back and forth with the news.

Now they knew the mob was still actively at work, and Mike knew he had to try to get the date of trial moved up, and provide more effective protection for his girls. He contacted their attorneys, and told them about Bella. When the lawyers conveyed the information to the court, the trial was moved up. They would be back in court on Monday, at nine a.m.

✝

David quickly became a beloved family friend, and soon, more like a part of the family. He asked Grace to mentor him in the Gospel, and she agreed. His heart was aching for the loss of Bella, and so was hers, so the time together became a chance to honor Bella's act of unselfish sharing and soon started a healing process in both their hearts. Gracie decided she needed to visit Tom, and wanted to take David with her. Mike drove them, and enlisted the help of one of the deputies as extra protection.

Once they'd arrived at the prison the three were led into a holding area, filled with metal tables and stools, which were securely bolted to the concrete floor. Three walls were constructed of the same concrete as the stained floor, and one was comprised of bars. The bars separated the visiting area, from the hallways leading to the main prison population, through a series of three connecting chambers. Grace noticed cameras in every corner, and guards behind bullet proof glass. The place smelled faintly of body odor, and urine, and there were several stains, on the concrete floor, of questionable origin. Grace began rocking gently on her metal stool, until Mike reached over and tenderly touched her arm, bringing her back to the here and now. She smiled at him, aware that he knew this was her go to coping mechanism. David sat wide eyed, and jumped at every small sound. Pretty soon they saw Tom walking toward them, feet in chains and hands in cuffs, led by a guard. As the guard reached each access chamber he called out and a barred door slid open. As he and his prisoner entered that chamber the door slid shut. He then called out again, and the next door opened, until finally, they were in the chamber before the visiting area. When the last door opened, David visibly jumped. "Are you okay, David?"

"I think so. I've never been in a prison before."

"Don't worry. Mike is here, and there are guards all around." Grace didn't mention that they were also surrounded by very large members of a heavenly army, in full battle gear."

"I know, don't worry about me. I'll get over it."

As Tom was led, shuffling, to their table, he began to smile. "Grace, I wondered who came to see me. I haven't had any visitors since you came to the county jail. As you can see, it's a little different here. I've gotten your letters. Did you get mine?"

"Yes, I did, Tom. And, you're right, it's very different here. Tom, I'd like you to meet my dad, and my brother David. Mike, David, this is my friend Tom."

Tom was visibly touched by the fact that Gracie called him friend. "Thank you, Grace. No one has ever called me friend before. I don't know if you realize how much that means to me. I'm pleased to meet you Mike, and you too, David. Thank you for visiting me. I don't get a lot of company in here. Hey, Grace, I wanted you to know I've been reading the Bible you left for me."

"Yes, you told me that in your last letter. Have you found a favorite verse yet?"

"I have. I'm sure you know it. "I know how to be brought low, and I know how to abound. In any and every circumstance, I have learned the secret of facing plenty and hunger, abundance and need. I can do all things through Christ, who strengthens me. Phil 4:12-13". This one has been important in getting me through each day."

"That's one of my favorites too!"

Mike, who had entered the visiting room with a scowl on his face, found that the easy conversation between Tom, and Grace, was softening him immensely. He'd expected to hate this man, who'd sold his foster daughter into slavery with the Russian mob; yet his heart began to warm to a man who had made mistakes and was paying the price. After all, who was he to judge?

"I'm pleased to meet you too, Tom. You look much different than the man I saw in court. Grace has told me about the letters that have been going back and forth between you two. I was all set to not like you, but I think I've changed my mind, and I'm glad you're doing so well."

"Yes Sir, I would have been all set to hate me too, if I were you, but your daughter has made a big difference in my life. I'm not the same man who was locked up after that trial. Grace's forgiveness has meant the world to me."

"Hi Tom. I'm glad to meet you too. I was a friend of Bella's, Gracie's sister. I've kind of adopted her family as my own, I guess, since we lost Bella. They have a way of making people feel loved, and included, and I think I really needed that."

"I agree, David. they do tend to make people feel important. You said, "Since we lost Bella". What happened?"

"The autopsy showed a massive drug overdose, but it also showed signs of a struggle, as if someone held her down to administer the drugs that killed her. We're guessing that the Russians got to her, so she couldn't testify, though we can't prove any of that."

"So, Gracie, you haven't had your day in court with Vladimir?"

"No, Tom, not yet. That will be coming on Monday. I'm a little nervous, but we need to get this taken care of. Lilly, my other foster sister, will be testifying too."

"You'll have to let me know how that turns out. I'll be praying for you."

"Thanks Tom. Keep reading your Bible, and I'll keep writing. I can't promise when I'll be able to visit again, but I will be back."

"Thanks Grace. And thank you, Mike, and David, for coming to see me. I appreciate it more than you know."

"Sure Tom, maybe we'll come again when Grace decides to visit in the future. It's been good to get to know you a little better. I do have to say that Gracie usually has good ideas, and I think this was one of her better ones. I'll talk to Nancy, my wife, and the whole family will be praying for you. I'll bet you'll even be getting some more letters."

"Me too, Tom. Even though I'm new to the family, I'll be praying for you too."

"Thanks everyone. It means a lot to have your support. I'll keep you in my prayers too."

†

Back at home, Grace and David went off to do some studying, for no other reason than to get their minds off the upcoming trial. Mike was left in the kitchen with Nancy, and she asked how the visit had gone. "You know, Nance, she just amazes me more and more every day. The way she treats people. The way she forgives. Here we were visiting the man who abused her, and sold her into sex slavery, and she talks with him like he's been an old friend for years. I'm just astounded."

"I hear what you're saying, Mike, but isn't that how we're all supposed to treat people? I mean, if we claim to be Christians."

"Sure it is, but have you ever actually met anyone before who did?"

"No, I guess I haven't. She is pretty amazing, and very strong. She's a little nervous about Monday, but I think she's actually looking forward to the whole thing. I can tell you she had a bigger impact on Bella than we knew."

"How's that?"

"Well, while the three of you were gone, I started going through Bella's things. I found a journal she's been keeping, and some of the things in there are eye opening. It broke my heart to read it, but I think you should see it too. I'm going to give it to Gracie to read first.. I know she's been struggling, and feeling a little angry with God for letting Bella be taken from us. I think the entries in Bella's journal will help her get some understanding, and some closure."

"Good. Anything that will help her get to a better place would be welcomed."

✝

Grace was a bit nervous about reading Bella's journal. It felt a little like eavesdropping, or snooping. But, she was thankful that Nancy had passed this portal into Bella's world, on to her. It was Sunday, and she intended to hunker down, by herself, and find out a little more about what had made sweet Bella tick. Tomorrow would come soon enough. Tomorrow she would concentrate on her testimony against Vladimir, and the Russian mob.

Gracie found a sunlit window seat, and settled down to read. What follows are some, not all, of the most poignant entries, in chronological order.

*"Today is the first day in my new family. Mike and Nancy have taken us on as foster kids, until they can officially adopt us. They are really great people. I can't believe it. We shopped for new clothes, I found this great journal, and then I took a bath in the most beautiful bathroom I've ever seen. I'm not quite sure how to act. These people don't know the things I've done, or the things that have been done to me. If they knew, they might not want to share

their home with me. I need to know lots more about them before I can share my whole past. They seem so good, and I'm just not. We watched a movie, as a family, with pizza and popcorn. It felt so warm and wonderful that I started to cry. I think Gracie saw me. She is amazing. Lilly, the other foster kid, seems a lot like me, but maybe not as crazy, but Grace has it all together. She's had the worst life of anyone I've ever met before, but none of it seems to get to her. She just wants to share Jesus with the world. She shared Him with me while we were locked up, and in trouble, when we were taken from the courthouse by the Russians. I asked Him to be my Savior. The whole thing was very surreal and beautiful. This experience makes me want to live the right way now, you know, as an example to other people, and maybe even get the courage up to share Him with others the way Grace does. I just hope I can measure up, and live in a way that will make Him happy with me."

*"First day of school today. I don't fit in, that's for sure. Most of the other kids just stared at me, and walked as far away as they could, like I had some kind of disease or something. I do tend to have my own style. I wonder if it had anything to do with all the butterflies I paint on my face? I made one friend. His name is David, and he just

might have more problems than I do, if that's possible. He wanted me to go out in back of the school to smoke a joint, but I told him I don't do that anymore. He seemed a little surprised at first, but then he decided to hang out with me and not smoke his weed. He seems nice enough, though a little confused. I wonder if he knows Jesus?"

*"I got an A in English today. It was for a short story I wrote. I couldn't wait to tell Mike and Nancy when I got home, and they seemed very pleased. We celebrated with ice cream and I felt pretty special. My grades have been so bad ever since I started back to school, I just haven't been able to get into it, and I'm sure they've been disappointed in me. It's so hard to play at being a regular teenager, trying to pretend nothing happened to me over these past years. It's really difficult to act like everything is just back to normal. Most of these kids have no idea what I've been through, as they go about their perfect little lives. I wish I could get it all together like Gracie. Her relationship with the Lord is so strong, and I want that for myself. A couple of boys started talking to me today. They asked if I could go to a party with them on Friday night. I know Mike won't let me go, especially with the Russians still hanging around out there. If I decide to go, I'm going to have to sneak out."

*"I had a long talk with David today. He asked me to go with him to smoke some crack. I told him a little bit about my past, and that I don't do drugs anymore. He seemed shocked about the stuff I've been through. I also told him a little bit about Grace, and started to talk about Jesus. He actually listened. I think he's more confused than I thought, and I might be able to help him. It felt really good to talk about the Lord. No wonder Gracie loves it so much."

*"I snuck out of the house tonight, to go to a party with people I thought were new friends. It wasn't easy, since we always have a deputy's car in front of our house. I wore a fun outfit, and painted new butterflies on my cheeks. When I got to the party there was only one other girl, so I started to leave. The two guys I'd met at school told me it would be okay, and gave me a drink. Things got a little blurry after that, and I couldn't control my legs. One of the guys grabbed me and started to kiss me. He and his buddy dragged me down a hallway, to a bedroom, and raped me. I fought as hard as I could, but I didn't have the strength. I passed out, and I guess several other guys joined in after that. When I woke up I was bloody, sore and confused. I cried, and I told them I was going to report them. They told me that everyone in the school already thought I was a

whore, because of the way I dress, so no one would believe me. I'm not sure what to do. I came in the back window, the same way I left, and I cleaned up, so no one would know I was gone, but I'm afraid. I can't tell Mike and Nancy, or they'll know I snuck out again. What do I do?"

*"The music at church today made me cry. I'm not sure why, but I think the Holy Spirit was filling my soul. I can't be sure, since it's never happened to me before, but if that was it, He can surely come in any time He wants to. By the time we left to come home, I felt stronger somehow. Maybe I can make it. Maybe Friday night doesn't matter. Those guys wouldn't be the first men in my life to use me and throw me away like trash. I'll just try to forget the whole thing, and no more parties for me. Gracie gave the message at church today, and when you listen to her it's hard to believe she's only fourteen years old. It's like she can see into our hearts, and knows just what we need to hear. I hope to have the same kind of relationship with Jesus some day. I'm pretty sure she's officially my hero."

*"Today was one of the worst days of my life. Some of the guys took pictures at the party on Friday night, and they were on everyone's phones by the time I got there. The looks I got were terrible. Even the girls were looking

at me like the whole thing was my fault. I guess some of their boyfriends were there, and now they hate me. I can't continue to come back to this place, it's sucking the life out of me, but I can't let Mike and Nancy know what's going on either. Grace and Lilly are in advanced classes, so I never see them. David was the only person who didn't desert me today. He's my only friend at school."

*"I feel so lost. I took a test in the bathroom at WalMart today. I'm pregnant. I can't tell anyone. I wish I was dead. I know Mike and Nancy can see something is wrong with me, just by the way I've been acting, but I can't seem to pretend everything is okay. I haven't talked to anyone since that Friday night a few weeks ago. I'm not trying to shut them out, but I don't know what to say. I hear Nancy crying at night, and I know it's because of me, but I don't know how to fix it. I'm sure they already think I'm the biggest mistake they've ever made. I quit going to most of my classes a while back, so I'm failing. I haven't even told David about the baby. I'm not sure who the father is. Gracie has asked me if I'm okay, until I want to scream. Lilly just leaves me alone. I know I've probably disappointed the Lord, and that makes me the saddest."

*"The family started counseling today. DHS thought

it might help me adjust better, but they don't know all the crap that's been going on. I guess I'll have to go, but I don't see how it will help. I know they're only trying to fix me, but I can't tell them about the things that have happened. I'm afraid they'll all hate me if they know. I should have been more careful. Now I've created all these problems for the only people in my life who've ever really loved me. I'm nothing but trouble. I wouldn't blame them if they just gave up on me. I wish I was dead."

*"I can't go back to school. The counselor says it would be a good idea, and Mike agreed with her, but they don't know what has been going on in my life. The kids there have made my life a living hell. My folks are pretty mad at me for skipping, but they have no idea, so I don't know what to do. I'm trying so hard to forgive myself for the stupid things I've done, and let Jesus' Grace and Mercy wash over me like Gracie says, but it's hard. I'm also trying to forgive all the people in my life who've hurt me. I don't know how Grace does it. She gave me a scripture to memorize, and I'm working on it. It goes, "Finally, all of you, have unity of mind, sympathy, brotherly love, a tender heart, and a humble mind. Do not repay evil for evil or reviling for reviling, but on the contrary, bless, for to this you were

called, that you may obtain a blessing." 1 Peter 3:8-9

*"I skipped school today. I promised the counselor I would give it a try again, but I couldn't take it. I can't go back to that place. The kids just get worse and worse every day, there isn't a safe place to go. I wish I could share my problem with Grace, or Lilly, but they seem to be in their own little world, and I barely see them even at home. They are both doing so well, and get such good grades. And, somehow, I can tell that neither of them has heard the gossip about me, or seen the pictures of that night, though how that's possible I don't know. I would be so ashamed to share my mess with anyone. Even David doesn't seem to know, or at least he's not letting on if he does. He met me in the park today. I guess he had to skip classes to do that, and I hate to get him in trouble, but we talked about Jesus, and he finally asked Him into his heart. It felt so good to help someone come to the Lord, and I think I would like to do this for the rest of my life. Maybe I'm starting to see how much God loves me, by putting my family, and David, into my life. No matter how much the kids at school hate me, I know I can count on David to be by my side. I noticed something strange today. While I was at the park, there was a black car parked on the street, and I was sure they were

watching me. Kind of creepy. Once David showed up they seemed to lose interest, and drove off. Probably just some old pervert."

*"I bailed on the counseling meetings. I know my family is upset with me, and I wish I could explain to them how much it hurts to talk about all the stuff from my past, but the sessions weren't helping at all. The whole thing seemed like a colossal waste of time, and life is too short to waste that much time. Maybe there is no help for me. I'm sure I'll start showing soon, and then I really don't know what to do. Grace and Lilly seem to have it all together. I don't know how they can file away all the stuff they've been through, but it doesn't seem to bother them. I'm a mess, and I know it. I don't know why Mike and Nancy even bother. They must have something better to do with their time than waste it on a loser like me."

*"I need to get out of this house. Mike told me that I can't expect the deputies to be at my beck and call whenever I want to go out. I really don't expect them to follow me. I think all the worry about the Russians is overblown anyway. I'm going to ask David to meet me tomorrow night. I need some fresh air. Maybe I'll go to the park and run barefoot in the grass. I hope it's not too cold out. I painted

some new butterflies on my face today. It would be so great to be able to fly free forever. I wonder what heaven is like?"

This was the last entry in Bella's journal, and was written the night before she was murdered. Gracie cried.

Now who is there to harm you if you are zealous for what is good? But even if you should suffer for righteousness sake you will be blessed. Have no fear of them, nor be troubled, but in your hearts honor Christ the Lord as holy, always being prepared to make a defense to anyone who asks you for a reason for the hope that is in you; yet do it with gentleness and respect, having a good conscience, so that, when you are slandered, those who revile your good behavior in Christ may be put to shame. For it is better to suffer for doing good, if that should be God's will, than for doing evil.

>   1 Peter 3:13-17

CHAPTER 21

Grace woke with a lump in her throat that didn't disappear with hot tea and toast. She knew it was fear, but refused to give it a name, or any more of her precious time. Vladimir Slochik had taken way too much of her life already, and she wouldn't allow him to take one more minute of her, or anyone else's, peace. Lilly was equally uneasy, and looked even more pale, than her usual porcelain loveliness. "Are you worried about today, Gracie?"

"My stomach is trying to be, but I'm not going to let it."

"Everything is always so easy for you."

"I didn't say it was easy. I'm just going to hand it all over to the Lord. You can do that too, if you want too."

"How?"

"Just pray about it, Lilly. Just say, "Lord, I know you watch over me. I'm not going to let all these worldly things get the best of me. I'm giving it to you. Thank you for your peace." If you do that you will feel a calm wash over you that will carry you through the day. I do this all the time."

"Okay, I'll try that. Just stay close to me today. Promise?"

"I will as much as I can. Remember the last court date? They put all the witnesses in different rooms. I don't know how it will work out today."

"I do remember. That's why I'm worried. The last time I was sitting in a room, waiting to testify, the world blew up and we were all kidnapped."

"That's not going to happen again, Lilly. We can't let fear overtake us. Keep this verse in your heart, it will help you. "For God has not given us a spirit of fear, but of power and of love and of a sound mind. 2 Tim 1:7. I lean on this every day."

"I guess I'm just not at a place, yet, where scripture leaps into my mind when I'm having a problem, like it does for you. I'm working on that. This one sounds like a good one to keep close to my heart. Thanks. I love you Gracie, and I'm so glad to have you in my life."

"I love you too, Lilly. We're both going to do just fine today. We are surrounded by God's love and protection, and we're doing what's best for everyone. The things Vladimir's organization did to us, to so many girls, were wrong. We're out to make sure he can never do that to any other woman again. Just give an honest testimony, and everything will go great."

"Hey girls, are we ready to go?"

"Yes, Mike, we're all set. Let's go get 'em."

"Are you okay, Lilly?"

"Yes Nancy, I'll be fine. Grace has been lifting me up with scripture. I really think everything will be great today. We're going to go out there and make a difference for all those girls who didn't have a voice."

"Good. If you need me, I'll be right there in the gallery, and I will be praying for you two girls all along."

Mike got all his ladies safely settled into the car. Though there was still a chill in the air, Grace opened her window. Mike glanced back at her, through the rear view mirror and smiled, so she gave him a small smile to reassure him that all was well. She just wanted to breathe in the fresh air, and settle her soul, before they reached the courthouse. She knew God was on her side, and that He had surrounded her with warrior angels. She also knew that Mike and Nancy would be there for moral support throughout the entire ordeal. She was actually more worried about how this would affect Lilly, than how she might be affected herself.

They drove slowly, knowing they had plenty of time to

arrive before their nine o'clock trial date, and Grace took in the tranquil sights and sounds of the town as they made their way; a lawn mower in the distance, and the smell of freshly mown grass; a dog barking somewhere nearby; and the sounds of children laughing and playing. As they approached Main Street, and proceeded to turn the corner for the courthouse Grace looked up and saw the cloud of demons swirling around in the sky above the courthouse, and then they saw the crowds. Gracie quickly closed her window. As with her previous trial, when she testified against Tom, there were two factions present, and holding signs which clearly stated their varying opinions, on their staked out sections of property. One group held posters that touted messages like: "We are praying for you Gracie", "God loves you Grace", and "Grace Always Wins". However, opposing forces pressed in angrily, shoving the peaceful lot out of the way, with placards which spewed political sayings such as: "Separation of Church and State, NOW", "Free Slochik, Stop American Imperialism", "White, Christian Supremacy Must End", "Your God is not the god of Grace". Grace saw the hurtful words, and shook her head. She knew that the positive posters were most likely held by those who had heard her speak, and those who were proponents of the

Gospel message; and the negative placards were probably brandished by the same groups who showed up at every pro-life, or pro-marriage march, held in town, usually to stir up hostility and anger. Several protesters stepped off the sidewalk in an effort to block traffic, which was clearly against the law, and just as quickly turned into rioters, joining in with the rest of the rowdy bunch. Suddenly, baseball bats appeared out of nowhere and people began beating on the windows of the car where the girls sat. Lilly started screaming, and Grace reached over to hold her hand. Mike gunned the engine, and people jumped back. He drove to the front of the courthouse, parked the car, and opened his door. Then the police came forward with shields and pepper spray, to quiet the rioters. Mike was angry. "What the heck! These idiots are threatening my girls! What are you people doing?" He shouted to the disruptive crowd. "These girls are the victims here." Several of the protesters rushed forward, only to be taken down by prepared police officers. They were cuffed, and led to awaiting cars.

"It's okay Mr. O'Sullivan. We've got it from here."

"I can't believe these people. These girls are my children, and they are here because this scumbag locked them up and abused them. Why would anyone be angry with my girls?"

"Sir, there are always people who disagree, even when we can't see anything a reasonable person would find to disagree with. Many people, especially these days, protest simply to protest. If they had a legitimate agenda at one time, we don't know, because it's been so long they forgot what it was. So, sometimes when we detain them, and ask for their reasoning, they don't know how to answer. We see a lot of anger out here on the streets, especially in this political climate. There are groups who believe all conservatives are fascists, and imperialists, it's just what we've come to know, and deal with."

"I don't envy you your jobs, men. It's hard to imagine there is this much hate out there for these girls, and I don't know how you deal with this every day. Thank you for helping us."

"You're welcome Sir. We will do our best to keep you, and your girls, safe.

Mike opened the back door of the car, to help the girls out; as Nancy exited on the passenger side, and quickly moved to join her family. Grace stepped out of the car and a protestor got close enough to make Mike angry. He put his hand out to keep the man at arm's length, but couldn't protect her from what came next. As the man approached he spit squarely in her face.

Her hands were shaking as she raised them up to wipe the mess from her face. Mike tackled the perpetrator to the ground, and police attempted to separate them. Grace wondered where her angels were, when she looked over and saw the hate dripping from the rioter's eyes, as he fought to be free to lunge at her again. Looking around she spotted them. They stood at the ready, but hadn't moved to help her.

She was slowly coming to realize that her angels weren't there to keep her from experiencing life, even when it reared its ugliest head in society's darker moments, but only to keep her alive to share the message she'd been given to distribute to the world to fulfill her earthly purpose. These Heavenly Host weren't her personal swat team, to order as she would. They were protectors of the Gospel. They would intervene to protect the message, as long as God needed her to be the vessel for that message. It was a humbling thought. She truly understood now, and suddenly the impact of the Gospel story she shared was even more miraculous. She was also flooded with insight about Bella's death.

Her sister had been tasked, even after all the hell she'd endured, with sharing Jesus with her friend David, a young man without many friends; probably a feat no one else in the world could have accomplished; and when she was finished, she was called home. We are all given a purpose, and we have the choice of fulfilling that purpose, or not. Most people think of life as the ultimate reward for a job well done, but the true reward for living in Him, is life everlasting; whether it be here on earth learning to rest in His will, or resting in His arms in the hereafter. This piece of revelation came as a shock to her. Gracie's anger softened to know that sweet Bella was at peace, and gone from this world where people spit in your face for having a different opinion than theirs. It is certainly true that to be called as a Christian is not a calling for wimps. More and more she was coming to understand the scripture in John that read, "These things I have spoken to you, that in me you may have peace. In the world you will have tribulation; but be of good cheer, I have overcome the world."

Nancy handed her a wet wipe, and she used it on her face and hands as she walked the length of sidewalk to the courthouse doors. As the door opened, she took a big breath and stepped into the marble halls of, she hoped, justice.

This time Grace and Lilly were placed in the same room. She didn't know whether it was due to the fact that they were sisters, and it would be supposed that they knew each other's thoughts on the whole case anyway; or if it would just be easier for the guards tasked with their protection to keep them together. The room was rather large, and had big windows, with safety screen built into the glass. The huge windows might have been a security concern, if they'd been on the back of the building, but Grace could see the picketers from where they sat. So, if anyone tried to enter by the windows they would have to go through reinforced glass, and dozens of witnesses. She watched for a moment, before turning her eyes away from the hateful signs, and the more hateful gestures coming their way.

There was hot coffee on the counter, and a small sign that said, "Help yourself", but the girls were already feeling jittery and coffee would probably make that worse. The leather chairs were comfortable, but both young ladies sat on the edge of their seats. Lilly had chosen to wear a grey, silk skirt and black sweater, with black pumps. Her hair was swept up in a chignon, and held with grey combs and pearls. Grace marveled that her sister always looked chic, even in situations of stress. Grace wore black pants and a white blouse, with comfortable, black flats. Never concerned with fashion, she was always about comfort, and conservatism. As they waited to be called, they held hands and prayed. Mike and Nancy sat in the front row of the spectator's gallery and prayed. There were people all over the city, and the state, praying. Today the armies of the Lord were in full battle armor.

The guards came for Lilly first. She was sworn in, holding her freshly manicured hand on a Bible, and looked out to the defense table where Vladimir was glaring at her with evil purpose. She gave the bailiff a small nervous smile. The attorney for the prosecution began.

"Ms. O'Sullivan, or would you prefer to be called Lilly?"

"Lilly would be fine."

"Okay, Lilly. Do you know why you're here?"

"Yes, I'm here because Vladimir Slochik held me prisoner for years, and you've finally caught him."

"Okay, when you say that Mr. Slochik held you prisoner, what do you mean by that?"

"I mean that I was sold to him by a man in my village. He took me against my will, to a brothel owned by him and the Russian mob, to force me to commit sexual acts with his clients."

"And, Lilly, I know this will be a hard question. What was your age when Mr. Slochik took you to live at the brothel?"

"I was six years old when I first went to serve at the brothel." Audible gasps filled the room.

"Lilly, can you point to the man who took you to that brothel, and forced you to commit sexual acts with grown men?"

"Yes, He's right there, sitting at the defense table, trying to bore holes in me with his eyes."

"Now, Lilly, this is another hard question. Did Vladimir Slochik ever have sex with you himself?"

"Actually, that isn't a difficult question. Vladimir made it a habit to have sex with all the girls, once they were no longer virgins. He had customers who wanted to be the first, you know the real sickos who like to be with the little virgins; which is why he bought so many girls who were very young; but he liked to test all the merchandise himself. The only girl I know for sure he had sex with, before she was with anyone else, was my foster sister Grace. She was pretty spunky. She'd already kicked a few clients in the groin, and most of the guys were afraid of her. He felt he had to put her in her place."

"And how did he put her in her place, Lilly?"

"He beat her within an inch of her life, and then he raped her himself, so she couldn't think she was too good to be like the other girls anymore. He never understood her. She never thought she was better than the rest of us, she just didn't want to be a part of any of it, and she was willing to die for what she believed was right."

"And how do you know about this, Lilly? Did Grace tell you this is what happened?"

"No, I was right there when it happened. I was there when he shot her in the head too. I was sure she was dead, and I envied her. To not have to be in that place anymore."

"I'm so terribly sorry, Lilly, that you have been through this ordeal. And, I'm so glad that you have found a family who cares about you. Your Honor, I have nothing else for now."

"Defense, do you have questions for this witness?"

"Yes Your Honor, we do. Do you mind if I call you Lilly, or would you prefer Ms. O'Sullivan?"

"Lilly is fine."

"Hi Lilly. You have identified my client as the owner of the brothel, along with the Russian mob. Do you have proof that the mob had any vested interest in the brothel

The Daze of Grace

where you were allegedly held?"

"Well, no, not proof I guess. But, I heard Vladimir talking to people, and in the conversations I'm sure there was talk about the mob. Besides he told me himself."

"So, he told you he worked for the Russian mob?"

"Well, not exactly. But he told me, when I was a small girl, that he owned me now, and that there were others who would not be as nice as he was, if I ever told anyone."

"Okay, so we've established that you allege Mr. Slochik told you that he owned you, but not that you actually heard anything about the Russian mob, can we agree on that?"

"I guess so."

At this point Vladimir was looking suspiciously at his defense attorney. The attorney who had been provided by his bosses in the mob. Were they trying to distance themselves from him now? Were they so sure he would be indicted that they were washing their hands of the whole situation? He needed to get hold of his contacts, and assure himself that they would be standing behind him as they always had.

"Fine, then let's move on. Is it true that the people in Mr. Slochik's operation knew you as his assistant. I mean, were you always locked up?"

"No, I wasn't anymore, but....."

"Did you help him with the preparation of, and discipline of the other girls?"

"Well, I kind of...."

"It's a simple enough question Ms. Lilly. Did you help Mr. Slochik get girls ready for customers? And, did you help in the discipline of the other girls?"

"Well, yes I......."

"Your Honor, the client's defense is badgering the witness."

"Your Honor, we, the defense request the removal of this witness, for her own good. She is making a better case for indicting herself in this supposed sex ring, than she is making a case for putting Mr. Slochik away. And she certainly hasn't given us any proof that the so called Russian mob had anything to do with any of this."

"Your Honor, I object. While it's true that Ms. O'Sullivan did act as an assistant to Mr. Slochik during her last year in captivity, she was doing so to keep herself out of harm's way. Our lead psychiatrist has told us this would be a perfectly normal way to behave in this type of hostage situation. He will be testifying later in the proceedings. The state is simply labeling the witness for their own purposes solely to try and discredit her. After all, Your Honor, what would any of us do in the same circumstances?"

"Defense, your move to have the witness removed is denied. Do either of you have any further questions for this witness?"

"No Your Honor."

"Are there any additional witnesses?"

"Yes Your Honor. The prosecution calls Grace O'Sullivan."

From the back of the courtroom, the sound of a door opening, and footsteps moving softly to the front of the room. Grace was led to the witness seat, and sworn in. As she placed her hand on the Bible, she said a quick prayer for God's favor. She looked out on the assembled company, and their otherworldly companions. By far there were more hissing, spitting demons, than there were armor clad angels, but she knew God was near. She could feel His presence. She closed her eyes, briefly, and took a deep breath. She was ready for anything. Well, almost anything.

The prosecution began, "Hello Ms. O' Sullivan. As with your sister, I will ask if you would prefer Ms. O'Sullivan, or Grace?"

"Grace would be fine."

"Okay Grace. Do you know why you are here?"

"Yes Sir. I'm here to give testimony in the trial of Vladimir Slochik."

"Good, and can you point to Vladimir Slochik?"

"Let the record show that the witness has identified the defendant."

Gracie noticed that Vladimir was surrounded by a vast army of demons. Many more than she'd seen the last time they were in the same room. From where she sat it looked as though his eyes glowed red, and she looked to her left and right to be sure her winged warriors were still present.

"Can I ask you, Grace, how you came to be in the company of Vladimir Slochik?"

"Yes, I was living in the cardboard village under the old bridge. A man there, named Tom, sold me to the Russian mob. When I was dropped off, I found myself in the brothel, and the possession of Mr. Slochik."

"Can you explain what you mean by, "In the possession of Mr. Slochik?"

"Yes, when my head was uncovered, in the room where I was dumped, there was a girl there who cut my wrists free and told me that I was now owned by the Russian mob. I argued with her, and told her it was against the law for one human to own another, and she told me that the men who owned me knew that, but that they made lots of money doing what they do, so that would be unlikely to change."

"Grace, I know this must be painful to recall, but can you tell us what you were forced to do while you were in the brothel?"

"I was expected to service the dirty old men who came there. The first couple of times they sent someone to my room I kicked them in their privates and scared them half to death. They left screaming mad. I was taken to Vladimir for punishment with each of those incidents. The first time he beat me and I was taken back to my room to recover. I was warned never to pull anything like that again. But, being the stubborn girl that I am I did the same thing with the next client who was sent to me. This time I was horribly beaten, and then raped by Mr. Slochik. Eventually, I think I got tired of fighting. It didn't look like I would ever get out of there, so I gave in."

"Is it true that you became pregnant while you were in the brothel?" This question caused Grace to tear up, and her answer was a small choked, "Yes".

"I know this is very painful for you, Grace, but we need to hear your answers in order to help make a determination."

"Yes, I said yes."

"May I ask you what became of that pregnancy?"

"I tried to keep it a secret, but when I got bigger, one of the clients snitched on me. When they found out, they sent me to their doctor, and he performed an abortion in his filthy, bloody baby killing room; then they sent me back to work. They murdered my baby, without a second thought, like she was nothing. After that, I just didn't care anymore. My baby had been kicking inside me for quite some time, and they simply killed her and ripped her from my body." At this point there were more audible gasps, and then murmuring in the gallery.

"Order. There will be order, or the courtroom will be cleared."

"Grace, I'm so sorry for your loss. You said you didn't care after that, so what happened then?"

"I refused to service their sick old men, so I was taken back to Mr. Slochik."

"And what did Mr. Slochik do?"

"He demanded that I do my job, or I would no longer be valuable to him. I refused again, and he shot me in the back of my head. I don't remember anything after that." Again the gallery was filled with gasps and voices that began to rise.

"Order. Order. I will not tell you again. Settle down, or the room will be cleared!"

"Grace, isn't it true that you were found washed up on the rocks in the river?"

"That's what they tell me. When I woke up, I was in the hospital. I guess a couple of little boys found me and called the police."

"Again, Grace, I'm very sorry for all you've been through. Your Honor, the prosecution reserves the right to cross examine. We are finished with this witness."

"Your right is reserved. Defense, do you have questions for this witness?"

"Yes Your Honor. We would like to request permission to handle this witness as extremely hostile."

"Proceed."

"Hello Ms. O'Sullivan."

"Hello."

"May I call you Grace?"

"You may."

"Well Grace, it sounds like you've had quite a tough time."

"Yes Sir."

"So, you have identified my client as the man who assaulted and shot you. Is that correct?'

"Yes it is."

"But I also heard you tell the court that the Russian mob had some involvement in all of this, is that correct?"

"Yes."

"May I ask how you came to the conclusion that the Russians were in any way involved in all of this?"

Grace's eyes shot up, and flashed with a new passion as she prepared to answer the question with quiet resolve.

Afterward He appeared to the eleven themselves as they were reclining at table, and He rebuked them for their unbelief and hardness of heart, because they had not believed those who saw Him after He had risen. And He said to them, go into all the world and proclaim the Gospel to the whole creation. Whoever believes and is baptized will be saved, but whoever does not believe will be condemned. And these signs will accompany those who believe: in my Name they will cast out demons; they will speak in new tongues; they will pick up serpents with their hands; and if they drink any deadly poison, it will not hurt them; they will lay their hands on the sick, and they will recover.

Mark 16:14-18

CHAPTER 22

At precisely the same moment the defense asked their most recent question, a man stood up in the back of the gallery; and pulling a 9mm out of his shirt; he fired a single shot across the room, which pierced Grace's chest less than an inch from her heart. Screams filled the space as court officials, and spectators alike, scrambled for cover. The gunman was quickly tackled to the ground, and willingly put his hands behind his back to accept the quickly applied cuffs.

It had been abundantly clear, throughout the proceedings, so far, that the mob didn't care much about how the case would pan out for Mr. Slochik, he was merely collateral damage in this situation if he was unable to run his business in a way which would not implicate them in multiple crimes, and upset their entire American operation.

As long as no evidence was brought to bear, which would link the Russian mob to the brothel, they were fine with losing an operative, even one who'd been as productive as Vladimir Slochik.. Much evidence had been presented concerning Vladimir, but so far the previous witness had only brought forth circumstantial evidence on the mob, evidence that was easily refuted by their crack legal team. However, the mob was fully aware that young Grace had a stronger case against them, and they weren't willing to take a chance that she would touch the hearts of those jury members who were already looking at her with sympathy. Simply put, the gunman was merely doing his pre arranged job.

Once the shooter was contained, attention was turned to Gracie. Where had her angel warriors been? They were standing very close by, and one of them had nudged her, just a bit, in order to keep the racing bullet from piercing her heart. Mike, Nancy, David, and Lilly were frantic. The judge ordered his bailiff to call for paramedics, as a nurse from the spectator's gallery began CPR.

Grace, once again in a place of comfort with the Savior; couldn't feel her body, or any of the severe pain she should have been experiencing after being shot. That would come soon enough. She had endured so much already, but she would live through this too. With the Lord by her side she asked, "Why is this happening, Jesus? What would be accomplished by my death now? I have so much more to do. And, what is the use of these big, strong, warrior angels if they can't protect me?"

"You're not dying Grace. You will live to serve the Kingdom, for a long, long time. Your angels saved your life. If not for them you would be with me permanently right now."

"Oh, Jesus, I would love that. Nothing sounds better to me than spending eternity with you. I only meant that I feel like there is more you've called me to do."

"You're correct Grace. There is much more for you to do. And, just as the injury to your head opened up your ability to see beyond what others could see with their mortal eyes; this injury, so close to your heart, will give you the ability to feel what others cannot feel with their mortal intuition. All the physical and emotional things that are going on in their lives will be opened to you.

You will know, simply by touching a brother or sister, what is happening in their bodies and minds. But, more than that, you will have a healing ministry bigger than any that has gone before you, which when linked together with the sacrifice I've already made for the salvation and healing of all who believe, will impact lives all over the world. I hope you're excited about the possibilities my daughter. First there will be a time of healing, and even pain, and then you will be very busy. Are you ready?"

"Yes, Lord. I'm ready for anything you have for me, but only with your help."

"And that is something you will always have my daughter."

As the two paramedics plied their trade, it was like watching a dance.

"I have a pulse. It's faint, but it's there."

"Good, bag her, hang an IV, and let's load her. I'll call it in. She's lost a lot of blood, this is going to be close."

"Is she going to be alright? Oh, my baby. We should never have let her do this, not after what happened last time."

"Nancy, she's going to be fine. I can feel it. And, we couldn't have stopped her if we'd tried. This is what she was determined to do. I believe she gave sound enough testimony to get Slochik locked up for good."

"But, what about the mob? I think their hit man got to her before she could say much about them. What if they come after her again?"

"I don't know about the mob. Nancy, calm down, honey. There's nothing we can do about that now. Let's just take Lilly and David, and go be with our girl. I have a feeling she's going to need us."

When Gracie woke in the hospital she opened her eyes and saw most of her family there with her. David was the first to notice. "Mike, Nancy, she's awake. Hey guys, she's up. Hey, Grace, we're all here."

"Oh, Grace, we were so worried."

"Nancy, don't fill her head with all that. We weren't worried at all Grace. We knew God would take care of our girl."

"Okay, Mike, maybe you weren't worried. David, go get Lilly. She went to get something to drink."

"Yes ma'am. Right away. I'll be right back Grace. I promise."

Grace tried to answer, but no noise emerged aside from a small croaking sound. Nancy leapt forward to get her some water, and practically shoved the straw down her throat in an effort to help. Surgery had been successful, and the bullet missed her heart, so she would be fine. She'd received six units of blood, so she would just need some time to rest and recover. Mike left the room to get Grace's doctor.

David and Lilly arrived back in the room, while Nancy tried to get Grace to drink a little more water. Grace gently pushed her hand away, and she backed up a step.

"Oh, Grace, I was so scared. I'm so glad you're awake. I've been so worried."

Grace made an attempt at a small smile, and said, in the gravelly voice of one who's gone through intubation for surgery, "I'm fine Lilly. I'll be just fine. They can't get rid of me that easy. They've tried before, remember?"

"Yes I do. I wondered, where do you go when you leave us Grace? You mumble, as if you're talking to someone, but you look so peaceful."

"I just spend a little time with Jesus, Lilly."

Right then Mike arrived back in the room with her surgeon in tow.

"There's our girl. It's good to see you up and at 'em. This is Doctor Phillips. I don't know if you remember him from the last time you were shot? He is the surgeon who works with Nancy."

"Yes, I do. It's nice to see you again, Doctor. Sorry that I seem to keep bringing so much business your way." She liked the fact that he had angels. So many doctors were extremely arrogant in their ability to save lives, and some even accredited the saving of lives to their own efforts, while leaving God out of the equation; but this man obviously knew the true value of life and its eternal rewards.

"Well, I'd say it's less your fault, and more the fault of the guys who keep shooting at you. You gave us quite a scare Miss Grace. If the bullet had been an inch more to the left, I doubt that you would be with us."

"Though you did have an excellent surgeon."

"Thank you, Nancy. I tend to do my best work under pressure, and our young Grace seems to provide plenty of pressure."

"Well, I'll try to bring you less work in the future."

"Good thing Grace, that would be a nice change. I'm going to send the nurse in for some vitals, and then our patient should get some sleep. I'll stop in to see you again before I leave, how's that?"

"Thank you, Doctor. And, thank you for being so good at your job."

"You are welcome Miss Grace. You obviously have angels watching over you. Try not to keep them so busy, okay?"

"Yes Sir. God bless you."

Doctor Phillips leaned over to give her a pat on the hand, and Grace knew immediately there was something wrong with him. She didn't know how she knew, only that she knew. Was this the new 'sight' Jesus had spoken of?

She wasn't sure how to hone it yet, but that would be a necessity if she was going to be useful for the Kingdom in this regard. She looked to her right, and to her left, to assure herself that she could still see her heavenly guards. They were there, and looked as powerful as ever. She didn't say anything to the doctor. A little unsure of her new gift, she thought she might need to have a little more contact with him, before making any true assessments. If truth be told, she was terribly afraid of looking like a fool. That was also probably the biggest reason she hadn't told her family about the winged warriors who escorted her everywhere she went; and them too; for that matter. This might be her chance to rectify that.

After the nurse took her vitals, and went about her way, Grace turned to her parents. "Mike and Nancy, I need to talk to you. You too Lilly and David. this is really important, and I need to have you listen till I'm done, before you try to say anything. Can you do that?" The whole family agreed that they would hear her out. The conversation took a very strange turn, and was not at all what any of them were expecting. "We have angels."

"Of course we have angels dear."

"Nancy, you promised you would hear me out."

"Yes, I did. I'm sorry. Go ahead."

"What I mean is that I can see them." Nancy looked as if she was going to speak again, and Mike gave her a look. "I'm serious. Ever since I was shot in the head, and lost my sight, I've been able to see them. Demons too. I see clouds of demons over the court house every time we go there. When I meet someone new they are either surrounded by protecting angels, or demons clinging on with yellow talons. When I walk down the street I see them everywhere. When someone is saved, I see their demons ripped away, to be replaced by towering angels. It's a beautiful thing." Mike and Nancy looked at each other a little unsure, and then back at Grace; while David just had a worried expression on his face, and Lilly simply closed her eyes and slowly shook her head.

"Are they here now?"

"Yes, Mike. Our angels are all around us."

"What do they look like?" At this question from Mike, David and Lilly looked a bit incredulous, as if they couldn't believe he was taking this seriously.

"They are enormous. Huge warriors with wings, clad in heavenly armor. they emit a slight glow, and they make me feel protected."

"If you are surrounded by angels, why do you keep getting hurt, Grace?"

"Well, Lilly, I'm finding out that if my angel hadn't nudged me, the bullet would have gone through my heart. He kept me from being killed. But, more than that, the angels are keeping the message of the Gospel safe. At first I thought of them as my own personal body guards, but I soon found out that they will only get involved when absolutely necessary. And those are the times when they are fighting the hardest to keep God's message of love safe for all those who would believe."

"Where were your angels when the mob blew up the walls of the courthouse, and took us prisoner?"

"Well, first of all, they are your angels too, Lilly. And, the angels were the ones who held Vladimir's arms, so he couldn't use his weapon. Don't you remember how he couldn't move his arms? They got involved that time, because our lives were in jeopardy, and so the message was in jeopardy. We are alive now, because they protected us."

"I didn't know. Why didn't you tell us before?"

"Well, I guess I was afraid of seeming like a fool; and of you looking at me the way you were just looking at me a minute ago, Lilly."

"I'm sorry. It's just when you started talking about angels and all."

"Yes, I know Lilly. That's what I'm talking about. Mike and Nancy, do you remember the day we went shopping before the first trial date, the one for Tom I mean?"

"Yes, of course."

"Remember how the Russian mob's men came to attack us, and suddenly they stopped and ran away?"

"Yes."

"The reason they ran, was because the angels revealed themselves, and the bad guys were scared half to death."

"Why couldn't we see them?"

"I'm not sure, Mike. Obviously they can reveal themselves to certain people, without everyone else being able to see them too. The way I can see them, even when no one else can."

"Are they here now?"

"Yes, Nancy, they are here now. They are always with us."

"Do I have angels too?"

"Yes, David. You have angels. When I met you at the funeral, that was one of the first things I noticed about you, that you had angels instead of demons. We all have angels.

Mike, Nancy, Lilly. Every one of us, we all have angels, once we believe. Now, there is something I've noticed, or I should say, something I've experienced. The angels aren't here to keep us from experiencing life. They won't stop us from making most of the foolish choices we make, and they won't keep us from seeing the ugliness in the world; even when the ugliness attacks us; unless the attack threatens the message. Their job is to protect God's message of salvation and Grace. We are simply the vessels of that message. But, now there is something new. While I was with Jesus this time...."

"What do you mean, "While I was with Jesus this time"?"

"I know it sounds crazy, Nancy, but each time I've been hurt I've spent some time with Jesus. He is the one who told me I would be able to see angels and demons. Now He has told me I will be able to see people's problems. You know, things like sickness, disease, emotional problems, that sort of thing. He said that I would be able to tell what the problems were, and through His power, those things would even be healed. I'm still new to all this, but when Doctor Phillips touched my hand, I could tell there is something wrong with him. I believe that's the only reason

I was able to tell you about all of this. I'm not positive, but I think he has cancer."

"Are you sure, Grace? How terrible. How do we tell him? Now we'll all sound crazy."

"I'm not expecting you to do this, Nancy. I'll tell him. I just wanted to tell you all everything that's been going on, so you wouldn't think I'd fallen off the deep end when I do tell him. I'm sure this is a pretty big shock, but this is what I've been living with for all these past months. What do you think?"

"I think it's wonderful, Gracie. I'm sure it feels like a lot of pressure, but I don't think God would have placed this on you, if He didn't think you could handle these kinds of demands. I do have to admit it sounds almost like science fiction, but we've seen lots of strange things since you came into our lives, so I guess this is just par for the course. It must be great to know that God trusts you with this much responsibility."

"It does feel great, but at the same time it's very frightening. I try not to wonder if I'm good enough, because I think it has a lot less to do with me and my worth, and a lot more to do with Him. This is all for God's glory. He is sending a message of love to the world through these miraculous things. Anyway, I needed to get right with all of you, before I approach Doctor Phillips, so you wouldn't think you needed to have me committed."

"We are all behind you, Grace. Thank you for sharing this with us. It feels wonderful to know there are angels with us, safer somehow. And, I think I can speak for us all when I say that if you need anything, at any time, we are here for you."

"Thank you, Nancy. I love you all very much, and it's nice to know you don't think I'm weird, or want to lock me up."

"Oh my dear, Of course we don't want to lock you up, but the weird part? We all know you're weird, or you wouldn't fit quite so perfectly into this weird little family." Everyone laughed, and hugged, and then they let Grace rest for awhile while they went to the hospital cafeteria to get something to eat.

Later that afternoon Doctor Phillips came back to visit Grace. "Hey there Grace, how are you feeling? I just thought I would check in on you before I went home."

"Hi Doc. I'm doing okay. A bit sore, and weak, but all in all glad to be alive."

"Well, you will be sore for awhile, and we did give you

six units of blood, so you will feel weak and tired for awhile too, but I think we will see all of that improve more each day."

"Thank you Doc. I'm grateful for everything you've done for me. I have something to ask you that doesn't have anything to do with me."

"Sure Grace, go ahead."

"Can I ask when was the last time you've had any kind of a checkup?"

"I can't really remember. Why do you ask?"

"I know it's probably none of my business, Doc, but when you touched my hand earlier I felt that there was something wrong with you. I know that sounds strange, but I think you have cancer. Don't ask me how I know, it's a feeling, and I care about you. I didn't say anything then, because I thought you might think I was crazy."

"Well, you're right, it does sound pretty strange young lady. I don't know what to say. If this wasn't you I was talking to I would have to say it does sound a little crazy, but I have also been feeling very tired and run down lately, and I guess I just kept making excuses for all of it. I have to say the world has been a stranger, and much more interesting, place since I found out you were in it."

"So, will you get yourself checked?"

"I will, for you Grace, I promise I will."

"Well, that wasn't as hard as I thought it would be. Maybe I really can do this."

"If anyone can, it would be you, Grace. thank you for putting yourself out there."

Doctor Phillips leaned over and gave Grace a hug before he left, and Grace was sure now that her assessment was right. It was cancer. Cancer of the liver to be precise. And it was in an advanced stage. She would wait to have it verified, before she employed her newest gift. She knew without a doubt that the healing gift would work, because Jesus told her it would; and she wanted to be sure He got every bit of the glory, so it would be beneficial that the doctor knew how bad things were before the Lord healed him.

The next morning, when her family arrived, Grace was excited to tell them how the exchange with Doctor Phillips had gone. "I'm so glad you guys are all here. I talked to Doc, and he's going to go in and get checked."

"Really? As easy as that? I work with the man every day, and I was sure he was much more stubborn than that. Were you able to tell how bad it was?"

"Yes, when he hugged me before he left yesterday, I

could tell clearly that it was liver cancer, and in a very advanced stage. I know that God is using this new gift as a way to make His love known, so I'm going to let his doctor confirm it before I do anything. I believe this will give Him the most glory, what do you think?"

"I think you're right. I can't wait to see the end result. Did you tell him about your gift?"

"No, Nancy, I thought I would wait to do that, so he won't have time to think about how crazy it sounds that God would give a gift like that to a girl like me."

"I think he, like the rest of us, has seen God use you in some pretty remarkable ways, Grace. I don't think he's going to be nearly as surprised as you think he might be."

"Oh, I don't know Mike. I think you might be a bit biased about the whole thing. I hope you're right. And I agree with you, Nancy, I can't wait to see how the end result changes his life. I believe the name of Jesus will be glorified, and that many will come to Him through this. I'm very excited."

"I'm sure you're right, Grace, and I think we all want to be part of it, isn't that right everyone?" This was followed by a chorus of "yes".

"That makes me so glad you guys. Of course I want

you to be part of this. And, it especially makes me happy to see you two wanting to get involved, Lilly and David. I think you will make a big difference with the younger generation."

"Are you calling us old?" Mike asked, which brought a laugh.

"I didn't mean decrepit, or anything, but way older than us. I'm not trying to hurt your feelings, Mike and Nancy. And, if it helps, you look way younger than you are. I just mean that someone of the same generation might have a bigger impact on kids our age."

"We know, Gracie. We're glad to see your sister and David wanting to be involved too."

Grace was feeling a bit better, so the family all gathered around and talked about plans for a family ministry, taking notes, sharing ideas and laughing. It was a time of closeness, until Nancy saw the weariness growing on Gracie's face. "Grace, they should be bringing your lunch soon. As soon as they get here we're going to go get lunch, and give you a chance to take a nap. We'll be back later."

"Okay. I'm so glad you came. I love you all so much. Thank you for being my family, and for loving me."

"Hey, Dave and I are just along for the free lunch."

"Yeah, right, Lilly. Love you sis."

"Love you too, Gracie." .

Right before her supper was delivered that evening, Gracie saw a distracted Doctor Phillips walk absently into her room. He looked up from his tablet, and she was saddened by the distraught look on his face.

"You okay, Doc?"

"Well, not exactly Gracie. I took your advice and came in very early this morning to see Doctor Lee. He's the resident Oncology expert here at the hospital. He rushed some tests through for me, and I'm sorry to tell you that your diagnosis was correct. I seem to have liver cancer, and it has gotten quite advanced as I tried to ignore all the signs. I saw all the scans, and pictures, and I know that my liver is extensively involved. It appears to have gotten into the lymph nodes as well, and has spread to other organs already. I need to talk to my wife, but I want to do that in person. Doctor Lee wants to start chemo as soon as possible. I can't believe you could tell that something was going on just by your touch. How did you do that?"

"I don't think I can explain that myself, at least not yet. It seems like the condition came on after I was shot. I don't want you to worry Doc., Jesus wants to heal you. Are you a

Christian, Doctor Phillips?" Of course Grace already knew the answer to that question. The doctor was surrounded by angels. But, she needed to get him to look at the potential of healing from God, as a real possibility, so she had to appeal to his more spiritual side.

"I am. I don't know if I'm a very good one. I don't go to church as often as I should, or pray as often as I should, but I do know Jesus as my Savior."

"Good. Jesus doesn't want to heal you because you've done a lot of things to deserve it, or because you go to church and sit in a pew a certain number of times a week. He just wants to heal you, because He loves you. He also wants you to know that He has taken care of it all. It was taken care of two thousand years ago, when He took our sin and sickness on the cross, and rose again to overcome it all."

"I don't know Grace. I don't deserve anything special from God."

"I don't either, Doc, but He healed me. Do you believe that He already covered it all? Do you believe that He can do this?"

"I do. I know that God is all powerful. I believe He can do anything He wants to do."

"Well, I can tell you that He wants to do this. To God be the glory. Will you come closer?"

"Okay, what do you want me to do?"

"Just believe, Doc. I'm going to put my hands on you. Is that okay?"

"Sure, Grace. Do what you need to do."

"Father God, we come to you today to receive the promises available to us in your Word, because of your sacrifice of love. We know Lord that "By Your stripes we are healed." We are confident that it is finished, and that, though we don't deserve Your great Grace, You love us enough to cover us anyway, simply for believing. As we come before You today, Lord, we are assured that we have been given a gift of Faith, and confidence, that could only come by Your hand. We know that Satan is doing his best to destroy your servant, Doctor Phillips, but we know that his powers are nothing compared to yours. Lord, we thank you for taking this cancer away, in Jesus' Name. And, to God be the glory for it all." At the end of her prayer, Gracie felt a strange heat leave her hands, and Doctor Phillips' eyes, which had been closed until that moment, opened wide, as he turned to face her.

"What was that? The strange heat that just filled me?"

"I'm sure that was God healing you."

"I feel different. Thank you Jesus. Thank you Lord. I'm going to go see Doctor Lee, Gracie. Is that okay?"

"Sure Doc. Come back and tell me what he says, okay? I'm excited to hear your good news."

"I will, Grace. Thank you for believing in the Lord, and for caring about me. I'll be back."

Grace laid back on her bed, closed her eyes, and smiled. She felt positively giddy. She was positive that the doctor was healed, in and through the Name of Jesus, and she couldn't wait for him to tell everyone he knew. All she wanted in her life was to give God glory, and share His message of love. What a wonderful vehicle this new gift would be.

Later Gracie's family returned and she greeted them with a big smile.

"Oh, it looks like somebody has good news."

"I do Mike. Doctor Phillips came in earlier. He told me he'd seen Doctor Lee, who is the resident Oncologist here at the hospital. The doctor did some tests, and rushed them through, as a favor for his friend. It seems that Doctor Phillips was diagnosed with Liver cancer. It has already advanced into other organs, and he was very concerned."

"Oh no, Grace. How terrible. Has he told his wife? Oh,

this makes me so sad. I've worked with this man for so many years, what can we do to help?"

"No, Nancy, you're getting upset about nothing."

"Nothing? How can you tell me that I'm upset about nothing?"

"I'm telling you this, because God has already healed him."

"What? How could you know? What happened? What did you do?"

"I laid my hands on him, we prayed, and a force that we both felt left my hands and entered him. I'm sure it was the Lord, and I'm sure he's healed. He's gone to see Doctor Lee, to confirm everything, but he is sure also."

"That's wonderful. Is he coming back here after he sees Doctor Lee?"

"Yes, he's assured me that he will let me know. I'm sure he's excited, and I'm sure he will be a great witness for the Lord."

"I'm so proud of you Grace. I knew God would use you for great things."

"Thank you, Mike, but I want to be sure that God gets all the glory, all the time, for every good thing."

"I understand, but I'm also glad that you've made yourself available for Him to use."

"Okay, Mike. I know you're just a proud daddy. All I can think of is how happy I am to see the doctor healed and well. I can't wait to hear how his wife takes all of this. As soon as I'm up and around, I want to begin doing healing services in church. There is so much work to do, and there are so many people to reach for the Kingdom."

"We'd all like to help in the ministry. We've been talking about this, and we want to support you in any way that we can. Nancy and your sister, and even David, have all told me that they believe in you."

"Thank you, all of you, but again I would ask you not to give me the credit for any of this. I'm not the one healing. Do you all understand? This is all Jesus."

"Yes, okay, we will try to remember that He is using your hands to do His work. It is still very exciting."

"Yes, very exciting. I am thrilled about all of this, but now I'm tired, and I need to sleep for awhile. Will you all come back tomorrow?"

"Of course. We love you Grace."

"I love you guys too. Thank you for being so supportive. I know that God will bless you for that. I'll see you tomorrow."

The Daze of Grace

Grace was exhausted; still recovering from her gunshot wound, and subsequent surgery; but it was more than that, her spirit was still hurting, and healing from the loss of dear Bella. There was a piece of her heart, deep down, that wondered if Bella would still be alive if she'd received her newest gift sooner, though she wasn't entirely sure how that might be. It was so easy to allow guilt to squirm its evil way in; she'd spent so much of her life thinking she was at fault for every terrible thing that happened to everyone around her. She would be leaning on the Lord as her total source and strength for everything going forward, or she'd never make it through what would now be expected of her. Her warrior angels towered over her, so she felt safe, but what pleased her more was to see the Heavenly host who flanked her family. Knowing that her loved ones were protected was a comforting thing, and tears suddenly sprang to her eyes with the relief of that revelation which washed over her soul.

Is anyone among you suffering? Let him pray. Is anyone cheerful? Let him sing praise. Is anyone among you sick? Let him call for the elders of the church, and let them pray over him, anointing him with oil in the Name of the Lord. And the prayer of faith will save the one that is sick, and the Lord will raise him up.

James 5:13-15

CHAPTER 23

It started off modestly at first. Grace and her family ministered in small churches; some of the same ones where she'd witnessed concerning God's message of Grace and love; with Doctor Phillips gladly sharing his testimony of miraculous healing at each meeting. Others were soon added who were anxious to describe their own miracles for the growing masses, and the numbers of excited grew with each new gathering. In those beginning times members of each church, who had illnesses and ailments, came forward a little shaky and embarrassed, not quite sure what to ask, or expect, to seek the help of Gracie's God. Mike and Nancy would ask them, out of sight of the congregation, what their particular problem was, and then when they'd ascertained the difficulty they'd bring the afflicted ones forward for Grace. She prayed a lot about how to lay her hands on those who came forward. Not wanting to be too dramatic, or to take away from the fact that this healing was entirely the doing of Jesus, and not of herself. She emphasized to those who came forward that they need do nothing, but believe in Jesus' ability and desire to help them. She stressed to each one that Jesus had already paid the price for their complete healing, over two thousand years ago on the cross. As she laid her hands on the part of the body effected, and one of her family members anointed the patient's foreheads with oil, she prayed; just as she had when Jesus healed the Doc., and the results were amazing to everyone present. Over and over again God performed His promises for the people.

She could usually tell, previous to their healing, which ones might be cured, and which ones wouldn't, not that she was judging. Those who came surrounded by angels were almost always made well. They had merely come forward to accept the promises already available to them in the Word, so that made sense. The difficulties came when someone with clinging demons showed up. Sometimes that individual was sincerely looking for help, and would give their life to Christ willingly; then the healing would follow as the demons were ripped away and replaced by heavenly guards; sometimes the individual would be healed first, and she could see their demons begin to panic and squirm as the miraculous healing touched something in their hearts so much that they decided then and there to take Jesus as

Lord, thereby leaving the demons with no body to cling to.

However, there were those entities who were simply out to discredit Grace, thereby, they hoped, discrediting the Lord and His finished work as an end result. Those who came with their demonic host, but who refused to acknowledge Jesus as Lord and Savior, or entertain a softened heart, were not healed, for obvious reasons, and then went about the area slandering Grace and her healing ministry for Christ. It was all part of the worldly cycle. Sadly, there would always be those who were willing to spend eternity in the depths of hell, to dishonor the sacrifice of God's Son; at least until the great day came when every knee would bow, and every tongue confess, that He is Lord.

Lilly and David became invaluable to the ministry. They both developed a way to speak to young people that Gracie felt she'd never quite managed. She'd felt like an old woman in a girl's body for most of her life, and just didn't fit in. Lilly, however, appealed to those who were a bit more shy and quiet, those who felt they didn't merit God's attention, but wanted desperately to be loved; while David, who was a more social and gregarious person, was able to reach out to those more brash, or outgoing, who felt unheard; and even those who'd gotten so mixed up in things that might kill them that they didn't know where to turn; those who might even think they didn't deserve the right to ask anything of God due to reasons of sin.

Sometimes our experiences, even those we aren't proud of, or those which were forced on us, are things that God can use to make us useful for the Kingdom. Gracie was amazed at how God worked, how He used these two important young people in her life, and the miracles which abounded by His hand.

After several verifiable healings were reported from these small church gatherings, the media got hold of the story. Soon Grace's assemblies started to grow, and became larger than any groups associated with her hugely successful evangelical meetings from before her last injury. Numbers healed in Jesus' Name, and by Grace's willing hands multiplied by the hundreds, and then the thousands. Many clamored to see her, for her obvious abilities; but others decided they would like to do her harm if only they could get close enough. Those who hated God, or worshiped gods of other names and religions, were not happy to see the Name of Jesus so venerated, and shortly they began to plot.

Doctor Phillips' witness was a highlight at each assembly. He'd acquired a fresh zeal for the Lord after his miraculous healing, and he wanted to share that new heart for Jesus as often as possible. Of course new testimonies were added regularly, and from each new group encounter, which kept the healing meetings positive, and energetic.

One night as Grace looked out over the crowd, before delivering her message, her eyes filled with tears and she became so choked up it was difficult to speak. She dried her eyes, and cleared her throat. "Thank you for coming. I want to begin by telling everyone here that God loves you. He gave His life for you, and He wants only the best for you. He offers you a place by His side, by extending His hand of Salvation, and Grace. If you would like to accept His offer of eternity through Grace, be sure to tell one of the ministry workers as you come up, and any one of them will be happy to pray with you to accept Jesus' invitation of eternal life. I am so humbled by the numbers I see in this auditorium. To listen to the hate spewing mainline media we might be forced to come to the conclusion that Christianity is on the decline, and that no one cares about Jesus anymore. Yet, when I look out over this assembly I see thousands of faces filled with hope, and a joy that can only come from the Lord. How can we ever believe anything but that God is still on the throne, and that He still watches over us. Please join me in giving Him praise." With that the entire congregation erupted in a vast and wonderful chorus of , "Praise God", "Thank you Jesus", "Glory to God", "Halleluiah", and "Come Lord Jesus". Gracie looked over at her parents, and her sister and brother, and saw that they were equally moved by the glory given to God during this grateful assembly. Certainly this was worth every moment of work and planning that went in to one of these gatherings. She nodded in the direction of her smiling family, and they began.

On this particular day a woman came forward holding her young son. His legs were so twisted with disease that it wasn't difficult to guess her prayer. Mike took the boy from his mother's arms and approached Grace. He'd come to expect the unexpected, and believe in the impossible, since he'd been involved in this ministry; but he was always amazed by the ways God chose to heal and grab hold of the hearts of believers, and non-believers alike. Nancy anointed the young fellow and Grace began to pray, laying her hands on the lad's legs. The congregation watched, with mouths agape, as the boy's legs began to untangle, and straighten before their eyes. The mother's face twisted first in disbelief, and then in softened acceptance and appreciation. The little boy, who had seemed totally without energy only moments ago, squirmed to get down, and Mike finally accommodated him. Grace smiled, as she watched his eyes grow wide when he looked down at his legs; the same legs which had never done as he'd expected them to in the past; and then up at his mom. He took his first steps, and smiled the biggest smile his mother had ever seen, and then he ran full tilt into her arms. She began to sob, and he reached up to put his little hands on her face. "Why are you crying Mommy. Jesus fixed my legs. I can run now. Thank you Jesus, thank you everybody." The crowd exploded in cheers and shouts of "Praise God", and "Thank you Jesus". Grace knew that she had the best job in the world. One that allowed her to help children, and grow the Kingdom of God. How could anything ever trump this experience? She was sure nothing could.

As the next person was advancing toward her for prayer, something very large caught in the periphery of her vision. She turned just in time to see a huge demon slither behind a pillar on the far side of the venue. What was going on? She motioned to Mike and he came to her quickly.

"I just saw a gigantic demon across the room. It hid behind that pillar. Please keep your eyes open for anything strange, okay?"

"Sure Gracie. You can count on me. I can't see the things you can see, but I'll keep an eye open for anything that looks out of the ordinary."

"Thanks Mike. I'm glad you're here."

"Me too baby girl."

The morning flowed into the afternoon, with many more miraculous healings and multiple souls won for the Kingdom. Grace, though exhausted, was filled with joy, knowing that this was the very purpose for which she was put on the earth. There would always be a part of her heart that longed for her sisters, her brother, and yes, even her mom. And she would never stop missing her dear friend Ruth, or sweet Bella; but where she was, right now, here in this place with her new dad and mom, Lilly, and David, making a difference for the Lord, was her true heart.

As the afternoon wound down, she saw the large demon several more times. It snuck and slithered about as if looking for a way to get closer to his target. Eventually he latched on to one of the many very ill patients, already surrounded by hissing, spitting demons, who had come with the express desire to do the ministry harm. The angry man came forward, surrounded by evil, and with this new hulking menace attached firmly to his back. Even those who couldn't see the demons, could feel the malevolence that enveloped him, and thereby radiated out from him. "Hello Grace."

"Hello. What can I do to help you?"

"I have only come to deliver a message, Grace."

"And, what message would that be?"

"You have made many angry, and there will be consequences for your actions if you do not stop this evangelizing."

"I don't know who sent you, but I will continue to fulfill the purpose that God has given me, for as long as I live, and you don't frighten me. Do you understand?"

"We will see my dear. We will see. This has been your final warning. We have sent many messages through other means, which you have not heeded. If you do not wish to see those you love harmed for your cause, you will take my advice."

After the gathering, Grace told her family they would all need to sit down and have a meeting.

"What's going on Gracie?"

"I felt that we needed to talk, David. Do you remember me telling you I'd seen a huge demon lurking around the meeting this afternoon, Mike?"

"Yes, I never saw anything out of the ordinary after that. Did I miss something?"

"No, you did fine. He managed to attach himself to a very angry man. The irritated man who wasn't healed toward the end of the meeting. Did any of you notice him?"

"Yes, he was putting up a pretty big fuss as he left. Should we have stopped him?"

"No, Nancy, there's nothing we could have done for him. He was surrounded by a great deal of evil, and he meant to share it with us to the best of his ability. He came with a warning."

"He threatened you?"

"It's okay, Mike. He came to tell me that there are those who are angry about what we are doing, and that they want us to stop. I told him we never would, and he threatened to hurt those that I love if we didn't. I guess the reason for this little meeting is that I want to give you all the opportunity to leave the ministry if you are frightened. I feel that his threat toward all of you was very real, and I couldn't bare it if anything happened to a single one of you."

"I don't know about anyone else, Grace, but I love what we're doing. It makes me feel close to Bella, and nothing has ever made me feel so positive about my place here on earth. I have learned how great God is, and I will never stop now."

"Thank you David. How about the rest of you?"

"You know how Nancy and I feel baby girl. God is good, and as long as He has things for us to do, He will provide what we need, when we need it. We're not going anywhere."

"Thank you Dad, and Mom. You have no idea how much that means to me. I don't have to tell you how much God loves you too."

At that, Nancy had to dab the tears from her eyes, and Mike had to clear his throat. They were both a little overwhelmed at hearing Grace call them, "Dad, and Mom", which wasn't a regular occurrence. Lilly stepped forward and took Grace's hand in hers, looked into her eyes, and smiled.

"I hope you know that you don't even have to ask me, Gracie. I spent most of my life doing things that I thought I would be paying for all the rest of my life. Now God has given me a place. A place where I have the opportunity to share life, instead of death. How could I ever turn my back on that, or on you? If you see that demon again, tell him to bring it on sister!"

"Thank you, all of you. How about you Doc? I would

understand if you don't want to be here for the meetings anymore. We know you have a wife and kids to think about."

"Hey Grace, I wouldn't even be here if it weren't for God's Grace, and your willingness to reach out, even when you were uncertain. I love what we're doing. I get to save lives in the daytime, and then save lives on the weekends too."

"Okay, so we're all agreed. Satan be damned, and God be glorified! Thank you all."

Grace knew that their warrior angels would stay close, and that they would step forward as long as it was necessary to protect the Word, but she would keep her eyes open for anything out of the ordinary. She smiled, and wondered how she had managed to get to such a place of blessing in her life. Not so very long ago it had seemed her life was over, and God had managed to take all of that pain, to use for her good, and His purpose.

That night, as she lay in bed studying, she looked around her bedroom, and shook her head. God had proved Himself to be faithful in her life, and to the promises in His Word. She would never stop working to give Him glory, and to grow the Kingdom.

See, I have set before you today life and good, death and evil. If you obey the commandments of the Lord your God that I command you today, by loving the Lord your God, by walking in His ways, and by keeping His commandments and His statutes and His rules, then you shall live and multiply, and the Lord your God will bless you in the land that you are entering to take possession of it. But if your heart turns away, and you will not hear, but are drawn away to worship other gods and serve them, I declare to you today, that you shall surely perish. You shall not live long in the land that you are going over the Jordan to enter and possess. I call Heaven and earth to witness against you today, that I have set before you life and death, blessing and curse. Therefore choose life, that you and your offspring may live, loving the Lord your God, obeying His voice and holding fast to Him, for He is your life and length of days, that you may dwell in the land that the Lord swore to your fathers, to Abraham, to Isaac, and to Jacob, to give them.

Deuteronomy 30:15-20

CHAPTER 24

"Did you give her the message?"

"Yes Master, I did, but she didn't seem to be as rattled by it as I'd expected her to be."

"She didn't back down?"

"No Master. As a matter of fact she told me she had no intention of ever stopping. I think she will be more of an obstacle than we thought."

"Shut up! Nobody asked you to think! Get me all the information you can on every member of her family, and her ministry team. There's more than one way to skin a cat!"

Kakos received his promotion, to 'Head Western Regional Demon' (in charge of forced Christian apostasy), only recently; and did not relish the idea of reporting to "the boss" that they had failed to sway this newest threat, to the work they'd been so successful in accomplishing over the past decades. Their territory, the Western region of the United States, which included Hollywood and Las Vegas, had been almost too easy to influence in the direction of Satan's plans and desires; especially in such a short period of time; so the armies assigned here had gotten a bit slack in their duties. His superiors would not be pleased by this new development, and he knew he would bear the brunt of their anger, even though he was relatively new to the position.

He'd not even worked for the regional office all those years ago, at the time when someone in the "Upcoming Threats" department had noticed the man upstairs employing extreme measures to ensure the survival of a certain young girl.

It seemed the Lord thought Grace was special, and apparently He had plans for her; and, let's face it, if He had plans for her, then Satan and his demons necessarily had plans for her too. Nothing this department had done, before Kakos arrived to act as supervisor, or since, had deterred her in her annoying heavenly purpose. And if anything was observed at all, it was that each traumatic event in her young life, events which would have leveled warriors much more experienced than she; including the death of her family and friends, living on the streets, being sold into slavery, being spat upon, beaten, used, shot, and dumped in a river, had softened her final resolve to be God's healing hands on earth. She was single handedly destroying their hard earned stats in the region, and it was imperative that they take her down as quickly as possible.

"You will get this young woman to give up her quest of bringing everyone she meets to the Son of God, or you will be dealt with", had been the latest command from his superiors, and so far nothing had worked. She didn't seem to have a single fear in the world, and simply would not back down. If he couldn't get her to cooperate, he would lose his position; and worse, demotions, particularly in this place, tended to be beyond anything the sane mind could comprehend.

As soldiers of the darkness, Kakos and his hordes of demons were never assigned to alter the beliefs of humans who practiced other religions. That would simply be a waste of time. Since their main function, in this realm, was to attempt to keep all humans from worshiping Jesus; in order that they couldn't receive His gift of eternal life as children of God; then those who already squandered their spiritual time by practicing false religions; such as Islam, Hinduism, Buddhism, etc.; or by worshipping and bowing down to various false gods; were not a threat to Satan's plans and desires. And, in many ways those people even helped to accomplish Kakos' evil assignment, of keeping humans from finding the Way, the Truth, and the Life.

On the other hand, this Christian thing was a huge inconvenience; bigger than anything they'd ever imagined; and getting worse all the time. Once a new soul came to believe upon the Son of God, they seldom deviated from that Way, even if they made human mistakes after their conversion. Jesus (wouldn't you know) was merciful, so if they messed up, all they had to do was come back to Him and accept His forgiveness, which made Kakos' job that much more difficult. And, this threat of Christianity was a wide reaching one, covering more of the globe now than ever before, especially due to evangelists such as this young woman. Grace had dug her heals in and wasn't about to give an inch. They would have to come up with some more inventive, and persuasive, ways to reach her. Perhaps she could be convinced through those she loved? This would be interesting indeed.

†

David hadn't touched any drugs, or even thought much about them, since meeting Bella before her death, but recently he'd had a hard time squelching his old cravings. He missed his best friend terribly; the sweet, free spirit who'd helped him feel loved and understood for the first time in his life; and still felt somewhat responsible for her death. That was a heavy burden to be sure, and seemed to be weighing on him more, and more, as time went by.

Oh, it wasn't that he'd decided he wasn't going to follow Jesus anymore, or anything like that. And, it certainly wasn't that he didn't enjoy the healing meetings where he assisted his family in bringing others to Christ. He was just so new to it all, this Grace stuff, and sometimes his feelings of guilt and low self worth crept up on him when he least expected it. Kakos had been busy trying to find weak spots in Grace's ministry team, and it seemed David was most likely it. Mike and Nancy were impenetrable tanks against the evil darts of the enemy, and Lilly proved to be much more solid in her faith than her years, and past, would have suggested she might be, but David....

Now David didn't realize demons had decided he was the chink in the armor that might get to Grace most effectively. Kakos' minions had been busy whispering in the young man's ears, week after week, and the negative message they were planting became more convincing with each passing day, as it wormed its evil way into his brain. The demons were sly, as they only showed up to torture him when Grace was not near, so they were infecting his mind during his most vulnerable moments. Only the brashest of demons were right for this job, as they had to work under the watchful eyes of the guardians. His family was all so busy with their crowded meetings, helping the poor lost souls of the world, that no one noticed the changes in him right away, and then the damage was done.

Kakos couldn't quite describe the thrill he experienced when he was able to tempt someone away, especially someone who professed to follow the Son of God. It was a special high he would never tire of. What made it better, was that David wasn't an easy sell. It was eminently more rewarding when he must work for his rewards, at least a little.

He had to give it to the young man though. He was fiercely dedicated to his work for God, and his loyalty to his friend Grace, so it looked like this would be a semi-loss for the darkness, at least in the ever important conversion column. He knew, despite his best efforts, David wouldn't inhabit hell; even if he was able to wipe him from the face of the earth; not since he'd accepted Christ as Savior. The young man would instead be with the Lord after his death, much to the aggravation of Kakos and his demons. But, if his earthly demise was enough to help take Grace down;

that infernally annoying girl; he would live with the loss of a soul.

Once Kakos began to concentrate on his new plan, and focused enough man power in that direction, all it really took was separating David from the family for longer, and longer, periods of time. Then when he was by himself it wasn't complicated to influence his mind and help him feel the loneliness, and hopelessness, that permeates this planet, apart from Christ. Soon he was feeling sufficiently depressed and despondent to look for other ways to feel better. Then, and only then, by simply bringing people into the situation who could supply him with a brand new drug that promised to take away the pain, did it become fairly easy to steer the young man in a destructive direction.

David's angels stood with heads bowed; unable to stop him; since he'd ultimately made the final conscious decision to do this thing on his own. They watched as he injected the poison into his vein, as he convulsed, and as he crumpled to the ground in an alley outside the local teen hangout. His last earthly thoughts, before he stepped out of this world and stood before the Lord, were of sweet Bella, and her beautiful butterflies.

"Has anyone seen David?"

"Not since this morning. Did you check his room?"

"Not yet, Dad. I'm going to do that now. Have you noticed anything different about him lately? I wonder if he's been missing Bella more than usual? It's been almost a year since we lost her."

"I'm sure he has. I know Mom and I miss her very much, and I'm sure that you young people do too. We'll have to give him some extra hugs and make sure he knows how much we all love him. I want to remind him that he can come talk to us any time he needs to. Why don't you bring Lilly down too? We've hardly seen her all day. I'd like an opportunity to talk to all you kids about several things that are coming up."

"Okay. I'll be right back down."

"I feel like a terrible mom, Mike. I've noticed that David has been kind of quiet and withdrawn lately, but we've all been so busy I just shoved that thought right to the back burner. These kids have all been through so much. They never really give us any trouble, and I tend to assume everything is fine, or if it's not then perhaps it will work itself out."

"Don't do that to yourself, Nancy. You're a good mom, and we have been really busy. David knows that just as much as we do. Don't worry about it. We'll talk to him and we'll do better. Everything will be fine."

Grace stood at the top of the stairs with Lilly. "Hey, Mom and Dad, David isn't in his room. Lilly thinks he went into town. We're going to look for him."

"Okay. Be sure you have your phone, and please let us know when you find him. I'm surprised he didn't say anything if he was going all the way into town."

"I know. That's why we're going to look. It's not like him to just take off. I'll call you when we find him." Mike and Nancy looked at each other with a combination of concern and puzzlement. It really wasn't like David to take off without letting anyone know. Well, the girls would find him and all would be right with the world. Once they had an opportunity to talk to him and reassure him of their love, and his importance to the ministry, they were sure things would be back to normal in no time.

Kakos was reveling in his win even before the girls found their brother. He couldn't wait to see their faces screw up in anguish. The joy he felt from their pain was his particular drug of choice. Grace and Lilly searched all the usual haunts, until one of his old acquaintances told them they might find him near the teen hangout. As they approached the street, where they should be looking, they saw a police car and an ambulance, both with lights flashing. Grace's stomach tightened and cramped in dread as they drew closer. Visions of small dead bodies littering the ground filled her panicked mind, as she found herself gasping for air. The girls made haste to the alley, and pushed their way through the gawking crowds to David's side. The officer on duty tried to hold them back, but they slipped through his grasp and knelt beside David's limp body. Grace lifted his head onto her lap, and began to smooth his hair, rocking back and forth in that way she had. Lilly took his hand and pulled it, trembling, to her cheek. The coroner's van pulled up, and the officer pulled the girls away, to give the workers a chance to do their job. The girls looked at each other, through tear filled eyes, and wondered how they would manage to tell their parents.

The officer was kind. He offered to drive the girls home, so they could be there as he told their parents. Mike would necessarily have to do another identification at the hospital's morgue, and Grace didn't envy him that. She wanted to be there to comfort him, while the police delivered the bad news. Her head reeled at the loss of yet another loved one. She was sure there had been plenty of signs that she'd missed. Why did people keep dying around her? What was she supposed to be learning from all this? How was it that she had the power in her hands to share God's healing with strangers, but she couldn't seem to keep those she loved from crumbling? How had she not seen her brother's pain? So much pain. Was this some kind of test?

When the officer, with whom they were riding, pulled up in front of their house, Mike and Nancy came to the door and stood, eyes wide, heads shaking slightly back and forth, waiting. The look in Mike's eyes told Grace he'd already figured out what was going on. Nancy looked wistfully hopeful, but ready to collapse if it weren't for Mike's strong arm around her waist. As the officer stepped closer, and she saw the look of condolence on his face, barely restrained tears broke free to track down her quivering face.

"Dad, Mom, they found David. I'm so sorry. It looks like it might have been drugs. He's been taken to the hospital morgue."

"I'm so sorry for your loss Ma'am, Sir. Sir, I'm going to have to ask you to come with me to do an identification, would that be alright?"

"Yes officer. Just let me get my sweater. Girls, look after your mom."

At that, Lilly ran to Nancy and buried her face in the woman's shoulder. Together they grieved. Grace felt her lip begin to tremble, but took a deep breath. She would need to remain strong for Mom, and Lilly. "We'll be okay, Dad. I'll look after them."

"Thank you Gracie. I'll be back when I can."

Familiarity didn't make the identification process any easier. The aging elevator, clanking itself downward, still opened to a long, semi dark hallway in the basement; the sound of footsteps, leather on concrete, still echoed in his ears all the way to the morgue's door; and smells of bleach and other chemicals were still strong enough to crisp the hairs in his nostrils. The florescent lights, which shone forth as the morgue door opened to stainless steel and glass, were still bright enough to blind him for several long seconds. He was led to a table. There, a white sheet was lifted just enough for him to see David's face. He choked back tears as he gazed at the face of the young man who was the closest he'd ever come to having a son. David's young face was pale, but to see him lying there, it seemed he could have been only sleeping. His hair was tousled, so without thinking, Mike reached out to smooth it down. His heart ached so badly at this new loss, that for a moment he thought he might be having a heart attack. "Sir? Is this your son?"

"Oh, sorry, yes it is."

"I'm so sorry, Sir."

"Thank you. You know it never gets any easier."

"I'm sure it doesn't, Sir."

"I really thought we were making a difference in his life. I just wish we'd recognized all the signs. I hope this was an accident. I would hate to think this happened on purpose. I thought he was so happy with us."

"Yes Sir. Again, I'm very sorry."

Mike signed appropriate papers and made arrangements for the same mortuary that handled Sweet Bella to come for David. As he walked the hallway back to the elevator he felt the weight of the world resting on his shoulders, and the flood of tears he'd been holding back flooded his face. As he entered the elevator, his sobs echoed through the hallway, and the hospital aide, standing in the doorway, lit from behind, shook her head sadly as she closed her door and went back to her work.

On the ride home from the hospital the skies opened up, and raindrops the size of marbles began to hit the windshield. Mike remembered his grandmother telling him, when he was a boy, that raindrops were God's tears, and he thought it only fitting that the universe would mourn the loss of another bright light for Christ. When he arrived home his family gathered round him and they wept together.

Kakos and his demons celebrated. His superiors would stay off his back for at least a little while, due to this new revelation of death and sadness in Grace's life. Keres approached her superior with her head appropriately down, and handed him the report he'd been waiting for. He viewed the file and threw the papers across the room, bellowing all the while. "What is this? What do you mean this seems to have brought them closer together? How can that be?"

"I'm sorry master. I only brought the file."

He kicked her, hard, and sent her flying across the space. The only thing worse than being a demon soldier in Kakos' evil forces, was being the bearer of bad news. Their immortal lives; those of the soldiers in his command; were not their own, as their eternity belonged unequivocally to Satan. Therefore they had no rights, and no fairness committee to complain to. They would spend eternity obeying the whims of Satan and his commanders, or they would be sent to the very bowels of hell to suffer pain unimaginable. Sometimes, as she endured Kakos' rage, she wondered if the bowels of hell really sounded so bad after all.

The Daze of Grace

✝

The memorial service for David was small. Mostly family, and a few faces from the weekly ministry meetings. He hadn't touched as many lives as outgoing Bella had in her colorful existence, and even her service had been poorly attended. And, though he would be missed by his new family, it appeared there weren't many others who felt they had been effected through his young life. That made Grace very sad. She knew David was with the Lord, but it seemed that his life here should have made more of an impact. He'd certainly made a difference in her life. Once again, she was feeling particularly angry with God, and found herself wandering off to engage in fervent prayer. At home she laid down, in an attempt to hold off a migraine which threatened to undo her. Rocking herself slowly, she prayed, as she dropped off to sleep.

"I don't understand, Lord. Why couldn't his angels protect him, just this once? Why have we lost another member of our family? When will this madness end? It's so hard to go on, to fix other people, day after day, when we are so broken. Even though you are the one doing all the work, it feels like we should at least appear to believe in what we are doing. Sometimes it's just hard to keep believing when we are surrounded by such loss."

"I know my daughter. Believing, when everything is not going just as we expect it to, is more difficult than believing when circumstances are ideal. I think we can all agree on that. However, I have given you the measure of faith, and even in complicated times, your faith will hold. David's angels were right there with him, until the end, Grace. The choice he made to take the drugs which stole his life, was his choice to make. I'm so sorry that this was the end result, but this world holds many evils and temptations which are harmful to man."

"At least tell me this. Is David with you Lord?"

"Yes Gracie, David is with me. Even an act of self destruction cannot undo my sacrifice. He asked me to come into his life while he was seeing Bella, and he believed in Me right up until the moment he left the earth."

"Thank you, Jesus. That means a lot to me. I love you Lord."

"And, I love you, Gracie. I always have, and I always will."

When she woke, she realized the time alone with her Savior had steadied her resolve, and she went downstairs to talk with Lilly, and her parents. "I need to know what you want to do. I can't ask you to continue to risk your lives anymore."

"You don't have to ask us, Grace. We've already talked this over, and we have no intention of stopping what we're doing. We should plan our next gathering. If Satan thinks he has us trapped, he can think again. Now, chin up and let's make preparations, the church told us they're expecting a huge turnout."

"Thanks, Dad, Mom, Lilly; what do you say we do this for David?"

"I say that's a great idea. This one's for David, and to God be the glory!"

†

Going forward, every gathering became an opportunity for the enemy to strike. The ministry team went on as if nothing was threatening them, for the sake of those who came for help, but as Kakos' demons slithered around every venue, and caused one 'accident' after another, Grace kept a watchful eye out to ensure their safety. She was encouraged when she saw their heavenly warriors step forward, more than once, to shield them from almost certain death. Everything from decorative building facades which suspiciously let loose at, what would have been the perfect time to hurt, or even kill one of their team; to lightening which struck sound equipment connected to microphones that family members were holding. One occurrence after another of mishaps, which were arranged by dark forces, and thwarted by heavenly ones. There was the night a man came screaming, face twisted in hate, and arm raised; rushing toward their group brandishing a jewel encrusted dagger; only to be halted by an armored warrior in his path. Or, the woman who, after claiming she'd come for healing, fell to the stage and began to convulse, while demons possessing her body twisted it into grotesque positions, and black viscous liquid poured from her mouth.

But, God was faithful, and people were healed. Many thousands were saved and added to the Kingdom, and Grace's family, though exhausted most of the time, were encouraged that they were moving in the Holy Spirit.

One of the biggest obstacles they encountered were religious people who called themselves Christians. These were not real Christians of course. These were the pompous, self aggrandizing, holier than thou individuals who thought themselves godly, by their own hand or accomplishments.

These pretend followers figured Grace's ministry group must be a bunch of charlatans, since they, themselves, had not been healed. Some of them attended events over and over. Each time standing in line, waiting to be healed, sure that they deserved healing for some pious and grand thing they had done themselves, and being disappointed when the healing didn't come. Jesus didn't play games with those who thought they deserved healing due to their own actions and holiness; who simply refused to understand that healing came only by the sacrifice He had made, Himself, on the cross.

Over and over Grace dealt with these usurpers of glory. Those who refused to humble themselves, and instead demanded. More than once her winged guards were forced to step forth and keep these so called Christians from killing Grace and her family. Grace made sure to tell the group every time this happened, so they would feel more secure in the protection God was supplying.

One night, as Grace stood on stage laying hands on one after another of those who came forward seeking Him, she suddenly looked up and into the eyes of her old friend Tony. He looked haggard, and much older than she remembered. She suddenly felt very guilty, as she couldn't remember the last time she'd even thought of him, much less visited him. "Tony, my goodness it's so good to see you. How have you been?"

"Well, I just figured that if Mohammed wouldn't come to the mountain, the mountain should go to Mohammed, so to speak."

"Are you okay, Tony? What brings you all the way over here?"

"I just wanted to see you again Grace. It's been a long time, and I didn't want to wait till it was too late."

"What do you mean, "too late", Tony? Are you ill?"

"Well, I've been diagnosed with ALS, Grace, and I just figured I should get some things out of the way before I couldn't manage to get around anymore."

"Oh Tony, I'm so sorry to hear about that, but you've come to the right place. God wants to heal you, right here, right now."

"Why would He want to heal me, Gracie? I haven't spent my life worshipping Him? I certainly don't deserve healing."

"Don't you see, Tony? You are exactly the person He wants to heal. A person who knows that you don't deserve it on your own. That way when it does happen, every witness realizes it was all due to Him; His goodness; His holiness; His Grace. Do you believe Tony? Do you want to receive His healing?"

Tony struggled to kneel, and Mike stepped forward to help him. Grace laid her hands on top of his head and prayed, giving God the glory, and evoking Jesus' Name for the healing of her dear friend.

When she was done Tony stood. His eyes were clearer, and his trembling had ceased. "I want you to go back to your doctor, Tony, and confirm, but I know that you will find God has healed you. Tony wept, and hugged each member of the ministry team, one, by one. Mike led him in a special prayer, and Tony became one of God's beloved family that night. All the loneliness and abuse of his childhood; all the pain of losing his sister; and the brokenness of his disabilities, caused by the terrible disease he'd been dealing with alone, gone forever. He showed up again, at the next gathering, and gave his testimony, and in no time at all, became a member of the family and an important part of the ministry team.

✝

"No Master, there hasn't been a change. If anything, she

seems to be more set in her thinking than she was before. We haven't been able to touch her."

Kakos was livid. He was due to stand before the council, for his quarterly report, in less than a month, and he had no good news to share. "I'm going to tell you one more time. Throw everything you have at her. She must be brought down, and her family with her. I can't believe that losing her brother, especially after all the other major losses in her life, didn't send her into a downward spiral of depression. I tell you, I'm not going to take the heat for this alone. If the council decides to take action on our department, they will have every one of your names. Do you understand me?"

"Yes Master. We'll do all we can. You can count on us."

"What a bunch of idiots. If this blows up in my face, I will take you all down with me. I swear to Satan!"

†

"Yes Sir? I've been expecting you to call. I'd assumed the trial would resume once things settled down. Thank you, we will be there. Gracie, would you come here please?"

"Coming Dad. what's going on?"

"That was the state's attorney. The trial will be resuming tomorrow. Now we can finally get some closure from this Vladimir Slochik. Are you nervous?"

"No, I'm good Dad. I'll be ready to go in the morning."

"I don't know how you can be okay about all this, Gracie. The man tried to kill you. He imprisoned us both, and made us do things no one should have to do. I pray they put him to death."

"I don't pray for his death, Lilly. I pray for him to know Jesus. I know that sounds strange, but I hope everyone comes to know the Lord. I know what it feels like not to have Christ in my life, and the difference it makes to know Jesus. Everyone should have that chance. If they refuse then, well, I believe that is what breaks the Father's heart."

"You're so strange, Grace. For your sake I hope he comes to know the Lord before he dies. But, I still believe he should suffer for all the lives he's destroyed."

"I Just believe we are supposed to forgive. Is that such a terrible thing?"

"I suppose we'll find out what the jury decides, after the testimony is all in. I'm glad I'm not in charge of his sentence. I don't know how objective I could be."

"Are all the arrangements made for the weekend? Dad, did you get in touch with Tony, and Doc, to see if they're coming?"

"Yes, they're going to ride together again, and they'll meet us there. They've become such great friends. Who would have ever thought those two could find so much in common? It's good to see them both happy."

"The one thing they do have in common is pretty extraordinary. How many people can say they've been healed of a terminal illness, by the miraculous Hand of God?"

"Well, there is that. They do love sharing their testimony, don't they?"

"I recognize the feeling, Dad. I guess when you don't have the answer for so long, and then, by the Grace of God, it hits you squarely in the heart; it's just so overwhelming you simply have to share, or you'd burst, you know?"

"I guess I get it, Gracie. Seeing you go from the brink of death, to alive again, was a miracle I'll never forget. It sure boosted my faith. God is certainly good."

"Yes He is. I don't have all the answers, Dad; but I do know that He doesn't want anyone to be lost. And, I feel I'm supposed to be figuring into that somehow. He has given me so much. How can I put the value of my own life above the life of someone else?"

The Daze of Grace

✝

Morning came and the family readied to leave. The state's attorney's office sent a car, and armed guards; though Grace knew no human agents could successfully thwart God's plans, she had to admit the security made her feel a bit more safe. She was surrounded by angels, but the sky was black with demon hordes. As they approached the court house she could see the streets filled with protesters, and was painfully aware there were more posters and signs against her, than there were for her.

"Why are so many against us, Mom? Why do they hate Jesus so?"

"I don't know my darling. I suppose it has something to do with the media, and how our case is portrayed in the press. From the reports I've seen, the media has made Mr. Slochik out to be some sort of mistreated immigrant, and we are the hateful Christians who just want to see him beaten down."

"Don't they remember my story? Have they already forgotten I was found on a riverbank, with a bullet hole in my head?"

"Many say there is no proof that Slochik was behind

that. Lilly's testimony helped, but they really need to hear it from you. I believe the Russians have abandoned their man. He's out there alone. They don't want to go down with him. After all there are too many business interests at stake here. There are actually factions out there who believe the whole thing is made up to put more strain on the immigration process. You know, the crazy right wing religious people who want to keep everyone out. We will have to be wary of the defense attorney trying to use that angle."

"It's really sad that the press is all about trying to pit one side against the other for their benefit. The things they'll come up with just to sell a story are amazing."

Approaching the front of the building she saw the crowds pressing in, and the security guards pushing back. Nancy grabbed Grace and Lilly by the arms and stood firmly behind Mike as he pushed his way through the throngs. By the time they all reached the court house steps they were out of breath and shaking. She shook her head. "Are you two girls okay? I can't believe the madness out there."

"I'm fine, Mom. How about you Lilly?"

"I'll live. What a mess. How can anyone tell us that we are safe here? After all the attempts on our lives that have been made from this place, I don't see how anyone can promise that they'll be able to protect us."

"We didn't receive any promises, Lilly. But, we need to show the world that we aren't afraid, and we need to put an end to the hold those people have on your lives, once and for all."

"I guess you're right, Mom. Well, I'm right behind you Gracie. Give 'em heck!"

Lilly sat with Mom, and Dad, in the gallery. When Grace was led in from the witness room, she was shocked by what she saw at the defense table. Slochik was a different man. He looked to have lost fifty, or more, pounds, and had been severely beaten, probably more than once since the last time she'd laid eyes on him. It was obvious that even the demon world didn't see him as much of a tool in their evil arsenal anymore, as the huge menacing devil which had been attached to him previously, was gone, and only puny, fledgling demons dug talons into what remained of his emaciated body now. Fire forever gone from his countenance, only vacant eyes stared out from grey, pasty skin, in a gaunt, expressionless face.

Grace swore to tell the truth, as, out of the corner of her eye, she saw Vladimir slip something into his mouth. She knew immediately that it was a means to his end, and wondered how the guards had missed it. Soon he was collapsed on the defense table, with foam trickling from his partially open mouth. Winged demons flew through the ceiling of the court house, and Grace wished she, like everyone else, wasn't able to see them; as they took hold of his eternal soul and flew to the depths of hell.

For I consider that the sufferings of this present time are not worth comparing with the glory that is to be revealed in us. For the creation waits with eager longing for the revealing of the sons of God. For the creation was subjected to futility, not willingly, but because of Him who subjected it in hope.

Romans 8:18-20

CHAPTER 25

Her family had survived the one year anniversary of David's death, only months before, and Grace found herself bone tired; more tired than she could ever remember being in her life. Having allowed grief, of all her past losses, to burrow so deep into her soul; she wasn't sure how to weed it out. One would have thought that hundreds of meetings, thousands of healings, and more family added to the kingdom of God than she could count, should have lifted her spirits, but the loss of so many close to her had simply, finally taken its toll. During this same period of time she'd also been bombarded with constant attempts on her life, threats toward her family; slander, and every other evil one could imagine piling onto any human being. So, today she would lay aside her responsibilities and take a much needed rest. With sun warming the top of her head, she slid back in the green, canvas lawn chair; noting somewhere in the back of her mind, that her chair was the same color as every canvas tent erected at every single funeral service she'd ever attended.

Closing her eyes she took a deep, shaky breath. It was strange, but she'd never been very good at relaxing, and she'd always thought it couldn't be so very difficult to learn. But, now, as she tried to loosen up, she thought there might be a distinct possibility she'd completely lost the ability to even try. She concluded she'd probably have to work at unwinding; but then, would she actually be releasing stress at all?

The luscious smell of grilled chicken filled the air, causing her mouth to water. Mike was determined he was going to make this fourth of July gathering a nice one for his family, and she could see how important it was to him, so she would try her hardest to enjoy. It'd been ages since they'd had time together, as a family, aside from healing meetings. Tony, and Doc were flinging horseshoes on the other side of the acreage, but even from here she could hear their light hearted banter through the still summer air, and they seemed to be coming up with more lame excuses than ringers. Doc's kids skipped down to the small creek on the back end of the property to catch tadpoles and pick wild flowers, while their mom hurried to keep up; as today's moms do; to be sure they remained safe.

Grace thought about following the kids down to the creek. The cool water would feel delicious on her bare feet. But, a larger part of her; the part that sometimes felt overwhelmed by people; didn't relish the company, so she remained in her green canvas sanctuary. Nancy and Lilly were finishing up in the house, with numerous side dishes, while Dad grilled and Grace rested. The whole family had been worried about her for months. These last years of responsibility had taken a toll on her. She tended to take the brunt of everything, no matter how hard others tried to help.

Considering the fact that she was not yet eighteen years old, she seemed beaten down, used up, and much older than her meager years would suggest. For these past months, and especially since David's death, she walked like someone carrying the weight of the world on her shoulders. Her special sight gave her knowledge the rest of them didn't possess, unless she shared, but it also gave her a degree of accountability none of them could imagine.

She rolled over in her chair, and watched a daddy long legs struggling to make its way through a thick forest of grass. Then, guilt kicking in, due to the tiny creature's obvious plight, she sighed and picked up a small stick. Rescuing the beleaguered spider from its vast, botanical maze, she walked to the back of the house and set it gently on the Swedish ivy growing there. She remembered someone telling her, once, that a daddy long legs had very powerful venom, but that it didn't have the power to pierce human flesh. This simple act most succinctly defined who she had become. Never able to leave anyone without a way, she found herself reaching out to all who struggled.

She wondered, when the small being looked up at her, did it see a giant? Did it understand the power she had over its life? Did it feel grateful? What did she look like through its many eyes? Smiling, she watched it long enough to assure it didn't fall from its new perch.

Inside the ivy she saw a small nest with three tiny spotted eggs; which would probably explain the mama bird squawking frantically nearby. Backing up a step, she said in a calm voice, "Settle down Mama. I'm not going to hurt your babies." For a sweet moment she felt excited by the possibility of new life, a feeling that had been missing in her life for far too long. She'd have to come back and check on the eggs in a few days, if she wasn't too busy. But, she sadly acknowledged, it seemed she was always too busy these days.

Wandering out by the family garden patch she saw how much work Dad and Mom had put into the well manicured plot this year. Every vegetable variety she could think of was taking up residence in every square inch of space. The sight made her smile and shake her head. She realized she didn't even know when her parents had accomplished this feat of magic. They were such amazing people, and took on so much responsibility. Mike still managed his restaurant, and even volunteered at the soup kitchen; where she'd met him years ago; twice a week, and Nancy still worked at the hospital, and cared for their family. Why was she so tired, when the rest of the family seemed to work so much harder than she did?

Was she really so wrapped up in her own, so called, divine purpose that she'd ignored everyone else's life for all these months? She would have to do something about that. Then, as she rounded a corner, the smell of roses hit her in the face like an aromatic cloud. The delightful scent almost knocked her over and she realized she'd made it clear over to the South side of the house in her meanderings. She stood for a moment and inhaled the heady fragrance, allowing the moment to seep into her soul. God was good. Life was good. And, she'd allowed herself to be so terribly busy she'd forgotten to enjoy it. Just then she heard Dad calling everyone to their meal. She arrived, much to everyone's delight, with a smile on her face.

Grilled chicken, slathered with homemade barbeque sauce; corn on the cob; coleslaw; potato salad; another kind of salad with miniature marshmallows and green fluffy stuff (she might skip that one); corn bread muffins; fresh fruit; and several delicious looking desserts, weighed down the gingham checked tablecloth, on the slightly lopsided picnic table Mike had lovingly constructed several years ago. They held hands to pray, and at that moment, to a one, they felt the loss of those family members who were no longer with them. The food was scrumptious, the company was wonderful, and the day was filled with fireworks and fun.

After their meal, stuffed to the gills with great food, Grace wandered down to the creek. Now that Doc's children were busy with some other grand adventure, she could sit and dangle her feet in the cool water. She hadn't done that in ages. Sun shone through leafy branches, in twirling patches of dappled light. It danced across the surface of the moving creek, creating small rainbows in the mist, where water hurried past rocks and rushed around small boulders. She took off her sandals and dipped a toe, frightening clouds of tadpoles into the shadows. The water was lovely, and she plunged both feet in clear up to her rolled pant legs. Tiny fish tickled her skin, as they came closer to investigate, and she found herself giggling as she sat on the mossy banks alone in the shade of ancient trees, surrounded by pink bleeding heart and lacey ferns. This is what is truly important, she reasoned, as she slowly began to unwind. Finding joy in the small things. She'd try to remember this the next time she was feeling overwhelmed.

Near a rock, in the crystal clear water, she saw a small crawdad, and teased it a bit with her foot, until it became determined to grab hold of its nemesis, and she got a little pinch.

Time away was important for her sanity, but it was in short supply, and today would have to be enough for now. There was much work to do, many to reach for the Kingdom, and she knew Satan would continue to do all he could to destroy what the Lord had built. It was good that they all realized their God was mighty, and that He who was in them, was more powerful than he who was in the world. Their next gathering would come soon enough, and there would be many who needed the healing touch of the Lord. She felt blessed to be His hands on the earth, and yet to be able to spend this precious time with her family.

✝

The weekly healing meetings had grown in size, until the only venue that could hold them these days was the area's local convention center. People came from all across the country, and the world, to avail themselves of God's healing power through His "Handmaiden of Healing" (the press' newest name for its favorite front page story), as the area became inundated with the world's hopeful. Grace thought it sad that so many of them didn't understand.

What they didn't understand is that God's healing power would be available to them anywhere in the world, including in their own homes. All they need do was believe He was able, and willing; and accept the gift which was earned by Jesus on the cross two thousand years ago, and freely given to His children, yes, all His children, just for the taking.

She found herself explaining over, and over, to those who came; that their healing had nothing to do with her, as they fawned over her, trying to bring her gifts and give her praise. If there was one thing to which she could attribute her ever growing exhaustion, and her feelings of depression, it would be that. The fact that so many wanted to give her the glory which belonged to the Lord; and the fact that she had to argue with them at every turn, and at every single meeting, was a grave disappointment to her. How could she have been doing this for so long, and yet so many still didn't get the most important message of all? The message of His Grace and goodness.

Newspapers, television, radio, and social media reporters followed her, harassed her, made up stories about her, and names for her. They wanted someone they could see, to which they could attribute the miracles abounding at the gatherings. In their minds, and to their way of thinking, it couldn't be some invisible godlike creature out in the universe somewhere, so it must be this slight, pale girl, with tired eyes. Her sadness, and exhaustion, came from believing she was somehow to blame for their misconceptions. Perhaps she hadn't explained herself well enough? Maybe she hadn't shared the Gospel in a relatable way? It was easy enough to accept the guilt for this. And she found herself once again becoming exhausted by their desire to credit her for their healing.

†

Kakos paced and waited for his latest update from the

field. Soon one of his minor demons came and knelt before him. "Tell me news from the field. How is this latest plan progressing?"

"Well Master. It seems we are finally making some headway. The girl is tired, and due to this, her sense of guilt and shame are growing. She is blaming herself for the lack of spiritual growth in her followers, just as you predicted she would."

"Good, good. Continue sending in those who will cause her the most remorse. Who knew it could be this easy? Instead of fighting her, all we had to do was cause her to doubt herself, to wallow in shame. As I said before, "There's more than one way to skin a cat!" Come back to me with another report as soon as you can."

†

Grace hadn't dreamt about her mother and siblings for years; which in itself caused her a certain amount of guilt; yet, for the past few weeks she was plagued by nightmares surrounding the day of the fire. Guilt is a funny thing. We all hate guilt, but when something terrible happens to our loved ones, we actually tend to feel more blame, if we don't feel we've suffered sufficiently in the aftermath of their tragedy. As human beings we have an innate need (definitely not from God) to feel that we've paid a price somehow for the things which have harmed the ones we love; it's called survivor's guilt; but how do you pay for the deaths of your mother and siblings? This question would have been enough to take down most who asked it. And, day after day, week after week, with less and less sleep, and Kakos' ministering, she'd been allowing it to erode her confidence. Exhaustion does funny things.

Grace, however, had something most young women don't possess. She had a personal, one-on-one relationship with Jesus. She walked with Him, and talked with Him, and He reminded her she was covered by the Grace He'd earned for her on the cross. So, He came to her through her dreams; the same dreams Kakos was trying to use for her harm; and reminded her of His undying love for her. "Oh, Lord, I'm so happy to see you."

"I'm glad to see you too, Gracie."

"I've been so tired, Lord, and I'm feeling like I can't do anything right. I must be a terrible teacher, because the people we've been healing through your Grace, don't seem to get it, no matter how hard I try to explain."

"I know, my daughter. It really isn't you sweet girl. There

will always be those who don't get it. All you can do is go forth to share the Gospel with those I put in your path. I always see you, and I always see your heart. You are not responsible for the hearts of others. They have choices of their own, and must follow who they will follow."

"Thank you Lord. I love you."

"And, I love you too, Grace. whenever you grow weary, turn to me and I will always answer. Bless you my child." With that, her determination to remain resolute grew. No matter what Kakos and his demons came up with, she knew she could turn to the Lord for her answers. She also knew her siblings were with Him in heaven, and there was nothing for her to regret. She would stand strong against every weapon, and every fiery dart, of the enemy.

This resolve caused her to gain a fresh perspective, and new energy. Kakos' scout sighed and shook his head. He didn't relish taking this news to Kakos, and knew the reaction it would inspire. He could only hope his master wouldn't shoot the messenger.

That morning her family was amazed at how a night's rest had revived her. Grace was as eager, and filled with Joy, as the girl they remembered from the beginning of this ministry journey. They all agreed it was time to branch out.

The Daze of Grace

✝

Grace received a letter from Tom, and immediately felt sorry that she hadn't gone to visit him for quite some time. The letter asked if she and her team could make arrangements to stopover at the prison in the near future. They all agreed it would be a wonderful next step. Grace was excited to minister in a place where she might make a great difference for the Lord. Measures were taken to make their appearance the following month and they began to prepare. She had no idea that Kakos was planning a trip as well, and there was no way to get ready for what he had in store for them.

Grace was more excited than she'd felt in ages. She couldn't wait to see Tom, and find out how his studies were going; but even more than that, the prospect of making a difference in the lives of men who had little hope, was singularly exhilarating. She prayed and asked for guidance. Once again, the Lord came to her in her sleep. "I need your help Jesus."

"I'm here my daughter."

"You know we're going to the prison where Tom is being held."

"Yes, and I have faith that you will do as you are called to do."

"These men may be hard to reach. What can I say to bring them hope?"

"Speak of my love. Tell them that my Grace isn't dependant on their actions, but on mine alone."

"I will, Lord. I'm excited to make a difference."

"Be careful Gracie. Satan's influence is strong in that place, and he will employ his demons to do their worst against you. You have my angels watching over you, but they will only intervene so much."

"I know, Lord. We're aware we may be walking into a situation, but we are prepared with your Word, and we won't back down."

"I'm very proud of you Grace. You are a brave girl, and I will be right there with you. Simply call on my Name."

"Thank you Jesus. I'm so grateful for your love and protection."

†

The family was packed up and ready for their road trip. Doc, and Tony; who'd become fast friends over these past months; were driving separately and would meet them there. "I want you all to know that the Lord will be with us on our trip to the prison, but Satan's minions will be there too."

"We know, Gracie. We're aware that the longer we share the Truth, the more we will be getting under the Devil's skin. We are prepared for anything he throws at us."

"I appreciate that Dad. Do you all feel the same way?"

"Yes we do, Dear. We love what we're doing, and nothing Satan does will change our minds."

"Me too, Gracie. I spent so many years being forced to do terrible things, and now that I'm free, because of the Lord and because of you, I love that we're helping people. I've never been happier in my life, Sis, so don't ever feel that you're trapping us here. This is where we genuinely want to be."

"Thank you all. I know we will have the opportunity to touch many lives, and I'm very excited!"

The drive was fraught with difficulties, expected, to a certain degree, considering who they were up against; a flat tire, an overheated radiator, and a near fatal accident, were a few of the featured obstacles. Angel warriors were working overtime to keep them safe, and they were all grateful to have Heavenly host on board.

The sky appeared to be getting ever darker the closer they got to their destination, and Grace wondered if they were approaching rain, until she stuck her head out the window, and looked to the heavens. A horizon of pink, which evolved into blood red above their objective, held clouds of circling demons which filled the sky over the prison. The hordes seemed to grow, in number and intent, by the minute. The sky, behind the growing threat, was lit with repeating lightning bolts, as if God was showing His displeasure at the heinous display of evil. As they drew closer to the prison the air cooled and become increasingly foul, and Grace felt the hair on the back of her neck stand on end. The family became very quiet, and Dad cleared his throat before he spoke. "Are you seeing anything strange, Gracie? Because I'm sure as heck feeling something strange."

"Yes Dad. the sky over the prison is filled with circling demons. Their intent seems pretty clear."

"Okay, as long as I know what we're facing. Do we still have our angels?"

"Yes Dad, our heavenly warriors are always with us, and they seem especially vigilant. They were the reason that van didn't hit us head on."

"Good. Is everyone still on board?"

"Yes, we're all on board Mike."

"I love you, Nancy."

"I love you too husband."

"I love you girls."

"We love you too, Dad."

At the gates of the penitentiary they were stopped and asked for identification, which they were happy to provide. Guards came forward, their car was parked for them, and they were loaded onto a transport for the rest of their journey. Once inside the facility, they endured a pat down, and were duly checked for contraband.

Led to an auditorium, which looked much like any other large meeting venue, except for the barred windows, and armed guards; Grace looked around and noticed peeling paint on the walls, and stains on the floor, which looked for all the world like patches of dried blood staining the concrete. The room reeked of body odor, and levels of testosterone she'd never encountered before.

Already filled with inmates in orange coveralls, the place held a sizable stage from which she assumed they'd be conducting their business. She didn't know how long the prisoners had been sitting, but it appeared they were getting restless, and she didn't want to keep them waiting any longer than she had to. Looking around she noticed some who appeared anxious to see what her group could offer, and some who looked ready to stab her.

One side of the stage held musical instruments, and microphones; the other side was set up with comfortable chairs, which Grace assumed were for their use, until such time as they were asked to proceed with their message. After about fifteen minutes, several inmates approached the stage, and headed for the instruments. Those men were accompanied by angels. But, it seemed they were among the very few in this place who were. Grace thought she'd never seen so many demons; hissing, spitting, and digging their talons into their victims; in one place. Then she spotted Tom. He seemed to be surrounded by a small contingent of Christians, probably those with which he'd shared Jesus during his incarceration. They were encircled about by a host of heavenly warriors. There was a space between his group, and the rest of the prison population, who were surrounded by a gulf, of sorts, and hordes of evil imps. When Tom noticed Grace looking in his direction he waved and smiled. She returned the gesture of welcome, and motioned him over. His group followed him, hoping for an introduction. "Oh Tom, it's so good to see you, old friend."

The Daze of Grace

"You too, Gracie. I'm so glad you could come. As you can see, I've been busy. My friends and I are a small minority here, but we meet for Bible study almost every day, and so far we've managed to stay out of any major trouble."

"I can see what you're saying, Tom. There is much evil here. I want you to know that there are angels watching over you."

"I figured as much. There have been a number of attempts made on my life, and the lives of my friends, but there always seems to be some kind of intervention, and the Lord has managed to keep us all safe."

"I'm glad to hear that you've recognized things for what they are. The sky is filled with opposition, and I want you to be prepared for whatever might happen."

"I will, Grace. Remember where I live. I've gotten pretty good at being prepared."

The musicians were warmed up, and they began to play. Grace was amazed at the talent these young men possessed. Playing a mixture of contemporary Christian pieces, and cherished old hymns, a few of the men, including Tom's group, in the auditorium began to sing along. Demons cringed and screamed to the music, as if someone were drilling holes into their temples with every sacred note, and

Grace was glad she was the only one who could see them. Her team equipped themselves to minister with scripture and fervent prayer.

Doc, and tony started the meeting off by giving their testimonies of healing, then Grace spoke about God's love, and mercy. She could tell she was speaking words that most of these men had never heard before, and she watched as demons held on tight to their hosts in desperation. She ended by inviting the men to come forward, against the advice of the warden and his guards. She knew, though, that she had to back up those words of Grace, by actions of Grace and love, or none of it would mean a thing. Men began to form a line to come on stage. At first some of the men seemed hesitant, but the team was warm and welcoming, and Grace looked at them with such compassion, that they soon felt comfortable and accepted. Grace kept her eyes open for the assaults she knew would be coming from the enemy, but until then, she simply shared Jesus with everyone who would listen and believe.

One after another, men were healed of various afflictions, from minor to very serious. A man came forward with a patch on his eye, and when the patch was removed they saw a gaping hole where his eye should be. An exercise yard brawl had led to his injury. When Gracie placed her hands over his eyes and spoke healing in the Name of Jesus, the crowd witnesses his eye growing back in its socket, and his face repairing, before their very eyes. So astounding was this miraculous healing that even some of the guards came forward to be healed. Many were introduced to the King of Kings, and made the decision to accept Christ as Savior. As each one did, their demons, screaming and flailing, were ripped away, and replaced by winged warriors. After over an hour of successful healings and conversions, she noticed a man ducking in and out behind others in line. At one point she caught a glimpse of his eyes, which were buried in a face covered in tattoos giving praise to Satan and the dark arts, and her heart skipped a beat. It was Satan in disguise or one of his most trusted demons, she was sure of it. She'd never seen so much evil in any other eyes.

Reminding herself she had nothing to fear; because she was protected by God and His angels; she calmed herself and went on to lay hands on another inmate who'd come forward. This gentleman looked into Gracie's eyes, and began to cry. "I'm sorry." He said. "No one has looked at me with kindness in a very long time. The things I did before I was locked away, were terrible, and even the other prisoners treat me with hatred. I guess I just don't know how God could ever forgive me, much less love me after all I've done."

"I'm sorry to hear about that, and to see the pain in your eyes. You see, to the Lord, we are all guilty, until we come to trust in Him for redemption. There is no sin greater, or lesser, than any other. That is simply a gage by which mankind judges himself unworthy, or more holy than another. When I look at you, I don't see evil, I see lost, and the moment you ask Jesus into your heart, I'll witness a brother who will live together with Jesus, in eternity with me, the very moment we leave this place."

"What do I need to do to have Jesus in my heart the way you do Grace?"

"First you must ask yourself if you believe that Jesus is the Son of God, and that He died and rose again to overcome death?"

"Yes, I do Grace. For the first time in my life someone has explained it in a way I understand, and I do believe."

"Wonderful, then together we will say a prayer and your place in eternity will be assured. What is your name?"

"Jim. My name is Jim.

Grace led Jim in a prayer of salvation, and he came eagerly into the arms of the Lord. This event had been one of the most rewarding in her ministry so far. Society had thrown these men away, and relegated them to second class citizenship. She understood the concept of paying a debt to society for one's crimes. But, just because society had given up on these individuals, didn't mean they were not of value to the Father. These were some of the very ones that Jesus died for, and she knew that God loved them just as much as He loved her. This experience had been eye opening for her, and she'd never be the same.

"Thank you Grace. I can't thank you enough for looking on me with love. I'll always remember you."

"And, I will always remember you, Jim. If you don't know my friend Tom, I will introduce you. He's been doing Bible studies here in the prison, and I'm sure he would welcome you into the group."

"Great, I'll be looking forward to it."

Again she saw the creature with red eyes. He was closer now, but still attempting to hide himself somewhat from her view.

Grace and her team answered questions, laid hands on the sick, and prayed with inmates well into the afternoon. Throughout that time she noticed other prisoners, all through the auditorium, with glowing eyes and obvious malevolent intent. It seemed that Satan's right hand minion possessed one of the men, and his many demons inhabited others.

As her time was winding down, she found herself looking longingly at the chairs on the other side of the stage. Even with threats looming, she found herself letting down her guard due to sheer exhaustion. Mike urged her to take a seat. He and the rest of the group could finish up. At precisely that moment the inmate who'd been successfully hiding himself stood before her. Looking into his eyes she instantly knew his goal. His eyes gleamed with an irrational hatred, which could only emanate from the depths of hell, and before she knew it the dagger came out. He lunged at Grace, but a vigilant angel stayed his hand. His eyes changed from anger to rage, as he tried with all his might to fight against God's emissary.

Once his minions saw the flash of the blade, they acted in unison to overtake Grace's team. He struggled again, against the hand of her warrior guard, but didn't stand a chance against God's sentry. He yanked his hand away, turned, and pounced on Lilly, but he was no match for her winged protector either. His irate screams and screeching echoed off the walls of the hall, and he ran into the crowd slashing as he went. Grace and Lilly were safe, but their newfound brother, Jim lay bleeding on the floor.

Inmates fought in a tale as old as time, good against evil, Satan's demons against God's newest children. Grace could see the difference between the two, but the prison's guards were at a loss as to who they should assail, to put an end to the riot. Soon, there were more bodies piled on the concrete floors, and the room ran red with the blood of the dead and injured from both sides. The prison sentries sent out a call for additional help, and it arrived halfway through the melee.

As the new guards arrived they slipped and slid on the bloodied floor, adding to the event's confusion. Grace watched as the bodies of those who'd been possessed contorted in death. Suddenly, at the end of their struggle, out of their mouths came something that looked like large, black frogs. These froglike creatures morphed into full-fledged demons before her eyes, and sailed through the air to join the cloud of evil circling the skies above the institution. She heard more screeching and looked up. Through the ceiling came large winged demons, arriving to cart off their prizes. Souls of all those who'd not been covered by the blood of

Jesus and had been possessed by the demons, those who tried to kill Grace and her team, were being taken away to an eternity in hell with Satan and his minions.

Mike tried to usher the girls off stage to safety, but Grace resisted. She could see many of the newly healed, and saved; hurt or dead; scattered throughout the place. She pulled away from Mike and ran to Jim's side. Taking his hand in hers, she brought it to her face and he gave hers a small squeeze. He smiled a grateful smile and mouthed, "Thank you, Sister", as he died. She laid her head on his chest, covering her cheek and hair in her new brother's warm blood, and cried, as war raged on around her. Her only consolation was that she knew he'd asked Jesus into his heart just moments before, so he would spend eternity with the Lord; but there were many others, just as dead, who'd lost their chance for an eternity of peace, and her heart broke for the wasted opportunities all around her.

Pretty soon swat teams arrived, and things were set straight, but not before many dozens were killed. Lost, so many lost. She looked frantically for Tom, and found him wounded, but alive. He was heartbroken, because several of his followers had succumbed to the battle, but he too commented that at least he knew he would meet them again;

that finally they were out of this terrible place, and resting in the arms of Jesus.

The warden gave instructions to have Grace and her team taken to a safe space, and the guards, and janitors, proceeded to clean up. She got word to Tom that she'd be back for a visit sometime soon. Apologizing about things getting so out of hand, the warden suggested that the next time they came to do a service, he would have more security on hand for their event. Oddly, the idea of not coming back never crossed Grace's mind. As frightening as the entire situation had been, Grace knew they must visit more prisons. When Jim told her she was the first person who'd looked at him with compassion in years, and that this was the first time salvation had been explained in a way he could understand, she wondered how many more Jims there might be in the world. How many of these men were easy prey for the devil, losing their lives, and their eternities in places like this, simply because no one had ever told them God loved them? She knew this would be one way she could make a big difference, so when she got home she began calling jails and prisons in the tri-state area, to set dates for meetings.

Grace had effectively found a new facet to her calling, and her team bought in wholeheartedly. They would teach men; men who the world had thrown away; how valuable they were in God's sight. Satan was boiling mad, and he was going to make someone pay. Kakos was the unlucky demon who happened to be in line for the boss's wrath, and when he was done dishing out that wrath, it would make its way down, step by step, to the lowest pits of hell, and to the lowliest demons. Nothing made Grace's heart happier than knowing she was putting a damper on the plans of the enemy.

The wicked plots against the righteous and gnashes his teeth at him, but the Lord laughs at the wicked, for He sees that his day is coming. The wicked draw the sword and bend their bows to bring down the poor and needy, to slay those whose way is upright; their sword shall enter their own heart, and their bows shall be broken.

Psalm 37:12-15

CHAPTER 26

"What happened? Are you telling me she outfoxed us again?"

"Yes Master. I'm sorry Master. There was nothing we could do. He had His angels posted everywhere."

"You knew they would be there! You were supposed to prepare for all contingencies! You are worse than useless! Get out of my sight. I will deal with you later."

Kakos was livid. He'd given specific instructions to all those in the attack forces, to concentrate on taking out that damnable girl. How was she still walking around? Did he have to do everything himself? His superiors wouldn't put up with this lack of results much longer, and he knew his time was running out. He had to come up with a plan so foolproof that even these bumbling idiots could get it right. This might be his last chance before the matter would make its way to the top.

†

Deciding to go with the family today had been a good idea. They'd talked about going to the cemetery for quite some time, but this week was the first opening they'd had, in their busy schedule, in recent memory. Grace didn't personally believe in burial. She preferred the idea of cremation, and had made her parents aware of her desires. But, she also knew humans well enough to know they needed a place to grieve, and a grave site was as good a place as any. As for herself, once they arrived she felt at peace in this pastoral retreat.

The graveyard was different now. On her visits here, twice before, the tranquility of the place had been obscured by tears and loss. Close by there was a small stream, hosting a beautiful falls, and the sound of water cascading down rock was relaxing to her soul. She reveled in the peace and quiet. Finding a bench, not far from where her family were paying their respects, she sat and prayed.

Scent of lilacs filled the air, and birdsong resonated through the small, perfect valley as she released all her stress and opened her heart for healing. She'd never completely let go of the resentments she harbored, or the remorse she felt, for the recent deaths of her brother and sister. And, if she was honest, it all tracked back to her feelings of guilt over the loss of her siblings when she was a child. God was working on her heart, but it was hard to let go. She stood to walk, and a butterfly floated down to land on her arm. The sight caused her to smile, and a single tear made its way down the gentle curve of her cheek.

Strolling through ancient grave markers, in the oldest part of the cemetery, she saw names and dates going back centuries, with comments eluding to cause of death, sweet sentiment, or some quirky aspect of a deceased's personality. "Our dear angel", or "Our baby", were common among graves which seemed to tie local, historical epidemics of small pox, or outbreaks of measles together. Her favorite was the verse on a very old gravestone, which read: "Here he lies". No name, no date. She patted the top of the stone, smiled and walked on.

Back, where the earliest dates on tombstones were prevalent, moss grew thick on the ground and covered Northern sides of trees and markers. Trees were older, and there were no obvious signs of upkeep by the grounds men. She supposed all the loved ones, of those occupying these ancient plots were long gone, so there would be no one left to complain to the establishment, but she quite enjoyed the feeling of absolute aloneness. An opportunity to stroll in the cool quiet, as squirrels watched and birds sang.

Grace didn't know if she would ever stop missing all

those who'd gone before her, though she knew God did not hold her responsible for their deaths. But, regardless, she would always assume some of the blame. She was, after all, only human.

Hearing the sound of footfalls behind her she turned to see Lilly approaching. "You okay, Gracie?"

"I'll be fine, Lilly. I just miss them all."

"I know what you mean. You know there's a part of me that feels like I just spoke to Bella this morning; and another piece that can't quite remember what she looks like. It makes me feel bad to think I might ever forget her. David was more recent, and his funeral is still fresh in my mind, so when I stand at his grave site all I want to do is cry."

"I'm sure we all just need time to heal. It was a terrible shock to lose them both so young, so it might take some time. How are Mom and Dad? I'm sorry I wandered off."

"They're okay, I guess. Mom cries and Dad holds her. I just had to walk away. I feel like I only have so many tears to cry before my insides dry up. That probably sounds selfish to you."

"No, not at all. why would you say that?"

"I just think of you as perfect Grace, you know? Everyone knows you're flawless and faultless. Sometimes I just find it hard to measure up, and I always feel like you put so much more effort into everything than the rest of us are even capable of, so I guess it's not strange that you would get all the attention."

"That's not true at all, Lilly. I'm no more perfect than anyone else. Jesus is the only perfect one. And, I certainly hope I'm not the one getting all the attention. All the glory is reserved for the Lord. I wish to take none of it from Him. Keep in mind, sweet sister, that God gives each of us a job to do, and you are doing your job just as well as I'm doing mine, maybe even better. Let's not lose sight of the fact that none of this is about us, okay?"

"I'm sorry, Grace. Sometimes I sound like such a brat."

"Not at all, Lilly. You just sound human like the rest of us. Let's get back. Mom and Dad are probably wondering what happened to us."

As the girls exited the trees, Mike and Nancy smiled and waved them forward. "We've decided to get ice cream. Anyone with us?"

The girls both agreed that ice cream sounded good, though neither of them felt much like having ice cream at all. Sometimes, when you love someone, you just go along because you can tell it means a great deal to them. Grace knew she was blessed. She couldn't ask for better parents than Mike and Nancy, and Lilly was the best sister in the world. She hadn't realized the girl felt so overwhelmingly overshadowed by her, and she certainly hadn't been trying to steal the show. She thought she'd made it abundantly clear to everyone that all the glory for every healing, every conversion, every good thing that happened, was to be attributed to God. She wondered again, where she'd gone wrong. Why didn't they get it?

Back in the car it was obvious that Mike and Nancy were trying to lighten the mood. "I scream, you scream, we all scream for ice cream." Mike sang, in a loud voice.

"Rocky Road for me!" Cried Nancy.

"Cherry Garcia is the only real choice in ice cream." Mike chimed in a mocking tone.

"What'll it be girls?"

"Vanilla", the girls said in unison.

"You two are so predictable." Nancy said with a chuckle.

"And, by predictable, she means boring." Mike laughed.

"Hey, we are not boring. We just know what we want."

"No, Lilly, we're boring. But better boring than crazy like the two of them." They all laughed and the sadness of the cemetery seemed to dissipate for the moment.

The Daze of Grace

✝

Grace was excited. She'd received a letter from the prison where Tom was incarcerated. His parole hearing was imminent, and they were offering her an opportunity to testify. She accepted gladly. The family went together to make an afternoon of it. Grace was sure the parole board had called her thinking she might fight his release, so imagine their surprise when the young woman he had harmed turned out to be his biggest fan and cheerleader. She told them of his new faith, and the Bible studies he was leading. As she spoke of the changes in his life, and her complete trust in the new man he'd become, Tom sat with tears streaming from his eyes. God was surely good, and he was blessed to have this forgiving young woman in his life. They would know the results of his parole hearing soon. Grace and her family visited with Tom before they left that day. She offered him a place on their ministry team, and Mike and Nancy offered him a place to stay. The house was certainly large enough. He was stunned, but accepted the loving offer immediately. He knew he was blessed to know this extraordinary young woman and her family.

✝

Excitement filled the air as the week's end approached. The ministry team would be appearing at one of the largest penitentiaries in the region. Once again Tony and Doc would ride together, and the family, in their trusty SUV, would lead the way. Grace was anxious to make sure all was perfect, so she'd made a list of supplies they'd take with them: Bibles, to pass out to those prisoners who wanted them; oil, to anoint the heads of those who came forward; an assortment of encouraging literature that the inmates could take back to their cells with them, all approved by the state's prison system; communion supplies; and her own notes. She checked everything twice and then a third time.

"Hey, Gracie, come and sit with me for awhile."

"I'll be right there, Dad."

Mike was sitting by himself, on the padded window seat, in their cozy upstairs landing, as the sun was going down on a beautiful pink and lavender sunset. The window was open, and white curtains fluttered around him like the gossamer wings of a guardian angel. Just as the fiery orb dipped below a blazing horizon, and the evening sky faded to dark purple and then black, Grace joined him.

"How are you doing baby girl?"

"I'm okay, Dad. I really am."

"You're not nervous about tomorrow? Even after what happened during our last ministry experience?"

"I'm really not. God was watching over us, and we all made it out just fine, didn't we? But, hey, are you okay, Dad?"

"I just know it's my job to keep all my girls safe, and I didn't feel like I did a very good job of it this last time."

"Don't be ridiculous, Dad. No one could have seen that coming. I can even see the spiritual realm, and I didn't see it coming. And besides, I'm pretty stubborn, so it's hard to keep a leash on me."

"So I noticed. I know you tell me over and over again that we have angels watching over us, Gracie, and of course I believe you; but you have to remember that only you can see them. It leaves the rest of us wondering how protected you, or any of us, are."

"I'll try to keep that in mind, Dad. I promise I'll be more careful." As they sat, Grace leaned her head on Mike's chest, and he put his arm around her shoulders. She closed her eyes, and they sat until darkness overtook the tiny space. Mike's eyes grew moist as he thought about all they had been through together, and how much he would miss his girl when she left, as she inevitably would. He imagined all dads must have these feelings, and it made him grateful to have been blessed with these young people in his life. He would never have had the joy of being a parent, if God hadn't blessed him in such a unique way.

✝

Everyone in the family was up bright and early, to load their ministry supplies and get on the road. The trip would take about six hours, and they would need time to set up and get the lay of the land before the meeting began that afternoon. Grace was more excited than she could remember being in a long time, believing they could really make a difference for the kingdom, and in the lives of these incarcerated men, with a new approach. She was also aware that Satan was firmly opposed to this current line of thinking, and expected plenty of backlash from the other side.

Meanwhile, at the prison where her team would be ministering later that day, opposition was readying its troops. As demons entered the unprotected hearts of unsaved inmates, their testosterone levels increased, as their confused minds began to work overtime in the direction of extreme violence; and most creepy of all, their eyes took on a dangerous red hue, which would be all too familiar to young Grace. Warden Miller, and the guards throughout the prison, could feel a change in the air. And, though they couldn't see the ever growing, and endlessly circling cloud of evil twisting round and round over the place, or see the signs of the possessed; the way Grace could; the hair on the backs of their collective necks stood on end, and a rising uneasiness washed over the entire institution.

Grace's team faced obstacles all along the way. Thankfully Mike was pretty handy, and gratefully, they'd taken every precaution imaginable. Emergencies, from a flat tire, to a local bridge washing out by some unknown force, and finally, a cracked radiator hose assailed them. They overcame every event that threatened to keep them from their destination. Then, only forty five minutes before they were scheduled to appear, they pulled up in front of the prison. Directed inside, they began to unpack the supplies they'd need, and get ready for their meeting.

Right away Grace noticed the menacingly red eyes of many of the men who were present. Having been in a similar situation at their previous prison meeting, she was more attuned to what might be going on at this one.

Their meeting space was a large gymnasium. Concrete walls of peeling paint, and torn padding on walls at both ends; faded wooden floors, with barely visible free throw and out of bounds lines; and old, rusted basketball hoops, sans nets, drooping from each side, told her so. A barrel of faded orange balls stood by the entrance door; and barred windows, way up high, plus a few flickering fluorescents barely supplied what light they would need for the meeting. Smells of ancient floor wax, sweat, and wisps of sulfur hung in the air. Grace looked around the room and encountered different moods from the prisoners. From one side looks of longing, perhaps for words that might encourage; and from the other, pent up rage and manic pacing. She knew Satan's minions were present here, not just in the demons who surrounded their hosts, holding on tightly with talons digging in deep, but also inside of those he inhabited. Angels were present too, but they stood around the periphery, awaiting the prayers needed to bring them to action.

As with their meeting in the first prison where they'd ministered, there was a stage set up and old, probably donated, musical instruments occupied one half of the platform. She remembered how talented the men were who'd played at their first prison event, and she couldn't wait to hear the music these fellows would produce.

On one side of the gym, which appeared to be occupied almost entirely by the enemy, she saw a man covered with satanic tattoos, who stood easily a head taller than any other man there. He watched Grace, as she went about her business, and each time she looked up from her work his lips curled into a sneer when their eyes met. He would be the ring leader. She was sure of it. She knew without doubt there would be trouble, but this time she would be prepared.

"Hey, Dad, would you fetch the warden? We need to check on security for the event."

"Sure Honey, have you seen something?"

"Yes. There are dozens in the crowd who are already possessed, I can see it in their eyes, and I expect there will be more. It's the same evidence I witnessed at our first prison event, only I wasn't sure what it meant then. Now that I know, I want to meet it head on. And, before you ask, there are indeed angels, lots of them, but remember they can only help if our very selves are in danger of being killed."

"I know, baby girl, but it's nice knowing they're here."

"I do understand, Dad. Being the protector of so many females has got to be overwhelming, especially under these circumstances. That is why I'd like to talk to the warden. Please pass along the situation as I've seen it, so the others on the team are prepared, would you?"

"Yes, Gracie. We'll make sure this gym is secure as a fortress. Anyone who wants you, is going to have to go through me first!"

Warden Miller was quite accommodating, and soon there were a number of guards posted within the venue, instead of just on the outer perimeter. Grace and her team felt safer already, which would have been perfectly normal, if the threat was coming from a physical presence. However, things work a bit differently in the spiritual realm.

When time approached for the meeting to begin, she looked out to the congregation and saw many more demon filled eyes looking back at her. The few who were not under Satan's spell were mostly off to one side, as if they could feel the evil influence filling the room. This time would be different. Jesus' words came to Grace's mind in a flash. "I will be with you. Simply call on my Name." Why hadn't she seen it before? The fiasco, which occurred at the last prison, needn't have happened. She'd remembered to call on His Name for each and every healing, but it hadn't occurred to her to call on Him in those moments of terror when

Satan's army attacked. This time she was armed with the knowledge that she only need call on His name to disarm the enemy!

She heard a bit of a commotion in the hall leading to the auditorium and saw a news crew making their way into the space. Word had gotten around to the media after the last episode and they were hoping to get a story for their local television stations and newspapers. Well, she wouldn't let that hinder the flow of the Spirit.

Men, surrounded by angels even in this wicked place, leaped onto the stage and went to their instruments. As they began to play she felt her spirit lifted higher. Her team was familiar with every song selection, and they all sang along. A few of the inmates, and some of the guards joined in, and before you knew it there was a full-fledged worship service going on.

At the end of a half hour, or so, of great praise and worship music, they were ready to begin addressing individual needs. Prisoners formed a line to come on stage for healing and salvation, and Grace could see there were many in line with demons firmly attached. However, she was not nearly as daunted as she'd been before, because this time she knew there was a tool in her arsenal that she'd forgotten previously.

Men, filled with pain, sorrow, guilt, and sickness advanced on the stage; and left healed and whole, filled with the spirit of God. Those who'd approached covered in ghastly, clinging demons, left freed from the foe, and surrounded by angels. Many were healed, and multitudes were saved for all eternity. But, now came the challenge. Suddenly, standing before her, was the inmate covered in satanic tattoos. He was followed by, and surrounded by, others who were possessed. Flocks of hideous demons with talons dug in deep, and others with black wings unfurled and flapping, hovered around and over the army of inmates. She stood her ground, and as Mike began to move closer to her side, she lifted her hand to keep him back. She looked Satan's minion square in the eye and said, "Back off Satan. In the Name of Jesus, every knee will bow, and every tongue confess that He is Lord! Come out of them demons, in the holy Name of the Lord Jesus Christ!"

The room became a dizzying scene to her eyes. No one else was able to view what she was seeing, but this was a moment she truly wished she could share. "Lord, God, they've all helped me so much. Let them see."

Suddenly the eyes of her team were opened, and they were witness to everything Grace could see. She continued to speak out to the Lord, to conquer Satan's demons, and their hold on the men. "Come out of them, demons. Release your hold, that they might draw near to God. Release them in the Name of Jesus! I command you, in the Name of our Savior, King of Kings, and Lord of Lords!"

What the ministry team saw was a miracle. Oh, they were used to regular miracles by this time. Healings of various sorts, and souls won for the kingdom, but this was different. This was a peek into the miraculous world of Grace's second sight, and they were awed by what they saw. Angels slaying demons, and Satan's minions being plucked from the backs of prisoners and cast away into darkness. A flurry of wings, white and black, in a battle older than mankind. As each demon was conquered, he lay writhing on the floor until carried away by huge flying demonic beings that looked like evil dragons. With eyes wide open, and mouths agape, Gracie's team watched the whole clash from the stage. Sadly, some new Christians were slain in the conflict, before the bloody melee was finished, but their eternal lives had just begun, and now they would be with Christ, instead of spending another day in this hell hole. The floor was littered with the bodies of men from both sides, but the demons had been forced to flee the bodies they possessed, through the power of His Name.

Grace approached her team, as they slumped to the floor shaking from all they'd seen, and held out her hand to help Lilly rise. "I never knew. I had no idea that this is what you see all the time, Gracie. How do you stand it?"

"I've mostly gotten used to it, Lilly. Now I consider it a weapon for our benefit."

"Wow, Grace. I've never seen anything like that in my life. And I thought I'd seen just about everything."

"There are many things present in the spiritual realm, Doc, that most people will never witness."

"Now that I know what is out there, I believe it will help me focus more on what's really important, Grace."

"I'm glad, Tony. I hope you can all see how much God loves you, and the power that can rise up, at the mere mention of His Name."

"That was amazing, baby girl. No wonder you are so tired every time we leave an event. I can't imagine having to deal with everything you see every day."

"It's not that bad, Dad. Knowing that God is watching over me, and that all I have to do is call out in Jesus' Name for protection, is actually a pretty good feeling."

"Well, I'm glad you're okay with it, Gracie, because I

don't need to see it again. I'm grateful to know that our protectors are there, and it makes the Bible come alive to see that there really are angels watching over us, but I certainly don't need to see it again."

"Okay, Mom. I'll keep that in mind."

"Now, that doesn't mean I don't want you to tell us when there is danger, or remind us when angels are watching, I just don't need to see it myself, if that's alright."

"I know, Mom. I just wanted you all to see what your prayers, and ministry work accomplish every time we enter a place like this. I'm very proud of all of you, and of the work we do. God is proud of you too, and He will continue to watch over us."

Warden Miller had been caught up in the battle, and was slightly wounded, but he would be fine. The guards were busy cleaning up the floors of the auditorium, and as they dragged away bodies, and righted chairs, they walked past reporters who were mostly unscathed, but shaking in their boots. The media had witnessed the entire battle, but from a wholly different perspective than Grace and her team. They were blind to the spiritual skirmish, but even the physical battle was beyond normal comprehension, and most of them were badly dazed.

"Are you guys okay?" Grace called out to them.

"Well, if this is the way your meetings usually wind up, it might be a lot safer for us to just stay home." One of the reporters hollered back.

"They don't all end up like this, but when they do, I figure we must be doing something right. Satan wouldn't feel the need to attack us if he didn't think we were making a difference. Don't you agree?"

"Whatever you say, Grace. Whatever you say."

Warden Miller made his way over to the group. "I should have known something like this would happen. I felt it in the air all day long. But, there was something that made me not call it off. I'm really sorry you all had to go through that."

"Warden, we wouldn't have had it any other way. And, that something which caused you not call it off, was God. He accomplished great things today. Men were healed, and a great many came to know Jesus as their Savior. You will see the difference in the attitude here in the prison in the coming days, I assure you."

"Thank you Grace, and all of you. Would you come back if we asked you to? I mean if we shore up our security?"

"We would be happy to come back. Please let us know

when you begin to see a difference."

"I will. Thank you all so much."

"God bless you, Warden. We will keep you in our prayers."

✝

"I can't believe you're here, Tom! This is wonderful! You're here in time to go with us to our next meeting, if you want to."

"I wouldn't miss it for the world. I can't thank you all enough for taking me in. I'm a little rusty on the manners, but I'll do my best."

"You'll do fine, friend. I ask that you help me out around the property a bit, and that you help me carry supplies when we have a meeting, and that is about it. You are very welcome here."

"Thank you, Mike. I appreciate all you've done for me, and I'll try to be the best help I can be. I do have another favor to ask of you. For years my sister wouldn't have anything to do with me, and wouldn't let me see my nephew; but now she has told me that Jason can come see his uncle, and spend time with me. Would it be alright if he stayed here when he visits, and if he came along to the meeting this weekend? I know it's a lot to ask, and I understand if the answer is no, so don't feel obligated."

"As long as you can keep the little fellow out of the way so he doesn't get hurt, I'm fine with that. Might as well train them while they're young."

"Thanks, Gracie. I'll call her today. Thank you again everyone. You don't know how much your kindness means to me."

†

Grace was grateful to have her friend on board. His witness would be wonderful for the ministry, as he had first-hand experience in the prison system. She spent the week volunteering at the food kitchen, and studying for the message she would share at the upcoming event. As she was serving, she saw a young girl, no more than twelve, coming through the line. She wore a backpack and dirty jeans. A torn hoodie partially covered a head of matted, blonde hair. She looked up suspiciously at every adult there, and avoided everyone's gaze as best she could. When Grace greeted her, she ignored the kind words and went on her way.

"Hey, Dad, did you see the girl who went through the line today?"

"Yes I did. I saw you try to talk to her too. Did she answer you back?"

"No, she didn't. She looked scared to death."

"She reminds me of another little girl I knew once."

"Did I look that pathetic? I feel terrible for her."

"Yes you did look that pathetic, or worse. I've tried to talk to her, but she doesn't answer. I don't want to push it, because I want to ensure that she feels comfortable coming back."

"Well, you're an adult. That's why she won't talk to you. She's afraid you'll turn her in. I remember the feeling. I think I might be able to get through to her. I'll try the next time she comes in."

"I think you're forgetting that you are an adult now too. What makes you think she'll talk to you before she talks to me?"

"Well, I might be an adult now, but I'm not ancient like some people I know."

"Oh, thanks daughter. You know how to make a guy feel great."

"You're welcome, Dad. Glad I could help."

Throughout the week Tom was as good as his word, and a blessing to his new found family. He cleaned up areas of the home property that Mike and Nancy hadn't been able to touch for years, due to their overly tight schedules. Then, he came with Mike and Grace to the soup kitchen and proceeded to organize storage spaces, and scrub floors. Mike couldn't think of enough great things to say about their new house guest, but Tom was simply grateful for the chance they'd all taken on him.

Curiosity brought Gracie back to the soup kitchen several times that week, as she tried for an opportunity to speak to the young, backpack girl she'd seen. On Friday her patience paid off. Fridays were meatloaf and mashed potatoes days, with vegetables, fruit salad, and chocolate pie, she remembered it well. That had been one of her favorites too, when she could count on one good meal a day from Mike. Dad still made meatloaf at home sometimes, but though it was good, there could never be a substitute for the feeling of filling a starving belly with food that good.

Grace saw her enter and walk by the 'FREE' table, giving it a quick once over. She walked up to the serving line and pushed her tray along, trying very hard not to make eye contact, but as she got to Grace she glanced up. "Hi, do you need an extra milk? I used to take extra milk, biscuits, and anything else I could get my hands on, so I wouldn't be hungry later."

That got her attention. "You used to come here?"

"Yep, for quite a long time actually, until my life took some very different turns. I could tell you about it sometime."

"I'd like that. And, thank you, I will take an extra milk and biscuits if that's alright."

"Sure, anything you want. I usually come a couple of days a week, or so, with my dad. He does the cooking, because he owns a restaurant up town. We can talk any time you want to."

"Okay, I'll keep that in mind. Thanks again."

"Have a great day.....I didn't get your name."

"It's Anna. You have a great day too. I'll see you around."

"So she actually talked to you?"

"Yes. I think she's just scared and lonely, Dad. I'd really like to be able to reach her. We might be able to save her from some of the stuff I went through."

"I'm all for that, and I know Mom will help in any way she can. Have I told you lately what a good daughter you are?"

"Yes, Dad, practically every five minutes. But, please don't ever stop. I love you, Dad."

"I love you too, Gracie, more than you will ever know."

"Thank you, Dad."

"Thank you for what?"

"Thank you for taking me in, for loving me, for believing in me, and for standing by me through all the crazy stuff that has happened."

"Crazy is right baby girl; but you are more than welcome. And, might I answer by saying, thank you for coming into our lives. We are grateful for you girls every day. You make us feel alive again. You've saved your mother. She was wasting away, feeling like she had no purpose, until you came along. God has blessed us greatly."

"Yep, God is good alright. God is very good."

And we know that for those who love God all things work together for good, for those who are called according to His purpose.

Romans 8:28

CHAPTER 27

Tom was anxious to see his nephew, and hoped the young fellow would be equally happy to see him. After all the negative press he was sure had come from his sister, he wondered how the reunion would turn out. The girls readied David's old room, adding a box of toys collected from various sources, to keep him busy when all the grownups were otherwise engaged. Tom was set up in one of the master suites, and therefore, had his own bathroom. That decision had been made and agreed upon by the whole family. Mom and Dad occupied the other master suite, and they all thought it appropriate, due to his age and circumstances, that Tom have the other. When he'd been shown his accommodations he'd cried like a baby. No one had ever treated him with so much love and care in his life, and as he looked around his new home he felt like a grand duke. He wasn't sure how he would ever repay the kindnesses of his hosts, but he intended to try.

Tom heard a car drive up, and figured it must be his sister dropping off the boy, but when he went to the door to let him in, he stood in the doorway, puzzled for a moment at what he saw. It wasn't his sister, and a young boy, but instead a full grown man getting out of a red sports coup. "Jason? Is that you?"

"Hi, Uncle Tom, yes it's me. You look surprised."

"I guess I didn't realize how much you'd grown. I was expecting a boy. It really has been a long time since I saw you."

"Mom sends her love, and said she will make arrangements to meet with you some other time. Well, are you going to invite me in?"

Tom, who had wandered out the door as he was speaking, led Jason up the walkway, and into the house. "Hey everyone, Jason is here."

The family hurried from the kitchen, to welcome their new guest, and stood dumbfounded in the entryway.

"Imagine my surprise. I guess I didn't realize how much time had gone by since the last time I saw him. He grew up on me."

"I guess he did, Tom. Well, somebody had better run up to his room and remove all the toys, before we are all completely embarrassed."

"I'll go Mom. I've got stuff to do before work anyway.

Nice to meet you Jason."

"Thank you Lilly. Well, you met Lilly; I'm Nancy, and this is my husband Mike. The young lady behind me is Grace."

Grace would have spoken, but she was too charmed by the handsome young man standing before her to form coherent sentences. Tall and slim, Jason had gentle features, blond hair, soulful brown eyes and a naturally quick smile. He was accompanied by angelic warriors, and that made her smile too. She searched for the right words, but none came, so she nodded and held out her hand. Jason took her hand and kissed it lightly, causing her heart to skip a beat. Mike's eyes flashed, until he noticed the way his daughter was looking back at the young stranger. Then he looked over at Nancy, put his head down, and sighed. It was possible that he would be losing his little girl even sooner than he'd imagined.

✝

It was settled, Jason would be helping at the upcoming meeting, and he seemed genuinely excited about it. Grace reminded herself to concentrate on the jobs at hand, so she wouldn't be swept up in things that did not give God glory.

She'd never had a boyfriend, and she wasn't sure how to act around a young man, at least one she was interested in. He seemed to be interested right back, and that made it even harder.

The night before their next big prison event they spent some time sorting and packing the supplies they'd need for the service. Tom was a huge help. Who would have known that he was so organized. He was very anxious to be of service, and couldn't wait for the big event the next day. As the sun was setting he walked out to the covered porch to take in the evening air after supper. Mike was already parked in one of the large rockers, so Tom sat down beside him and began to rock. "I want to thank you again for taking me in. I feel very blessed to have such wonderful friends."

"You really need to quit thanking us so much Tom. We're glad to do it, and you've been a huge help to us, so I'd say the favor is returned. If you want to give thanks, give the glory to God."

"I will. I'm also very excited about the service tomorrow. Ever since Gracie introduced me to the Lord, I've been dreaming of being in the ministry."

"You've already accomplished that, Tom. You had quite the Bible study going at the prison. Many men came to know the Lord because of your sharing."

"I guess you're right. God is very good. Jason is also thrilled about the meeting. He jabbered on about it all afternoon, while we were packing supplies."

"I'm glad he's eager to help. I'm guessing though, that he and Gracie are both pretty excited about spending more time together. You can't tell me you don't notice how they look at each other.""

"Does it bother you that they seemed to take to each other so quickly? I can talk to him if you'd like me to."

"No, Grace is a grown woman, and he seems like a nice young man. I'm just feeling a little lost at the moment, because I have a feeling it won't be much longer before I lose my little girl. I know I can't keep her from growing up, and I don't think I'd even want to, but it's hard."

"I'm sure it is. I was never blessed with a wife and kids. I made too many stupid mistakes along the way. And since I didn't know the Lord it only got worse. I should probably be grateful I never brought kids into the mess I'd made. That would certainly be more to regret. I am so blessed now that Grace has forgiven me, and allowed me to be a part of her life. It's brought me into this family, and surrounded me with the best friends I've ever had."

"No, no, no, Tom; you don't get off that easy. You are kin, and that is all there is to it. You fit right in here. We are an entire family of people who owe everything to the Lord, so you are now, and always will be, my brother."

"Thank you Mike. You have no idea how much that means to me. And, with God's help, I will try to live up to the blessings you've shared. I never had a brother before, but if I could have ordered one, he'd be you."

"Hey you two, what are you doing out here?"

"Just catching up on our fresh air, Babe. Supper was great by the way."

"I'll second that, Nancy"

"Thank you boys. I do my best. And, that isn't always an easy thing when I have to compete against a professional chef."

"You do a great job, Nance. And, after cooking at the restaurant it's nice to be able to come home to a great supper."

"I can cook a little too, Nancy. Before I ended up on the streets I used to put together a couple nice dishes. I'd be happy to take turns if you want a break."

"You've got a deal, Tom. As soon as we get home from the prison trip you can show us what you've got. How does that sound?"

The Daze of Grace

✝

"Do you need any help?"

"Thanks, Jason, but I think I've got it." Grace's face turned an adorable shade of scarlet, just being within arm's length of the handsome young man. No one had ever made her feel quite like this, and though the feeling was pleasant, it was also a bit uncomfortable.

Jason felt the same way, just the sound of Gracie's voice made him gasp for breath; and since he wasn't what anyone would likely call a lady's man, he couldn't tell if Grace liked him or not. Was she shy? Was she playing hard to get? Did she just flat out not like him? That would be awful! He couldn't stand the suspense. "I don't mean to bother you, Grace. I'm just trying to help. I like being around you, but if you want me to leave, I'll respect your wishes."

Grace was thrilled to hear his confession. "No, Jason, I don't want you to leave. I like being around you too. I was just feeling a little self conscious I guess. I've never had a boyfriend before, and, I, not that you're my boyfriend or anything, I mean....."

"That's okay, Grace. I know we've just barely met, but I feel the same way about you. There's something about you that just draws me in. And, it doesn't hurt that you're surrounded by warrior angels."

"What do you mean? You can see them?"

"Yes, for most of my life. I can see the bad ones too. I've never told anyone before. When I was younger it used to scare me; then I got a little older, and I thought it would drive me crazy; but now I use it to help me know who to share Jesus with, or sometimes, who to steer clear of. It's helped me lots of times, when something bad was about to happen, and I needed angels."

"I just can't believe it. I thought I was the only one."

"That's part of the reason I came. When my uncle told me about you, and your special gifts, I knew I had to come meet you. I just didn't know there would be this kind of connection between us, so I wasn't prepared for that."

"I liked you as soon as I saw you too, Jason. Part of the reason I did, was because I could see your guardian angels as well. It was a shock to me when you got here, because I was expecting a small boy, and then there you were, a man."

"Uncle Tom told me I surprised everyone. It'd been a long time since we'd seen each other; and growing up, well, that tends to happen as the years pass. When my uncle told me about your healing gift, I had to come. How did you learn you had that ability?"

"Well, I don't consider it an ability, since I'm not the one doing the healing. I feel like I just listen real hard, and God tells me what is wrong with the person in question, and then I invoke the power of Jesus' Name, and the individual is healed. I was shot in the head a number of years ago, and while I was visiting with the Lord in my coma, He told me I would be able to see things that the rest of the world couldn't see; then I was shot again during a court trial for the man who'd held me prisoner for a very long time, and after they brought me back God had given me a knowledge of what was going on with people, their health, mental state, and other things about them. He is the one who taught me how to call on Him. It's really Jesus who does it all. I don't want any of the glory for any of this."

"I understand. And, I would never try to steal God's glory. I just want to help, any way I can. I'm very excited about the prison ministry, especially after my Uncle having been an inmate for so long. I won't get in the way, I promise."

"No, Jason, you're not in the way, and I want you to help, if that's what you want to do. I'm sure God can use your hands, just as easily as He uses mine. Anyone can be an instrument of healing, as long as they understand that the power, all of it, comes from the Lord, and from using the majesty, and authority, of Jesus' Name. I'm actually very happy you will be with us, and more so now that I know you can see everything that's going on. We can watch each other's backs."

"I would like that. And, I'm the lucky one, since you have such a pretty back."

"Oh, stop, Jason." Grace giggled, hoping deep down inside that he wouldn't.

†

Morning dawned bright and cool. Doc and Tony were already headed in their direction, so they could get an early start. Nancy made a quick breakfast of sausage and egg burritos, wrapping each one in parchment paper so they could eat on the road. Some apples and a big thermos of coffee rounded out their meal. After loading all their supplies into the back of the SUV, and getting out onto the highway, Mom started passing the sandwiches around; unwrapping Mike's halfway down, so he could manage with one hand. The family was already accustomed to the crisis' that would happen along the way, as Satan did his best to keep the healing meeting from happening once again.

After a flat tire, and another cracked hose; but before a large herd of pigs parked themselves in the middle of the road, and decided they weren't going anywhere fast; Jason sat back and shook his head. "So this kind of thing happens every single time you are headed to a meeting?"

"Yep", Nancy answered. "We figure we must be doing something right if Satan is trying this hard to stop us."

"I'm sure of it. Good thing Mike is so handy, huh?"

"We have just taken to carrying one or two of everything we might need, and we do repairs as we go."

"So, that's why we leave so early in the morning? I wondered. I know the prison where we're going, and it's only a couple hours up the road."

"Yes Tom. It's gotten to be our regular routine to give ourselves a few extra hours for all the emergencies we'll run into. Sad that it has to be this way, but we'll do whatever it takes to get where we're going."

"Well, I'm pretty handy with a lug wrench too, so if you need me to spell you, Mike, just give a holler."

"I'll keep that in mind. Expect to be called on for help with our next flat."

As they drew closer to the prison, which would be this

day's venue, the sky began to grow dark. Grace looked out her rear driver's side window to check out the swirling clouds of evil. When Jason leaned out the rear passenger side to take a peek he whistled and pulled his head back inside.

"Whoa, Jason, can you see them too?"

"Yes, Lilly, I can, and I can tell you they are out in force today."

"We didn't know that, Jason. You can see the angels and demons just like Gracie can?"

"Since I was a little boy, Mike. My mom always made me hide it, so people wouldn't think I was crazy or something like that."

"I didn't even have this particular bit of information, and I'm your uncle. Though, I should have figured it out. You always were a bit of a strange duck if I do say so."

"Thanks a lot Uncle Tom. Though, there might be a small chance that I get the "strange duck" part from you."

"Okay, I give. This could come in really handy at the prison; having two of them who can see things in the spiritual realm. Does anyone else agree?"

"I agree, Tom. This could be a very good thing. We'll figure out how to use it to our best advantage. God is good!"

"Yes, husband, God is very good!"

Inside the penitentiary the group was led to an auditorium, which, just like the others they'd seen, had obviously celebrated better days. This gymnasium lacked the basketball paraphernalia present at the last location, but boasted bleachers along one wall. Ancient musical instruments had been set up opposite the seats, in an area, it appeared, they would be using as a stage of sorts. Peeling cement walls, and floors, seemed to be a general theme in these institutions, and it hurt Grace's heart to think of humans living in these conditions. But, she also understood the general thinking, that these men shouldn't be rewarded for committing crimes. And, admittedly she knew of several characters she'd met along her life's path who probably belonged in a place like this. If only there was a better way.

Warden Jones met them in the auditorium, and introduced himself. "I wish I could offer better conditions for your meeting, but it is what it is."

"This is fine Warden. We've actually seen worse."

"Well, that's hard to imagine, but if there is anything you need, let us know. We will be bringing the men in soon. I don't like to make them wait in here too long. I find the waiting gets them a little riled up."

"Hmm, I wonder if that had anything to do with our

experiences before?"

"I don't know, Gracie, but it could be a factor I suppose. We'll have to see how things go this time."

"You're right, Dad. We'll have to compare everything from all the different meetings, and see how it goes. Well, we'd better get set up. Everyone know what to do?"

"No I don't, but I'm open to anything you need."

"You can come with me Jason. Tom, why don't you help Dad?"

Tom and Mike looked meaningfully at each other, and Mike rolled his eyes before they both laughed.

"What's so funny?"

"Nothing, Grace. We're setting up."

"Leave her alone husband! She's going to clobber you if you don't quit kidding her, and I might just help."

"Yes wife, I'll behave."

"Oh, you two are just hilarious! Come on Jason."

The work went smoothly, and in no time at all they were ready to start. The inmates were marched in single file; most with hissing, spitting demons clinging to their backs; and directed where to sit. Things seemed much more organized this time, and Grace wondered how much of a difference it would make, until she looked to the bleachers and saw the eyes of the men. Most were inhabited by the same red hue that filled the eyes of every possessed man she'd seen so far. They were obviously prisoners in more way than one. Well, she and the team would try to change that with God's help.

Several young men came forward and took to the instruments. Before long they were deep into praise and worship. Much to Grace's delight, and Jason's as well, the demons were screaming with pain over the wonderful music, and as they were singing, she saw several inmates, even some with demons attached, joining in. This would be a grand day, she could feel it. "I didn't realize how concentrated the number of demons could be in such a confined space. I just had no idea at all. Kind of disturbing isn't it?"

"Just wait, Jason. It gets more exciting when they make their way up for prayer."

"Oh, they come right to us? That doesn't sound very safe now does it?"

"Don't go all soft on me. This is just how we do it, that's all. Up close and personal."

"Okay, Grace. Lead on."

Grace shared her message for the day. It was filled with Love and Compassion. She couldn't talk about the Lord these days, without sharing the wonderful ways in which she had been blessed. Doc, Tony, and Tom each shared their testimony, and she could see hearts softening, and demons holding on for dear life. When the invitation was played, the bleachers emptied and lines formed for healing, salvation, and encouragement. Each need was different; but she could also see Satan's minions, those with the red eyes, intermingled in with those who were truly seeking.

"What's with the red eyes, Grace? Do you see all the men with red eyes?"

"Yes, Jason. That's what we've been running into at every prison we visit. Satan is out to shut us down, and he sends his armies out to the most vulnerable, those who are unsaved. That's one of the reasons we keep doing what we're doing. We can't let him scare us off, and we can't let all these men die without the Lord. Just keep your eyes open for the ring leader. I haven't been able to spot him yet, but when he makes his way up, he'll be the one to start trouble."

"Okay, my lady. I will protect you from the demon hordes, at risk of life and limb."

"I'll take you up on that, but we do have angels you know."

"Yes, but I never like to assume. They won't intervene for just any little thing, so I like to be prepared. I was a boy scout. Made it all the way to Eagle!"

"Somehow that doesn't surprise me. Good, I'm glad you have mad Boy Scout skills. They might come in handy."

The afternoon was humming along with healings, in the Name of Jesus; salvations galore; and mental issues addressed. The warden stood by, nodding his head in grateful agreement, as he watched men being saved. He knew from personal experience that men who claimed Christianity were less likely to make trouble at the prison; and usually joined Bible study groups, versus one of the many gangs who ruled supreme in every penitentiary in the land.

Grace and Jason exchanged knowing looks, when men who were saved had demons ripped from their backs, and gained guardian angels. Grace could tell, looking into Jason's eyes, that he enjoyed the glorious vision as much as she did. Moments like that made all the difference in the world to her, and it thrilled her heart to see they were also making an impact on him. Jason had never felt so productive, or useful, in his life; and it made sense now that he'd carried this gift all his life and was led here to meet the woman who'd been saved for him.

Jason knew, without a doubt, that Grace would be his wife; and that they'd spend the rest of their lives bringing people into the Kingdom of God together.

Suddenly, the ring leader appeared. Eyes glowing red; malevolent smirk on his face; and dagger in his hand. He raised his arm. "Where do all these daggers come from? Why is there always a dagger?" Grace thought. Obviously these prisons were awash with compliant guards, and systems of bribery that could cause any desired item to materialize.

Jason saw the dagger only seconds after Grace saw it, and his heart froze. He was far enough away that he wouldn't be able to make a difference if this animal's arm came down holding the knife. The thought of losing the woman of his heart, after just meeting her, was enough to spur him to action. He turned and started to rush to Grace's side. When Grace saw from the corner of her eye that Jason was making his way to her, her first thought was for his safety. Then, just as quickly, she remembered the Lord's words to her, and she shouted in her most powerful voice. "In the Name of Jesus, demon be gone!" As she uttered these words, the inmate's eyes returned to normal, and he looked around in a state of confusion, dropping the dagger and backing up a step.

Warden Jones ordered the guards to grab the prisoner, but Grace stopped them. "Please, Warden, don't take him away. He needs our help, maybe even more than some of the others."

"Are you sure, Miss? I have to tell you that it would be against my better judgment. What he deserves is......"

"I know Warden, but if we are honest, we all deserve the same thing; and by turning our hearts to Jesus we don't get what we deserve, we get what He deserves. Please let me talk to him."

"Alright, but we will be close. My men will frisk him, and then you may speak to him. Is that acceptable?"

"Yes Warden, thank you. First let me say something to the rest of the men."

"Yes, by all means."

"Again I say, in the holy Name of our Lord and Savior Jesus the Christ, demons you must flee. Release your hold on these men, and fly away to Satan. In Jesus' Name."

Again, as before in other prison venues, men collapsed to the floor and small frog like creatures crawled from their mouths, growing in size and morphing into full fledged demons. This didn't remove demons from the men's backs, only salvation would cause that to occur, but at least the possessions were now a thing of the past for these prisoners. Now, in the place of angry men with red eyes, there were fellows shaking their heads, with blank stares on their faces. It was obvious they hadn't known what they were doing. Many men were saved that day. Many demons were plucked from the backs of men who were now children of the Most High King, and many hearts were healed. For the first time in her prison ministry Grace had not been part of an uprising, and she was very happy about that change.

But, something else happened that day as well. Grace saw that Jason had been willing to put himself in harm's way to rescue her, and now when she looked at him, all she saw was her very own hero, and she felt long awaited love blossoming in her heart.

She took the time to speak with the man who tried to kill her. He didn't know what had come over him, and he didn't know what to say. He didn't want to go into solitary confinement. He'd been there before, for long periods of time. Grace shared her idea of a perfect life in the Lord, with the man who only moments ago had raised a dagger into the air with the intention of taking her life. His name was Robert. He'd been in this place for years, with no hope of probation. She shared the Gospel message of Grace and love, and he cried. He asked Jesus into his heart that day, and his demons were torn away. She hugged him before he was carted off to his cell, and promised to write. A promise she would keep.

Warden Jones invited them back, and they agreed, though it would be some time before they could manage a return engagement. It seemed they were in demand in venues farther away all the time, and the calls kept coming.

†

Kakos was livid. "Are you telling me she got away again? What do you need from me? I gave you all the information you'd need to finally take care of her, and she's still out there? This isn't over, not by a long shot. And, you will all feel my wrath."

"Master, she knows all the right words to make us leave, you know we don't have the power to overcome those words. And, when we inhabit the inmates at the prisons, she always seems to figure it out in time, so we are of little consequence. This time we had hold of dozens, and dozens of hosts, but no one could get close enough, before she started throwing around the 'J' word. And, it doesn't help that there is another one now too."

"Another one? What do you mean another one?"

"I mean another one who can see us. And, he is living right in the same house with her. I think they might be interested in each other for more than one reason. If they join forces, we may never be able to overwhelm their defenses."

"Don't even say that. This is catastrophic. You said it always seems like she can see you, and knows what is going on before you can get the job done?"

"Yes, Master. I believe she expects these attacks now; and why wouldn't she, when we continually use the same plan. I don't think it's a far reach for anyone to think inmates in a prison could be bad guys, so she's got her guard up all the time."

"Well, well, well, remember I told you there's more than one way to skin a cat? We will just have to show a little restraint, and be patient. I know that's a quality I'm in pretty short supply of myself, but if it means I can finally get this damnable girl out of my hair once and for all, I think I can do it. If she expects evil from those men in the prison, we will have to find a way to relax her and get past her guard. I think I have a plan that will work, but it will take some planning, and a great deal of cooperation from all of you.

We have to surprise her, and when we catch her unawares, we will finally conquer her, and the young man too. Now, come here so we can get the details worked out."

☦

Back at home Gracie couldn't wait to get back to the food kitchen. She'd had young Anna on her mind since their last meeting. Lunch rush was almost over before she saw the girl's worn, dirty backpack by the 'FREE' table. She waved and called out, "Anna, over here."

The girl turned around and smiled. They'd really hit it off over their similar stories, and it seemed young Anna wasn't so frightened anymore. Grace had already decided she was going to do something to help this girl. Something more than the usual free meals and clothing. She intended to get Anna off the streets. She hadn't heard all the girl's stories yet, but when she looked at her, she saw herself, and it caused her heart to ache in a way she couldn't ignore.

Anna arrived at the cafeteria line, and grabbed a tray. Lunch today was spaghetti with meatballs; garlic bread; salad, with all the fixings, including those yummy, buttery, crunchy little croutons; and carrot cake for dessert. Grace loaded her up with extras; and put several cartons of milk in a bag, along with leftover donuts from that morning's breakfast, for tomorrow. "Can I come sit with you while you eat?" Grace looked over at her dad, to be sure she had a green light, and he nodded his approval.

"Sure, I guess. I got places to go after, but I can talk for a while if you don't wait too long."

"I'm coming right now. Though, I'm going to grab a couple pieces of that cake and some milk before I do." Smiling, Grace cut herself a large piece of carrot cake, and scraped all the extra frosting from the plate, that didn't have its own piece of cake to call home. Grabbing two small cartons of milk, and a fork, she set out for the farthest table in the room. Anna was already there, and had already put a huge meatball in her mouth. "Should we say a prayer before we start eating?" Grace asked.

"I guess", Anna mumbled through chewed up meat and sauce. "I ain't ever been much on saying prayers." She looked a little embarrassed and that made Grace feel bad.

"Oh, don't feel uncomfortable, Anna. I didn't used to say prayers before I started coming here either. My Dad, Mike taught me, and now it's a really great part of my life. I'll say the grace if you'd like."

Anna shrugged, and Grace figured she'd better say something worth listening to, or she might lose her young friend on this one. "Thank you, Father, for the food we're about to eat; and thank you for being here when we need you. For watching over us, and for loving us no matter what is going on in our lives. Amen."

"Amen. How do you know?"

"How do I know what?

"That He's watching over us, and loves us no matter what."

"Well now, that is a very good question. A long time ago my family was killed, and I lived on the streets. I made it through some pretty tough things that I can tell you about when you get a little older. I lost friends, and I did some things I'm not very proud of; but the Lord watched over me and kept me alive. When I was shot in the head and dumped in the river for dead, He preserved me and helped me make it through. After I got better, Mike and Nancy, my mom, adopted me. I've never been happier in my life than I am right now, and I know I have only Jesus to thank for all of it. Now He has given me a special gift. I heal people in His Name, and people come to know Him as Lord and Savior through our ministry."

"You got shot in the head? How can you still be alive if

you got shot in the head?"

"Here, I'll show you," Pulling her hair over enough for Anna to see the bullet's entry wound, she took hold of the girl's hand and pulled it up to the back of her head.

"Wow, you really got shot? I've never known anyone who got shot before. I haven't gone through nearly as much stuff as you did. My father left when I was a baby. He and my mom never got married. She married my step dad when I was seven. He was always a jerk. Last year my mom died. I ain't got no other relatives. I couldn't stay with my step dad anymore. He was beating me, and when he was drunk he tried to, you know. Anyway, I couldn't stay there no more, so I've been finding other places to sleep for about a year now. I used to live on the other side of town, so I just found out about this place a few weeks ago."

"How old are you, Anna? I was just wondering because I think you're about the same age I was when I found the soup kitchen."

"I'm eleven. Just turned eleven as a matter of fact."

"So, you're even younger than I was. I'd like to try to help you if I can. Will you accept my help if I offer?"

"I might. Depends on what it is, and what you want in return. I've met some real weirdoes since I've been on my own."

"I assure you. I met plenty of them too, and I am not one of them, Anna. Let me see what I am even able to do for you, and I'll get back to you. As long as you come back. Is that acceptable? And, do you have a place to sleep tonight?"

"Yeah, that's acceptable, and yeah, I have a place to sleep. I'm going to finish eating, and then I gotta go. I'll be back another time. Is that okay?"

"That's fine. Let me see what I can figure out."

That night at supper the family talked about Anna. What their options were, and how far they wanted to get involved, until Nancy said, "Why can't we just take her in? Mike? Grace and Lilly are both getting old enough that they will be out on their own soon. We don't have Bella, and David here anymore. And, Jason doesn't need me to be his mom. Certainly Tom takes care of himself. Why can't we just take her in?"

"That's certainly an option, Nance. Are you sure you want to get that involved? Don't you already feel overwhelmed?"

"Honey, taking these kids in, and having them be part of our family, is the best thing I've ever done in my life, besides marrying you. I haven't even met Anna yet, and I feel like she's mine."

Grace wanted to shout out loud. She couldn't have been more happy. She loved her family, but knew that she and Jason would one day marry; probably sooner than later; and Lilly had plans to go to college in the Fall. Anna would be the perfect addition to their family. She needed a place to belong, and Nancy needed someone else to mother. They all agreed, and Mike and Grace would offer that news as an option when they saw the girl again. Everyone smiled and hugged, and went on to their evening plans.

Grace walked out the door and onto the front porch, where she opened her arms wide, and took in huge breaths of fresh air. August had been warm, but this evening was pleasantly cool, and she looked out over the property to the lights of the town beyond. Anna would like it here, she was sure of it. There would be a time of adjustment, as there was in all things, but before long she would fit right in. Mike and Nancy were two of the most loving people in the world, and they would change her life forever. They would be a solid influence, and she would have a real chance here. True, she wasn't a Christian yet; but she hadn't been saved herself, when Mike first met her. It would all work out, she was positive.

She heard the front door open, and before she knew it Jason was standing next to her. He reached over and took her small hand in his. Their fingers intertwined, and he spoke, "You want to take a walk?"

"Sure. It's a lovely evening, and the fresh air feels great."

"I hadn't noticed. I only have eyes for you my dear."

"Don't you think it's wonderful how Mike and Nancy were so willing to take Anna in? They were the same way with me, and we've never looked back. They're terrific people."

"They are pretty great, though it isn't hard to raise someone as wonderful as you, so they had an advantage."

"You're just biased, that's all."

"I'll admit it. I believe you are the most perfect woman in the world."

"Oh, Jason, please don't do that to me. I don't think I can ever live up to the woman you think you see through your rose colored glasses. I'm not perfect, and I come with just as many faults, and foibles as any other human being on this earth."

"Nope, you are perfect. And, I have a question to ask you," Jason said as he lowered himself to one knee. He reached into his pocket, and pulled out a small box. Opening it he showed her an exquisite, antique ring. She gasped and raised her hands to her mouth. "Grace, would you do me the honor of being my wife? I will do my utmost to be the kind of husband you deserve, and I will spend my life worshipping, and serving the Lord together with you."

"Oh, Jason. It's beautiful. Are you sure? We have known each other for such a short time. How can you know?"

"Oh, I know, and I've never been more sure of anything in my life. You are the woman for me, and I believe God has brought me here for such a time as this, so I am doing the only thing I can possibly do. I think I knew the first moment I saw you. I love you Gracie."

"I love you too, Jason; and yes, of course I will marry you."

From the house Grace heard a chorus of "Yays", "Yippees", and "Woo Hoos". She turned around, and blushed when she saw her whole family crowded around the picture window in the living room, watching their romantic exchange.

"I suppose you were all in on this? Well, you sure kept it a secret. That might be a first for you, Lilly!"

"Hey, I can keep a secret!"

Everyone crowded out onto the porch for hugs and congratulations. The women huddled together, soon after, to begin making wedding plans. Jason asked to borrow Nancy for a moment, and gave her a big hug, "Thank you so much for the advice, and the ring. I don't know how I will ever repay you."

"Now, don't you even speak of it. Why would I want repayment? You've just made my daughter so happy, and that young woman has had way fewer moments of joy in her life than any human being deserves. My grandmother would be proud that her great granddaughter will be wearing her ring, and I knew Grace would like it. She is kind of an old fashioned girl."

"I believe that's one of the reasons I love her so much. She seems to be from another time; a time when women were more modest, and the world was a simpler place. She's smart, and beautiful, and one of the most caring people I've met in my life; she's everything I ever dreamed of in a wife."

"That's all I ever needed to hear young man. If you can help her find her joy, I will be forever grateful."

He turned and shook Mike's hand. "Thank you too, for everything. I was afraid you'd say no when I came and asked for Gracie's hand. I was sure you'd tell me we hadn't known each other long enough."

"Well, Jason, I can see the way you two look at each other. It would have been like trying to dam up a creek during a spring storm. Gracie has had so little happiness in her life, why would I deny her this? Besides, you two would have found a way to be together, even if I'd said no, so why try to halt the inevitable?"

†

Next day, at the soup kitchen, Gracie waited for Anna to arrive. Pacing back and forth; straightening the 'FREE' table, five, or six times; sweeping the floor in the storage room; and mixing potato salad, to go with the fried chicken, coleslaw, and banana pudding they were serving for lunch. She was excited to share the recent decision to offer Anna a home, if she wanted to be a part of their family; and the thrilling news of her own upcoming wedding. She was fairly bursting to tell her new little friend.

"Settle down, Gracie. She'll be here. You're going to give yourself fits if you don't calm down."

"I'm just excited, Dad. If someone had offered me a home, right after I'd lost my family in that fire, there are so many things I wouldn't have had to endure. I understand that God is using me, and I want to be part of that, but it would be great if Anna could have a normal life."

"And you think she's going to get that living with us? Then you'd better think again. There is no such thing as a normal life, Grace. It just is what it is. If those things hadn't happened the way they did, you wouldn't be with us, I wouldn't have you for a daughter, and you wouldn't be in a place where God could gift you, and then use your gift. Besides, you would never have met Jason, if things hadn't unfolded the way they did." Tom and Jason were back in the kitchen frying up the rest of the chicken. With the extra two sets of hands, work here went pretty quickly these days, and they both liked to be useful. Mike was quite sure Gracie had been right about these two.

"You're right of course. So, let's just say I'm excited to have another sister, and I'm very anxious to tell people about the wedding."

"Okay, that makes more sense. I'm anxious to tell her too."

The front door of the soup kitchen "dinged", and Anna walked in. When she saw the looks on Mike's and Gracie's faces, she looked frightened and took a step back. "Oh,

Anna, don't be afraid. Everything is fine. As a matter of fact, everything is great, if you truly want it to be."

"What do you mean? You didn't turn me in, did you? You need to tell me if you did, so I can leave. I'm not going to let them put me in one of those places, do you hear me?"

"No, no, it's nothing like that, Anna. Our family talked, and we'd like you to come and live with us. To be a part of our family, if you want to. What do you say?"

Anna, who'd been walking closer, as Grace spoke, stopped in her tracks and burst into tears. She sank to her knees, covered her face with her hands, and bawled. "I can't believe it. I just can't believe it. A real home."

"Well, believe it honey. We all want you to come. This is the way Grace came to us; and her sister Lilly; we think it would be great if you would say yes. We can start out as foster parents, like we did with the other kids, and then if you'd like us to, we can start adoption proceedings. My wife Nancy is so excited, she's home getting a bedroom ready for you."

"A room for me? You mean my own bedroom? I've never had my own room before."

"You'll love it with us, Anna. And we'd love to have you. You're right about the same age as I was when my first family was killed, and I was on the streets for a very long time. God is good, Anna, and He wants to do some exciting things in your life, if you'll let him."

"And it's okay with your whole family? Everyone wants me there?"

"Yes, Anna, we all want you to be a part of our family. Please say yes."

"Yes, yes, of course yes. But, does that mean I can't eat here anymore? The food here is terrific, and I smell fried chicken." Mike and Grace both laughed, and Grace grabbed young Anna, to give her a big squeeze.

"You can eat here whenever you want, but the food is great at home too."

"Home, that sounds nice. Thank you. I really don't know what to say."

"You don't have to say a thing, my dear. Now, let's get you some food. After lunch is over, you can help us clean up, and then we'll take you home to meet your new mom, and the rest of your family. How does that sound?"

"That sounds pretty good to me." Grace sat to eat lunch with Anna. It warmed her heart to see the difference the news had made to the girl. Her face was utterly changed. Pretty soon Tom, and Jason came out of the kitchen, and filled a couple of trays for themselves. Then Mike finished serving those few stragglers who'd come in to peruse the clothing table, and he joined them too. Introductions to Tom, and Jason, followed, and then they began to talk about the weather. Before anyone realized it, they were joking, telling stories, and laughing. Anna already felt as if she belonged.

Mike said he wanted to get a move on, before Mom had an anxiety attack waiting for them to come home, so they finished up, and began to bus tables. Neither of the girls was afraid of hard work, so they kept up with the men easily; and by the time Mike had the steamer table apart and clean, the dining room was finished. As a big happy team, they'd all washed and dried trays, and pans; swept and mopped the floors; tidied the bathrooms; and dealt with leftovers. To see Anna, one would have thought she was born to this. She fit right in, and did it all with a smile on her face. The men were huffing and puffing, but the girls took it in stride, then it was time to be on their way.

"Before we head home, we should go pick up the rest of your things."

"This is it. What I'm wearing, and the backpack. I don't have anything else."

"Well, young lady, we will fix that. Your mom will want to take you shopping."

"I don't want to be a bother. I can wash these, and they'll be fine."

"No, you don't want to tell this woman you don't want to shop. You'll give her apoplexy. She is already sad that Grace isn't a shopper, but thankfully her sister, Lilly, enjoys those outings with her mom. She'll have you properly outfitted in no time."

"It's true I've not been a shopper up to this point, but that could change, Dad. We have a wedding to prepare for, remember? That is my other good news, Anna. I'm engaged to this gentleman right here." Anna grinned and congratulated them, happy that she would be there for a wedding.

At home, Nancy was anxiously waiting to meet the young girl who would be her daughter. She was every bit as nervous as a new mom in labor. She'd prepared a room for their new charge, and hoped she'd like it as much as the rest of the kids liked theirs. Anna's new room had light lavender walls; a queen sized, four poster bed; white bedding, and white lacey curtains over a lovely window seat; a large fireplace, for chilly evenings; beautiful wood floors, with a dark purple throw rug, and purple and white pillows and accents. She was thrilled to have another bedroom filled, and couldn't wait to take the girl shopping for the things she'd need. Anna was going to be here in time to start the new school year, so she'd need all sorts of supplies, and with Lilly going to college this Fall, clear over in the next state, it would be nice to have another young person in the house. Another shopping buddy.

Nancy ran to the door as Mike drove up honking his horn. Lilly was right behind her. When the doors to the SUV swung open her heart soared to see the young girl she would be mother to. She looked so small and frightened. Everyone exited the automobile, and Anna began to walk slowly toward the house; knees shaking and lip quivering. Would this woman she'd heard so much about be happy to see her? Her eyes connected with Nancy's, tears welled up, and they ran into each other's arms crying. It was as if they belonged to one another, and had been waiting for this moment their whole lives. Grace and Lilly, who would both be leaving in the near future; and had worried about how their departure would affect Nancy; felt a combination of relief, and gratitude that the meeting had gone so well. With Mom's overwhelming approval, Anna was now officially a part of the family.